THE FORGETTING

THE FORGETTING

SHARON CAMERON

Scholastic Press
New York

Library of Congress Cataloging-in-Publication Data

Names: Cameron, Sharon, 1970– author.
Title: The Forgetting / Sharon Cameron.
Description: First edition. | New York : Scholastic Press, 2016. | ©2016 |
Summary: Canaan is a quiet city on an idyllic world, hemmed in by high walls,
but every twelve years the town breaks out in a chaos of bloody violence,
after which all the people undergo the Forgetting, in which they are left
without any trace of memory of themselves, their families, or their lives—but
somehow seventeen-year-old Nadia has never forgotten, and she is determined to
find out what causes it and how to put a stop to the Forgetting forever.
Identifiers: LCCN 2016007978 | ISBN 9780545945219
Subjects: LCSH: Memory—Juvenile fiction. | Amnesia—Juvenile fiction. |
Conspiracy—Juvenile fiction. | Friendship—Juvenile fiction. | CYAC: Science
fiction. | Memory—Fiction. | Amnesia—Fiction. | Conspiracies—Fiction. |
Friendship—Fiction. | LCGFT: Science fiction. | Psychological fiction.
Classification: LCC PZ7.C1438 Fo 2016 | DDC 813.6—dc23
LC record available at http://lccn.loc.gov/2016007978

10 9 8 7 6 5 4 3 2 1   16 17 18 19 20

Printed in the U.S.A.   23

First edition, September 2016

Book design by Becky Terhune

For all who remember
they can change their world

I have forgotten.

When I first opened my eyes I saw a room of white stone, and the light was bright, too bright, coming into the room from two high windows. I have never been so afraid. I don't know this room. I don't know this girl who woke with me, or these children who cry, their faces streaked with black lines. They've forgotten, too. But this book was tied to my wrist, and the book says I have a family, and that my family will be marked with dye so I'll know them. I think I have to believe the book.

There is violence outside. We've barred the door. I don't know what else is outside this room, but I think there are more of us, and that they did not wake up with a book. I want to scream like they are. I want to cry like the children. I want to claw my own skin and find out what's buried inside. I want to know who I've been.

The book says I knew this Forgetting would come. That it's happened before and will happen again. We have to write it all down. Everything about us, as the book has told me to do now. The children with the marks on their cheeks run from me. I think I am their mother. I will read them this book. I'll tell them their names and I will tell myself mine.

We are made of our memories. Now we are nothing. It feels like death.

What have we done to deserve this piece of hell?

THE FIRST BOOK OF THE FORGETTING

PAGE 41

CHAPTER ONE

I am going to be flogged, and I don't know why I'm so surprised about it. No one could take this many risks and never get caught. I don't want to be caught. I drop flat onto my back without a sound, stretching full length along the top of the wall, a wall that's only a little wider than I am. There's a long drop on either side. I clutch my pack to my chest, squint my eyes against the brightness of the sky. No. I've always known I would get caught. I just didn't think it would be today.

I chance another quick glimpse over the edge of the wall. There are two people down there, standing close together in the shaded alley, my rope ladder dangling just above their heads. I don't think they've seen it, and I don't think they've seen me, though practically everyone else can. The walled city of Canaan spreads like a wide and shallow bowl of winking glass and white stone below me, and here I lie, ten meters high on its rim. Just one set of eyes on the streets during the resting, awake—as I am, as those two below me are—one pair of hands pulling aside a sleeping curtain from a well-positioned window, and they will see. And they will come for me.

My fingers find the twisted rope of the ladder, tied to a metal ring sun-hot and burning through the cloth of my leggings. I could pull up the ladder, flip it back over to the forbidden side of the wall, climb down, and wait until they've gone. Or I could try jumping for the roof of the Archives. That would be an easy drop, only the width of the alley and a meter or so down. But that roof is thatch instead of turf, the pitch steep, and how could either of those people in the alley not notice a girl jumping over their heads? Or the ladder pulling back up, for that matter? It's a miracle they missed it coming over the wall the first time.

And so I force myself into stillness, into patience. Balanced high inside the dome of the blue-violet sky, the white city on one side, a wilderness of mountain and waterfall on the other, eight weeks of the sun's trapped heat scorching my back through the wall stones. I'm not good at patience. The wind blows, a hot, swirling breath, and I wonder if it can push me off this wall; I wonder which side I'd rather fall on. Two words float up from the shaded alley.

"How many?"

It's the kind of question asked when you think you haven't heard right. I know most of the people of Canaan, at least by sight, though not by the tops of their heads. But the murmur of the answering voice I know right away. Polite. Always pleasant. It's Jonathan of the Council, enforcer of Canaan's many rules. Finding him in defiance of those rules is my second non-surprise of the day. Jonathan will have me flogged all right. And enjoy it. I wonder how many stripes you get for climbing over the wall.

"Eleven," says Jonathan.

It takes a heartbeat to understand this answer wasn't for me.

The other voice replies, much louder, "And what am I supposed to say to these people when they request their books? What reason am I supposed to give?"

This is Gretchen of the Archives Jonathan is talking to.

"The reason is mine, Archivist. What you tell them is your affair."

I hold my pack tighter to my body. My own book is inside, its tether worked through a hole in the cloth, tied to the braided belt at my waist. Surely Jonathan can't be telling Gretchen to not let eleven people read their archived books. Your books are your memories, who you are. The thought of being denied one of my books brings a familiar tingle to my fingers, my legs. I shove the feeling down. I can't afford to panic, not here, on the wall, right over Jonathan's head and in full sight of the city. Then I catch a movement from the corner of my eye. One of my braids is free from its pins, dangling over the wall edge like a long blond banner.

And there's no more talk in the alley. The pause grows so long I can almost see the two necks craning upward, watching my braid flutter and the rope ladder sway. I think of the ridge of scars I saw on Hedda in the bathhouse, her back like a badly plowed field, and I make a decision. If they come for me, I'm going to pull up the ladder, climb down the other side of the wall, and go back into the mountains. Then I decide the opposite. Hedda survived. And my mother and my sisters need me. Even if they don't know it. It's only seventy days until the Forgetting.

The moment passes when Jonathan's pleasant voice says, "Here is your list." After a soft word from Gretchen his voice comes back, this time with an edge. "And what if your food ration depended on doing what you're told?"

I pretend to be Gretchen of the Archives. *Well, Jonathan of the Council, if your own ration depended on how much you love punishing a rule-breaker, I'm pretty sure there would be nothing left to eat in Canaan. And if you'd just look up, you could see one great big rule being broken right now . . .*

Gretchen says none of these things, of course. I never say them, either. But I almost wish she would. I need for her to end this so I can get off this wall. I snag my wayward braid, tuck it up behind my head, and wonder what Janis, Canaan's Head of Council and Jonathan's grandmother, might have to say about back-alley meetings during the resting. I'd bet she doesn't know anything about them.

More muttering from Gretchen, and then the air settles into quiet, lulled by the *chick chick* of the suncricket song. I risk another look over the edge of the wall. The dim alley is empty. No feet on the flagstones, no creak of an opening window, no shout that means I've been seen. As far as I can see, the city sleeps.

I move. The pack goes to my back, feet over the wall as I roll onto my stomach. My sandals find the rope ladder and I shinny down, but only halfway, a meter or so above Jin the Signmaker's roof garden. I get my feet planted sideways, push hard, and make the short drop into the garden, half turning as I fall. I land feet, knees, then hands in the prickling grasses, the view from below now obscured by the huge, hulking, windowless building that is the Archives.

I hurry to a bed of dusk-orange oil plants and pull out a pole made from a fern stalk, light and thin, its end carved into a hook. I reach out, catch the hanging ladder with the hook, and work the ropes up and over the wall, letting the weighted last rung finish the job of pulling the ladder over to the other side. Then I slide the pole back into its hiding place and straighten, listening.

The streets below are quiet, the low, slanting sun making the shadows long, blocking out patches of bright light, leaving others in a shrouded dim. Jin's house is one of the old buildings, and even dry and untended it's pretty up here, white stone arches mimicking the curve and flow of the fern forest I've just been hiking through. Shaping stone like this is a skill we've forgotten. Jin doesn't spend much time in his roof garden, especially in the last, hot days of full sun. He's old, with no wife, no children he can remember or identify. That, and his nearness to the wall, and the privacy created by the Archives, makes this roof a good one to jump into. Not to mention that the old man is nearly deaf.

I lower my pack to my feet, its tether snaking down around my leg, and for the first time feel my pulse begin to slow. I'm not caught. I'm not going to be flogged. At least not today. I reach for my falling braids, seven or eight of them out of their pins and brushing the bare skin of my waist. I've taken the tail end of my tunic and tucked it back through my collar in a way that makes my mother frown, but it's cooler like this, and useful when the foliage is dense. Extra fabric snags. I re-braid and pin, braid and pin, fast, getting them as neat as I can. I have to get home before my mother sees my empty bed. Sometimes I think she knows when I've been out, deep down, but appearing at least somewhat presentable helps her keep up the sham.

Did you have a good resting, Nadia? she'll say to me, even though my tunic will be wrinkled where it was pulled through my collar and I'll have dirt on my knees that wasn't there when the curtains closed. *You've brought the water? Thank you . . .*

And I'll say nothing, because I never do, and she'll say nothing about the yellow apple on the table, an apple she would know didn't come from our stores if she'd bothered to count. But once in a while her brow will crease, as if she's unsure. Confused. Maybe she is. I'm not sure how many Forgettings my mother has lived through. She wears her book on twine, heavy around her neck, but I know she doesn't remember me. Not really.

"Have a good resting, Nadia the Dyer's daughter?"

I snatch up my tethered pack, my last hairpin lost to the grasses. That voice was not my mother's. It was deep and very male, coming from the shaded shadows beyond the arches, beneath the covered corner of Jin's garden. I step back, glancing once at the place I've hidden the pole. I'll never get the ladder back in time. The roof is too high to jump from and the voice is between me and the stairs to the street. Correction: Today is the day I'm caught. I feel sweat on my neck, and not from the sun.

The shadows in the corner shift, reshape, become a person, and then the person steps into the light. Not Jonathan, or any other member of the Council. It's Gray. The glassblower's son. Of all people. He's taller since we finished our time in the Learning Center, the weeks of sunlight leaving deep gold in the dark brown of his hair. But that smile he wears is the same. "Cheeky" is what his own mother might call him. I just call him a *zopa*, a word my mother sometimes uses, though not if she thinks I can hear.

Gray hooks a thumb on the lower end of the book strap that crosses his chest, waiting for me to do something. I think what I would say if I were a normal person. *Hey.* Or maybe, *How long have you been on this roof?* Or, *Why, exactly, are you on this roof? Which way did you take to sneak up here during the resting? Does your hair really grow all wild and curly like that?*

He just stands there, grinning at me. I wish I'd listened to Mother and never tucked up the end of my tunic. But it's much more important to know what else Gray the Glassblower's son has seen. I break my ban against frivolous conversation and say, "What are you doing here?"

The grin widens. "Nadia speaks. I'm impressed. What else have you learned to do since school?"

Zopa, I think. He seems to think this is funny. I don't. I notice he hasn't answered my question. I decide not to answer his.

"So," he says, "come up to Jin's often?"

I can't tell if he's teasing me or threatening me. The quiet stretches out long, waiting for my explanation, until I say, "I've come to request from Jin, that's all. We need signs."

"True. The Forgetting is coming. We could all use a few more labels, I guess. Probably worth a flogging to get them an hour before the leaving bell, ten weeks ahead of time. No, I agree with you, Nadia. Plan ahead. Avoid that last-minute rush."

Sarcasm. Perfect. I think of the only other time I've spoken actual words to the glassblower's son. He was at least a third of a meter shorter then, in the learning room, and we were meant to be self-exploring the seeds for planting. Gray was self-exploring the art of teasing me. I ignored him through two bells, the same way I ignored everyone, until finally he tugged on the cord of my book, worn hanging from my belt in those days. I looked him in the eye and said one word: "Stop." And then he grabbed my book and opened it. My book. I'd have rather found him peeking through the door of the latrine. I slapped his face, hard, and then I slapped it again. Gray left me alone after that, and I've carried my book in a pack ever since. I doubt the same strategy is going to work here. But the memory has done me good; it's reminded me of my temper, which always helps me speak. And I need to know what he's seen. This time I look him in the face.

"You must have an urgent need for signs yourself," I observe, "since you seem to be taking the same risk."

"Well spotted, Dyer's daughter." He moves across the garden to sit on the low stone wall that runs along the edge, crosses one ankle over the other, and leans back, relaxed. There's a two-story drop behind him. "But I came straight here. You took the long way around to Jin's, didn't you? The really long way."

Question answered. He's seen everything. Whatever this game is, I'm done playing. "I'll be long gone before you can get Jonathan here," I say. Jonathan might not be easily found, since he was just wandering the streets.

"I'm sure I can find someone who would be interested."

"I'll deny it. It will be your word against mine."

"And you don't have one thing in that pack, or in your house, that has come from over the wall?"

The apples. I can feel the weight of them alongside my book. And there are the plant cuttings. They'll have to be gotten rid of. Quick. Plus the crystals in my resting room. I won't be able to do it. Not in time. Something inside me tightens, and I realize just how much I did not want today to be my day. Gray gets up and crosses the garden grasses, his trademark smirk for once not present. He stands right over me.

"Tell me how many times you've been over the wall."

I watch the empty sky beyond his shoulder.

"Tell me, or I bring them."

I put my gaze on his. "Once."

"Liar."

The word feels like he's finally slapped me back. One clear bell rings out over the city. The first of the day, for waking. Mother will check my bed soon. I have to go. We both have to go. "What do you want?"

"I'm glad you asked. I want you to take me with you."

Where? I think. But that smile is back, and I realize he means over the wall. He wants me, Nadia, to take him, Gray, over the wall. This strikes me as the single most stupid thing I've heard in a lifetime of stupid things. "No."

"Yes."

I glare at him.

"I go with you, or I bring the Council," he says. "Take it or leave it."

I'm more than mad now. I'm afraid. Would he turn me in, watch my back being laid open like Hedda's? I don't know the answer, and that means I'm cornered. He's intent, watching me think. His eyelashes are startlingly long. I drop my gaze and nod once.

"When?" he asks.

"Three days."

"The sun will be setting by then."

I look him again in the eye. "Take it or leave it."

"I'll take it, then." And here comes the smirk. "I'll meet you here. First bell of the resting."

"Fourth bell."

"Oh, no. You'll come at the first. Like you always do. Three days, Nadia the Dyer's daughter." He moves backward into the shadows, still grinning at me. And right before he disappears down the stairs, he says, "Don't forget."

I stay exactly where I am until his footsteps have faded, then dart to the edge of the roof to see how he manages the streets before the leaving bell. I don't see him. He's gone another way. I move out of the sun and sink down into the dark corner where Gray must have been, watching me lie on top of the wall, jump into Jin's garden, get rid of the ladder. Braid my hair. And now that I'm alone and out of the heat, I'm shaking inside. I'm not going to be flogged. Not today. But I have been caught. *Don't forget,* he said.

I measure my breaths, take my book out of my pack and run a hand over its thick cover, feel the long, connected tether that keeps it tied to my belt. I've been taught to write truth in my book since I was old enough to hold a pen. Our books are our sole identity after the Forgetting, the string that connects us to who we were before. The one thing we should never, ever be separated from. *Don't forget.* I hear the words again in my head, this time in the voice of a child. Gray doesn't know it, but he's said that to me before.

And then the shaking in my middle shoots outward—legs, arms, fingers, scalp—the panic I managed to fend off on the wall slamming hard into my chest, squeezing out the air. I hear my mother's screams, her fists banging on the barred door of her resting room, my older sister with her, pleading with my father. The baby cries in her cradle seat, and I flatten myself against the wall beneath the window, where pots of seedlings make a line across the sill above my head. I was Nadia the Planter's daughter then, in my sixth year, and my father had let me plant those seeds, touch the tiny shoots of green and orange springing up to meet the light. I'd been so sure that he loved me.

My father takes my hand, leads me away from the window, and sits me in my chair, feet dangling, the light of sunrising painting our walls with blotches of pink and gold. Then he picks up our knife and cuts the tether of my book. I see the book leave my body, watch it cross the room without me in my father's hands.

"Don't cry, Nadia," he says while he cries, "it's almost time to forget."

He is a stranger. My father has become a stranger who did what he said I should never do, who cut off a piece of me and took it away. And so I run. As fast as I can, out the door, losing the sound of his voice as he calls, and it's as if the pain and confusion inside me have somehow bled into the streets. Everything is noise and stinging smoke, breaking glass and laughter—laughter that is more frightening than my mother's screams. I don't know where I am. Ribbons hang from the trees. Nothing looks the same. My book doesn't bump against my leg. The stone walk is slippery and I fall and someone tries to grab me and then I run and I run more and that is when I see the brown-headed boy in the place where they make the glass.

The furnace is glowing, and the boy is squirming and kicking. A man has him by the arm, and the man has taken the boy's book. The glassblower shouts at the man, shakes his head no, and I am angry, so angry that someone else's book has been cut, and then I see the man throw the boy's book, watch it land near the bright orange opening of the furnace.

I run into the workshop and I hit the man. I hit and hit him and then someone hits me and I land hard on the ground, heavy tools clattering down onto my legs. The man and the glassblower are fighting, the heat of the furnace pushing on my face. The cover of the boy's book has caught fire, flames eating his pages, and the boy reaches through the heat and grabs it. He drops his book to the floor, smothering the fire with his hands and chest, yelling because he is burned. The men hit each other, and when the fire is gone the boy holds his smoking book with red hands, and he looks at me and says, "Don't forget."

I find my feet and run, down the white stone streets, between the white houses. Light is peeking over the edge of the mountains, from beyond the walls, and the sun comes in a sliver of gold. Then the sky bursts. A broken-glass sky like in the boy's shop—sharp, bright light that pierces the gold with dazzling shards. The trees bloom, just like Father said they would, all the white flowers opening one by one while the ribbons flutter, as far as I can see on either side of the street. The air is sweet. Stone, light, flowers—it's too bright. I crouch and cover my eyes.

When I can open them again I see a man leaning against a locked door. His hand falls down to the book at his side, and I watch his face empty, like when Mother pours water from a pitcher. When there is nothing left in the man's face he wanders away, past a baby lying in its blanket in the middle of the street. I can't see whether the baby has a book or not, and then

I hear a woman cry. And even though I can't make sense of my world I do understand that this noise is different. The woman isn't crying because she's afraid she might die; she cries because she has lost her life. She has forgotten. Everyone has forgotten, and the sound of it hurts my ears.

I push myself up and go home, slipping on the stones. I don't know where else to go. I'm bruised and tired and I hurt. I want my mother. My father isn't there when I open the door, and even this room looks unfamiliar in the cracked white light. The baby has cried herself to sleep in the cradle seat. There are no seedlings in the window, but on the table is a book, open to the first page. It says *Nadia the Dyer's daughter.* But that is not my book. I push until I lift the bar across the door to my mother's resting room.

"Mother?" I call.

And there she is, just as she's always been, my sister huddling in the corner. Mother blinks once, twice, and when her eyes find me she jumps back. Scrambles away.

"Who are you?" my mother yells. "Get away from me! Get away!"

I go away and sit on the floor beneath our table. I hug my knees and I rock and rock. And then I know what has made me slip and fall in the streets. I'm sticky with blood.

I rock now, hugging my shaking knees in the shade of Jin's garden, beneath his beautiful arches, my book tight against my chest. A book must contain the truth. We are supposed to write the truth, for no one to see but ourselves. But how easily that truth can be twisted. Bend a little here, omit a little there, make yourself into the person you wish you were instead of the person you are. How easy to cut the truth away, to throw it in a fire, open your eyes, and have the whole world remember nothing of who you are. Nothing of what you've done. When you will not remember who you are or what you've done. My father lives on the other side of Canaan now, with Lydia the Weaver. He has two children, girls, and passes me in the street without a second glance. He got what he wanted and got rid of what he didn't. What a victimless crime. Like everything before the Forgetting. Guiltless. Forgotten. Unless you can remember.

Don't forget, Gray the Glassblower's son has said to me. Twice.

And he's said it to the only person in Canaan who never has.

Two days ago I went to Arthur of the Metals to have my mother's knife sharpened, even though we'll hide it from her as soon as I get home. I didn't write it down because it wasn't worth remembering, but while Arthur was talking scythes I looked at his whetstone. It had a smooth, shallow groove where knife blades had been run over and over across the surface. When you sharpen a knife, tiny pieces of metal are filed away to make a new edge, and now I see that tiny bits of the rock go as well.

Today I walked through Canaan, running my hands over the stone of the old buildings, the ones we've forgotten how to make. Sharp corners, no blunted edges. No ruts in the flagstones of the street, where the metal-banded wheels of the harvest carts pass back and forth. Even the leaf edges on the columns and arches are crisp, not worn. Nothing like Arthur's whetstone.

There is only one answer I can think of. We have not been in Canaan long enough to wear down the stone. And if we have not been here that long, then we must have come from somewhere else. And somewhere else can only be one place. Outside the walls . . .

NADIA THE DYER'S DAUGHTER
BOOK 11, PAGE 14, 10 YEARS AFTER THE FORGETTING

CHAPTER TWO

I wait for the leaving bell to ring before I go home. Normally I wouldn't. It's not far to my house if I cut through the back alleys, hop three small dividing walls, and duck beneath some windows. But today Jonathan of the Council is on the streets. Today I've been caught. And I need time to stop shaking. Which means my mother will not be able to pretend I was in my bed when she woke.

But I've also used my time to make a decision. I will not be taking the glassblower's son over the wall. Gray is used to getting his way: lovestruck girls, trouble-loving boys, irritated teachers, all ready to adore, be exasperated, forgive, and then adore him again. But he made a mistake letting me get away from Jin's, giving me time to hide my contraband. Now it really will be his word against mine, and my explorations on the other side of the wall do not require his help. Or hindrance. He can do his rebelling or thrill-seeking or boredom-relieving without me.

I slip down Jin's stairs and into the street, taking the proper way home, hair mostly neat, tunic where it should be. I have two arms, two legs, one book, and still somehow manage to be the opposite of every person I pass. The people of Canaan move with purpose but without hurry, safe inside their walls, measuring days into even, logical steps. Unquestioning. Unthinking. And even on this back street there are too many of them. I brush walls and bump shoulders, avoiding books and eyes until I round the corner into the noise of Meridian.

Water flows through the center of this street, glinting as it rushes down a white stone channel that cuts Canaan in half, all the way from the spring at the top end, down the gentle slope through the city, through the fields, and out beneath the lower wall. The thoroughfares on either side of the running channel are choked with comings and goings: children in cloth of reds and purples and yellows running pitchers back and forth to the water, craftsman requesting their supplies, one or two my age loitering beneath the long, slender limbs of the forgetting trees, where the buds are just beginning to show. A reminder of what's coming. I duck beneath the trees and out onto First Bridge, a delicate arch of the same pale stone that everything is made of, then pause at the highest point and look down the channel.

Jonathan of the Council is in the amphitheater, at the bottom of a slope of terraced seats, standing on the speaking platform in front of a tall tower of latticed stone, a spike that marks the center of the city. The tower houses our water clock, run perpetually by the channel that cascades down the terraces, passing under the platform and directly beneath it. There are three dials on each side of the clock, high, where everyone can see. The first says it's the second hour of waking. The next says that today is the fifty-sixth day of sunlight, that tomorrow will begin the seven days of sunsetting, followed by fifty-six dark days and another seven of sunrising. The third dial is for the two seasons of light and two seasons of dark that make a year, and the twelve years between Forgettings.

We know all this because there's a chiseled plaque on the tower, helpfully marked "Water Clock of Canaan," complete with instructions. So we can't forget. There's also another plaque, more simply carved, that says "I Am Made of My Memories." That's where Jonathan of the Council tied Hedda for taking more than her share at the granary, when her family had increased by two sets of twins and her ration had not. I won't forget that, either.

My glance at the Water Clock of Canaan has told me three things I knew already. That it will be mid-sunset when I break my promise to take Gray over the wall, that in exactly seventy days this entire city will descend into chaos, and, most important for the moment, that my mother is probably very upset right now.

"Mother is upset," a voice says near my waist. Genivee, my younger sister, stands beside me on the bridge, book strapped to her back, in an orange dress and with two yellow flowers in her hair. She's one of the only people in the world who can coax my smile. So I smile.

"What kind of upset?"

"Scared upset."

My smile goes away. My sisters know I tend to ramble during the resting, just not that my ramblings take me over the wall. Until an hour ago, I would have said nobody did. Liliya, the oldest, never bothers with my activities, resting or waking, mostly because she can't stand the sight of me. Genivee, the youngest, always does, because she loves me. But what our mother needs is lies, and the three of us have an unspoken agreement to give them to her. Today, I haven't held up my end of the bargain.

Genivee says, "I'll run home and tell Mother that I saw you at the channel, that you left for the baths just before the bell and that you were very, very sorry you didn't wake her before you went." She stares up at me. "And then I'll tell her you offered to stay home and do the rest of the baking so Liliya can take her to the dye house."

I look down at my little sister, her big eyes dark and innocent. She's saving me from Mother and laying down my punishment at the same time. "Cruel," I say.

She can't quite hide her grin. Then we both turn at a rattling noise. The harvest carts are coming down Equator Street from the fields, crossing Meridian to the granary, a group of Lost women and children working together to pull them over the flagstones. Genivee pushes out her lower lip. She thinks it isn't fair that the Lost should get undyed cloth and the worst of the work just because they didn't have a book after the Forgetting. Just because they don't know who they are. I think it's more than unfair. If you didn't have a book and became one of the Lost, you are twice a victim.

A supervisor walks with them, urging them on faster, and behind the carts comes a group of growers and planters, overseeing the last of the harvest and the preparation of the fields for sunsetting. One head is easy to spot above the others, tall, fair hair fading with some gray. It's Anson the Planter. Our father. I pretend I'm not Nadia, that I'm someone else, someone who would have the courage to speak to him.

Hello, Anson. You don't remember me, and when I knew you, your name wasn't Anson at all. It was Raynor. I just called you Father. But you don't remember that, either. You took my book, and if I had forgotten, then I wouldn't have found my way home to the false one you wrote for me, would I? I would've been wandering the streets without a book at all, and one of those Lost girls you're walking behind today would have been me. With no name, no age, no family, kept penned behind the fences until it's time to burn the dead or dig out the latrines. Or pull your harvest carts. But you wouldn't know the difference, would you? And neither would I . . .

I hear my father laugh over the racket of the carts, the sound still familiar after all this time. If I could make them believe what I know, then the man they now call Anson would be condemned. His book would be taken, destroyed, and not only would he be living with the Lost, removed from his current wife and children, he'd be living with the knowledge that when the Forgetting came, he'd lose even the memories he had left. So I keep my secret, and it makes me angry that I do. And frightened that I won't.

"Nadia," Genivee whispers. "You're doing it again."

She means I'm staring at people as if I want to fertilize the fields with their insides. I study Jonathan of the Council instead, in the long black robes that mark him as Council, brown hair neatly clipped, surveying the gathering people from his little place of power. This Forgetting will not be like the last one. I won't let it. No one is going to take my book, or Mother's, or my sisters'. No one will separate us. I've made sure of that. I'm careful not to look as our father passes, taking the gentle turn around the edge of the amphitheater behind the carts.

"You should go down to the baths so that what I tell Mother will turn out to be true," Genivee says. She pats my hand once, another of her privileges. "And don't forget the bread!"

I watch the yellow flowers in Genivee's hair bounce as she skips away. Somehow I don't mind the irony of being told not to forget when it comes from Genivee. She's too young to remember what that means. And it won't be long before she doesn't know me at all.

I look around and realize that the people of Canaan have been moving in a slow but steady stream, working their way down to the shaded side of the amphitheater. Janis, Head of Council for as long as anyone can remember, is now in her chair on the platform, back straight, white hair elegant against black robes, her expression kind. A mother with her children. Reese and Li, Council members chosen very obviously for their size, stand just behind her. The impression is subtle but clear. Janis is going to talk, but it's Jonathan, not his grandmother, who is really in control of the city.

I turn to go, pushing myself the wrong way through the line trying to cross the bridge. In seventy days Jonathan of the Council will forget; Janis, Head of Council, will forget; and these people are going to turn on one another.

～❧～

I enter the baths on the women's side. This is one of the old buildings, a circle of white columns with arches carved to look like blowing wheat on the edge of the harvested fields, vines of green and blue twining down from the roof's flower garden. A Lost girl waits in the changing rooms, with smooth olive skin and a mask of an expression. I know her, though not by name.

I've never asked. Every now and then the Lost don't give themselves a new name, and anyway, people, Lost or otherwise, are safer kept at a distance.

I set my pack on the ground and untie my tether. The Lost girl takes my dirty tunic, leggings, belt, and sandals, exchanging them for a drying cloth large enough to wrap around my body, her face unchanging. I wonder if she's lonely. My mother told me once that the Lost will always be lonely, because who could form an understanding with one of them? They could be anyone. Cousins, sisters, brothers. So many go missing after the Forgettings. The Lost are removed from our gene pool. Or they're supposed to be. This girl, I notice, is filling out her tunic rather well.

"No," I say abruptly when she tries to take my pack, then, more softly, "No. Thank you." There are small cupboards here, with a numbered key on a string that can be worn around the neck after a book is locked inside. I'll risk the damp and keep my book with me. My pack is full of contraband anyway. "A private room?" I ask. "Warm?"

She nods, my dirty clothes over one arm, and I follow her into the cool room, past an enormous pool that takes up most of the floor space, fed by a waterfall diverted from the main channel. Since it is the last, hot day of sunlight, the room is loud with women and girls, many of them just a year or two younger than me, unlucky enough to have finished their learning too close to a Forgetting, when it's impossible to apprentice long enough to retain any of your skills. The hum of chat echoes weirdly as we pass into the quiet of the warm side. This pool is empty, bubbling from beneath, the air here thick and wet.

The girl with the olive skin hands me off to another Lost woman, small and round, as wrinkled and familiar as my dirty tunic. I walk with her to a row of doors across the back of the room. The wrinkled Lost woman opens one, stepping back to let me go in first. A deep basin is sunk into the floor stones, lined with glazed tiles the same green as our dishes, set against a curving back wall in a bluish light shining through a vine-covered window in the ceiling. The Lost woman closes the door, opens a sluice gate in the wall, and a stream of water, cloudy with steam, arcs out into the basin.

I drop the drying cloth and step down, shivering once at the first touch of heat. The bathhouse was built over a hot spring, "hot" being the all-important adjective. I settle onto the little bench built inside the basin, enveloped in a vapor cloud, waiting for the water to inch up deliciously and cover me.

"Would you like me to bring you a jug of cool?" the woman asks.

I shake my head. Two or three degrees from scalding is exactly how I like it.

A quick smile creases her face. "I don't know why I asked. You never do."

I look up, surprised. It's funny that she remembers this about me, when every female in Canaan must come in and out of these bathing rooms. I watch her bend to pick up my drying cloth in the fog, but what I see is the glassblower's son materializing out of Jin's dark corner. How often are we all being observed without knowing it? So many times the Lost are dismissed, ignored, and women gossip in these baths. They gossip a lot. All at once I'm willing to bet this little Lost woman knows everything about us.

I lean over, swirl the water with a hand, and for the second time in one day I start a conversation. "Could I . . ." I try again. "Do you have a name?"

The woman's forehead wrinkles more at my question, but she only places the folded cloth neatly on the bench, careful not to touch my pack, and says, "My name is Rose, Nadia the Dyer's daughter."

So she knows me. As suspected. I say quietly, "Do you happen to know the glassblower's son?" I begin to undo my braids, as if my question is casual, and she steps over to touch the running water, as if its temperature might have changed.

"The glassblower's son?" she repeats, voice soft beneath the water splash. "I thought you might have asked your sister about that."

"My sister? Which one?"

"Liliya."

I frown. Why would I ask Liliya about Gray? I never voluntarily ask Liliya about anything.

Rose says, "They have an understanding, or are approaching one. That is what the potter's wife says. She lives across the street from the glassblower."

I huddle in the water, stunned by this news. I have no trouble believing that Liliya would be interested in Gray. He probably has some sort of line queuing. But I just can't picture him choosing my sister. Then again, he is a *zopa*. I say, "But why start an understanding this close to the Forgetting?" The whole thing will be over in seventy days. Unless they choose each other again.

Rose watches me closely. "Maybe it's only a dalliance."

Now I'm shocked. Would Liliya really allow that? It would be easy for her to have an understanding with Gray. Just go to the Council and show that they've both written it in their books. And if they don't choose each other again after the Forgetting, then take themselves back to the Council and cross it out. That's what everyone does, unless they decide to stay for any children. Or take the coward's way out, like my father. But a dalliance, a relationship of convenience, unwritten, that is shameful. And stupid. Two or three months after a Forgetting a girl could find a child in her belly and have no idea how it got there. And since that child's name will not be written in the books of two parents, that child will be taken, and that child will be Lost. I jerk loose another braid. Liliya, I have decided, is also a *zopa*.

"Or it may only be a rumor," the wrinkled woman says in her quiet voice. "It's best not to trust everything that is heard in the—"

A blast of cool air disturbs my steam. My head jerks up, the Lost woman turns, and there, standing in the doorway, is Liliya, wrapped in a drying cloth. I stare at her, torn between irritation and fear of what she might have overheard. Liliya puts two dark eyes on the Lost woman.

"You can go."

The old woman shuffles out without a backward glance. Liliya closes the door behind her and it's just the two of us and the sound of water splashing. I sink back into the basin. If Liliya is seeking me out, that can't be good. She sits daintily on the bench, adjusting the drying cloth as she crosses her legs, a key dangling from a string around her neck. I examine her anew from beneath half-lidded eyes. My sister is pretty, in a curly-headed, big-eyed, curvy sort of way. Very curvy sort of way. Everything about me is tall and straight. We look like two different species. Maybe we are.

"Mother was upset this morning," she says sweetly.

I spread my arms along the rim of the basin, careful to show that her presence doesn't affect me. The water is up to my knees now. "She knows I left early for the baths."

Liliya snorts. "Genivee is such a little liar."

I narrow my eyes. I will not stand for her insulting Genivee.

"I was concerned when I saw you come in," Liliya says. "Running about during the resting, going who knows where, with who knows who. I was so worried, I dropped off Mother and came here instead. I couldn't even go to the granary today."

Which means she knows she could get away with not going today. The granary is a perfect apprenticeship for Liliya, learning to decide how much everyone in Canaan can or can't have to eat. She'll be one who retains her work skills after the Forgetting, I think. Telling other people how to live must have become second nature by now. She's still smiling.

"So where have you been, Nadia?"

I don't move, but I can feel my body tensing in the heat. Only now am I connecting the Lost woman's words about my sister and the glassblower's son and his sudden appearance in Jin's roof garden. Liliya dislikes me; I've always known that. But the idea that she might actually hate me enough to find out what I'm up to, to get me caught, that thought has never occurred. I look at her smug face through the steam.

"Nothing to say?" she asks.

Would it give Liliya some sort of twisted satisfaction to see me flogged? Any guilt she might feel would be gone in seventy days.

"You're so quiet, Nadia." She eyes my pack, snatches it, and sets it in her lap.

"Liliya," I say.

She twists the clasp and opens the flap. I know she can see my book now, and I feel much more exposed by that than my naked body in the bath.

"Stop, Liliya. Now." If she touches my book, I will scream the bathhouse down.

"Apples!" She nearly squeals. "Not many of these left in the city now, are there? But what's this?" She pulls a small bundle from my pack, folds back the cloth to show a purple branch studded with pale, round fruits. Like the dark day moons. "Are they silvercurrants?" she asks. And before she's even finished speaking she has two of them popped into her mouth.

I watch her swallow, paralyzed. Those aren't silvercurrants. I actually have no idea what they are. I brought that plant from over the wall. I'd intended to show it to Mother, see if she'd seen anything like it in the dye house. She's actually very knowledgeable about plants, some of it retained from my father, probably. But even my half-insane mother wouldn't put something in her mouth when she didn't know for sure what it was. Liliya is such a *zopa*. She makes a face.

"Needs sugar sap." She sighs. "You know there's something wrong, don't you, Nadia?"

There are a lot of things wrong. I'm waiting for Liliya to convulse, or at least froth at the mouth. She talks on.

"You know you only apprenticed at the dye house to be with Mother. But that hasn't worked out for you, has it? Why do you think that is?"

This is pulling at a still-fresh wound, as my sister is aware. I did apprentice at the dye house for a time, to be with Mother, and no, it didn't make a difference. But Mother had loved me once. I remember it.

Liliya leans forward, squishing my pack against her ample chest.

"You weren't with Mother and me when we woke up from the Forgetting. You probably think I was too confused, but I remember when the door opened and the sky was sparkling. Genivee was in her cradle seat, all the little seedlings in the window, and you—you picked up your book from the table, and you know what you said next, don't you? You said the book wasn't yours."

I'd also said her name was Lisbeth, because it was, before Father wrote her a new book. But she doesn't remember that. The water gurgles and rises, my body half ivory, half sunrise pink. I think I'm getting too hot this time.

"You know it's not you she cares about seeing in that bed. It could be anyone. And you don't look like us," Liliya says. "You don't act like us."

I'm the only one who favors our father. Finally I whisper, "My name is written in Mother's book."

Liliya leans back against the wall, arms comfortably around my pack. "Oh, we had a Nadia, I think, before Father died. But I think we lost her and got you instead. We all know it's true, and it's time we admitted it."

So this is what Liliya thinks. Really thinks. While I've been risking my back to make sure the Forgetting never separates our family again. My head feels like the swirling currents. She balances my battered pack on her lap, plays with the soft twine of the tether.

"I could toss your book in right now, you know. Ruin it. And you wouldn't say anything if I did, would you? Because if you did, I might tell about all your running around during the restings."

I watch her hands.

"But I won't do that. Because I think it's better if you do. And that's why I've come to say that I want you to apprentice at the Archives. Think about it. You would have access to all your old books there. You would have the chance to fix them."

I know I'm getting too hot. There's a blurriness at the edge of my vision.

"Change your books. Let Nadia be lost in the Forgetting. Like she was last time. Find your real family, or something close, and stop making Mother miserable. We'll all forget soon and then everything will be like it should. Unless you're still there when we wake up."

My sister tosses my pack to the floor and stands, adjusting her cloth. "How can you take the heat in here?" she asks. I watch her walk to the door, every step sure, confident that something necessary has now been done. She looks back at me.

"Do it, Nadia, or I'll make it happen myself. You know I will. Just let me know when you've taken care of things. No reason to talk about it again." Liliya waits to see if I'll respond.

When I don't, she says, "You know you're miserable, too." Then the door shuts and I am alone.

I need to get out of the basin. My knees are on the ledge beneath the water, elbows on the rim, then my hand covers my mouth and I am racked with one silent sob. I wouldn't have thought Liliya could slice my insides to ribbons, but she has done it, ruthless and precise, like a harvester with a scythe. I'm dizzy, heart throbbing in my chest, and the little breath I can find feels more like water than air.

The shock of cold water on my back jolts my eyes into opening. The sluice gate has been shut, and Rose sets down the water jug.

"Sit on the edge, then," she says. "Head down."

I do as she says, and feel the wind of a swaying fern frond in Rose's hand. The moving air has an instant cooling effect, though my chest still heaves. When some of the dizziness has passed, Rose deftly unbraids the rest of my hair and pours soap on my head. I can't believe I let her. I don't let anyone deliberately touch me except Genivee. But I close my eyes and allow Rose to work the soap through, keeping them closed when she pours more cool water to rinse. I feel the nudge of the drying cloth next to me and wrap myself in it.

"Come to the bench," Rose says. I walk on unsteady legs to sit on the cooler stone. I'm not crying anymore. I never cry. Except for today. Today is the exception to everything.

"Better?" Rose asks from beside me.

I nod my head, but I can't look up at her wrinkled face. "Do you ever wish you could remember?" I ask. "Because I don't want to remember."

The steamy air moves. I think she nods. "I've wanted to remember before. But not now."

"Why?"

"Because the Lost girls need me. They don't have anyone else."

I close my eyes. I am a lost girl, I think. Without being Lost. Liliya's words seep back through my mind, leaving a dark, slimy trail behind them. *You weren't with Mother and me when we woke up from the Forgetting. You probably think I was too confused, but I remember when the door opened and the sky was sparkling. Genivee was in her cradle seat, all the little seedlings in the window, and you—you picked up your book from the table, and you know what you said next, don't you? You said the book wasn't—*

My eyes fly open. What did Liliya mean, *seedlings in the window?* There were no seedlings in the window after the Forgetting because our father took them with him. I know he did. And I have never seen another plant inside our house again. "Put it on the roof," Mother says every time, as if she unconsciously avoids it. I suck in a breath, and then another.

"Are you well?" Rose asks.

I look wildly for my pack, relieved to see that Rose has set it back on the bench, out of the splashed water on the floor. My cleaned clothes are beside it, still a little damp. I jump up and jerk the tunic over my head, pulling the leggings onto my skin with difficulty before sliding into my sandals. The pack goes to my back, tether tied to my belt, but not before I stuff the bundle with the bare purple shoot that I brought from over the wall inside it. I rush for the door, then dash straight back, swing my pack onto the bench, and dig inside. I place one yellow apple in Rose's startled hands.

"Thank you," I whisper.

I run out of the bathing room and past the pools, damp hair flying, the slap of my sandals loud in the echoing space, through the changing room and into the low, hot sunshine and overcrowded streets.

Little seedlings in the window. That's what she said.

Liliya has had a memory.

I am Nadia the Planter's daughter. I am writing in a book that says Dyer's daughter because Father went away and Mother says that's who I am. She does not remember before. Nobody remembers before. I remember. Now I am going to write all of what our teacher taught us to say.

At the first sunrising of the twelfth year, they will forget. They will lose their memories, and without their memories, they are lost. Their books will be their memories, their written past selves. They will write in their books. They will keep their books. They will write the truth, and the books will tell them who they have been. If a book is lost, then so are they Lost. I am made of my memories. Without memories, they are nothing.

1. Books will be written in every day. In our books we are to write the truth.

2. Truth is not good, and truth is not bad. When we write truth, we write who we are.

3. Books will be tied at all times to the body. When we keep our books, we remember who we are.

4. Books that are full will be taken to the Archive. When we register our books, we learn our truth.

5. When we forget, we are to read our books. When we read our books, we remember our truth.

6. When a book is changed, the truth is changed. When a book is destroyed, then we are destroyed.

I got a good grade for writing that and spelling all the words. Now I'll think about how many of these words aren't true.

NADIA THE DYER'S DAUGHTER

BOOK 1, PAGE 65, 2 SEASONS AFTER THE FORGETTING

CHAPTER THREE

I keep running, up Meridian, around the edge of the gathering in the amphitheater. Janis is talking, voice amplified by the bowl she stands in, Jonathan behind her, flanked by Reese and Li. I skirt the high ground, and when I look to the side I see her eyes fix on me, tracking my progress around the rim. I dodge behind a group of bodies, escaping her gaze and a few curious expressions, leap over some flower pots, then across Second Bridge to duck right down Hubble Street. I pass the potter's and the glassblower's. Gray is in the open-air part of the workshop, where I found him just before the last Forgetting, hair wet and curling, shirt dark with sweat from the furnace where his book nearly burned. He glances up, straightening as I run past, but I don't have time to think about him now. I have to get home.

Two streets to Hawking, then I turn the corner into the little alley between our house and the neighbors' and burst through my front door. The sitting room smells of hot wind, baking, and dry herbs. I run through it and stick my head into the storeroom. The wrapped loaves of dark days bread are stacked above rows and rows of sealed jars, the harvest of this sunlight's garden, dried apple and pepper braids hanging from the ceiling. No one is there, or in the resting rooms, so out the door again, up the outside stairs, two at a time, to a roof garden almost identical to Jin's, only ours is well-tended and one story up instead of two. Genivee has moved the bread oven into the sun for me, I see, to heat while I was at the baths. But I'm alone on the rooftop.

I make my way back down to the sitting room, slam the door, set my pack on the shining metal top of our long table. The window stands open to the breeze, the constant footsteps and clanging and calling of the city barely muted. I take out the cloth bundle with the shoot now bare of its fruit and touch the smooth skin of the leaves. Liliya ate this, I think, and Liliya had a memory. Of seedlings on our windowsill. Such a small, insignificant detail, a thought easily discarded, but its existence rocks the stone beneath my feet. I lift the cutting to my nose. A fresh smell, sharp, almost with a tingle. What if the Forgetting doesn't drain our memories away forever, like Rose pulling the plug in the basin, but only locks them up, like a book in a bathhouse cupboard? Could we unlock what's inside our heads? I jump at the sound of a voice.

"My mother said I had to come and check on you."

It's Imogene the Inkmaker's daughter, standing in our alley, her wispy brown head stuck inside my open window. Her twin, Eshan, is a little behind her, his arms crossed. I turn my back to them quick, blocking their view of the plant cutting with my body.

"She said you came running down the street like you were crazy."

I don't know what to say to that. I probably was. I probably am.

I hear Imogene sigh when I don't answer. "I'll just tell her you're fine, shall I?"

I've known Imogene and Eshan all my life. Their mother is Hedda, and the whole family is blue-eyed, brown-haired, and perfectly nice. It's the nice ones who can hurt you the most. When I peek over my shoulder Imogene is gone from the window and Eshan has taken her place.

"You really are all right?" he asks. Eshan caught me leaving contraband in their garden once. Nothing they couldn't have grown or been assigned, and just enough to make sure Hedda wasn't feeling so desperate that she would take more than her meager share at the granary again. I wonder if Eshan ever told Imogene. We've never mentioned it. I give him a tiny nod, but he doesn't leave. He says, "Can I come in?"

And before I can look back to give him any sort of nonverbal response, I hear the door opening. I grab the tattered cloth, fling it over the purple plant before I turn around. My hands grip the table behind me, the whole bundle just hidden behind my back. Eshan shuts the front door and, being male, looks completely alien in my sitting room. He gets straight to the point.

"Things can't go on like they are. Already the fields aren't quite big enough to feed us. Someday soon, we'll have to go outside the walls. I know they say we don't know what's out there, that the walls must have been built for a reason, that we don't know what we've forgotten. But if that's so, then Janis and the Council should let some of us volunteer to go over and find out. Or, if they know a reason why we shouldn't, say so."

I study the mat at my feet as if it's the most fascinating thing the city has to offer, but I'm listening. And agreeing.

"Janis has been a good leader, but she's getting old. Already the Council is making decisions she would have never allowed . . ."

Like his mother's flogging. I didn't know a braided rope could cut.

". . . and you know that's all Jonathan. If we're not careful, we're going to wake up after the Forgetting and discover that he's the one in charge." He pauses. "Did you hear Jonathan's announcement today?"

I shake my head.

"They're doing a count, of all of us, this sunsetting, to see exactly how many are in the city. They're also going to start giving rewards. Turn in a rule-breaker, extra rations. Now how does that make sense when we're not even sure if the grain will last through the dark days?"

It doesn't make sense at all.

"And it's stupid, don't you think, to just sit around and see which half of us starves? Some of us are meeting today, tenth bell, on my garden roof, to talk about going over the wall. I thought you might be interested."

For the first time I lift my eyes. "Why do you think that?"

Eshan starts at the unexpected sound of my voice. "I just . . . did," he says. "I do." I see now that he's nervous. He's playing with the tether of his book. "When we know how many of us there are, we'll know just how bad the next harvest is going to be, and then it will be the time to approach the Council. I haven't mentioned your name. I wouldn't . . . I just mean to say, I appreciate what you've done."

Now he's talking about the contraband in his garden. Surely Eshan and Imogene can't know where those things really came from. Surely they think it came from our own stores? Yesterday I would have been certain; today, I can't be certain about anything. The fraying edge of the cloth over the plant cutting brushes my fingers behind my back. I don't like all this talk about rule-breaking and rewards.

"You should come," he says. "Think about it."

In what realm of reality Eshan the Inkmaker's son thinks I will sit on his roof and talk injustice with our old schoolmates is beyond me. No matter how much I might agree with him. But I nod, and after a moment he nods, too, hesitates, then nods again and slips out the door.

I watch him pass by the window, hands behind his head. Frustrated. I don't blame him any more than his sister. But I wonder if what he said about the size of the fields is true, if the city really will be forced to move outside. We've always been taught to fear the unknown beyond the walls. But what if it wasn't unknown? What if someone besides me could remember?

I turn back to the table, take off the cloth. The smell wafts up, so clean it clears my head. Assuming Liliya is not poisoned by the resting I could quiz her, see if there are other memories lurking that I might share, but something tells me she's not going to cooperate. Genivee has no memories before the Forgetting at all, and Mother . . . It would be hard to know what's a true memory with her and what isn't, no matter what I fed her. Not that I actually have anything to give them, of course. Thanks to Liliya's greed or her lack of breakfast, I'm going to have to go back over the wall before I can do anything at all. And I cannot get caught this time. Not yet. And not now.

I split the end of the cutting, get it in a water jar, and, as soon as I'm sure no one is lurking outside, run up the stairs to the roof and nestle it among the dying breadfruits. Then I'm back inside, dropping the bar across our door, down the silent hall, and into the resting room I share with Genivee. Light beams from one high window, open now for the cross-breeze from the door, leaving a bright warm patch on the pale green matting. I go to my knees, shove aside my mattress and blankets, and, using a broken metal hinge confiscated for the purpose, pry up a floor stone. Beneath the stone is a hole.

It took me weeks to dig out the hole. Sneaking jars of soil up to the garden every day, digging only when I had the house to myself, and without leaving the smallest speck of dirt for the all-too-observant Genivee. I reach in and carefully move aside extra ink, a pen, and a wad of thick sacking that holds a book. A true book, for all four of us, sewn page by stolen page. A book that, when finished, will contain everything that's happened to our family since the last Forgetting. Everything except Anson the Planter. I think that memory could only hurt them now.

I also have a jar of stain in the hole, waterproof, made from oil and the shells of the blacknut trees in the lower-quadrant grove. I've been testing it on my own knees, which, now that I think of it, has probably been a bit of a bathhouse riddle for poor Rose. But when the Forgetting comes, my mother and sisters will be marked with this, all of us locked in this room together, with our books. And if something happens to one of our books, if there's any question about the truth,

I'll show them the alternate one, hidden in the same room, under a floor stone marked with the symbol that is stained on their skin. No one will be able to separate our family again.

I slide my pack off my back. All this is written in my book, too, in detail. I can't count on not forgetting myself, just because I didn't the first time. Though part of me hopes that I will. Then I sit back on my heels, one hand still propping up the stone lid of my hiding hole. Liliya is not going to cooperate with this plan, I realize. Not anymore. She'll fight to get rid of me. The sister that isn't. The thought makes me feel sore, bruised inside.

Into the hole goes everything that came with me over the wall. Soil samples, pressed leaves, the apples I'll have to retrieve again soon, to get them dried and into our storeroom. And I drop in the rocks I've collected on the mountainside as well, my one and only attempt at decoration, a row of deep, sparkling blue crystals lined up on a single shelf. I replace the floor stone, my mattress and blankets, leaving my side of the room plain and impersonal. Genivee's is an explosion.

I half braid my hair, swinging it to the side to avoid my pack, lost in thought as I go back to the sitting room. Genivee, being Genivee, has left flour, oil, spoon, bowl, and an apron sitting on the table for me. I measure, pour, and stir, but I'm not thinking about bread at all. I'm thinking about sickness.

I've never been sick, and I've never met anyone who's been sick, at least not in their body. But we talked about it in the learning room once, when one of the doctors came as part of our apprentice exploration. The ways people die, she had explained, are from age, accidents, childbirth, or poison, but sometimes there can be an internal malfunction. Nothing to be done about that, though there are certain chemicals from leaves or fruits that can relieve pain or, rarely, correct the malfunction and make the person well again. My spoon slows.

What if the Forgetting is not something inescapable, like Jin's age, but more like a malfunction? A sickness? And if so, did Liliya, while being a *zopa*, eat something that would correct it? If our memories aren't gone, but still inside our heads, could we get them back out? What if I didn't have to convince Liliya that I belong in our family? What if she, or Mother, could remember one glimpse of my face from before? What if none of us ever forgot in the first place?

I stir with a vengeance, arms aching. I have to know if it could be true. I have to go up the mountain, get more of that plant, and give it to Liliya. See if any more memories come, to compare them with my own. There's nothing else to do. And then my stirring slows, and it hits me. There is someone else I could give that plant to. Someone I share a memory with from before. Someone who already knows I've been going over the wall.

I jerk off the apron, leave the dough in the bowl, and hurry out the door, careful not to run, so as not to alarm Hedda. I cut between houses, past the Learning Center, where the children are chanting: "If a book is lost, then so are they Lost. I am made of my memories . . ." Then across Newton Street, then Sagan, darting into the alley beside the potter's workshop, directly across the street from the glassblower's. And there I pause.

Gray and his father—I think his name is Nash—are working together on a large cylinder of glowing orange glass on the end of a blowing tube. His father takes the tube from his mouth, still spinning it, then quickly rolls it back and forth across a sheet of metal. Gray hits the tube, the glass breaks off, and then he cuts it fast with scissors. Bright sparks fly, and, like a piece of cloth, the molten glass falls and lays flat on the sheet. Now it's a long, thin pane, clearing as it cools, nearly ready for a window.

His father lifts the metal sheet and slides it back into another furnace. Gray wipes his forehead with the back of his arm, almost exactly like I did with the bread. Only he is smiling, from amusement, pleasure, happiness, I don't know. I'm unfamiliar. It strikes me as beautiful, unexpected, and I've never wanted to approach a place less in my life. I have no business here, or nothing I can admit to. Then Gray turns his head and sees me standing across the street.

He wipes his face again and says something to his father. The glassblower shoves him once, playfully I think, and steps through a door into their house. Gray looks at me again and waits. I force my steps, pulse racing as hard as when he caught me at the wall. I wonder what the potter's wife will have to say about this in the baths.

The heat from the firing furnace is a barrier to be breached. I push through, Gray wiping down tools as I inch into his workspace. He's much larger than his father, a black apron tied over a shirt of light blue that is stained with sweat, smudges of soot and stubble on his jaw. He grins just a little.

"The dyer's daughter seeks me out. We make—"

"It has to be today," I say.

"Why?"

I don't answer this. He puts what looks like a very thick spoon into a bucket of water, and I'm surprised to hear the water hiss. He looks at me sidelong. "Anything to do with why you came racing through here earlier like your hair was on fire?"

I shake my head, a dismissal more than a denial. He's thoughtful, a tiny line between his brows. Again I notice the dark smear that is his eyelashes. Oh, I can see why Liliya is interested. But why does Gray want to go over the wall? Or does he?

"Whatever is going on with my sister is none of my business," I say in a rush. "And what I do is none of hers. Swear to me you're not trying to help her get me caught."

The frown deepens. I'm not sure I've ever seen Gray go so long without a smirk. "I . . ."

"Never mind," I say quickly. I can't believe I asked. Anyone who would dally or otherwise with Liliya is probably not trustworthy in any case. "First bell of the resting, be on Jin's roof."

"Okay. But—"

"Fine," I say, cutting off whatever he was going to add. The whole plan is stupid, and I don't like to be stupid. First, assume Gray is somehow not trying to get me flogged or earn extra rations or my sister's admiration by getting me caught. Second, get him over the wall without being seen, traipse about the mountainside, trick him into eating an unfamiliar berry and telling me things he probably doesn't remember, and third, get us both back over the wall and home without anyone the wiser. The thought of just how much could go wrong makes me long for the bed I will again not sleep in. The thought of what we could gain if Gray does remember makes me determined to do it, stupid or not. The thought of nothing going wrong, of being over the wall, alone with the glassblower's son, makes me turn to go.

"Nadia," he says.

I look back. The smirk has returned, so I glare at him.

"You have flour on your nose."

I do go then, and as soon as I'm out of sight I use the end of my tunic to scrub my face.

⤦

I drop into my place at the long table to eat with my mother and my sisters, feeling every second of the last resting I missed. Mother is small, slender, with the coloring of the rest of the family, only her dark hair is threaded with gray. She runs her hand back and forth along her book, still upset by the empty bed at waking. Liliya looks the most like her, Genivee a close second, the two of them almost identical in their curly-headed prettiness, even if what's inside their heads is so completely different. I am like the pale bruise on the rich brown of a honeyfruit.

"Did you hear about the counting today?" Liliya asks. She's slicing up the bread I baked, serving everyone but me. She doesn't seem poisoned. "Council members will be coming to every house in our quadrant, tomorrow after the leaving bell."

I lean over to take the knife, to cut my own slice. The blade has the entwining letters "NWSE" stamped into its blade, like most of the metal tools in the city, another of Canaan's little mysteries. Mother shakes her head and pushes my hand away. "It's Liliya's turn to cut."

Liliya looks amused before she turns back to Mother. "Do you understand that means we have to stay home in the morning, Mother?"

"We're not going to the dye house?" Mother pushes the food on her plate back and forth with a spoon.

"Only for a little while, until the Council comes," says Genivee. "I'm staying home, too. Then, when the Council says it's time to go, we can all go. Nothing to worry about."

I stir the mix of greens on my breadless plate. "I think we should force some of our seeds from the garden," I say abruptly. "We could have seedlings by sunrising, and get our harvest sooner that way. We might even get two."

There's a shocked little silence at our table. That was quite a speech from me. It's just that kind of day. I look down at my plate, but at an angle that gives me an easy view of my sisters and mother across the table.

"We could put them in pots," I say slowly, "and put the seedlings in the window."

Genivee shoots me a questioning glance, while Mother just looks unhappy, like I knew she would. But it's Liliya's expression that interests me. A slight frown, a passing confusion quickly dismissed.

"I don't like plants in the house," Mother says. She runs a hand absentmindedly over the book around her neck. "It's so untidy."

Mother used to tease our father about all the different plants he brought in during the dark days. The house had been full of them.

Genivee says, "You should ask Liliya where she's going before resting, Mother. I heard she was sitting with a boy."

"Genivee!" Liliya protests, but this is just the sort of thing Liliya and my mother love. It wakes Mother from her stupor.

I thank Genivee with my eyes and prick up my ears for Liliya's answer.

"Is he handsome?" Mother asks, as if the Forgetting isn't almost here.

"I heard that he is," Genivee answers, giggling. "Liliya says he'll be the head of his trade one day."

Well, that's not hard, I think. There's only his own father to pass up for the job. I reach for my water cup. *Actually, just by the way, Liliya, as soon as you're done sitting with your boy, I'm taking him over the wall with me. And not to pry or anything, but you're an idiot if you're not making him write this down.*

Liliya pretends to be embarrassed. "You shouldn't talk like that, Genivee." Which means she wants her to.

"That's good," my mother says dreamily. "It's good for children to have a father, if they can. Never forget that you had a father once, girls."

But she doesn't look at me when she says it.

๑

Genivee watches me during the writing time, her book in her lap. Kenny the beetle, a gift from over the wall, now living out his days in a jar beside Genivee's mattress, sits like a bright yellow, multilegged apple, eating leftover greens on the palm of her hand. Genivee is watching me because I'm not writing, and also because I'm not getting ready to sleep. I'm braiding my hair down tight, retying the tether of my book, waiting for Mother to come see two full beds. Genivee says, "She's jealous, you know. Liliya, I mean."

I drop my tether, startled into speech. "Why?"

"Because she's pretty and you're not."

"That makes zero sense, Genivee." I go back to tying.

"See, that's what I mean. She's pretty, but you make people stare when you walk down the street."

They look at me because I'm an oddity of nature. Or crazy.

"You're exactly what she wants to be, and you don't try, and you don't even notice, and that's really annoying, Nadia."

I have to smile at Genivee. She can be very perceptive, but I think she might be unaware of our oldest sister's plan to get rid of me.

"You should ask her about her boy. It will make her feel better since you don't have one."

Something tells me this would also be an unpleasant conversation.

Genivee lets Kenny crawl up her arm, and asks, "Why do you have to go over the wall?"

I go still. Yes, Genivee is perceptive. Very perceptive. I don't know exactly how she knows I've been going over the wall, but she does. I'm starting to wonder if everybody does. Answers flit through my brain, but I can't think of a single one fit for my sister. Before, I'd wanted to understand where we came from, to know if there could be others out there, people like me, who never forgot. But today is different. Maybe today I can find a way to stop the Forgetting altogether. "Why do you think I do it, Genivee?"

"Because the city is too small for you," she says. She looks thirty-five instead of twelve.

"Don't tell Liliya, okay?"

Genivee just rolls her eyes. "Please."

And here is yet another reason to go over the wall. Because I won't be able to bear it when Genivee forgets me.

❧

The streets are emptying this close to the resting, the sun a sliver of gold behind the mountains, sky showing its first hazy stripes of pink. Tomorrow will be sunsetting, and I won't see the light again until the Forgetting. I take the back way to Jin's and sneak up his garden stairs well before the bell. I'd planned to be there first, to see Gray arrive, make sure he hadn't brought Jonathan or someone else with him. But the glassblower's son is already in his dark corner, waiting for me.

"Eager?" he asks. "No, don't tell me. I don't think Jin is in bed yet, and we all know how talkative you can get."

I ignore him, move to the edge of the garden, and look down into the alley, then on the other side, down to the street. I can feel Gray's gaze like a pressure on my back.

He says, "If I didn't know better, I'd say you don't trust me."

"I don't trust you."

He only grins. "Tell me how we do this."

"The same as you saw before."

"Simple, then. And the sun will help."

My brows come down.

"The sun is low," he says, "and we're going straight into it. If anyone does have their curtains open, or is out when they shouldn't be, the light will be in their eyes."

I hadn't thought of this, and I don't like that Gray the Glassblower's son thought of something before I did. I sit, back to a column, adrenaline taking away any thoughts of being tired. We wait until the water clock strikes once, the first bell of resting ringing out over the city. Deep silence settles into the air of the garden. I wonder what he talks about with Liliya. We wait a little more, and then Gray says, "Shall we?"

I make him go first. I reach up with the long hook, feel along the top of the wall until I snag the rope ladder, and pull it back over to our side, stretching it across the empty space so he can get a foot in the bottom rung. He rides the swing of the ladder across the alley to the wall better than I think he will, though I'm sure he'll have a decent-size bruise on his shoulder. Gray climbs quickly, straddles the wall, then lies flat on his stomach.

I feel a sudden flutter of nerves. Unless someone is in the alley or in this garden with us, we can't be seen . . . until we reach the top of the wall, and Gray is already up there. I guess I had expected something to happen. To see Jonathan arrive, trying to catch me in the act, telling Gray he's earned his reward. But Gray's back is in just as much danger as mine now.

I ride the ladder and climb fast to the top, flip it over, and as soon as Gray's feet hit the grasses at the base of the wall, I follow him down, get my hands on a lower rung, and make the short drop. The ground is higher on this side, the rock face that is the lowest slope of the near mountain rising blue-gray and sparkling where it's not in shadow, the tall golden grasses rippling in the breeze. I can smell the forest, and I am over the wall with the glassblower's son.

Gray looks at me, gives me his grin. And then he runs.

I went over the wall.

When we were young in the learning room, Eshan once asked why Canaan had a wall around it. Our teacher said that we'd forgotten what was outside Canaan, but that was exactly why we needed the wall in the first place. To keep us safe from what we did not know. What if there were insects that could sting or bite? What if you fell off a cliff or into a deep hole? What if there was no food, and you starved? What if, the teacher said, you were outside the walls and you forgot? You'd wander alone, forever, never able to find a way home again. We stay inside the walls because that is what we know, and where we are safe.

It made me wonder, does the wall protect us, or keep us in?

Today I found I'm not afraid of the unknown. Today I discovered that the unknown loved me, and that I loved it back.

NADIA THE DYER'S DAUGHTER
BOOK 13, PAGE 64, 11 YEARS AFTER THE FORGETTING

CHAPTER FOUR

I watch Gray bound through the grasses, angling off to one side to go around the cliff face and climb the steep slope. This is the Gray I knew in learning, a little wild, with more energy than he can hold. Part of me wants to let him run. But I don't need him on the windy, rocky scree at the top of the mountain. I need him at the waterfall, where that plant is twining through the fern trees. I run after him.

He's faster than I expected, his legs much longer. Another minute and he's out of my sight, but it isn't hard to know where he's gone. The suncrickets and the blueflies chirp and click wherever he passes, clouds of tiny white dust moths rising up from the leaves to make patterns in the air. I follow the noise and the moth clouds until I am up and around to the top of the cliff.

And there is Gray, standing stock-still at the very edge, toes hanging over the rocks. Nothing moves but his shirt, tightening and loosening as he breathes deep from his run. He's looking out over Canaan, a white stone circle washed in a slanting gold light. I stand beside him. I'd almost forgotten the city could be like that. Beautiful. And this Gray, with the serious, settled face, is not the Gray I know at all.

"We'll be seen," I whisper. I'm not certain that's true. I think we're too high. But I need to redirect him. His sleeves are pushed up, and for the first time I see the scars on the inside of his right wrist and forearm, where it looks as if the skin has been melted. Burn scars. Yes, he would have scars from the Forgetting. I hadn't realized that's why he's always worn sleeves. He turns his head to me, smiles once.

"Let's go."

❧

We hike around the mountain, down a natural path through the thick foliage in light that has grown a little dimmer since I was last here. One or two glowworms have already started to leave strands of luminescent silk as they travel between the fronds. By the first of the dark days this part of the mountain will have its own light from thousands of tiny threads. Gray doesn't run anymore, or not as much, but he does veer off course when he sees something interesting. Which is often. I steer him back.

He asks me questions. What have I seen? Where else have I gone? I shrug, or nod, or shake my head when appropriate. The truth is I've been a resting's walk away from my ladder in every direction and I've never seen anyone or anything to fear outside the walls, only rock, water, insects, and plants. Which is part of why I love it on my mountain; no people to complicate things. It's strange to see another body here, unsettling, but at the same time Gray enjoys it so much, his enthusiasm rubs off. I show him a completely innocent-looking hole in a rock, let him be surprised when without warning the hole shoots a spout of water ten meters up into the air. But somewhere in Canaan the water clock is ticking. I have to get him up to those vines.

Finally I maneuver him to the two towering ferns I've been aiming for, skirt down the hill where the forgetting trees grow wild, and when we break free of the leaves, there's a shallow canyon stretching wide between the cliffs, the foliage going dark purple and blue for sunsetting. To our left and just a little higher up is a waterfall, gushing and spraying four or five meters down to a pool at its base.

"Are we going up there?" he asks.

I nod and start uphill, fast, not letting him stop until we're above the falls, at a watercourse gurgling around tumbled stone, where the low light can't directly penetrate the dense, twisting leaves. It's like a small room here, a room with a stream and a spectacular view of a canyon. Having Gray in this place is harder than on the mountainside; it feels a little bit like the time he opened my book. But there are the silver-white berries, only two or three bunches left, and I'm guessing we have an hour before we need to start back. A straight course back.

Gray squats down beside the water, drinks from his hand, then splashes some on his head and neck, turning the ends of his hair into loose, dark spirals. I turn away, wander toward the berry vines.

"Do you swim here?" Gray asks.

I look back and find him right on the edge of the rocks again, leaning forward, looking over the waterfall and down to the pool. Gray the Glassblower's son has obviously missed developing some key survival skills. I'm not particularly afraid of heights, but I do respect the fact that they will kill me. He glances over his shoulder.

"Come on, Nadia. Speak. Do you swim down there?"

"Yes," I say, cautious.

He grins wide, all the way across his mouth, and starts working at the buckle of his book strap. "Let's go, then."

"There's not time to hike down and back around before the resting is over." This is mostly a lie. He has to stay up here. But his smile has gotten even bigger. He seems to consider it some kind of personal triumph every time I manage a full sentence.

"Who said anything about hiking down?"

And then I realize that Gray means to jump. Off the cliff. And swim. Without our books. I step back. He sets his book on a boulder, well away from the water, and looks at me.

"Coming?"

I shake my head, and his brow wrinkles.

"Isn't the water deep enough?"

"It probably is. I've never found the bottom." He relaxes again.

"Good. Let's . . ."

I shake my head again, harder, and this time he goes still. The small smile is back on his lips, the sarcastic one.

"Is it the jump, or me?" he asks.

I clutch the straps of my pack. I am not jumping over a waterfall. And while I might swim with my book in sight when I'm completely alone in a vast and unexplored wilderness, I will never separate from my book in the presence of another person.

"I see," he says. He picks up his book, slowly buckling it back on.

Now I feel guilty. And annoyed. I turn my back, pretend to be very, very interested in the berry vine. The quiet grows loud in my ears. "Are you hungry?" I say, and break off a shoot heavy with the round white fruit, holding it out without actually looking at his face. But I see his feet as he comes and takes it, watch as he finds a spot to sit with his back to a boulder, running his fingers down the length of the branch.

He says, "Let's play a game, Dyer's daughter. Answer for answers. You answer my question, and I have to answer two of yours, no matter what."

I think this through. Since I doubt Gray will ask anything that allows me to merely nod or shake my head, giving answers implies that I'll have to talk. But getting Gray to answer, that is exactly what I want. Just as soon as he's eaten what's in his hand.

He gives me a little of his smirk. "You can't say no to such a generous offer."

I turn around, find a small flat rock beside the stream and sit on it. "Okay," I reply.

The smirk gets bigger. He settles his elbows on his knees, the shoot of berries dangling from his fingers. I am so tense the muscles in my shoulders ache.

"Then this is my first question. Tell me, Nadia the Dyer's daughter, why do you go over the wall?"

Answers shoot one by one through my brain, like when Genivee asked just a few hours before. But this time I need an answer that will keep Gray talking. I decide to offer him part of the truth. I lean over to the bank of the watercourse, pick up a stone from beneath the rushing flow. It's the same blue-gray as the cliff face, rounded and smooth, with a little sparkle. I hold it up.

"This was probably jagged once," I say, "broken off from a larger stone." My words are halting. "But the water has worn it down, like the whetstone at Arthur's. Use and time wear away the edges. Make them smooth." He leans forward, so intent on my face I have to pause. Speaking is difficult, being looked at like that even more so. Saying thoughts aloud I have never shared with another living soul? Excruciating. "But the stone in the city . . . it isn't worn at all. It looks . . . freshly cut."

"So you think we haven't lived in the city long?"

I shake my head.

"You think we came from somewhere else, outside the walls?"

I nod.

"So your question is, where did we come from before Canaan?"

I look up in time to see him lean back, thoughtful, no need for me to answer at all. He's getting this quicker than I thought, and I'm glad, because I'm not sure I can go on. Then, as if to justify my sacrifice of speech, he eats a berry.

Gray says, "So what are you looking for, exactly, outside the walls?"

I take a breath. "Roads. Paths. A dropped tool. Anything."

"And what have you found?"

"One pit where we've dug out the metal ore, one where we've dug out clay. Nothing for the sand for the glass."

"We've got masses of sand. Sacked and stored. No idea where it came from. And nothing else?"

I shake my head. He eats a handful of berries. I note the number.

"And what about a pit for the stone?"

I frown at him, and then at the running water.

"Have you found where they dug or cut the stone?"

All this time I've been thinking about that stone and taking its existence for granted. An entire city of unworn stone. Where had it come from? The hole would have to be massive, the cuts incredibly obvious. I'm on my feet and to the cliff beside the waterfall in an instant, where Gray had been earlier, looking out over the canyon, a wide scoop in the landscape of hills. Then I drop flat onto my stomach and put my head over the edge, push aside the wet, hanging foliage to expose the rock. Mist sprays my face. More of the blue-gray stone, not white, and no man-made cuts, at least not that I can see. I look back over my shoulder, where Gray is watching me, and shake my head as I get to my feet.

"It could have filled with water," Gray says. "You should think about that as well."

I eye him warily as I brush off the dirt. When he's still like this, I can almost see the little boy before the Forgetting instead of the Gray from the learning room. Is he that different, I wonder, or did I just never really know him at all? He's much smarter than I'd given him credit for. Then he eyes me, a little sly.

"Maybe you should go swimming with me after all. We could look for tool marks. You don't mind getting your tunic wet? Or, you don't have to get it wet at all. What do you think, Dyer's daughter?"

Meaning my tunic is not required, I take it. No, I decide. He's not that different. But I also note that he's tossed away the shoot I gave him, stripped clean. Now is my time. I go back to sit on my rock and for once meet his eyes. "What I think,"

I say, "is that you've asked me nine questions. That gives me eighteen answers, doesn't it, Glassblower's son?"

"I did not ask you nine questions."

I hug my knees.

"That was conversation!"

"It's not my fault if you didn't specify."

He looks like he's going to argue, but then he grins and cocks his head once, as if to acknowledge my point. He leans back and puts his arms behind his head. "Go."

Questions swirl through my mind like the dust moths, and there are so many to tempt me. *Is Jonathan of the Council waiting for me on Jin's roof? What is your relationship with my sister? Why did you want to come over the wall with me?* But instead I ask the thing I need to know the most: "What is your earliest memory?"

He frowns, an unusual expression for his face. I wait for his answer, heart thumping so hard I'm afraid I could look down and see the movement. Finally he says, "I would think it would be the same as yours. Waking up after the Forgetting. Why would you ask me that?"

"No questions," I say, "only answers, and that wasn't one." *Think, Gray,* I beg in my mind. *Remember what happened when I came into the workshop before the Forgetting.*

"I don't want to talk about that, Nadia," he says. And he's not teasing or joking.

"Okay," I say, thinking quickly. "Then tell me how you got the scars on your arms."

He jerks his arms down from behind his head, glancing once at his forearm. "You know, this isn't as fun as I thought it was going to be."

I wait. Wind ruffles the tops of the fern trees.

"Fine. I don't know how I got them."

"What do you mean, you don't know?"

He looks at me in confusion, maybe a little bit of anger. "You know what I mean."

"No, I don't." *Think,* I'm silently pleading. *Try to think back to before the Forgetting. Please have a memory.*

"I mean that when I woke up, I was burned."

"Who tended the burns? Your mother?"

"No."

"Was there anything in your book about it?"

"No." Gray is calm on the outside, but I can see that he's mad now. Boiling beneath his skin. It's possible I've never actually seen the glassblower's son angry. I hadn't bargained on being so completely alone with someone who is bigger than me, faster than me, and mad. And having him agitated won't help his memory.

I say, "I'm sorry if it . . . it seems like I'm . . ." I stop. I really am terrible at this. I decide to offer him another part of the truth. "I'm just trying to understand some things . . . about the Forgetting."

"What things?"

"No questions," I say. But I did hear the subtle shift in Gray's mood. "What if you tried to remember how you got those burns? Can you remember what it felt like?"

"I'm telling you they were there when I woke up. But yes. It hurt. A lot."

This is like shaking a tree, trying to get one particular nut to fall. "Think backward," I say. "You realize your hands and arms are burned. Was one before the other, or both at the same time?"

"What happened right before that is I opened my eyes. Pain is something you tend to notice right away, Nadia."

He's upset again, and I'm worried. What if he's not trying? This is too important for him not to try. "What about—"

"Wait," he interrupts. "What do you mean, 'hands'?"

I stare at him, puzzled. He jumps up from his position against the rock and before I can blink he's squatting in front of me. Trying to make me look at him. I don't want to. He holds out his arms, wrists to the sky, sleeves pushed up.

I feel my breath come fast, the slight tingle in my fingers and legs. How could I have made such a mistake? Such a stupid mistake? His right wrist and forearm are marred with rippling patches. But the skin of his left arm is a smooth, muscled strip of pale surrounded by tan. His hands haven't scarred at all. Somewhere deep in my mind, I hear him yell as he reaches into the fire.

"How did you know I had burns on both my arms? And my hands?"

I don't know what to say, so I don't. I'd just assumed both sides had scarred. Stupid.

"You asked if I burned them at the same time. How did you know they were both burned?" he demands.

I can't look up at him. "I must have seen you after the Forgetting. With your arms bandaged. I'm sure I did."

"Liar," he says to me, and just like before, I feel the slap of the word. This time I think I'm meant to, and it makes me mad, too, which is good. The anger distracts me from the panic I could feel lurking just below the surface. "You did not see that," he says.

"Why?"

"Because you didn't."

"I say I did."

His voice is deadly serious. And close. "If you know something about me I need you to say it. Now, Nadia. While we're out here, alone. Tell me when you saw me with those burns."

No, I need for him to say it. I need for him to remember. I want so much for those berries to make him remember it's like an ache inside.

"If you know it, say it!" he yells. The suncrickets raise a chorus of chirping, and then immediately go quiet. "Please."

I can't say anything. He's on his feet now, and I can hear him moving, pacing, trying to keep his frustration in check. I hug my knees, my own anger turning inward. This is my fault, for being so careless, reckless. Overconfident. I have to find a way out, a way to explain without explaining, and these are not tools I often find ready and waiting in my box.

When Gray speaks again, it sounds like barely controlled rage. "Then just tell me how you know, Nadia. How were you there?"

My gaze leaps upward, pulse jumping in my veins. He has both hands in his hair, and his expression is not what I thought it would be at all. He's not angry; he's afraid. But he said *How were you there?* like he knew what it meant, like a memory. "Do you remember me being there?" I ask.

"No." His voice is a whisper. "How could you have been?"

"Tell me what you remember about being there."

He drops his hands and sits against the rock, head back, eyes closed. "Just that I was confused. I didn't understand where I was, or why I'd been taken. Everyone was a stranger, all penned up together. And"—he grimaces once, maybe at the memory of pain—"no one remembered what to do about burns, except for Rose. She got oil for my arms, made tea to dull the pain and make me sleep. She took care of everyone, on the men's and women's sides. I think maybe she was a doctor once. She—"

"You don't mean Rose in the bathhouse?" His eyes dart up, and I see that he does. I don't understand what he's talking about. I don't understand anything. "But . . . Rose is Lost."

He goes completely still. "Isn't that what we're talking about?"

"But . . ." I sift through his words and the realization comes to me slow, like a leaf falling from a high limb. "Were you . . . Lost?"

And again I see it in his face. He was.

I don't know what to do with my body. I stand, turn away, try to escape from his stare so that I have time to think. How could he have been Lost? He pulled his book from the fire. He put the fire out with his own hands. He had his book; the cover was burned, but almost all of the pages were there. I saw it. "You can't have been Lost," I say to the fern trees.

"But, Nadia, how could you have known—"

"You live with the glassblower!" I shout. Now I'm out of control, just like I was back then. What happened in the glassblower's workshop was the only thing I did right that sunrising. Hitting the man so Gray could rescue his book from the fire. I will not believe it went wrong. How could it have gone wrong? "You weren't Lost," I say again.

I hear him cursing beneath his breath. He must be up and about because I think he's kicking bushes. Then my little vine-covered space goes quiet again, nothing but the music of the crickets and the stream. When Gray speaks again he's perfectly calm. On the outside. "What do you know about me?"

I close my eyes.

"Is there something in your book?" When I don't respond he just says, "Please tell me."

I don't know what to do. This is cruel. For both of us.

"Then would you . . . would you at least turn around and sit?"

I turn and I sit down hard on my little rock. I'm not sure how much longer I could have stood anyway. I'm shaking inside. Gray sits on the ground in front of me, his book in his lap on its strap.

"I'm going to tell you something," he says. "But only if you say to me you will never write it down. You cannot write it down." I drag my eyes up to his. They are a deep, deep brown. "Do you swear it?"

I nod, pressing my fingers into my legs to push away the shaking.

"When I woke up after the Forgetting, I was burned and in the streets without a book. I was afraid. I hid, and after a day or so, two members of the Council found me in a roof garden. They were searching for people like me, and they locked me in with the Lost. I was there almost until sunsetting, my hands and my arm nearly healed, and then the glassblower came. He'd lost a son in the Forgetting, and he mostly remembered how to do his work, but he needed help, and he didn't want an apprentice. He wanted a son back, and . . . You understand that nothing was organized. We were barely fed. I don't even know how he got in, but he picked me out from the other boys, took me home, and gave me a book. He'd seen my scars, so we sat together, with my mother, too, and we watched him turn back the pages of his book and write, 'Gray was burned at the furnace today.' And he's been a father to me ever since, just as if it was true . . ."

My head drops to my hands. He'd lost his book after all. He'd been Lost. And then his own father came and got him. Chose him out of a crowd. Was the memory lodged so deep inside the glassblower's head that he gravitated to his own son without knowing it? Did he feel the tug of his own blood? And if so, why had no one in my family ever felt even an inkling of the same? What was wrong with me? What is wrong with me? I look up again and realize that Gray is trying to gauge my response.

"You know what will happen to me and my father and mother if they find out," he says. "I'm trusting you. But . . . if you know something about me, then please . . ."

He puts a hand on my arm and I flinch, as if I were the one who'd been burned, and he pulls it back. I hug my knees. He probably thinks I reacted that way because he was Lost. I don't know how to explain. I don't know what to do. I think of running. I think of screaming. I think of telling the glass-blower's son everything. What I can't do is breathe properly.

"This game hasn't gone the way I'd planned," Gray comments.

I actually almost laugh. Except that it's not funny. He's not laughing, either. He tents his fingers over his face, eyes closed.

"I don't understand. I know you weren't with the Lost, and I know I didn't see you on the streets after the Forgetting.

I would have remembered you. I know I would . . . But how could you know I was burned on my other arm?"

I shake my head.

"Nadia, what do you know about me? Please."

I shake my head again, but I don't know who I'm telling no. This is so different from my mother. What I know about her would hurt deeply when she's too fragile for hurt of any kind. What I know about Gray would only make something right. Something I thought in my own childish way I had helped make right before.

Gray, listen to me. You are the glassblower's son. When he chose you from the Lost, he chose his own child. You burned your hands in your own furnace, saving your book. I thought I'd helped you. I thought you had your book. I thought I'd saved you. But I didn't.

"Please," he whispers. "Do you know who I am?"

I think I'm going to cry. I never cry. I hear the boy with the soot-streaked face in the glow of the furnace, telling me not to forget.

"You are the glassblower's son," I say. "And you're going to have to trust me again, because I can't tell you why I know."

Again there is only the rush of water in the dim, vine-covered grove. I try to breathe, and when I dare to look up again Gray is exactly as he was, each muscle unchanged, his voice so quiet it sounds like the breeze. "You know this? You're sure?"

"Yes."

He closes his eyes. For a long time. I know he's going to question me. I think through my answers. But when he opens his eyes again he only looks at me. Really looks at me. A look that has nothing to do with the boy with the burned hands, and nothing to do with the Gray of the learning room. This is a razor-sharp gaze that cuts straight through my planned lies.

"You didn't know I was with the Lost," he says, "and you didn't see me after the Forgetting. I know you didn't. I hid, and I would have remembered. But you know where I was burned. And you say you know who I am . . ."

I'm afraid. Afraid to my core. I can see Gray's quick mind working, turning the problem inside and out.

"I was burned before the Forgetting," he says. "But you know." And then he goes completely still again, a tree without wind, and says two simple words: "You remember."

No. Of course I don't. That's impossible. But when I open my mouth to say these things, I can say nothing. Nothing at all.

"You remember, don't you?"

I cling to my one last crumb of hope. "Do you remember me?" I ask. I am shaking, trembling inside.

"No," he says. "No, I don't remember you at all."

And that is when my tears fall, and when, very faint, the first bell of the waking echoes across the mountainside.

Hedda was flogged today, and today, for the first time, I'm glad the Forgetting will come.

NADIA THE DYER'S DAUGHTER
BOOK 14, PAGE 12, 3 SEASONS UNTIL THE FORGETTING

CHAPTER FIVE

We run through the fern fronds, down and around the slope of the mountain. Streaks of deep, rich pink stretch across the violet sky. By the time we hit the grasses at the base of the slope Gray is ahead of me again. He waits for me at the wall beneath the rope ladder, sweat darkening the front of his shirt. He takes a step forward, as if to lift me to the ladder, but he hesitates. I don't. I jump.

I grab it on the first try this time, walk my feet up the wall, pull myself up far enough to get a sandal on the lowest rung. I climb up the ladder, straddle the wall, lie flat, and check the other side. The wall is cooler than the day before, the city quiet, the alley empty, as is Jin's garden. There's no space in my mind to worry about staring eyes. If we can get to Jin's before the second bell, the leaving bell, we can blend in with the people on the streets. I'll be late, Mother upset, and I have no idea what Gray will face. But we'll remain unflogged. For today. I feel the ladder move as Gray climbs.

As soon as he's up, he lies flat while I flip the ladder back to the city side of the wall. I climb down, jump into the roof garden, and turn to watch Gray. He makes the jump, falling much heavier than I did. He'll be bruised. Again. We get the pole, push the ladder back over the wall, hide the pole again. Gray collapses in the dry grass, arms outstretched, face to the striped sky.

"Do you think we were seen?" He's panting.

I sit exactly where I'd been standing a moment before. I don't know. I never know. I can't believe we've gotten here before the bell.

He turns his head. "You know we have to talk about this."

I've done more talking today than since the last Forgetting. The bell rings, and I am on my feet, to the edge of the garden, looking down. As soon as there are people out and about, I'll run home. Maybe Genivee will tell Mother the same thing she did yesterday, that I left early for the baths. Surely she would think to do that for me? I'll bake bread until the dark days if she does.

I wait for the familiar bustle, the sound of doors opening, feet on the street stones. I only hear a child cry, a muffled noise from behind walls and curtained windows. The breeze twists through the dry and dying stalks. The quiet of the resting. I spin around.

"They're counting us!"

"Is your quadrant today?" Gray is getting to his feet before I can answer. We're in my quadrant now. Only we're both in the wrong house, and Gray is in the wrong quadrant altogether. "Where are they starting?"

I shake my head. We're both moving toward the stairs. "Just take the quickest way out and I'll try to get inside before they get there."

"No. I'm with you. Quickest way out is past your house, and I'm betting you know the shortcut. If they see us, we run in two different directions."

There's no argument. Jin's curtains are closed, and Gray is already following me down the back alley, behind the Archives, then over the dividing walls, around latrines, beneath windows, a quick hop across the small water channel diverted from the main. We approach my house from the side, and then I see the black robes coming out of Hedda's across the street, three backs grouped around her door, still talking to someone inside. Jonathan, Tessa of the Granary, also on the Council, and . . . my father.

I freeze, in full view of Hedda's door. Anson is on the Council. Is he really coming inside our house? His house? Hedda's door begins to shut, the backs start to move, and Gray jerks my arm, pulling me to the small bit of safety around the corner.

"What's wrong with you?" he whispers. I lean over, hands on knees. He's learned not to wait long for an answer. "Where are they going?"

"Clothesmaker's."

"How many live there?"

I hold up five fingers.

"Are they in?"

I peek once around the corner. The door to the Clothesmaker's is closing, so I skirt around my house wall, moving along the street. Gray is just behind me. I look back over my shoulder, questioning.

"I'm seeing you to your door!" he hisses. The glassblower's son is developing an uncanny ability to answer what I did not ask, with, of course, a large dollop of sarcasm.

We round the corner into the alley between the houses, the Clothesmaker's in plain sight of my front door. I push the latch and my stomach drops. I push it again, and my stomach climbs right back up my throat and chokes me. It's locked. Who locked our door? Never mind. I know exactly who. The door to the Clothesmaker's opens, voices spilling into the street.

"Up," Gray says. We slip around the back corner to the garden stairs and run crouching onto my roof. My plant cutting is invisible among the dying leaves, but there's nowhere for us to stay so well hidden. We stand there, trying to breathe silently in the harvested space. Gray looks at me and shrugs. Today is my day, I think. And his, too. Why didn't he run the other way? My insides tighten.

I hear the knock on our front door, Liliya's voice inviting the Council members inside. Then I run to one side of the garden, lean out, glance once over the low wall. I sit on it, throw a leg over the edge, and look at Gray.

"Grab my arms," I whisper. He does, and there's no time to flinch or even think about it. In my mind I am thanking Genivee over and over again for leaving our window open. I look at Gray for confirmation, he nods, and I go over the side, stretching out until my feet find the window ledge.

Gray lets my arms slide through his hands one at a time, until he only has me by one wrist. But now I have two feet on the ledge, one hand on the open window frame. He lets me go. I get a knee down and slither backward into the window, hanging by my hands from the interior ledge until I drop onto the matted floor.

I spin around. There are voices in the hallway, and Genivee is on her mattress, Kenny the beetle in his jar on her lap, her eyes large and on me.

"Did you have a good resting?" she asks. And then I watch her eyes grow wider.

My gaze follows hers to the two male feet lowering themselves through our window. I can hear the door to Liliya's resting room opening right next to us, Liliya giving her name in a way that's overbright and false. Gray's legs follow his feet. He's got his hands on the upper ledge, coming in on his back. Liliya's door shuts. I want to yell for him to stop, to shove his feet right back through and up to the garden. His book gets stuck on the windowsill, he twists until it clears, drops to the matting, grins once at Genivee, and then the door latch turns. Gray takes one giant step backward and slides into the corner behind the opening door while I sit straight down on the edge of my mattress.

Jonathan of the Council stands in the doorway, a large book in hand, his own book hanging around his waist in a bag covered with fancy stitching. There's a key on a string around his neck. Liliya is with him, and I can see by her wide-open mouth that she did not think I was in this room. Until very recently, she was correct. The open door has completely covered Gray, though from my angle two feet are clearly visible beneath the bottom edge. I jerk my eyes back up to Jonathan, who is giving us a beatific smile. It's a nice smile, really, on a pleasant face, but there is no light in his hazel eyes. No light at all. I feel a sudden sense of satisfaction at the thought of all the contraband hidden in the floor just below me. I'm not sure what I think about what's hidden behind the door.

Liliya moves forward, inviting Jonathan to step into the room with her, and then Anson the Planter comes to the doorway. His eyes sweep impersonally over the interior of the room, over Genivee, over me, and I am stiff, frozen, like I was in the street. Jonathan hands the large book to him, and my father opens it, pen in hand, flipping slowly to the right page in a way I have seen many times before. I can feel the lack of air burning inside my chest.

"Names?" Anson says.

Genivee jumps up from her mattress like a seedling springing free of its pod. She stands right in front of the two men, smiles, holds up her beetle for inspection. She doesn't look thirty-five, nor does she look anything near twelve, and she has the attention of the room. And everyone's back turned toward Gray's corner.

"Name?" Anson asks.

"I'm Genivee," she replies, "the Dyer's daughter. Would you like me to spell it for you? G-E-N-I—"

"Genivee," Liliya warns.

"V and double E," she finishes. I see Gray's feet move slightly behind the door. Genivee looks at Jonathan and asks, "How many names has he written in your book?"

Jonathan looks up from straightening his long, hanging sleeve. I don't think children talk to Jonathan very often. "I don't know. I—"

"Is it twenty? Is it more than fifty?"

"I'm sure I don't—"

"Genivee!" Liliya says. "Our Council members want to be on their way." I snap my gaze to her. She's already ushering them back out the door. "I'm sure they have other places—"

"I think you're forgetting someone," Anson says, nodding his head toward me.

The words hit me like a fist, and I see the cracks form in Liliya's smile. She'd hoped they would leave without writing me down. Some kind of small, petty triumph. The thought unfreezes me, gives me a surge of welcome rage. Though not at her. When you get down to the root of it, this whole, horrible situation is really only one person's fault: Anson the Planter.

I look straight at my father when I say, "I'm Nadia, Dyer's daughter. Would you like me to spell it?"

Anson's pen slows, then stops scratching. He stares at me, brows down just slightly.

Jonathan raises his chin. "Is that everyone? Yes?"

My father breaks his gaze, finishes scribbling in the book.

"Well, thank you"—Jonathan looks over at the book in Anson's hands, runs a finger down the page, makes a show of checking the names—"Liliya. Thank you very much, Liliya." He repulses me with his smile. "Good waking."

Feet shuffle, bodies move, the door shuts, and there is Gray in his corner. He runs a hand over his face and slides down the wall to sit on the floor in the corner, wearing his glassblower's grin. Genivee watches this, expression serious, waiting until the voices are out of the corridor to whisper, "Did you have a good resting?"

"Very," Gray replies. "You?"

"Waking was better." Genivee turns her eyes on me and giggles. "Liliya is going to be so mad at you."

I close my eyes. It's not today. Today is not the day I'm caught. The loss of anger and adrenaline is leaving me with nothing.

"Why did you come through the window?" I hear Genivee ask. She must not have been asking me, because Gray answers immediately, matching her seriousness.

"I have my reasons."

"Can you tell me what they are?"

"I heard them sending Tessa of the Granary up to look in the garden."

"That seems like a good reason."

I curl up on my side on the mattress and discover that it feels incredibly good.

"You'll be staying, won't you?" Genivee says. "Until they finish counting?"

"I think I should. Would you mind, though, if I talked to your sister for a little while?"

"Which one?" Genivee asks.

"Nadia."

"Oh. Does Nadia talk to you?"

"Sometimes."

I open my eyes in time to see Genivee slap Gray's palm once with her own on the way out the door. Then she sticks her head back in and says, "Be really quiet. I'll keep the others busy." Gray cocks his head once at the closing door.

"I like her," he says. And then he looks at me. Really looks at me. Again. The grin is gone, and the Gray from the waterfall is sitting on my floor. I wrap my blankets over my shoulders; it's a poor kind of protection.

"So," he says. "You remember."

And you don't, I think. I shut my eyes. The berries didn't work. I didn't even leave with more of them, to try again if

I could. I've told the one secret I never imagined I would. I've failed. At everything.

"Come on, Nadia," Gray says quietly. "Your sister will say I'm a liar."

I know why he wants me to talk. He wants me to tell him what happened before the Forgetting. He wants his life. I understand. I don't blame him. It just feels so good to be still.

He says, "When was the last time you slept?"

Two restings ago. But I think I forgot to say it aloud.

"Then just tell me this, yes or no. What you told me about my father. That's true?"

Even in my clouded state I know he needs a real answer to this. "Yes," I tell him.

"And my mother, too?"

"Yes." The room is full of stillness. It matches the darkness behind my eyelids. I manage to say, "They'll be worried . . . about where you are."

I hear him let out a long, slow breath. "They will, won't they?" And he sounds happy about it. Not that his parents are worried, but that the people doing the worrying are his parents. What a fortunate son. I suppose he can't help it.

"You asked two more questions," I murmur. "That means I get . . . four more answers." I slide a little deeper into my warm fog before I realize that he's chuckling.

"Go to sleep, Dyer's daughter."

꿈

I must have done it, because when I wake I can hear the noise of a moving city outside my open window. For a minute I'm disoriented, head filled with vague thoughts and half dreams that have left me unquiet. Upset. I don't know what bell it is, and I think I've been having nightmares. Then I remember Anson the Planter's face when he asked me my name; Gray's sandals coming through my window; hugging my knees and spilling secrets on the rock above the waterfall. My eyes pop open. The light has gone dim with a glaze of red, the breeze from the window cooler. But my room is empty. No one sitting in the corner. It feels lonelier than I expect it to.

I push myself upright, and something crinkles beneath my hand. A small piece of torn paper with tiny, cramped writing. *Blacknut grove, ninth bell.* Did Gray tear this out of his book? Did he sit in that corner, writing while I slept? I run a hand over my messy hair, shiver slightly. It's unnerving to think of the glassblower's son watching me sleep. It's unnerving to think of seeing him again at all, after what was exchanged at the waterfall. But he's not going to let this rest. How could he? I look down. My sandals are still on, my pack tied and on my back. I feel terrible.

I wander out into the dimming hall. There are voices coming from my mother's resting room, and through the crack of the half-open door I can see Liliya brushing her hair, Genivee on the side of the mattress, doodling in the margins of her book. I watch, like a stranger through the window. Mother looks like the mother I knew before the Forgetting. Eyes closed, smiling. Happy. Liliya says something I don't catch, and Genivee laughs.

I could join them, I think. I could walk in and offer to brush Genivee's hair, could laugh with them when they find a leaf in mine. I could ask Liliya to show me how she twists hers up. Or I could leave them as they are. With everything they could want and need within reach. Nothing to bother or disturb them. Maybe Liliya was right. Maybe Nadia should be lost to the Forgetting. For everyone's sake.

I move softly past my mother's door, down the hall, through the sitting room, and into the storeroom. They've already had the last day meal, I see. The bread is still on the counter. I start to cut a large piece, then move the knife and cut it smaller, thinking of what Eshan said, about too many people and the size of the fields. I eat the bread standing up, staring back out at the empty room, our empty windowsill, at the long, shining table where we all sat together before I took Gray over the wall. Gray, who was Lost, and somehow managed not to be. Who hides on rooftops and in my room, blackmails me into spending a resting with him, leaves notes for meetings in the blacknut grove. And all of it, as far as I can tell, without my sister's knowledge. Something will have to be done about that. And even though my experiment at the waterfall failed, none of it takes away the fact that Liliya had a memory. Something will have to be done about that, too.

When I've poured water from the pitcher and drunk, I wipe out my cup and put it back with my plate and bowl, stacked between Liliya's and Genivee's. I'll meet Gray and tell him what he needs to know. And then I'll tell him a few other things he needs to know. About my sister, and if he won't write her name down I'll put a stop to it. At least I can do that much. I'll take care of Liliya, whether she deserves it or not, and then there will be sixty-nine days. Maybe what's hidden in our heads can still be found.

The sound of Genivee's laughter comes distant and sweet from the other room. Or maybe, after sixty-nine days, it will just be best if there isn't a Nadia here at all.

∼♥

The city changed to sunsetting while I slept. The air has lost its heat, freshened, glazed the sky with red. Longer sleeves have replaced the sunlight shirts and tunics. The signs of the Forgetting are everywhere, too. The ripening tree buds, Karl of the Books working late to keep up with the last-minute demand, the sandalmaker hanging a new sign. Not for those who need sandals, but for his own family, so they can find their house. I see Frances the Doctor walking with a man who is not her husband, and I wonder if she's considering making a change after the Forgetting. It's so easy, I think some people consider a new partner just because they can.

I pass the water clock and the baths, and there the crowds begin to thin. One group jogs past, heading for the paths around the walls, getting in their requisite exercise now that the air has cooled. I wonder if Jonathan will start flogging us for missing a run, too. Then the road between the fields loses its flagstones, becoming a dirt lane that is nearly deserted. Open ground stretches long and barren on either side, a huge expanse ready for the days of dark and rain before sunrising. I can smell the turned soil. In the distance to my left is the Council House, where Janis and Jonathan live, standing large, white, and alone beside the wall. In the distance on my right are the fenced houses of the Lost, also large, also white, and also alone. The two places could not be more unalike.

The blacknuts grow in a wide, curving swath between the fields and the wall, and I'm early for the ninth bell when I stop and lean against one. Rough-barked branches arch over my head, tangling together in bare, twisted knots that make shadows against the reddening sky. I try to re-pin my hair, but strands are still flying loose all around my face. I give it up, and then I hear, "You came."

I peer though the dim and straighten. It's not Gray. It's Eshan, weaving his way through the trunks, a large sack thrown over one shoulder.

"Didn't expect to see you," he says, stopping beside me. "But, I mean . . . I'm glad you came." He smiles, a little awkward. Being a seasoned expert on awkwardness, I understand this. He's tan from the sun, making his eyes particularly blue, especially in this light. My skin remains pale no matter how much sunlight you apply to it. "We're setting up over here," Eshan says.

I have no idea what he's talking about, but I follow rather than ask, and by the time we reach the center of the grove Imogene has come strolling up, Veronika at her side, and Michael, Chi, Ilsa, Elijah . . . fifteen, maybe twenty of the people I've interacted with as little as was humanly possible for the past twelve years. Some of the girls are in dresses, almost as fancy as for the Dark Days Festival, bits of colored cloth twisted through their hair, books worn on a belt tight to their hips. Gray seems to have invited me to some sort of . . . party? Celebration? Meeting? Whatever it is, he's not here, and I'm getting glances that run the gamut from indifference to hate. I'm hyperaware of my loosening braids, the smudges on the knees of my leggings. They might even match a few on my face.

"Sit here," Eshan says. He's crouching now in front of a small stack of biofuel from his sack, blowing and waving to get his spark of a fire going.

I sit, trying not to notice the others around me. Is this the sort of thing people do while I'm climbing the wall, or sewing new books, or concocting stains to mark my own family? Other than Eshan, I'm in a sphere to myself, a sphere I don't know how to leave without becoming more of a spectacle than I already am. Plus I need to see Gray about Liliya. Or maybe Gray is coming here with Liliya? She was doing her hair, and there are probably quite a few girls here who wish they were in Liliya's place. My sister would like that. I hear Veronika's voice rise above the hum, her little group close behind my back.

"But how did she get to be Head of Council? Who wrote it down? Doesn't anybody think that's a question that should be asked before we all forget?"

An extension of the meetings on Eshan's roof, then, with a fair amount of socializing thrown in. I see a couple slip away, hand in hand, deeper into the grove. I hug my knees. Eshan has pulled a corked bottle from his bag, and many of those around me seemed to know to bring cups. If that's moonshine, which I think from the smell that it is, he's sneakier than I thought. And braver. Moonshine is made for the Dark Days Festival, when the moons rise, and it gets stronger every day it exists. That bottle is bound to be weeks old. But surely no one here would turn Eshan in? I wish that offer of extra rations didn't make the idea possible.

Veronika is still behind me, going on and on about the Council, when the question she should really be asking is who would do the work if we decided not to punish the Lost for being Lost. Eshan puts his hands out before the fire, still with me in my sphere, and then my bubble is broken by a body right beside me, shoulder brushing mine. It's the glassblower's son, looking clean and rested and with his hair tied back.

"Hey, Eshan," he says, cheerful.

"Hey," Eshan replies, not cheerful at all. His brows are drawn down. Other greetings are called to Gray from the groups of threes and fours, but they trail away into murmurs when they see who he's sitting with. And how. This nearness, I suddenly understand, is some kind of statement. A deliberate statement. Or that's how everyone is interpreting it, anyway, and I don't like what that means for my sister. At all. I sit forward, scoot just a little, to escape the proximity, and Gray leans back on his hands, spreading out his arms. Now it almost looks like he has an arm around me. He glances at the surrounding grove.

"Nice party," he says. "Is—"

"Where's Liliya?" I interrupt.

Eshan looks a little shocked, by the words or who's spoken the words or the anger behind them, I'm not sure. Gray only gazes at me, a brow up, that tiny little grin on his mouth. "Who?" he asks.

I'd been ready to make the sacrifice of speech, like I had at the waterfall, to tell him what he needed to know about what happened before the Forgetting. But this is not the Gray of the waterfall. This is the Gray I knew at school, the one who gets exactly what he wants and somehow makes everyone love him for it. This is a public slap to my sister. One that I'm sure

Imogene and Veronika and every other girl in Canaan will be discussing in the baths. Liliya may be stupid and scheming, she may spit on the ground I walk on, but she's still my sister, and I'm not helping anyone who dallies with her. I look Gray in the face.

"You," I say loudly, "are a *zopa*."

And then I'm on my feet, walking away from the fire, moving fast out of the crowd, not caring that they're looking at me while I go. Gray calls my name, and when he calls it again I break into a jog, through the blacknut grove, past the startled couple, out onto the path that runs along the edge of the wall. There I run. I want to keep going all the way around to Jin's garden. I want to climb the wall and head straight up the mountainside, where I never feel alone. I'm not even sure I know exactly why I'm so mad. Except that I am. Nobody deserves to be treated like that. Even Liliya. Even if she's allowing it.

I hear footsteps on the path behind me, heavier than mine. I put on some speed, follow the wall's gentle curve until the way is blocked by a high, rickety fence, a jumble of a new building beyond it. The houses of the Lost. I move to sprint around it, but my feet slow, and then stop without me telling them to. There's a woman standing just outside the fence, holding a section of it askew. Like she's just opened her front door.

"Nadia the Dyer's daughter. I've been thinking of you." It's Rose, with her smock of undyed cloth and her round, wrinkled cheeks.

The heavier tread comes pounding down the path, catches up, and falters. I know who it is. Why can't he just leave me alone? Rose's glance moves to just beyond my shoulder, and her wrinkles change direction.

"Oh," she says. "So it's you, is it? I should've known." She pulls the sagging section of fence a little wider. "You'd better come in, too, so I can take a switch to your back."

I wonder if she needs any help.

There was a day when I was very young that I went to the fields with Father. When he was busy, I snuck away and looked through the fence at the houses of the Lost. I saw dirt, and I saw a plaque above the door that I didn't know how to read. And I saw a man, a supervisor, and he was hitting a girl. I cried, and Father came and hugged me and said I was never to go inside the fences, even if a nice person asked me to, because bad things can happen inside the Lost houses. That's why we have the fence.

I'd thought of this today, when I saw Tessa of the Granary, who is Council, go next door with Reese and take Roberta's unwritten baby. Now, of course, I know what the plaque says: "Without Their Memories, They Are Lost."

I wonder who protects the ones inside the fences.

NADIA THE DYER'S DAUGHTER
BOOK 14, PAGE 52, 1 SEASON UNTIL THE FORGETTING

CHAPTER SIX

I sit where Rose shows me, on a frayed woven mat laid over a pressed-dirt floor in a room where it's almost too dark to see. She points for Gray to sit as well—I don't know or care whether he got a mat—then she goes to the far wall to pick up the room's only light, a small jar of glowworms. When she moves the jar I catch a glimpse of shelves, rows and rows of bottles and tied sheaves of leaves and herbs, a thin blanket, neatly folded on the floor. I think we're in Rose's resting room.

Rose sets the jar between us, leaving the blanket and the shelves to the darkness. The houses of the Lost were made without windows or glass, and we came to this room through a maze of rooms, full of women and girls moving half-seen in the semidark, not bothered by our passing. I don't know how I've ended up here, other than being so furious I couldn't think of an excuse. And not knowing whether I would hurt Rose's feelings. I don't know how much trouble I'm in if we're caught. But surely Rose must think it's safe, if she invited me? Rose walks up to Gray and smacks him on the top of his head. Then she bends down and kisses the same spot.

"I've been neglected," she says, ruffling his hair so that it's no longer neat.

"I know."

He's rueful, and I'm annoyed. First, because I've had to stop myself wondering what it would feel like to mess up his hair like that, which is an idiotic thought when I am so incredibly mad at every tiny piece of him. Eyelashes included. Second, because Gray the Glassblower's son seems to attract affection like the blacknuts draw the bees. Maybe I just never bloomed. Whatever he's done, Rose has already forgiven him.

"I'll be back," says Rose. She finds the door and leaves, no trouble negotiating the dark. I don't think I'd have such an easy time trying to get out of here. I pull my knees up to my chest. The air is stuffy, thick with the scent of people and herbs, heavy with our angry silence.

Finally Gray says, "Why don't you tell me what your problem is, Dyer's daughter?"

That makes me want to laugh. I don't want to tell him anything.

"All right, then," he says, "let's review. I sit down, you ask where your sister is, I don't know what you're talking about, so you insult me, go crazy, and run off. Do I have that right?"

No. *My problem is the fact that you are an arrogant* zopa *who sits too close to one sister and dallies with the other.* But I only stare at the glowworms.

"Right," he says, drawing out the word. "And now that we're having this stimulating conversation, I'm remembering one or two other choice comments from the dyer's daughter, comments that at the time all seemed like part of the mysterious charm. But I think I might be seeing a little more clearly now." I feel his gaze on the side of my face. "Do you really think I would have an understanding with your sister?"

I narrow my eyes. Gray's tone had been incredulous, which is exactly what I was afraid of hearing.

"Oh, I see. Not even that good! A dalliance, is it? While I'm running around with you over the wall and sitting next to you at Eshan's . . . whatever?"

Now I look at him. He's pulling out the tie from the back of his hair so he can run a hand through the mess Rose made. "Nadia," he says, "why would you think something so stupid?"

When I open my mouth no sound comes out. On the second try, I say, "The potter's wife . . ." and nothing else. Gray rolls his eyes.

"Liliya came to see me a few times at the workshop, but . . . I told her no, okay? That was all. The end of it. It was a while ago. Tell the potter's wife to find a new window to stare out."

I hug my knees, trying to decide if I believe it. And I think I do. I'm relieved, and also feeling just about as idiotic as Gray thought the whole idea was in the first place. Who, then, has Liliya been going out to sit with?

"So, new rule," Gray says. "Next time you need to ask me about something, you get to say 'free question' or 'time-out,' and as long as you don't run off, I won't count it against you in our game. It will save me some aching muscles, I think."

I lift my eyes. "Maybe I wouldn't run if you didn't sit so close."

"Maybe you'd have been glad of it if you'd seen the way Eshan was looking at you."

Rose comes in, walking straight through the tension left hanging by that statement. Gray looks up at her.

"This is all your fault, isn't it? And you smacked me on the head."

I'm not sure, but I think I see Rose wink at me in the blue-white light. She gives each of us a mug, and I'm surprised to feel the warmth.

"Taste it before you thank her," Gray says. Rose just ruffles his hair again. The tea is strong, very strong, with a tang that gives me one violent shudder.

"Leaves of the oil plant," says Rose. "The liking will come to you."

She smiles at me and I try to smile back. I think I succeed. Maybe she can't even see it. She shuffles out again, and somewhere in this maze of a house, a baby cries.

Gray says, "I didn't know they were meeting out there. I thought it was still on Eshan's roof. Just so you know. And you should be careful of Eshan."

Says the boy who threatened me with the Council if I didn't take him over the wall. "I thought you and Eshan were friends."

"We are. That's why I know."

I shake my head, sip the horrible tea. I can't think of anyone more harmless.

"I think it's still your turn."

I look over the cracked rim of my mug. Gray has leaned his head back against the wall, eyes two deep shadows.

"Our game," he says. "You had fifteen or sixteen questions left, didn't you? Plus the four while you were falling asleep?"

This is generous. I know he wants to ask his own. But I nod, and I think this means we've forgiven each other. I say, "Do you come to see Rose a lot?"

"Not as often as I should, but yes."

"On the women's side?"

He laughs without humor. "Lots of men come to the women's side. The supervisors don't bother much about the Lost until it's time for them to show up for work." I keep my eyes down, and after a moment he says, "But to avoid any more uncomfortable mix-ups, I just come to visit Rose."

I smile while I sip.

"But it's only a dalliance, sorry to say."

I nearly spit my tea, and then I realize it's because I'm laughing. Actually laughing. I choke and laugh more, and Gray laughs, too. I can't remember the last time I laughed. I wipe my mouth with the back of my hand, catching my breath. I don't know what to say now, which is no great surprise. So I study my tea. And then I hear the last thing I'd expected in the houses of the Lost, besides laughter. A flute.

Gray sits quiet for once, listening, and then someone sings. The song is picked up by one and then another, scattering from room to room. The tune isn't sad, but there's something lovely and wild about not being able to see where it comes from, hearing some notes closer, others down hallways and beyond walls. It takes on a life of its own. I watch the glowworms writhe in their jar, living for no other reason than to emit their weird light. I have sixty-nine days to try to change the life I have, or to decide to leave it behind.

I start talking, like a bucket overfull, tilting, spilling more and more as the minutes go by. About Liliya's memory, what

I was trying to do at the waterfall, what I think it could mean for the Forgetting. Gray gets up once to shut the door, sits closer to hear, though he's careful and leaves me my space. I don't tell him about Anson the Planter, or the things I saw before and after the last Forgetting, or what I might decide to do before this one, but I do tell him how he burned his hands, about the man and his book, how he told me not to forget. About Mother. Gray is intent, like he was on the mountainside, sometimes asking me questions, mostly just listening, watching me talk. When I'm done the tea is gone, the music is gone, and my voice is hoarse. Gray sits still, thinking.

"The man who tried to burn my book," he says, voice low. "Would you recognize him?"

I shake my head. My memory is all legs.

Gray says, "He was trying to make me Lost. On purpose."

This gives me a feeling I think is like sickness. Maybe there are Lost in this house right now who had their books taken. Who were deliberately put here. Maybe Rose is one of them.

"So why haven't you taken it to the Council?" Gray asks. "Just walked up to Janis and told her you remember? She might know what to do."

I've thought this out many times before. "I can't prove it. Not without hurting someone else. And neither can you," I remind him. His father took one of the Lost and falsified a book. My father destroyed and falsified books on a grand scale. Evidently I'll go a long way to protect people who wouldn't do the same for me. My entire life is proof. "You know . . . you understand that you can't tell your parents?"

He laughs once, a brief whoosh of air. "Can't have one without the other, can I?" He means he can't tell them without giving me away. "And I'm not sure they would believe me even if I could explain . . ."

Truth can look so flimsy and feeble sometimes. It's one of the things I hold against it.

"But what I can't get over isn't so much Liliya's memory," he says, "but the fact that you never forgot at all. Why? Why didn't you forget?"

I shrug. "No way to know."

"Well, there's a lot of that going around, isn't there? Answers we take for granted that there's 'no way to know.' Who wrote the First Book of the Forgetting? No way to know. Who built the city? No way to know. How long have we been forgetting? How old is Rose? There's no way to know anything. What we need," he says, "is to read everyone's books. Compare them all and make a history." He looks at me from the corner of his eye. "We should read them aloud. On the platform, beneath the water clock. We'd take turns. Everyone would come, don't you think?"

The absurdity makes me smile, even though the thought of someone reading my book is horrifying. Who could write truth, the real truth, if someone else was going to read it? Not many. And if your book doesn't have the truth, then you don't have yourself after the Forgetting. My father taught me that. Gray sits forward again, restless.

"Eshan's little band have their points, you know. The Council reads the rules from the First Book of the Forgetting twice a year, practically ruin the Dark Days Festivals with it, but they're not reading the whole book, are they? How do we know what's in there? How do we know what really happened before? For all we know that book is full of people who never forgot, or"—he pauses—"maybe there's just never been anyone like you at all."

It's the last one that seems more likely. I glance at Gray, but his eyes are already on me, hair a mess, chin shadowed. *Time-out*, I want to say, *this question doesn't count. If you weren't in Jin's garden because of Liliya, then why were you on that rooftop at all, and why did you want to go over the wall with me?* But this time he doesn't answer what I didn't ask. Suddenly I'm aware of our tiny dark room, the quiet, the circle of blue-white light that has seemed like the entirety of the world for a long while now. I sit up, look around us. Gray smiles.

"First bell of the resting was a long time ago. You're here with me until waking. Unless you want to try and get all the way across the city."

I sink back against the wall. I didn't go home. Again. Mother will see an empty bed. Again. I look at Gray. "When is your counting?"

"Not this waking, but the next. I checked."

"Are you in trouble?"

"Loads. But it's worth it."

I wrinkle my forehead.

"You're not nearly as afraid of me now. Look. Watch this." He lifts his hands, shows me both sides, so I can see that they're harmless, then he reaches out very slowly, picks up my wrist, and puts my hand in his outstretched one. I can feel the ridge of scars on his wrist beginning just at my fingertips. He shakes my hand.

"See," he says. "Not scary."

His hand is warm, the palm rough. *No, Gray the Glass-blower's son,* I think. *I'm much more afraid of you now than I ever was before.*

"Come on," he says, keeping a firm hold of my hand, using it to pull me up with him as he gets to his feet. He doesn't let go. He picks up our jar of light and walks backward five steps, leading me to the other side of the room. "You can have the bed. Such as it is."

I hesitate. "What about Rose?"

"She'll have gone in with one of the other girls a long time ago. I'll be over here. I'm thinking, not sleeping."

I must seem unsure because he lifts my hand, still in his. "Not scary, remember?"

I nod, and he doesn't let me go until I've sat down beside the folded blanket. I settle in on my side, using the blanket like a pillow while Gray puts down the light. He seems stiff after sitting for so long; he's probably black and blue beneath his shirt, from jumping onto Jin's roof and swinging into the wall. I watch him unbuckle the strap of his book, letting it go free from his side, and then I feel guilty about it, like I should have looked away.

"Mind if I write?" he asks.

I shake my head. He sits facing me in the little corner made by the wall and the shelves, long legs crossed, opens his book, takes the pen and vial of ink out of their niches in the thick inner cover. Soon I can hear the scratch against the paper. I've missed writing for two straight restings now, both in my book and the hidden one. But it's not as critical for me. I will remember. Probably. And I don't think I could write here, not in front of Gray. The pen moves in his circle of light, then I realize the pen has paused, and Gray is looking at me again.

"You can take off your pack, you know."

I slide my hand up the strap over my shoulder, hold it tighter. I see his brows come down.

"What? You think I'm going to jump across the room and wrestle that pack from your body just so I can get a look at your book?"

"I've had to correct you about it before."

I'd meant to think that, not say it; the words just popped out. He was being such an idiot when I gave him those two slaps in the learning room, and I was so full of very righteous indignation. For the first time, the memory strikes me as funny. When I look up Gray is smiling across his whole face.

"I think Nadia the Dyer's daughter has just teased me," he says. "This is a key life event that I will now write in my book."

"You will not."

He makes a show of dipping his pen. "Nadia," he says slowly while he writes, "is a terrible tease . . . who abuses her peers . . . during learning . . ."

"Stop!"

". . . and holds . . . grudges for decades . . . against those who are otherwise agreeable . . . intelligent . . . and awestruck by her glittering . . . beauty . . ."

Glittering? I'm unwashed, unbrushed, and lying on a dirt floor. I pretend I'm going to sleep, to show I know he really isn't writing any of that, slightly nervous that maybe he is. His pen scratches for a few more minutes, then stops again. I open my eyes.

"You were dreaming. When I was in your room."

I shut my eyes again. I don't want to talk about that.

"Before the Forgetting, what you saw. Was it bad?"

I wasn't ready, hadn't steeled myself against the question, and my mind shifts, jumps as easily as I might step over a rivulet running down the mountainside. There is the trickle of laughter, the smell of smoke. I feel my body curling into the blanket, into myself. I sit up to breathe, to uncurl, to fight the shaking, the answer I will not say rolling through my head.

They all know it's coming, you see, like knowing you're about to die. And they know that whatever they do will be forgotten, even by themselves. There are no consequences. No guilt. And so they give in. Take what they want, do what's never been allowed, get their revenge. I think some of them try on wrong like they would try on a new shirt, just to see if it fits. To see what it feels like on their skin. I saw things I didn't understand, but that I understand so much better now. And I see it again. And again. And again . . .

I know where I am right now. I'm in the houses of the Lost, but I have every muscle tensed, ready to run. Somewhere deep in my memory a woman is screaming, and they laugh because she does. "Yes," I whisper. "It was bad." And it's coming again.

"I'm sorry."

I open my eyes. Those words had force. I think because they've never been said. I think because he meant them.

After a minute Gray says, "I think you're right about the Forgetting being like a sickness. You wouldn't understand this, but forgetting feels so . . . wrong. I don't think we're supposed to forget. We're not made for it." He pauses, thinking. "So the question is, are you cured, Dyer's daughter, or were you never sick at all?"

I don't know. But sicknesses have a cause, and they can have a cure. If we could find either, the horror of the Forgetting wouldn't have to happen at all. Ever again. I lean my head back against the wall, eyes closed, the trembling inside me almost gone.

"Think," Gray says. "Is there something you do differently than the rest of your family? Or something they do that you don't?"

I've been down this path before, and it's gotten me nowhere.

"How about something you eat? Did you eat anything different right before the Forgetting?"

I can't think of a thing.

"Wait. I know what it is."

My eyes snap open.

"Silence. Silence cures the Forgetting."

"You're ridiculous," I say, closing my eyes again. Though I know he can see me smiling.

"You realize, though, that this means everything we've been taught about the Forgetting is wrong."

Yes. And so we should question those teachings. All of them. I think of the passage we recite in school.

At the first sunrising of the twelfth year, they will forget . . . Their books will be their memories, their written past selves. They will write in their books . . . They will write the truth . . . If a book is lost, then so are they lost. I am made of my memories. Without memories, they are . . .

I sit up. "Whoever wrote the First Book of the Forgetting, how did they know it happens every twelve years?"

He sets the pen in the valley between his pages. "He, or she, whoever, would've kept entries, I guess, from before one Forgetting to the next. Like we do."

"So the writer of the First Book wrote more than rules and laws. They wrote entries? Twenty-four years' worth, to figure out that it comes every twelve?"

"I don't know . . ." Gray's brows come together. "If you didn't have a First Book to tell you, and the Forgetting happens, how do you know it's going to happen again at all? You probably wouldn't understand the first time, not for a long while. And you would've forgotten what happened the time before that. I'd guess more like three Forgettings to work it all out. Thirty-six years, maybe?"

I've seen the First Book of the Forgetting. During the Dark Day Readings. It's not a large book, not any bigger than ours. I shake my head. "How can one book have thirty-six or even twenty-four years' worth of entries? Did they not write everything down?"

"Well, they made a pretty big point about telling everyone else to. Is there another book?"

I don't know. I put my chin on my knees. Gray was joking earlier, when he said the First Book could be full of people who've never forgotten. Or I'd taken it as a joke. Just like I had when he suggested comparing the books. *I am made of my memories. Without memories, they are nothing . . .* My mind is humming. "That whole passage," I say. "The words are 'they,' and 'them,' and 'their.' Why change to 'I'? It should be 'we.'"

Gray puts his hands behind his head, thoughtful.

"If you were thinking about everyone, you'd say 'we.' It's like there's a difference between himself, or herself . . . and the people who have no memories."

"So what are you saying?"

"That maybe that's why there aren't so many years' worth of entries. Because whoever wrote the First Book of the Forgetting . . ."

"Didn't forget?" Gray finishes for me. He's forward again, tenting his fingers over his nose, thinking. "It makes sense. If a person didn't forget, like you didn't, then they'd know what happened to everyone else the first time, and by the second, they'd know everything. Twelve years."

"And," I say, "if there are entries in the First Book from someone who didn't forget, I could compare them to what I remember."

"You're the only person in Canaan who could."

We look at each other. Rose's room is quiet, dark.

"I might be wrong," I say.

"You might be right."

What if I could find . . . anything? Cause or cure. Could I do something to stop all this? How can I not try? It's like I've just seen a mountain I have to climb.

"You know you can't just walk into the Archives and read that book," Gray says, though it goes without saying. "They're not going to let you."

Of course they're not going to let me. They didn't let me go over the wall, either. Gray's expression doesn't change, except for a slight lifting of his mouth.

"You're going to read it anyway."

It's true.

"You're going to steal it."

If I can.

"You'll be flogged."

What else is new?

"No," Gray says.

I feel my brows rise at that. "Yes."

"I mean no, not you. Me. I mean we. You and me. We steal the First Book of the Forgetting. Together."

My gaze drops to the dim space between us. This is just like when he said we were going over the wall, only without the threats. I don't understand what he was doing then, or what he's doing now. "Why?" I ask.

"Because someone tried to make me Lost, that's why. To punish me, or my parents, I don't know. And look at Rose; do you think she was running around without a book? There's something wrong here, Nadia." He throws up a hand. "We're in a whole house of something wrong." I watch his brows come together. "Answer a question for me. I'll answer four of yours if you do. Just say yes or no. Is your father really dead?"

I feel the cool dirt of Rose's floor beneath my fingers, smell the herbs from her shelf, feel the breath in my chest. And then I say, "No."

He sits back, and again I drop my eyes. I know this is a mistake. I broke my own rules when I let Genivee in, and I'm going to suffer for that. Now I'm about to do the same again, and I think I will pay for it. I think I'm going to do it anyway.

"Okay," I say. "We steal it together."

Last resting I slept in the garden after Mother checked my bed. Jemma the Clothesmaker's baby came early and Pratim brought their youngest to sleep in our house. I let him have my mattress, took a blanket to the roof, and made a tent to hide my face from the sun. When I woke Mother was next to me, digging tomatoes. I don't know how long she'd been there. I didn't know whether Liliya had hidden the knife. I could see that Mother wasn't hurt, but I told her I was sorry not to have been in my bed when she checked. Mother told me not to be silly, there were no empty beds.

Now I understand it's the emptiness she remembers, not me.

NADIA THE DYER'S DAUGHTER
BOOK 5, PAGE 8, 6 YEARS AFTER THE FORGETTING

CHAPTER SEVEN

adia!"

"Is that your sister?" Gray asks.

I look around. We're walking where Meridian splits and curves around the rim of the amphitheater, while I fold two squares of undyed cloth that Rose brought to us, to cover our colored clothing when we left the fences with the Lost. The sun-setting mists came and the supervisor didn't, so in the end, we didn't really need the cloth. The gates weren't locked, the fences not in good enough repair for it to matter if they were. Where can the Lost go anyway? Everyone knows everyone inside the walls. Gray hugged Rose for a long time before we left, which made me think that's what always happens when people love you. You love them right back. Like Genivee.

I need to be careful.

"Nadia!"

The fog trails the ground thick and white, the walled complex of the granary rising tall and pale on our right, and it takes a three-quarter turn for me to find Genivee appearing from the haze. She's out of breath, no flowers in her hair.

Something about the way she runs, the way she holds her mouth, squeezes me from the inside out. I squat down, look her in the face, and whisper, "Mother?"

She nods, breathing hard.

"The knife?" I don't know how she even hears me, but she nods.

It's been a long time since Mother did something like this, and I know exactly why she did it now. She found an empty bed. Twice. I knew, sitting on the floor of Rose's room, that I would pay for my choice, but the truth is I'd partly made that choice long before, while the Lost women sang. I could have demanded to be led out, made sure of the bells. But I was exactly where I wanted to be, wasn't I? The first payment has come soon. I'm already moving.

"Liliya says we can't get the doctor," Genivee says. "That's why I came to find you . . ."

"Nadia."

I look back. I've forgotten Gray. In lieu of actual information, Gray sat up the whole resting, making absurd plans to steal the First Book that had me laughing until my eyes ran. Since we left the Lost, he's hardly spoken. Right now, I can't find the word for his expression. He only hooks a thumb in his book strap and says, "Clock tower, seventh bell."

I nod, we hurry away, and I'm making the turn onto Hawking with Genivee before I realize which word fits the look on Gray's face. I think it's "regretful."

❦

As soon as I get through our front door, I bar it, then close the curtains. There's blood everywhere, on the floor stones, on the table, a trail down the hallway. Guilt has a bitter taste, stronger than Rose's tea. I start down the hall, then look back to Genivee.

"If Mother needs a doctor, I'll get one. You can come in with me, but you don't have to."

Genivee wipes her face, thinks about it, then turns left. To our room. I hurry to our mother's room, drop the bundles of cloth I'd forgotten I was carrying, and open the door.

It's warmer than I expected. The window is shut, the red light outside smearing the wall and the bed curtains pink, making Liliya and Mother look as if they're flushing. I don't think Mother is flushing. I think she's pale. Her eyes are closed, her left forearm tied with a stained cloth. I want to look beneath that. Liliya is sitting on the floor next to the mattress, holding Mother's hand, curls bouncing when she turns to me. Mother doesn't move.

"She's resting right now," she says.

This is a warning. Mother is not asleep, so don't say anything she shouldn't hear. I jerk my chin toward the hall. Liliya hesitates, then lets go of Mother and follows me back through the door, shutting it after us.

Before I can speak she says, "No one can know about this. Not the neighbors, no one. They can't know she did it to herself. If someone happens to see it, we'll tell them it was an accident. No, don't argue with me . . ."

I hadn't planned to. This is no different from what we've always done. Except that in the past, we got the doctor. "Where's the knife?" I ask her.

"What?"

"The knife, Liliya!"

"Still in the storeroom . . ."

I hurry down the hall, around the blood, through the sitting room, and into the storeroom, Liliya right behind me. It's worse in here. The knife is on the counter, the "NWSE" stamped in its blade now etched in red. It's been almost two years since Mother used the knife on herself; we've gotten careless about leaving it out. I clench my fists, breath coming hard. Why couldn't she just be like any other mother? Mad that I was breaking the rules? Out with a boy when I shouldn't have been? Why did she have to do this?

"Nadia, swear to me you're not going to say anything," Liliya hisses. "The doctor might suspect."

I turn to glare at her. "What do you know about the doctor?"

"Nothing." But she knows I won't accept that answer. Liliya's dark eyes look beyond me, at the mess on the counter. Now that I'm staring right at her, I see fear beneath my sister's usual confidence. "There could be a . . . mistake," she says. "About Mother. That's all. Just swear to me you won't say anything."

"What kind of mistake?"

"Swear it, Nadia!"

"Does she need the doctor?"

"I don't think so."

That's not actually good enough. I go to the counter, wash my hands in the water bowl, find the garlic leaves, pick up the knife with a cloth, and take it all back to Mother's room.

"What are you doing?" Liliya is saying, still following me. I kneel beside Mother's mattress, move the oil lamp closer, work the knot in her bandage.

"Mother," I whisper, "it's Nadia. I'm just going to look . . ."

I wince when I see the wound. Right in the center of her forearm, not too terribly wide, but still bleeding. She put the blade straight in. I pick up the knife, throw a glance of contempt at Liliya's noise of protest, and study the tapered metal end. For the wound to be that wide, the depth would have to be about the length of my index finger, up to the first knuckle. I examine Mother's arm. She's slender. She might have hit the bone.

"Can she move her fingers?" I ask. I turn back to Mother when Liliya doesn't know. "Can you wiggle your fingers?" She does it, which means Liliya was right. She's awake and listening behind her eyes. I lay the clean leaves along the wound, then wrap the bandage around it again, a little tighter this time. As far as I can tell, the doctor wouldn't have done any different. I stand, careful to take the knife with me back into the hall, Liliya trailing me.

When she shuts Mother in, I say, "All right. I swear it."

Liliya brushes back her hair, clearly relieved, one of her fingers a little bloody. Then she cocks her head, studying me. "I hope you've been thinking about our conversation."

She means the baths. My disappearance after the Forgetting.

"This could help you with that decision," she goes on. "Just imagine, after the Forgetting, if Mother didn't have to worry about that third bed . . ."

What I can imagine, Liliya, is finding a way to make you remember me and eat your words.

"You could do what you want, and Mother wouldn't have to hurt herself anymore. She could go back to—"

"You know what, Liliya. How about you just shut up?"

"Oh." My sister looks taken aback, then amused. "Well, in that case, I have some news for you. Today is your first day at the Archives."

Now it's my turn to be taken aback, but I have to smile at my sister and all her curly-headed efficiency. She'd said she would take care of things if I didn't. I just hadn't expected her to do it so quickly, or for her schemes to play so exactly into my hands. The First Book of the Forgetting is in the Archives, too. Exactly where I want to be.

"Fine," I say.

"Really?"

"Yes."

"You're very . . . reasonable today," she comments. "And talkative."

We stare at each other. She thinks she's won. That I'm leaving.

"I heard you left Eshan's with Gray," she says, "and that he didn't come back for the resting, either."

Left Eshan's with Gray is not a fair statement, in my opinion, considering I ran and Gray chased. But thanks to Liliya's tone, the implications of neither one of us coming home after running off like that have only just now hit me. And here I stand, hair falling, still in the clothes I wore over the wall, two bundles of undyed cloth not unlike blankets lying where I dropped them on the floor outside Mother's door, doing quite a respectable impression of a person who has just slept outside. With someone else. I feel heat slide up my neck, and then I look at Liliya. Her hair is done, but she's still in a sleeping dress.

"How did you hear that? Have you even been outside?"

"I was in the garden. And Roberta was in hers next door. People do talk, you know."

I wonder what she told Roberta. Probably that it's true. Since it is. Sort of. Except not.

"You should make him write it down," Liliya says.

My mouth opens, and then I close it. There's just so much irony in that statement I don't know what to say. So I don't.

"And make sure he uses your new name," she adds, taking the knife from my hand, "whatever you decide that is. And by the way, you should've been at the Archives already. Just so you know."

I watch my sister sashay down the hall, sure in her ability to put everyone and everything into its rightful place. But I don't forget the fear I saw on her face. If it's not Gray she's dangling at the end of her string, then who?

⌇

By the next bell I'm walking slowly up Copernicus Street to the Archives, having seen a mostly comforted Genivee off late to the Learning Center, leaving Liliya to look after Mother and clean up the mess. The Archives is huge, shapeless, and windowless, made of white plaster instead of stone, two enormous plaques on either side of the doors that say "Write Our Truth" and "Remember Our Truth." I hate it.

I can see Jin the Signmaker's house through the sunsetting light. I wish I wasn't in this dark blue dress of Liliya's. I wish I was in my stained leggings and belt, looking for my moment to sneak up to Jin's roof and climb the wall. I wonder what Gray went home to. Whether he's heard the talk. If that parting expression meant he was sorry I was going, or that he wished it hadn't happened at all. Then I remember that whether the glassblower's son regrets it or not, I'm going to steal that book. Unless they've left it out somewhere for me to read. I climb the steps between the plaques and walk through the door of the Archives.

The waiting area is full of people, more than I would have expected. A penmaker, weaver, grinder, fuelmaker, others I don't glance at long enough to recognize, all lined up on the benches. What could so many want with their old books this close to a Forgetting? It's after a Forgetting that people need to come, to match their tied books to their archived ones. To find out who they are. The room hums with quiet talk.

In the back wall of the waiting area is a door, and standing grim-faced, arms-crossed beside it is Reese, Li on the other side, on watch for the Council, flanking the way in to the books the way they flanked Janis as she announced the counting. It's not Janis whom Reese and Li answer to, I feel certain about that. They're Jonathan's men. And seated at a table in front of them is Imogene, wispy hair tamed into a knot, her expression twisted into the same. I didn't know she was apprenticing here. She's finished writing my name on the paper in front of her before I'm halfway to her, and when I do get there, I hesitate. She tilts her head, impatient.

"I'm here to apprentice," I say. The words feel like a shout.

Imogene's brows rise, and then Gretchen of the Archives breezes out the door between Reese and Li, a book in her hands. She calls a name, and a supervisor of the Lost rises from the benches and goes with her toward a reading room. I think of the top of Gretchen's head, which is the way I saw her last, being coerced by Jonathan while I lay flat on my back on top of the wall. This supervisor, it seems, was not on Jonathan's no-reading list. I haven't had time to dwell on the conversation I overheard that day, but I think about it now. I'm not sure Gretchen can be trusted. Which might not be her fault. I watch the supervisor being searched by Deming of the Council, also on watch in front of the hall that leads to the reading rooms. When Gretchen returns Imogene waves her over.

"This is Nadia," says Imogene. "Dyer's daughter. She says she's come to apprentice."

Gretchen inspects me. Her skin is as pale as mine, her hair mist gray, book worn strapped smartly to her stomach. She gives Imogene a curt nod.

"Take your pen and ink from your book, please," Imogene says, formal in front of Gretchen. I set my pack on the desk, take out my book, and crack it open, turning it so she can't see while I remove the pen and small, flat ink vial from the inner cover. Imogene puts them in a box below her table.

"I have to see inside your cover," she says.

I open the book a bit more, so that she can see the empty niches for my writing tools. I always keep a blank page in the front anyway. As soon as I shut my book Reese looks through my pack, even taking out the pieces of dried apple I brought, then without warning runs his hands up and down my body, looking for hidden ink or pens, I suppose. I manage to hold in my protests, and when he's done, Gretchen says, "Come with me."

I put on my pack and follow her through the door without giving Imogene another look. We're in a sort of anteroom, a room that exists, apparently, solely to hold doors. There are three, including the one I just came through. Gretchen leads me to the door on our right. Inside is what can only be her workspace: a table, two chairs, papers precisely stacked, a small pot of blue paint, and a set of brushes. There's a mattress, too. Someone has been sleeping here. Gretchen sits, and so do I. She folds her hands.

"Why do you want to apprentice?" she asks.

Because I want to read what I'm not supposed to and steal the most important book you have. But after a slow minute, I say, "Because . . . I'd like to be an archivist." I only just keep the question out of my statement.

"You'll remember nothing, of course."

I don't respond until it's obvious that she expects me to. "I can write it down."

She sighs. "Well, we do need the help. I've had one not show up at all today, and you were late." She eyes me, but I don't have anything to say about that. "Everyone wants to see their books right now, or turn in the ones they've finished, for safekeeping, and every day it's only going to get worse. Afterward, it will be impossible. So the more hands returning the better, no matter how little they know. Do you know why, Nadia the Dyer's daughter, so many people want to see their books at this time?"

I don't.

"Because they want to change them."

I blink.

"They're hoping to put a pen in their sandal and a bottle of ink down their shirt and get into a reading room to alter the truth." She sighs again, as if her book is heavy. Or maybe it's the weight of the Archives. "No one changes a book on my watch. Is that understood?"

I nod, and she sits a little straighter. "You will be searched when you arrive and searched before you leave. You are never to enter or leave the building without being cleared. Imogene will sign you in and out. Pen and ink are strictly forbidden in the stacks, as is, of course, any sort of flame . . ."

My eyes dart upward. Glowworms in glass, hanging from the ceiling. A hundred times the number Rose had.

"We do not open books in the stacks," Gretchen continues, "even our own. If you want to read your own book, you can request and go to a reading room like everyone else. Opening a book is an automatic referral to the Council. No more than two archivists at a time in the stacks. Books may only be removed or returned to the shelves by the head archivist, which is me. No one else touches the books. Questions, so far?"

I shake my head. I wonder if Liliya was aware of all these rules when she decided I could just waltz in here and change my books. I know I wasn't when I decided to steal one.

"Inventory is done twice a week, more while training, and is what you'll be doing today. If," she adds, "I allow you to do so at all. I'll be frank and say that I have difficulty believing that you have a sudden wish to be an archivist just a few weeks before a Forgetting, Nadia. Do you know why someone might want to apprentice in the Archives right before a Forgetting?"

I shake my head again.

"For the same reason the waiting room is full. Because they want access to their books. Because they have the mistaken impression that they can change their books while I am in charge. Again I am telling you that this will not happen. Do you understand that this won't happen?"

I nod, and Gretchen considers my silent face.

"Well. From the standpoint of noise, at least, I think this could work out rather well."

I notice she didn't mention leaving with a book that isn't yours.

❧

Gretchen takes me back into the anteroom and through the only door I haven't entered. Then I discover why the Archives are so good at blocking the view from Jin's rooftop. I've never seen a room so large, not even in the baths. Rows and rows of freestanding shelves, as far as I can see, lit with the blue-white glare of glowworms. There must be thousands of them up there, giving the whole enormous room a strange brilliance.

"A Lost girl comes once a week to feed and clean out the lights," Gretchen says when she sees me looking. "Not the task of an archivist, happy to say."

She leads me to one side of the room, our footsteps hushed, to the farthest row of shelves, where a massive book is lying open on a table with wheels on its legs. I've already noticed that each shelved book we've passed has a code of letters and numbers painted on its spine, with the blue paint I saw on Gretchen's table. The books in front of me start with A. I look at the immensity of the room, at the far, far side where the other shelves must end, and feel the tedium coming on. If the First Book is in this room, how to find it, and how to get it out?

Gretchen says, "Each person's set of books has a letter-and-number code; multiple books for the same person are numbered below that. There is a page here"—she points to the book on the rolling table—"for each code and its multiple books. You will make sure that the page here"—she taps the massive book—"matches what is actually on the shelves. You do not correct an anomaly. Any anomaly found, you come straight to me." She pauses. "It goes without saying that you will not find an anomaly. I'll come and let you know when it's time for a break. No need to ask."

I wait, and she waits, and then I realize she means for me to get started. She watches me for a few minutes, then goes about her business. It is at A51-3 that I think I'm going to scream. I do not scream. Li comes into the Archives and walks its edges, strolling down the row where I work. A little later, and Reese does the same thing. He stops for a few seconds, silently watching, and I have a bad feeling they've been told to keep an eye on me. I have another bad feeling that by the time I reach Z and this inventory is done, it will be just about time to cross the room and start back with A again.

I reach the B section, which feels like an accomplishment, and I have to go and find Gretchen to tell her there's a book missing. She lets me know it's being read, and a minute or so later comes and replaces the book on the shelf. She smiles at me, very satisfied, which makes me think the book wasn't being read at all, and that I have just passed some sort of test.

A long time later—minutes, hours, days for all I know—I'm rubbing my aching eyes at the end of the row, ready to turn into the next, when I see there's a door in the back wall of the Archives. A door Gretchen failed to mention, just visible from where I stand. I glance around, at the empty rows of quiet shelves. I've already learned that the door to the anteroom squeaks, alerting me every few minutes to Gretchen, or the Council watchers' comings and goings. Right now, it's silent in the stacks.

I steal quickly along the back wall of the Archives, almost glad for the risk if only for a break in the monotony, and push down on the door latch. Locked. I run my hands over the door. Heavy and old, metallic, like the ones in our house, not light and new and made of fern stalks, like the rest of Archives. Then I see that this back wall is not plaster but stone, painted to match. The Archives has been built around this older room. The door to the anteroom squeaks.

I run with silent footfalls. The front of the room is only visible in faraway sections as I move, brief glimpses of empty space between the shelves. I make the turn and pop up from behind the rolling table just as Gretchen rounds the corner into the B row from the other end, a book in hand. I squat back down, as if I'm reading the numbers on the bottom shelf, use the moment to get control of my breath.

I stand, check the next book, and when Gretchen starts to pass me by I say, "Where does that go?" I nod toward the door in the back wall.

"Council members only," Gretchen says.

My brain latches on to this fact. "Is that where the Council members keep their books?"

"That room doesn't concern you. You will not be working there."

"But you work there?"

She examines me, like she did in her workspace. "Inquisitiveness is not a quality we prize in the Archives," she warns. "But the answer is no. It's for Council members only."

She moves on, and so do I, in opposite directions. My mind is on that door. If the Council members are the only ones to read the First Book, then surely it would be in a room that only the Council can enter? Does Gretchen have a key? Maybe she doesn't. If I had a key, I would be curious, and they wouldn't want that, though I can't imagine Gretchen being curious. Curiosity was probably drummed out of her by the boredom. But if the room is kept locked even from her, then I would say there's something in there worth reading. It's certainly the first place we'll have to look.

I pause before the shelves. "We" is not a word I use all that often. It gives me a pleasant, agreeable sort of feeling. I'm looking forward to telling Gray about this, I realize. I've been looking forward to it ever since I walked through the doors. Storing up the details for when I meet him at the clock. Which is exactly the sort of thing I warned myself about before we left the houses of the Lost. If we don't succeed, if we can't find a way, any clue to cure the Forgetting, then Gray is going to open his eyes and he will not know me. I know how that feels; I have the internal scarring to prove it. The more I'm not alone now, the more alone I'll be afterward. Something I should remember.

Because it's boring, I put my mind on the work, where there's no room for the glassblower's son. I flip through a few pages of the massive book, holding my place with a finger, glancing over the names that go along with the painted numbers on the spines. There's no order to them. Gretchen must have another book, organized by name instead of code, or she'd never find anything in here at all. My gaze falls on *Eshan, Inkmaker's son*. He has fourteen books in the Archives, two of them from before the last Forgetting by their submittal dates, lined up in a row on the shelf to my right. I remember what Gray said about how Eshan was looking at me, to be careful. Eshan is not the boy I think I need to be careful with at all.

And then, all at once in the silent stacks, I feel the true temptation of the Archives. Gray's books are in here, and so are my mother's. Liliya's. My father's. The curiosity is an itch, burning, begging to be scratched. Gray said that we could know so many things just by comparing the books. How many of these books have entries about the Forgetting? It's hard to write during the chaos, especially if you have a family . . . But there must be some. People who tried to record it all the way to the moment they drop their pen.

My hand lifts to the nearest book, the spine rough beneath my fingers. And then I think of Gray touching my book, of Liliya just looking at my book when she opened my pack, the panic of someone else seeing my words. My soul. I drop my hand, step back from the books, and roll the table farther down the row. Oh, yes. I can see why inquisitiveness isn't appreciated at the Archives.

The door squeaks and Gretchen comes to tell me I can have a break. I leave the table where it is, go out into the ante-room and through to let Imogene sign me out, Reese search me, then do it all again after I come back from the latrines. Later in the day this happens once more, and when Gretchen comes the next time I say, "There's a book missing."

She frowns, slows her walk. I'm in section F now. Gretchen stands next to me, looking at the number beside my finger, then running her eyes over the shelf. She does it again, checks the numbers surrounding, and does it again.

"Yes," she says finally, "thank you, Nadia. I'll take care of it. You're done here for the day. Please arrive tomorrow as soon as you can after the leaving bell."

I pick up my pack and she stays where she is, hand casually covering the name on the page of the book. But it's too late for that. I've already seen the name that goes with the missing book. It's hers. And I don't think she knew about that one.

Liliya started going out to sit with a bookmaker's son, and she would come home and tell Mother all about it, and Mother would listen to everything she said. Mother even helped her twist up her hair, darken the edges around her eyes, and remembered when Liliya was supposed to come home. I couldn't understand why this would be the thing to make Mother pay attention, but it was, and it made me wonder if talking to other people might be worth the risk after all. Then Liliya came home and she was crying. She cried for two days. This I could understand.

I think pain is a thing that, when it fills your cup, you shouldn't keep pouring from the pitcher.

NADIA THE DYER'S DAUGHTER
BOOK 11, PAGE 31, 10 YEARS AFTER THE FORGETTING

CHAPTER EIGHT

I come flying out from my first day in the Archives like I used to come flying out of the Learning Center on the last day of school.

"You know he was sitting with Veronika not three weeks ago."

I turn. Imogene is at the bottom of the steps, leaning against the Archives wall, smiling the smile of someone who wants to be friendly, but to someone they don't particularly like. I stop and wait, like I don't know what she's talking about. I know what she's talking about. But I didn't know about Veronika.

"Gray has run around with a lot of the girls."

This I did know.

"But he dropped Veronika cold. He's been acting weird, disappearing a lot. And he slept on our roof the other resting for no reason I could tell. He'll charm the book right out of your hand, but he hides more than you think. And he likes a challenge. You should be careful. It's almost the Forgetting."

Your words are wasted, Imogene, because that's exactly what I've been telling myself. And funny, it's also the same thing Gray said about your brother. But I don't really want to say any of that to Imogene. Imogene can't make sense of me, prefers not to be around me. I've never blamed her for that, and I've also never seen her try to hurt someone else. I take a deep breath.

"This is . . ." I try again. "It's not what you think. People just like to talk."

Imogene looks a little like Eshan, especially right now, when I've startled her with my voice. She laughs once. "Don't they ever. Nobody has anything to do in this city but talk." Then she says, "You should probably know a lot goes around about your mother, too. People worry about . . . what she might do."

So do I.

"And get Deming to do your search, when you can. He can be bribed. If you need it."

I take another deep breath. "Thanks, Imogene."

She nods, still looking a little surprised, and I watch her as she goes on her way, blending into the other bright clothes in the dimming street. It worries me, what she said about my mother. Neither Liliya nor Genivee had thought to close the sitting room curtains before I got home. As soon as she's out of sight, I trot down Copernicus and get between the buildings where I can see the dials of the clock. It's nearly the sixth bell. Over an hour before I meet Gray. I decide I have just enough time to go see Rose.

It's crowded when I get to the baths, but most of the women on the warm side are in the big pool, eager to chat at the end of the day. The girl with the olive skin leads me to the last private room, where I take out my braids and dunk my head almost immediately under the stream of hot water. I'm rinsing my hair when Rose comes in. She has a drying cloth in her hand. I already have a drying cloth, but I doubt that's why she's here. Being clean is not the only reason I'm here, either.

I submerge myself in the heat, coming up close to the side of the basin where she stands, wiping the water from my eyes. Rose has her fingers under the water flowing from the sluice, as if she's feeling the temperature. This is a favorite trick, evidently.

"Did you have a good resting, Nadia the Dyer's daughter?" she asks.

Probably better than yours, I think. "I'm sorry we stayed so long in your room. We were . . . talking."

She waves her dry hand, as if giving up her resting room to the unlost happens every day. Then I feel my stomach squeeze. Does Gray have a girl in there every week?

"There has been talk in the baths today."

My stomach squeezes again, for a different reason.

"Plenty to be had about you, of course." She smiles as she squats down, picking up the bottles of soaps and oils to study them one by one. "But that isn't the talk I mean. This is something I happened to hear Lydia the Weaver say to Essie the Wheelmaker."

Lydia. My father's wife. I lean forward, elbows on the basin. Rose's soft voice is once again masked by the running water.

"She said that Jonathan of the Council has formed an understanding, a secret one, because Janis would not approve. Lydia's husband is on the Council now, and has seen . . ."

I droop just a bit. Whatever I had expected Rose to come in here to say, it wasn't this. This really is gossip, through and through. What do I care who Jonathan of the Council is sitting with? Other than to feel sorry for her.

"The understanding," Rose says, "is with Liliya."

It feels like I stare at Rose for half a bell. Then I'm out of the water rubbing my legs and back fiercely with the drying cloth. I need to go so I won't be late, but I also need to do something because I'm mad.

"I think you should be cautious," she says.

I take her meaning. It's what everyone is telling me today, even myself. I jerk the blue dress back over my head. Jonathan is older than Liliya, much older. He can't be serious. And he can be cruel. Which means everything that I worried about with the glassblower's son is still fair game for worrying. More so, and with greater consequences. I think of the fear I saw on Liliya's face, and the new possible source for her anxiety about Mother. I sit down on the bench, still drying my legs.

"Rose, have you heard anything that . . ." I stop to think, rephrase. "If someone had a malfunction that was more . . . in their head, is there anything that would make that person need to be . . . concerned?" I don't even know how to ask what I'm asking.

Rose frowns while she thinks. "You're speaking of your mother?" She waves a hand again. "Please. Rose knows everything. But the answer is no, though I'd say you have a reason for asking."

"Would you listen for me? And if you do hear anything that would be important to someone . . . like my mother, would you tell me?"

Rose smiles her answer. And then she says, "If I could say something without offense . . ."

I stop in the act of slipping on my sandals. Rose is sitting on the bench beside me now, folding and refolding the extra towel.

"I'm glad that what I first told you about your sister was not true," she says. "Gray is dear to me, and I'm glad he chose differently."

I put on embarrassment in the same way I put on Liliya's dress. It clings to my skin. Rose has overshot the mark, like everyone has, but I care much more about what she thinks than Imogene. At the same time, saying that she would prefer me as a choice has me questioning her intelligence, so in the end, the only word that comes out of my mouth is "Why?"

Rose's wrinkles go deep, spreading curving lines around her cheeks and outward from her eyes. I think she's laughing at me. "Because you had to ask," she says, "and because you do. That is your answer. Now, you're in a hurry. Come and let Rose fix your hair."

She doesn't wait for me to come, she just does, so I let her. She rubs my hair until it is only damp, not dripping, running her fingers through the long tendrils until it's as good as brushed. What a funny, strange, odd, and remarkable thing this is. Last week, I wouldn't have allowed it. This week I close my eyes and am comforted. I can't decide if this is a new weakness or a strength.

Before I can puzzle it out she has my damp hair braided up and pinned, and from somewhere in her smock she has produced a long string. She crisscrosses the string over my shoulders and across my chest, tucks, folds, ties, and when I look, down the loose blue dress has become something different. The belt goes on, so I can tie my tether, and when I leave the baths, I have kissed Rose's cheek and I'm not exactly sure who I am.

❧

I wait for Gray at the water clock, on the opposite side of the speaking platform, the clang of the seventh bell long faded from my ears. The sky is a beautiful, deep red, a red that, if you look carefully, varies in waves from a hint of pink to the color of old blood. I know most people miss the light, but I love the sunsetting almost as much as I love the dark day moons. What I do not love is waiting, especially when I am so incredibly, obviously waiting, with my hair so incredibly and obviously done.

I remember a story that the little girls used to tell in the learning room, about how Janis had a place inside the clock tower, high up, where you couldn't see her but she could see you. Follow the rules, or Janis would see. I always thought this story had its roots in my schoolmates' imaginations, or maybe our teacher's fear of showing Janis our test scores. But now I'm left with the uncomfortable feeling that even the Head of Council of Canaan is somewhere just above, watching me be abandoned at the water clock.

A pair of women cross the green that is the low end of the amphitheater, one of them Essie the Wheelmaker, her baby on her back, banging its fists, a small book dangling from its jumper. The woman walking with Essie looks me over, and they whisper. I think of that regretful expression right before I ran off with Genivee. Rose's room was like some kind of separate existence. Now that we've reentered our worlds, maybe

Gray has decided to leave that existence to the Lost. Maybe I'm going to steal this book without his help. The "without" hurts more than I'd anticipated, no matter what my good intentions at the Archives, and I'm irritated and a little frightened that it does.

I push off the clock tower and go. I should be home anyway. Tending to Mother. Taking care of Genivee. Enduring Liliya, trying to understand why she would make the choice of position and power when Jonathan of the Council comes with it. Or does she think he'll forget and she can make him into someone else? But I think he liked seeing Hedda flogged, and cruelty is a trait that doesn't get unmade in the Forgetting.

I'm more than halfway home, ducking beneath the tree buds on Meridian, when I look up and see the glassblower's son crossing Third Bridge, striding fast, his back to me. I track him with my eyes. Now I'm more than irritated. I'm mad. I had things to tell him. I did tedious work. Maybe found where the First Book is kept. Put up with gossiping women. I even fixed my hair. I pick up my pace and follow him.

I see Gray lift a hand to someone, turn left onto Einstein, then dodge into the alley between two houses. I start to trot, stepping over moonflowers in their pots by the doors. He's taking the shortcut to Jin's. To the wall. When we're almost to the Archives again, I slow, letting him get farther ahead, and then I stop, watching as he crosses to the other side of Copernicus. But instead of going up the garden stairs, Gray knocks on Jin's front door. Yellow lamplight flares as the door opens, is extinguished as it shuts. Gray is inside.

I stand, awkward, across the street. There aren't many people in this back corner of Canaan, even during the waking hours. I lean against a wall, pack in hand, as if I'm digging through it, avoiding the eyes of one or two passersby, positioned exactly where I can see Gray sitting at the table through Jin's front window. Jin sits beside Gray, hair pure white, thinner than the last time I saw him, an oil lamp hanging overhead. I watch Gray opening a book, dipping a pen.

I forget to dig in my pack. Gray was writing in a book with a brown cover last resting, I'm sure of it, the one he wears in the open, strapped across his chest. This book is a deep sky red. Is that Jin's book Gray is writing in? Has Jin grown too feeble to write? Who's been making his signs, then? I think I might know the answer to that, too, and how I was caught coming over the wall. I watch Jin's hands moving through the air as he talks. Gray has his hair tied back, out of his face, and he pauses once, to ask a question, then Jin pushes himself up, hobbling toward the window.

I remember where I am and start moving again. When I glance over my shoulder, I'm halfway down the street, and Jin has pulled the curtain, shutting them inside. I stop walking. I don't want to go home and tend and take care of things and endure. Not yet. And what, exactly, was stopping Gray from coming to the clock? From telling me he had something else to do? And I'm tired of being told to be careful. Especially by myself. I turn around, march back to Jin's, and knock on his front door. Before I can change my mind. I have about half a minute to consider whether this is a mistake before Gray answers. His brows go up a little.

"Hey," he says.

The table has been rearranged, I see. Or the people. Now the red book, and the pen and ink, are directly in front of Jin.

I suppose it's still against the rules to write in someone else's book, even if they ask you to. I look to Jin, to see if he minds my presence, and the man is waving his hands again, beckoning me inside. Gray is still staring at me. I walk past him and sit down at the table. Jin leans across and grabs my hand and shakes it. Over and over. I'm getting good at shaking hands. Gray shuts the door.

"Welcome," Jin says, much too loud. "Welcome! You are a Dyer's daughter. Which . . ."

"Nadia," I whisper. Gray drops into the chair beside Jin. Jin squints, wrinkles his forehead. He's still shaking my hand.

"This is Nadia," Gray says, much louder than I did. His eyes are on me.

"Yes!" Jin agrees. "I'll get you water. Or tea. Do you like tea?"

I nod.

"The water is hot!" Jin shouts. He shambles off toward his storeroom, so happy I feel guilty for not knocking on his door forty times before now. I look around. Most of the houses in Canaan have the same, basic floor plan, with one or two re-arrangements. But Jin has hung pieces of cloth in shades of red and gold all over the walls. It makes his sitting room warmer, cozy. Gray crosses his arms, leans back in the chair, a bit of his smirk lurking.

"You followed me," he says.

"You didn't come to the clock."

"You look nice."

"Rose did my hair."

Gray shakes his head. "What do you girls do over there on that side? The men just get clean."

"And shove each other and jump into the pools."

"You've been?" The smile is pulling his mouth upward now.

"You didn't come to the clock," I repeat.

Smile gone.

"You like it sweet?" Jin's shout from the doorway of the storeroom makes me jump. I nod at him again. He smiles, waves his hands in the air for no reason I can think of, and goes back in the other room. I look at Gray.

"The clock?"

Gray leans forward, like Jin could hear us if he didn't talk low. "I was going to come by your house after this, on the way back, to explain. See, the fact is, I've been asked . . . told not to see you anymore."

I sit back. "Oh."

"Not," Gray continues, "like that's going to have anything to do with what actually happens, you understand."

"Oh?"

"You see, I didn't come home two restings in a row and everyone in this city thinks they know what I was up to and who with."

"I had the same problem."

"Did you? There's a coincidence. And what did your mother have to say about it?"

Not much. She just stuck a knife in her arm.

"Mine had plenty. You're an odd one, Delia says, and so's your mother. And ever since the potter's wife saw you come by the shop, I haven't been myself. You're what they call a bad influence. That's what Delia the Planter says."

I look him over. "You don't seem too upset about it." What he seems is amused.

"I'm having a hard time being annoyed with either one of my parents right now. I found out we share the same biology. And anyway, I like being influenced for the worse. Usually it's the other way around."

Jin comes in then with a steaming cup of tea, offering it to me with two hands like a sunrise celebration cake. I blow, take a tiny sip, give Jin a weak smile. It tastes almost exactly like a sunrise celebration cake.

"Jin," Gray says, full voice, "can Nadia wait on your roof until we've finished our talk?" Gray glances once at me and I nod. If he's writing in Jin's book for him, they'll want some privacy.

"Yes, yes," says Jin, shooing me away, his grin huge.

I take my sweet tea and climb the stairs to the garden, stand at the edge on the far end, where I can see down the street. The whole city is blushing pink in the light. I watch a Lost man cleaning out the hanging lamps outside the Archives, getting ready for the dark days. After a long while, Gray comes and stands next to me.

"What are you thinking about?" he asks.

I really don't want to tell him.

"Come on, Dyer's daughter. Talk."

I keep my eyes straight ahead. "If I do, you'll owe me thirty-seven answers."

"And how many answers do you owe me again?"

"Four." I'm making this up and we both know it.

"I'll take it," he says.

I tilt my head toward the Archives. "I was thinking about going through that roof. I could get on it easy enough, just drop down from the wall, though bare feet might be better than sandals. I'm not sure how slippery it is. And I'd need a knife, to cut my way in, and a light that I could hide until it was time to use it. But there's a ceiling below that thatch, maybe stone, I couldn't tell, everything's painted, so even if I get through I'm not sure it would work. And there's getting back up and out and down again. So . . ."

When I glance over Gray is looking at me, really looking, like at the waterfall. He says, "I should've gotten you talking a long time ago. Once you get going, the most interesting things come out of your head."

I drink the now cold sweet tea and put my eyes on the street. Because I don't know what else to do.

"So I take it you were in the Archives today?"

"I work there now. It was my sister's doing . . ." Or was it Jonathan's? I think suddenly. "But I might know where the book is." And I tell him about Gretchen, and the locked door, and how they protect the books. "So even if I could get in the locked door, I don't know if I could get out with the book. It might have to be read in place."

"Which you won't have time to do."

"And if we do take it out, it will either have to be returned before the Dark Days Festival, for Janis's reading, or we'll have to wait and steal it after. I'd rather no one ever knew it was gone."

Gray rubs his chin.

"So if I'm caught," I go on, "it's going to be red-handed. Or they're going to know it was me. Only Gretchen and I go in the big room, except for Reese and Li, and that's to check on me. And Deming sleeps in the waiting area, and maybe Gretchen in her workspace. That's why I think your parents have a good idea. You shouldn't be seen with me."

"That's what you think, is it?"

"I didn't say you shouldn't see me, just that you shouldn't be seen."

He grins. I wonder if all this makes me more of a challenge. "Here's what I think," Gray says. "We go to the Dark Days Festival, we let Janis get going with her rule reading, then I give her a hard shove, you grab the book and go." Gray glances over at me, smirk in place. "She's not very fast."

"Oh, you're full of excellent ideas."

Gray says, "You should go this time."

"To the festival? Why?" I'm amazed he knows I don't.

"You're the only person in Canaan who would have to ask that. Because it's fun, Nadia. You might like it. And think of all the opportunities for crime . . ." But then Gray's voice lowers, and he says, "Look."

I move my gaze back to the street and there is Jonathan, his black robes unmistakable in the red light, and he has Reese and Li with him, plus Rachel the Supervisor, also on the Council.

Gray reaches out and takes my hand, with much less caution than in Rose's room, this time using it to pull me down, out of any line of sight from the street. I go to my knees behind the low garden wall as he sits, still tall enough to see Jonathan and his group turn down Copernicus away from Jin's, walking with purpose to a door four or five houses down. Jonathan knocks, and someone lets all of them in. Gray still has my hand. I pull it away, gently, and immediately wish I hadn't. He doesn't say anything. His gaze is fixed on the house the Council members have entered.

I hear yelling from down the street. Doors open one by one, heads sticking out of windows, turning to the noise, and then Reese and Li half drag a man out of the house we've been watching. His hands are tied. I lean closer to Gray.

"Who is it?" I whisper.

"Rhaman the Fuelmaker."

"They're taking him? What could he have done?" Rhaman's yells are echoing all around us. I hear Jin open his door.

"I saw him today," Gray says, "just before the leaving bell. In the houses of the Lost."

"On the women's side?"

"Yes, but . . . It's not always like that, you know. This is . . . it's mutual."

And Gray would know. Is this what would happen if Jonathan found out Gray goes to the Lost? Even just to see Rose? "Has Rhaman seen you there?"

"Yes."

"Would he say anything?"

"I don't know."

Rhaman has quieted a little, and I can hear the buzz and whisper of talk from the gathering people as Jonathan drags him down the street. I wonder if any of those whisperers will be claiming their reward. The thought disgusts me.

"But why now?" Gray is saying, voice held low. "Rhaman has been going down there for years. No one's ever done anything about it before." His gaze is sharp, focused by anger. "He," Gray says, looking at Jonathan of the Council, "is trying to make us afraid. He wants us afraid."

When the group rounds the corner off Copernicus I say, "Rose told me today that Liliya is sitting with Jonathan of the Council."

Gray turns his face to me.

"Rose says they have an understanding in secret, because Janis doesn't approve."

"Does Liliya know you've been going over the wall?"

"No. Or I don't think so."

I hear him curse once beneath his breath. "Can you get out the window in your room?" I wrinkle my brow, and he doesn't wait for me to speak. "Put something there to climb on, and if they come for you, get out, run to Jin's, and go over the wall. Promise me you'll do that."

"I will if you will." We look at each other, and again I see an expression on Gray's face that I don't understand. Maybe it's many things at once. I wonder why he's sitting up here with me, instead of running around with Veronika, or Imogene, or one of the others.

"Come here tomorrow," he says. "To Jin's roof. Come up when no one can see you."

He's so still, except for his breath, except for that place in his jaw that's clenched.

"Come," he says again. "And we'll take that book, and we'll find a way to make them remember."

And that's when I have a revelation. Liliya isn't going to turn me in to Jonathan, not even if she wants to, not even for a reward. Because I have something she wants: access to the Archives and the ability to make myself disappear, something I could never pull off tied to the plaque on the water clock. And now Liliya has access to·something I want, too.

That key hanging around Jonathan of the Council's neck.

I saw Lydia the Weaver at the water channel, with the two little girls who are my half sisters. The youngest is named Kari, and she was explaining to her mother how to write truth in a book. You write your mistakes and the bad things about yourself just like you write down the good things you want to remember, too. So you can always know who you really are. This is my father's teaching. I remember it.

I decided to go to the Archives to look at what is now my first book, the false one my father made before the Forgetting, to read what he wanted me to remember about who I am. I read about my pretty eyes and chattering ways and playing with my sister. I read about the death of my father. I have never seen so many lies.

NADIA THE DYER'S DAUGHTER
BOOK 7, PAGE 14, 8 YEARS AFTER THE FORGETTING

CHAPTER NINE

I work the first two bells at the Archives without taking much notice of what I'm doing. Rhaman the Fuelmaker was flogged right after the leaving bell, seven days after he was taken, for mixing with the Lost. I made sure I wasn't there, and I made sure Genivee wasn't, either. Just like I've made sure that all of us are nowhere that isn't our bed at the resting and at the waking bell. Mother hasn't gotten up to check yet. Liliya has been staying home with Mother during the waking hours, while I take over for the resting, and she's in her bed exactly when she's supposed to be, when Mother might check. But in between, I'm not so sure.

"I know who you've been going out to sit with," I'd said three restings ago, cornering my sister in the storeroom before she could escape to her room.

Liliya had set down the plate she was drying like it was made of weak glass. "How do you know that?"

And it was only then I'd realized it was true. Really true. Jonathan of the Council. Part of me hadn't quite believed it.

"So what are you going to do about it?" she'd said, without any of her usual bravado.

"I don't want to do anything about your . . . dalliance." It pleased me at the time, to see my jab hit home. "But if you want me to do that thing we've been discussing, in the Archives, and if you want me to forget about any other particular thing I might know, I'll need . . . some help."

Liliya had narrowed her eyes. "What kind of help?"

Now, in the silent stacks of the Archives, the image of Jonathan of the Council in our house comes back to my mind, that key around his neck, the exaggerated point he'd made of looking up Liliya's name. Janis disapproves of our family—evidently everyone does—and I'd be willing to bet a week of rations that Liliya means to have Jonathan write down her name right before the Forgetting, right before Janis will also forget her objections.

The idea of Jonathan becoming Head of Council one day, with Liliya at his side, is terrifying, but I wonder if Jonathan's plans actually match my sister's. I'm afraid they don't. I'm afraid my sister is in over her head, and if Gray and I steal the First Book of the Forgetting, using a key Liliya has stolen from Jonathan, it's Liliya who will be blamed. I was angry when I asked her to do it, upset about Mother, Jonathan, our family, about her asking me to change my books at the Archives. I'm not even considering changing my books anymore. When I go home, I'm going to call it off. That key might be to something else anyway. Except I can't imagine what. I'm sure it is the right key. Mostly.

"Nadia!"

I jump at Gretchen's voice near my ear.

"Are you asleep standing up?"

"Sorry. I'll work quicker to make up the time."

She makes a noise like *hmph*, gets the book she's come for, and glides away. I find my place on the shelf, find my place in the book on the rolling table, think of how many pages there are left, how many books there are on all of these shelves, and just like the first day, consider screaming. I decide not to scream. I read through the next names and then I stop, freeze, finger just below a set of inked letters.

R382-1   Nadia, Planter's daughter

This is my name. My old name, from before. It can't be right. Father destroyed my old book. And Mother's and Liliya's, baby Genivee's, and, I assume, his own. He changed everyone's name but mine. It must be another Nadia, daughter of another planter. Someone who died. Or became Lost. I look at the date. One volume only, submitted almost twelve years ago. Right after the Forgetting.

I listen. The stacks are silent, but I haven't been paying attention. I don't know how long it's been since Gretchen squeaked the door. I have to open that book. Just long enough to know if it's mine. Or not. The wheels creak softly as I push the rolling cart to the next shelf, skip down to the corresponding numbers in the book, so it will look like I've made progress. If there's an anomaly, Gretchen can find it. I'm more concerned with the anomaly of a book archived in my real name.

The door squeaks, I make sure I have the look of doing my job, and this time it's Reese wandering through. He stands at the end of the shelf, hair slicked back, leaning with his thick arms crossed, just to put some fear in me. I don't look at him.

I keep my eyes on the work I'm not doing. He tires of this after a few minutes, and as soon as the door closes I hurry back to R382-1. I yank the book off the shelf and open it to the first page.

NADIA, BORN TO RENATA, PLANTER,
AND RAYNOR, PLANTER
4TH DARK DAY, 2ND SEASON,
6 YEARS AFTER THE FORGETTING

I close the book without noise, put it back on the shelf. My head feels like I've gotten too hot in the baths, dizzy. Raynor is my father's name, from before. I hadn't known my mother was a planter, but I remember the writing like I remember my own face. That book is mine. The book I watched being cut from my body.

I walk back to the rolling cart, hang on to it, as if the floor might collapse underneath me. We've discussed our plans every day, Gray and I, heads together in the chill of Jin's dead garden, speaking low and where we can't be seen. I talk to him like I've never talked to Genivee. I'd thought I'd be wait-ing days, weeks maybe, perfecting a clever plan, a foolproof plan. It turns out there will be no plan, or not much of one. Because I'm going to steal a book today. Right now.

The door squeaks and Gretchen comes to tell me I can have a break. I leave, submit to my search from Li, visit the latrines, stand outside, breathe the dark air. Think. When I slip back inside Gretchen has just called the name of a teacher. I don't think she's noticed me. Imogene starts writing my name as Gretchen takes the teacher to Deming and the read-ing rooms. I set my pack on the table, let Li start my search, and then there's a disturbance from the other end of the waiting room. I think Deming has found a pen. I snatch up my pack.

"Eager to work, are you?" says Imogene.

I don't have time to answer. I walk into the anteroom, but the moment the door shuts I alter course to Gretchen's workspace. The door is standing partially open, which is a shame, because now I can't close it without risking her notice. I slip inside, leaving the door as I found it. Gretchen's desk is still neat, the blue paint that marks the spine of every book in the stacks in a small pot, the brushes beside it. My tethered book comes out of my pack. I dip a brush in the blue paint, bend down to the desk, and on the spine of my book write a painstaking R, then 3, and 8.

The door to the anteroom opens. Instantly I step back, book and brush with me, out of sight of the door. Sandals slap sharp against the floor. Everything depends on Gretchen going straight into the stacks—not into her workspace—and coming straight back out again—not into her workspace—without realizing that I've been signed back in. The footsteps pass, fade into the squeak of the door to the stacks.

I dart back to the desk, paint a slightly messy 2, then a 1 beneath that, blowing on the spine of my book. Then I look at the wet paintbrush. The door to the stacks squeaks and I back out of sight again, rubbing the wet brush on the wrong side of my hem as the footsteps cross the anteroom. They pause before the cracked door, then continue on, a little faster. "Imogene," I hear Gretchen call, "where is . . ."

The door shuts, but I can easily fill in the missing word of Gretchen's sentence. It was "Nadia." The brush goes back in its place, book in my pack, and I sprint into the anteroom, making for the door to the stacks. I wish now that door didn't squeak. I slip through just as the door to the waiting room opens and run full out to the R shelves, where the rolling table waits. When Gretchen rounds the corner of my row I am studiously comparing numbers. She stops, stares, and I look up, expectant.

Gretchen asks, "Were you . . . here just a minute ago?"

I look around and over my shoulder, as if evaluating the surroundings will help my fake confusion. "Yes," I say. "You mean when you came into the stacks?"

Gretchen's brows knit.

"I was probably checking the bottom row," I say helpfully. My pack is open and undone, behind the cart at my feet. I'm hoping my lack of breath isn't showing. Gretchen looks at me, head tilted, then gives it up.

"Carry on," she says.

I carry on. When the door squeaks again and Gretchen is gone, I reach down and untie my book from its tether, walk deliberately to R382-1. The long-lost book of Nadia the Planter's daughter looks down at me from the shelf. I replace it with my current one, with its brand-new blue numbers, squeezing my book into the blank, tight space between the others. My old book was smaller, child-size, and now that is the book that gets tied to my tether, goes into my pack.

The next bells are the longest I've ever lived through. But finally, after a steady pace through shelves I'm fairly positive I never checked, Gretchen comes to compliment me on a job well done and tell me my day is over. I leave the rolling table at W, thinking exclusively about the R section. It's risky, leaving my book there. It feels wrong. But I'm not in danger of forgetting where it is. Or what's in it. Probably.

I make my way through the empty anteroom, approach the door to the waiting room. The beating in my chest becomes a throb, a painful dance I can both feel and hear as I open the door and put my pack on the table beside Imogene for inspection. Reese or Li will see only a book there, tied to my tether, but it will be a book a little too small, and with blue numbers on the spine. Numbers it should not have. I've turned it spine downward.

Li pats me down while Reese opens my pack. He does the worst job of searching I've ever seen, barely glancing at the interior, one hand just swishing around the things that live there. Imogene hands me my ink and pen, and then I am out the door, in the dark of a late sunsetting, and the book I thought was burned, shredded, buried, or destroyed is out of the Archives and in my pack.

I turn toward Jin's, choose a moment when the streets are empty, and run up the stairs to his roof, settle in the prickling grass with my pack in my lap and my back to a column. The air is cool, but I'm hot, the throbbing in my chest speeding up to the rhythm of a run. I open my pack, take out the book, run my hand over the dark blue cover, over an even darker black splotch along the edge. There's something I'd forgotten. The ink stain. I open it, lean down to get closer to the pages. There's just enough light to read by. The first pages are written by my parents, alternating between Mother's and my father's hand.

Nadia is a strong baby. The first child to take after me . . .
Nadia found her toes.
Nadia ate a bug in the garden. She liked it; her mother didn't.

Nadia went with her mother to request new clothes today. Lisbeth asked if the dyers could please make Nadia's hair the right color . . .

Lisbeth, I think. Liliya's old name.

Nadia took four steps in a row. She'll soon be running. Her eyes have settled into her grandmother's shade of blue . . .

My grandmother. Who was my grandmother? The pages start to be interspersed with my own childish writing. *N A D I A* sprawls across one, the following pages mostly my father's hand when it's not mine, though still written for my book. He wrote:

Nadia went with her father to the fields today. On the way through the city she stopped on a bridge and asked about the water. She listened while her father explained the spring that brings water up from the ground to run through the channel from one end of the city to the other so that everyone can have clean water to use. Then Nadia asked her father what would happen if she put a leaf in the channel. It took some time for him to understand that she wasn't asking about making the water dirty, she was asking where the leaf would go, where it would be after it traveled out of the city. She wanted to know what was beyond the wall. Nadia has a fine, inquisitive mind . . .

I can remember this, just around the edges. I was three or something close, and it was the first time I'd realized my father did not have all the world's answers. After the Forgetting, I'd wondered what would happen if I threw myself in the channel instead, if I could just float out of Canaan to a new place. I turn the page. Reading these entries is wonderful. And exquisitely painful. I had adored my father. The next passage is written in my mother's hand.

Nadia does not like the resting-time game. Lisbeth wants to race to see who can win and get to her bed first, but Nadia says having to rest first is not a good thing to win. She lets Anna take her to bed instead, because if Anna says it's time to sleep that must be right, because Anna knows "lots and lots of things." Nadia will be just like her.

I stare at this passage. Who is Anna? The name ripples out to the edges of my mind. Anna. I can almost hear the word; I think in my mother's voice. It's eerie. And familiar. I start flipping the pages, one by one, scanning the words. The entries change over to only my own writing, but I don't see the name Anna again. I keep turning the pages, even when they become blank, but there's nothing there.

Except there is something there. Wedged into the crack between the cover and the last page, inside my book so long the paper is permanently molded to its shape. A small piece of metal, delicate links making a kind of short rope attached to both ends. I pry it out, hold it dangling in the dim. The center piece is smooth and thin, polished and reflective, and carved into it are bold block symbols: потому что я смею.

What is this? Why is it in my book? And why does my book even exist? If Raynor, now known as Anson, had wanted to remove himself from his wife and the responsibility of his children, he would have destroyed this. Why didn't he? Did the Forgetting come too soon? But if so, how did my book end up registered in the Archives? And the name Anna . . . It all leaves me with a sense of confusion, a deep, tickling frustration of things just beyond my grasp. I wonder if this is what it feels like to have forgotten. Really forgotten.

I look at the metal more closely. On the reverse side is a row of numbers, not carved but crude, scratched with something sharp. 39413958467871x2. Random or very specific—I can't tell which. But on one end of the metal rope there's a link that's different, a bump I can feel when I run my finger over it, a bump I discover is the tiniest of levers. When I push, the other side of the link opens. I feel my eyes widen. I've never seen metalwork with such fine parts. Maybe it's not only the big things we've forgotten how to make.

The other end of the metal rope does not have a fancy link. So I loop it around, push down the lever, slide the plain one into the opening, let it close. Now the metal rope makes a circle. I hold it up, let the circle hang around my splayed fingers. It's a bracelet, I think, like some of the girls make with strips of braided cloth. Though this is much too big for my wrist. I unhook the link, put the piece of metal around my ankle, and hook it back. It feels cool, heavy. A thing that was inside my book. My real book, from before. I run my hand over the cover and it's like rubbing a sore, a pain that only gets worse when you touch it. Why did he do it? Why did he leave us, and take this away?

I sit up. There's a knock at Jin's door, and I hear Gray's voice, indistinct from the street. The closing of the door cuts it off again. I get to my feet, put my book into my pack. I tell myself that I need to get home because I need to stop Liliya from doing something stupid, even if I was the one who asked her to do it. I need to check on Mother, make sure her wound is healing. I go without noise down the stairs. Jin's curtains are already closed. I'm sliding past his front door when it opens, and then Gray is looking out at me. He's messy today, straight from the furnace. He didn't come straight from the furnace for Jin.

"Change your mind?" he asks.

I don't answer. I can't even think what I'd say if I could.

Gray says, "So it's like that today, is it?"

It is like that today. I don't want Gray to know that my father took my book or that Liliya thinks I'm not her sister. I don't want him to know how easily I can be forgotten.

I turn and walk away down the street, and when I hear Jin's front door slam, I wince.

∽

When I walk into my sitting room, I stop short, the air pulled straight out of me. Genivee sits beside a lamp glowing on the sparkling metal of our tabletop, and standing in the doorway to our storeroom is Reese, much like he guards the door into the Archives. There's noise from near the resting rooms, Liliya's voice and at least two others, and then Tessa of the Granary walks down the hall. I find Genivee's eyes first.

"We're being searched," she says. My mind goes instantly to my pack, to the book Reese failed once to find today, then to my hiding hole, then to the cutting in the garden. Is today unexpectedly my day? Or has Liliya, in her own efficient way, already done something she shouldn't? I think about what Gray said, to get out of the house, get to Jin's, go over the wall.

"Why?" I direct the question to Reese, but he only holds his hands behind his back, ready to chase, I suppose, if someone says chase. Did he stand there, looking at me today in the Archives, knowing he was going to do this?

"Just a routine inspection. Nothing to be concerned with," Tessa says from the hallway.

Oh, it's something to be concerned with. We don't have routine inspections. At least we didn't yesterday.

"Who ordered it?" I demand.

Tessa says, "Council vote. We—" Then I recognize one of the voices from down the hall, from my mother's room. I should have known. I start a march to the hallway.

"Ah, wait . . ."

I push past Tessa and down the hall. She doesn't try very hard to stop me.

Liliya's voice is coming through Mother's open doorway, telling people what they can and cannot do, and when I burst inside I can see it isn't doing any good. Arthur of the Metals is going through my mother's clothes, shaking them out, inspecting each piece, while Anson the Planter is bent over my mother. She looks like she's sleeping.

"Don't touch her!"

I didn't know I was going to yell; it just happened. Liliya closes her mouth, and Anson looks up, startled.

"No harm meant," he says. His voice was always like that, so calm and reasonable, even while he's cutting a tether.

I go and sit on the floor beside Mother, as if I'm guarding something instead of Reese, and Anson decides not to fight that any harder than Tessa. He goes to help Arthur. Mother is sleeping soundly, no sign of any staining on her sleeve, so unless they've inspected her arms, the wound is hidden. I wonder if Liliya has given her one of the sleeping tonics we saved from the doctor.

I take Mother's hand. I don't know what I'm doing. I should have stayed in Jin's garden. They cannot search my pack. But I also can't stand the thought of Anson touching my mother. I think he might be the one who made her this way.

Liliya comes and leans against the wall at the foot of the mattress, hands behind her back, quiet for once while Arthur reaches up and runs his hand over the top of Mother's cabinet. Anson shakes out one of her tunics. This is horrible. Violating. Could that really be the man who held my hand on the bridge, telling me where the water went? What are they looking for?

And then I feel a touch on my leg. I see Mother's hand, her unwounded arm stretching out from beneath the blanket. Her eyes are open, and she's smiling. She whispers something, not words, just sounds, gibberish. It's frightening. Arthur turns around.

She begins to say it again and Liliya starts talking, loud. "How much longer is this going to take?" My sister marches up to Anson and Arthur, hands on hips, pulling their attention away from Mother. And now I think I know where Genivee learned this tactic. "If you'll tell me what you're looking for maybe I can help. Because the two of you are making a mess . . ."

Mother is on her side now, smiling at me. She says the gibberish words again, and then I realize what's caught her attention. She's brushing her fingers over the metal around my ankle, exposed now that my leggings have drawn up while I'm sitting. How much of that sleeping tonic did Liliya give her?

"Don't worry, Mother," I whisper, trying to keep her quiet. "They'll be gone soon, I promise."

"We're done now," Arthur is saying. Liliya backs off, Anson nods to me, and the two men file out, moving away down the hall. I stand, Liliya beside me.

"They're going to yours," Liliya whispers. "What are they going to find?"

"Nothing," I reply. And I hope it's true. They'll have to be thorough to find my hiding hole. I don't know how thorough they're being. Mother's fingers brush my ankle again. "Are they searching us? Personally?"

"Not yet."

"I can't be searched."

"Neither can I."

We look at each other, and then away. "What are they looking for?"

"I don't think they're looking for anything," Liliya replies. "I think they were looking at Mother. Who did you tell about her arm?"

No one. Not even Gray. "Anyone who came past our window could have seen. You left the curtains wide open."

"Oh, I don't know, we might have been busy trying to keep Mother from killing herself while you were running around all resting and leaving your bed empty!"

Liliya let her voice rise just a little that time, and Mother mumbles something from her mattress. "Because I dare," she says, smiling.

I glare at my sister. "She's not even making sense. How much sleeping tonic has she had?"

"I don't want to hear it, Nadia. It was a bad day."

"Could you have stopped this?" I mean the search. The inspection.

"And how could I have stopped this?"

"I thought you had connections."

Liliya doesn't answer. She's staring at the floor. I wonder if she went to Rhaman's flogging, and what she thought of her understanding—or whatever it is she has with Jonathan—after that. I can hear the two men talking with Tessa and Genivee now. I think this means they're already done with my room. I let go of some fear. As long as they don't count our stores. "Nadia."

My eyes dart to my sister. That was not a usual Liliya tone. She drops her voice to a bare whisper.

"If you had to, could you get Mother over the wall?"

I blink. "What makes you think I could get over the wall?"

"Nothing," she says. "Never mind." And there's that fear again, an ugly emotion passing across her face. What could be making Liliya so afraid? And what, after all this time, makes her think I go over the wall? I haven't been since I went with Gray, in the last of the sunlight. I look down at Mother's dreaming face. I don't think I could get her to make the jump, climb the ladder. Not quickly, anyway. But the fact that Liliya is asking frightens me more than anything else that's happened.

We both hear the front door open, Genivee talking nonstop to whoever will listen to her.

"Here," Liliya says quickly, reaching right down the front of her dress and coming back up with a cloth bundle. If I tried to store something there, it would fall to the floor. She puts the bundle in my hand. "Take it," she says, "and don't squeeze. It's still soft, and I'm not getting you another."

Beneath the cloth is a piece of clay like a misshapen stone, which is confusing until I realize the clay is in two pieces. I open the lump like a book and inside is the perfect impression of a key. I decide I don't want to know what Liliya had to do to get this, but one thing is as clear as freshly cleaned glass: She's willing to risk a lot to get rid of me.

"I'm going to go check the storeroom," Liliya says.

I listen to her walk away. For a few minutes during the search, it had felt like Liliya and I were on the same side. A team. Like before the Forgetting. Like the entries in my book, when we were a family. Right now I feel every bit of what I have lost.

I sit down beside Mother's mattress. She has her eyes closed again, her hair a streaked cloud of dark smoke on the pillow.

"Mother," I whisper, "who is Anna?"

She smiles, eyes still closed, and says the gibberish words again. What can she think she's saying? I take her hand and put it on the metal around my ankle.

"Have you seen this before?" I don't know why I'm asking these things. I know she can't remember.

"Nadia," she says, very softly.

I lean forward, straining to hear. Her expression has changed, drawn, as if in pain.

"She's gone," she whispers. "The bed is empty."

"Who, Mother?"

"Nadia," she says again. "Her book is wrong. It's not Nadia's book."

I know, Mother. But it was only ever the book that was wrong. Not the daughter. Never the daughter.

After the search, I ran the back way to Jin's with the impression of the key, and when Gray opened the door, before I could say a word, before he said a word, I realized something important, something I didn't expect. I was the face he'd wanted to see at the door.

NADIA THE DYER'S DAUGHTER
IN THE BLANK PAGES OF
NADIA THE PLANTER'S DAUGHTER
BOOK 1

CHAPTER TEN

I sneak into the alley behind the wheelmaker's, coming up to the glassblower's workshop from behind. It's been ten days since I went running to Jin's with those two pieces of clay, the impression of Jonathan's key in their center. Gray had sat listening to my breathless explanation while Jin tottered about getting tea. It was clever of my sister, I'd thought. A way to steal a key without stealing it. Gray held the pieces of clay in his hands, studying them. There's little to no extra metal in Canaan, no good way to shape one key out of another, even if one of us had the skill. Then he'd just grinned, shrugged a shoulder, and said, "I'll make it. Out of glass."

We've both been to Jin's every day since then, there's no thinking we won't, and I've replaced much of Jin's tea. The light is gone and so it's easy now to avoid the streetlamps, to slip over from the Archives and up the garden stairs unseen. In the garden we talk about nothing, and we talk about everything, except the secrets I want to keep, sometimes with blankets and lately with a fire. He makes me laugh, prods me about going to the festival, which I will not do, and if I can stand it, we talk about the Forgetting, trying to find some characteristic, some circumstance or hidden fact. Then we ignore each other in the street. I've seen Gray walking twice with Veronika.

But this also means the talk has mostly blown by. Gray has another conquest and now he's moved on, nothing new there, and there are always other interesting topics to keep our neighbors' minds occupied. Like how Karl of the Books has all but stopped working before the Forgetting, whether Frances the Doctor will cross out her husband before the Forgetting, the unknown reason for the fight between the potter and Nathan the Penmaker, and if this is why Nathan has boarded up his lower windows before the Forgetting. Or the rumors about the harvest not being big enough, or the bloodstains of two curfew-breakers left on the plaque at the water clock. Or the supervisor who was condemned for tearing pages from his books in the Archives. I wonder how he'll fare, being Lost, living with the people he oppressed. If Jonathan's goal was to make us afraid, then he's done it. I sleep with a chair beneath my resting room window. But I'm certain it wouldn't take much to get the potter's wife and those other ladies in the baths talking again. Like me, right now, creeping over to Gray's when his parents aren't home, just to watch him make a key. That would do the trick. I really don't know how I let Gray talk me into these things. Well, yes I do.

I wait for my moment. Hubble Street is busy, half the city that's of age on their way to the granary to press the honeyfruit and make the moonshine, drunk twice a year, at every first rising of the moons. Or at least every rising we can remember. Moonshine is thick, sweet, and because it gets stronger every day, is best made about a week before the festival, which tends to become a party before the party, with lots of sampling to go with the boiling and bottling. I remember when Mother used to go. It's where Gray's parents are now. But I wonder if it will be such a party this time. The buds have grown thicker on the forgetting trees, and yesterday I saw Roberta next door, trying to ink the likenesses of her remaining children in her book. Thirty-seven days to the Forgetting. Eight days until we steal a book.

The street clears, and I take my moment and slip up to Gray's door. He has the curtains closed, maybe only one lamp lit, somewhere deep in the house. I've barely put my knuckles to the metal before the door opens and he pulls me inside.

"Sorry," he says, shutting it quick. "Potter's wife. Get here safely?"

He wants to know if I got here without being seen, and the answer is yes, of course. He has his sleeves rolled up, which means he's been working already. I watch the scars on his right arm become visible as he lights another lamp. Gray's house is more like Jin's than ours, two stories instead of one, the roof garden high on the third. But there are the same white walls, the same table with the sparkling metallic top, only Gray's mother has dark day plants around the windows, waiting for moonlight to make them bloom. And some of the chairs have been moved to the other wall, I see, clustered in a half circle. Just for sitting. For talking.

"Come through," Gray says, waving for me to follow. "I need to eat. Have you eaten?"

We step into the storeroom, where there's a pot on the counter-top flame, bread and a jar of pepper preserves on the opposite side. This room is almost exactly like ours, from the fruit braids hanging from the ceiling to the rows of glass jars and wrapped bread. It smells spicier, though. Gray's mother must dry different herbs. And I would never eat someone else's stores during the dark days.

"Nadia," Gray says. "You're forgetting to speak."

"Yes," I say aloud. "I got here safely, and yes, I've eaten." He grins to himself while he slices bread. I think Gray is sometimes afraid that if I don't speak once, I'll stop altogether. I lean over the pot. "What's in here?"

"Potatoes."

"And what else?"

"More potatoes."

I set my pack on the floor between my feet, to free up my arms, and start rooting through his shelves. Gray hops up on the counter beside the bread, his feet swinging. Last sunlight if someone had told me that by the dark days I'd be standing in a storeroom with the glassblower's son, seasoning his soup, I would've called them a liar.

"Did you hear that Anson the Planter's house was searched?"

I set down the little pot of salt, glad that Gray is behind me, where he can't see my face. That doesn't make sense. Anson is Council.

"And Karl of the Books, and Nathan the Penmaker, and Gretchen of the Archives."

I stir the soup, sprinkle in the garlic leaves. I'm waiting on a new book from Karl, if he'll ever finish it, a book I'm going to paint numbers on and switch for mine on the Archives shelves. My old book with my old name I'm keeping. I'd never be able to request it, since it isn't registered to me. But Nathan is where I get my pens, and Gretchen . . . This can't have to do with me. No one knows about Anson. But it leaves me disquieted, like there's something there, invisible. As if I'm locked in a shrinking room that I cannot see. What is it all about? Liliya? Anna? The Forgetting? Stolen books or going over the wall? "This is done," I tell him.

"That's it? All you have to say?"

I hear Gray jump down from the counter. He reaches around from behind me with a spoon, leaning close to taste the soup. Gray is usually wary with my space, cautious about the way he touches me, as if I might run. Which, I suppose, I might. But he's not being cautious now. His body is against mine, his face just above my shoulder, where I can see the stubble on his jaw, the length of his eyelashes as they close. He smells like soap and the furnace.

"Oh," he says. "It's actually good. Are you smart at everything?"

No, Glassblower's son. I really must not be, because I'm letting myself stand here like this. With you.

"Here," he says, setting down the spoon. "Let me fix this before you catch it on fire."

I feel him pick up a fallen braid, wind it around my knot of myriad other braids, looking for a place to tuck it back in.

"How much hair do you have in here—" he begins, then I jump as his front door slams.

"Gray! Hey, I was going to see if you wanted . . ."

Eshan stops just outside the doorway of the storeroom while Gray goes on very deliberately fiddling with my hair.

"Hey, Eshan. What were you saying?"

Eshan looks back and forth between the two of us. "Just . . . to see if you wanted to run the walls. I need to go . . . soon."

"I have glassblowing today," Gray says. He gets the end of my braid tucked in. "Sorry. Do you want to go on or wait until tomorrow?"

Eshan hesitates. I turn now that Gray has released my hair, and there's a beat of awkward silence. Gray says, "Don't say anything, Eshan. You know my mother."

I don't know what to make of Eshan's face. It's like stone in the lamplight. "Whatever you say," he replies. "I'll see you at the wall tomorrow." He walks out and I hear the door shut, not slam. Just a click. Gray goes through the sitting room and drops the bar down.

"He," Gray says, coming back into the storeroom and grabbing the soup pot, "is going to punch me in the face."

"I thought you were friends."

"That, Dyer's daughter, is exactly why he's going to punch me in the face."

Gray blows out the flame and hops back up on the counter, soup pot and spoon in hand. I'm betting he doesn't do that when his mother is here. I do the same on the opposite counter, prop my feet up beside him, making a bridge of his black leggings and my blue ones.

"Don't look so glum," Gray says. "I'll hit him back, of course."

"Because you're friends," I say.

"Exactly. And he doesn't want to run anyway. He wants to drink. He'll have a bottle stowed away somewhere, mark my words. It's his one perk for apprenticing at the granary."

Gray eats soup from the pot, somehow managing to do it neatly. "When are you going to tell me about this?" he asks, setting down the spoon to hook a finger beneath the bracelet around my ankle, showing now that I have my feet up. I flinch just a little, not because he touched my ankle, but because I don't want to answer.

"What do you mean?"

His smile goes indulgent. "I mean, where did you get it? Did someone give it to you?"

I shake my head. He eats soup, watching me. "I found it."

"You found it. You know, if I'd found a piece of metal like that, I think I'd have mentioned a little something about it. Just in passing."

I make a face at his sarcasm, but the beating in my chest is picking up speed. I don't want to tell him where I found it. I shouldn't be wearing it at all. But it was in my book, my first book, and there's something about it, something solid that says Nadia the Planter's daughter was real. That I am who I was.

"Don't worry," he says, "I'm not going pry out all your secrets. Can I look?" I nod, and he sets down the pot, gets off the counter, and studies the bracelet, lifting it, running a finger over the carving, touching the links. "It's so fine," he says. "Do you know what the symbols mean, or the numbers?"

I shake my head again, and Gray straightens.

"I don't think you should wear this. Not where anyone can see it."

"Why?" It's underneath the cloth when I stand or walk.

Gray looks at my outstretched leg. "If you don't want to be asked about it, then you shouldn't offer it up for questions, that's all. I'll get you a cord or a string, you can wear it underneath your tunic. Okay?"

I'm puzzled by this. But then he grins at me.

"Let's go see about a key."

There's another door at the end of Gray's storeroom, leading out into the open, covered workshop. Before he lights the lamps, he gives me a stool behind the tool shelf, where I'm invisible to the street, but have an unobstructed view of the covered, orange-glowing furnace. I also have a bowl of broken glass in my lap, a jar sacrificed as my excuse for being here, should either of Gray's parents come home. We always bring them our broken glass.

I look around my little corner. There's a makeshift mattress back here, and the green shirt Gray was wearing yesterday. Is he sleeping in the workshop? I glance at him putting on the apron, testing the heat of the furnace. I'm glad he's sleeping out here, even if the weather is cool. The resting rooms in his house are on the second story. If the Council came for him, he wouldn't be able to get out. This way, he can run.

The clay with the key impression has dried by now, Gray measuring it carefully over several days to make sure it didn't shrink. He made a key from it already, out of resin, while the clay was still soft. To be safe. The resin key isn't strong enough to turn a lock, but it will make another mold if we have to start over. In case this doesn't work. And it might not work. The glass could shatter while it cools, break in the lock when we use it. But the key is small and thick, and Gray says he filled the mold with the pulverized glass his father calls the "strong stuff," which is exactly how my father always referred to the moonshine. Gray fired the mold, filled it again, fired it, filled it again, and fired it again before I ever got here. Now he's taken it out, dunked it quick in water on the end of some tongs, making a huge puff of steam, and laid it carefully on a metal tray. It sits there, too hot to touch, taunting me.

Gray picks up a long tube of glass, a dark color, holds it in the fire, spinning it until there's a luminous molten ball on the end. The heat of the furnace almost feels good from where I sit, but it must be unbelievable right in front of it. He gets another tube of glass and uses it to work the first one, every few seconds pulling it out of the fire, then back in, pressing it with metal, then back in to glow again. The glass seems alive, lit from the inside, and he looks like he's playing. Play that is calm and concentrated. I have no idea what he's doing. He takes the glass out of the fire again and bends the top with tweezers, making a loop, as if the glass is really only very hot, very sticky string.

He breaks his piece of glass off the other tube and sets it aside, somewhere near the furnace, and then he starts blowing bottles to replace the ones his father took for the moonshine. The way the glass changes form fascinates me. I watch him manipulate the shape of something too hot to touch, coax it into doing what he wants with a roll or turn or puff of air. One minute it's brittle and breakable, the next fiery, glowing, and malleable, becoming something new. It reminds me of me. I watch him shape the glass again and again. With ease.

"You're a funny sort of company," Gray comments. There are fifteen or sixteen bottles lined up in the cooling kiln. "More of a presence, really."

I hold in my smile. "I don't want to distract you."

"It's more distracting looking over there to see what you're up to."

I'm pleased that he's looking. Which means that I'm an idiot. "I'm just . . . thinking."

"I know. How's anyone supposed to concentrate when you're doing that?"

He lays the blowing tube across a rack, hot end pointed away, takes the tweezers, and picks up the bit of glass he played with earlier. He gazes at it, then comes to me. He's sweat-stained and sooty, the hair that's not pulled back wet and curling. I'm not sure how he manages to make that look good, but he does. He squats down in front of me. A piece of glass dangles from the tweezers, shaped like a water drop with an open loop at the top, deep blue and sparkling, embedded with one white crystal. Like one moon in the dark day sky.

"What is it?" I ask.

"Just leftover bits. It's to wear," he says. "Do you like it?"

I nod my head. I've never seen anything like it.

"Would you like to have it?"

I look up.

"Well, you can't."

He closes his fingers around the glass, and I raise my brows. The glassblower's smirk is all over his face.

"Unless," he continues, "you come to the festival. Dance with me one time, to prove that you came, and you can have it. Very simple."

I think my brows actually rise higher. "So it's a bribe."

"No. Well, yes, it's a bribe."

"I thought we weren't being seen together."

"I'll dance with all the girls and be above suspicion."

I bet he will, too.

"It will be a pre-celebration of our crime spree," he says, "assuming that key isn't in a thousand pieces. And you have to decide soon, or the potter's wife will think I'm talking to myself." He moves the tweezers back and forth, making his creation sparkle. I've never seen glass that color blue before. Then I realize that I've never seen glass that color because he made that color. On purpose. And I think it was for me.

"How do you wear it?" I whisper.

"I don't, you do," he says, which sounds like the usual way he teases me, only he isn't.

He touches the glass with a finger again, then wraps it with his hand, testing the heat before he reaches back behind him and pulls the string that ties his hair. He goes to his knees, threads the string through the glass loop before putting it around my neck. I lean forward, move some of the escaping hair from my knot of braids to let him tie it.

Time-out, I want to say, *free question. If we can't stop the Forgetting and you don't know me anymore, you'll know you made that necklace as soon as you see it, won't you, Glassblower's son? Is that why you want me to wear it? Is it written in your book?*

"How long did it take you to make this?" I ask while he ties.

His breath is on my neck. "Just a few minutes. You watched me."

"You know what I think?"

"Never."

"That you're the liar this time."

He laughs once, leans back to look me over. "Wait." He picks up my ankle and plays with the latch until he figures out how to unhook the metal bracelet. He hooks the link end to the string right behind the piece of glass, and drops the whole thing gently down my tunic. I feel the metal dangling all the way to my stomach. The necklace is heavy, the glass hanging low, almost inside my neckline, still warm against my body. I'm afraid it's moving up and down with my heartbeat. I touch it and frown.

"Did I just let you talk me into dancing at the Dark Days Festival?"

This time he really laughs. "That's it," he says. "No more questions. I'm cutting you off." And he gets to his feet and walks over to his workbench to put away tools. My hand drifts back to the piece of glass. Something inside me pushes and pulls between aching and pain. *The thing is, Gray, that when you forget, whatever it is that made you want to make this necklace for me, you're going to forget that, too. And I won't.* The thought makes my body shudder.

Gray is bringing the metal sheet with our mold of fired clay and a knife to where I sit, still hidden behind his tool racks. He sets the tray on the ground at my feet, the "NWSE" stamped on it, just like our knife. I lean down, peering at the clay while he touches it gingerly, to see if it will burn him. It will, but not badly. He uses the end of his apron to hold the brown lump, slips the knife between the pieces, and twists.

The top half of the clay comes off, and inside, as if it grew from a stone, is a key of white glass. I watch his smile grow.

"We're going to steal a book, aren't we, Dyer's daughter?"

I think we are.

I wish it was time to steal it already. But it's not. It's the Dark Days Festival, and Janis will be reading from the First Book to everyone in Canaan. The Archives is closed, and the Learning Center, and by the fourth bell of waking, everyone will be gathering in the amphitheater seats, and in the streets surrounding, waiting to listen, waiting for the moons to rise to start their eating and dancing under the stars. For fun, or so I hear. But something about the laughter, the smoke of the torches, tends to conjure feelings I don't want to remember. I've taken out my nervousness on the storeroom, scrubbing it like it's seldom been scrubbed.

Mother is up now, puttering around the house, checking our beds, sometimes coming to watch me clean. For the past five or six festivals she's been my welcome excuse for staying home; she gets confused with so many people at once, needs someone to be with her. This time she needs to be watched. I haven't spoken to Liliya, but I'm sure she isn't planning on staying home, and I would never ask Genivee to. I don't know how I could have made that promise to Gray, if that's what it was. Or what I'm going to do about it.

I showed Genivee the necklace of blue glass after I came back from Gray's, since she was going to notice it anyway, explaining how it was actually a bribe to make me dance. I'd thought she would think this was funny. Instead she'd just set down her pen and listened, wide-eyed and serious. I couldn't understand her reaction.

I don't understand her now, either, standing in the sitting room, nearly jumping up and down with excitement as she beckons me forward. She's been holed up ever since waking, and when she drags me back into our room I discover why. My mattress is covered with . . . things. Brushes and little pots and colored cloth, and there's a white tunic, long, with leggings to go underneath it. I'm not sure this is actually my side of the room. Genivee shuts the door and, for my second surprise of the day, drops the bar across it.

"Now you listen to me," says Genivee, hands on hips. "Nope! Not a word. Just listen. You have a boy"—she says the word "boy" as if it were something as odd as Kenny the beetle—"a boy who went to a lot of trouble to bribe you just so you would dance with him once." The word "once" gets the same treatment as "boy."

"Genivee, it isn't like—"

"It isn't? What's it like?"

I don't actually know what it's like. Not exactly.

"Nadia." She speaks very slowly. "Eyes on my eyes, and try to understand. You like him. You talk to him. He climbs things. And he made you glass the color of your eyes."

I touch the necklace hanging just beneath my tunic. Is that what it is? We have a mirror, in Mother's room. But I don't spend any time in front of it.

"Of. Your. Eyes. Nadia. Do not be such a *zopa*."

She doesn't understand. How could she? Taking that book next waking is what has to be focused on. The Forgetting is what has to be focused on.

Genivee closes her eyes. "You are so worried about what's happened before and what will happen next that you forget there's a *now*, Nadia. Do you know"—her voice trembles— "how hard it is to watch your own sister miss every opportunity for her own happiness?"

I think she's going to cry. I reach out a hand.

"Oh, seriously!" Genivee stomps her foot. I step back. "What else do I have to do? Get on my knees and beg? Sit!"

I gaze at my spitfire of a little sister. Despite her dramatics, I'm considering what she's really saying. Why does every "now" have to be ruined by what will be?

Genivee clenches her fists. "I will fight you if I have to. Sit, Nadia!"

I sit. And I enjoy myself. I think it's funny how I know Genivee loves me the same amount she did at the last resting, and yet something about this, about the attention, makes me feel it more keenly. She has me strip down into an old, big tunic I've always suspected might have belonged to Anson, washes my face like I am a baby, and uses Liliya's lotion on my arms and legs. I'm guessing Liliya's room is where most of these supplies have been confiscated from. Then Genivee puts me directly under the lamp and starts painting my face, chatting about her friends, and who won the spelling competition, which was her, and how her teacher really isn't as smart as she is. It doesn't surprise me that Genivee thinks this. It's probably true.

At some point the thought arises that I'm letting a twelve-year-old paint my face right before I go out in public, and that paint is not really the best word for what's she been using. That little pot of dark brown now smudging my lashes and lining my eyes has blacknut in it, and maybe, it suddenly occurs to me, if I'd been more prone to painting my face, I wouldn't have spent all those hours concocting the stain beneath our floor. The marks on my knees have only just faded. Some of these thoughts must show on my face, which Genivee is paying very close attention to, because she says, "Please. I am an artist," and goes on chatting.

When she's done, Genivee takes out all my tiny braids, tilts her head, squints a critical eye, and says it's fluffy and that we are going to go with that, except for two pins to pull the front pieces back, so they won't drive me crazy, two long strips of blue cloth attached to each of the pins. Genivee informs me that all the girls wear these. Then she makes me step out of the old tunic and into the white one. The material is thin, a cross between a dress and a shirt, the top mid-length and wide, flowing with a low collar, leggings for underneath.

"Where did you get this?"

"Requested it a week ago. Jemma the Clothesmaker was very"—the "very" gets the same emphasis as "boy" did—"excited to make it for you. In fact, I think she was dying to."

"A week ago?" I ask.

"You should always have hope. That's what I think. And white looks good in moonlight. Why are you wearing this here instead of on your ankle?" She rattles the piece of metal hanging from my necklace.

"Just am." My answer must have been defensive because Genivee pretends to shudder. When I have my sandals on Genivee steps back, looks me over. I reach down for my pack, to tie my tether.

"No!" she yells.

I jump.

"You can't take that dirty old thing! Don't be stupid."

"Genivee . . ."

"Can't you wear your book on the outside for once?"

Nope. That book is stolen. But now that I look at my pack next to the new white of my dress, I do see that it's a little . . . battered.

Genivee waves her hand. "No. Of course you can't. Okay, okay. Thinking . . ."

A moment later she unbars the door, dashes from the room, and comes back with the knife. This means she's been in the potatoes, where we've hidden it. Mother doesn't like potatoes. Without hesitation or remorse, Genivee takes Liliya's dark blue dress and slits a huge piece of cloth from the bottom of it. There will be wrath tomorrow, but today I have a piece of blue cloth like a sack to wrap around my book. Genivee cuts another long slit to use for a tie, and lets my tether run out of the tied blue sack to attach to a white belt. She steps back and smiles. Very satisfied. Then she narrows her eyes.

"Okay, Nadia. It's time to go out there. Can you do it?"

I'm not sure. "Wait, who's staying with Mother?"

Genivee rolls her eyes. "I am, of course. Now, here's what I want you to do. I want you to visualize. This party is a wall. A wall that you must climb. Go climb your wall and don't think about anything else until you're done climbing the wall. It's one day. For once in your life, have fun. For one day."

I look at the mess of paint and cloth and discarded clothes, and know I'm going to try. "Thank you, Genivee," I say.

"Of course you should thank me," she replies. "It took me the whole last resting to think that up. And anyway, you look really good."

❧

When I open my front door the streetlights are glowing, the air chill, sky dark blue, and the noises of the street are different.

Quiet around me, loud in the distance. Music, voices—many, many voices—beyond the buildings, footsteps moving in the same direction. It's strange, like a city I don't know, which is a feeling from the Forgetting I have to push away. I'm self-conscious, nervous, and I decided not to look in a mirror or I might lose my courage. I'm determined not to lose my courage.

I take my first step into the street and move directly into the path of Janis.

I remembered something today. A woman came to our door after the Forgetting. She asked our names, asked after our books, after our stores. Did we need anything? She told my sister that the Learning Center would be open again by sunsetting, encouraged us to go read our old books as soon as the archivist was retrained.

I couldn't speak to her or answer her questions. I pretended to be asleep. I did that a lot then. I hurt, and I was so tired. But she made Mother smile, and even I could see that this woman, unlike my father who left me, unlike my mother who forgot me, cared about what happened to me. Today, I realized for the first time that woman had been Janis.

NADIA THE DYER'S DAUGHTER
BOOK 13, PAGE 2, 11 YEARS AFTER THE FORGETTING

CHAPTER ELEVEN

Hello," Janis says, taking a graceful step back so I don't knock her down. "It's a Dyer's daughter, isn't it? Which one?"

"Nadia," I whisper, though the book covered up in a piece of Liliya's dress at my side says a little different. I'm shocked that Janis knows even part of my name, that she knows where my mother lives. And then I'm not shocked at all. Liliya. She may not approve of her, but then again, I don't approve of her grandson.

"Well, Nadia, you are looking very lovely indeed, I must say. Are you going to the clock? Would you like to walk with me?"

She extends an arm, her black robe flowing, as if showing me the way. I fall into step, *no thanks* not really seeming like an offered option. Janis is striking, tall, dark-eyed, with piled hair that is pure white. Her accent is very neat, clipped—a sound I could never quite manage in school, no matter how hard they tried to correct my pronunciation. Liliya was better at that. But what is Janis doing on Hawking Street? There are people walking in the same direction we are, and they are staring.

"I enjoy the Dark Days Festivals," Janis says. "The cele-bration, the crisp air. And the rise of the moons is one of the best sights Canaan offers. But I think the children are my favorite. It's so interesting to watch how they grow, consider who and what they might become. I like to walk the streets before we read the First Book, to see how the people and the city are faring. How are you faring, Nadia?"

After some consideration, "Well" is the word I settle on. I have a wild vision of knocking Janis down, finding the First Book of the Forgetting hidden somewhere beneath those black robes, making a run for it. And that, I think wryly, is all the fault of the glassblower's son. Janis doesn't deserve to be knocked down. Unless it's about Jonathan.

"Oh, I'm glad," Janis is saying. "You had excellent test scores, I remember. Quite high."

Surely Janis doesn't remember my test scores.

"Where are you apprenticing?"

"The Archives."

"Oh, yes. A position of trust. We'll be needing you soon, won't we?"

We're almost to the corner of Meridian, loud, thronged with people and squealing children. The forgetting trees rise over our heads. Janis stops to pat a passing beribboned child, and smiles at me.

"I would hope, Nadia," she says, "that you feel you could come to me, if you have any questions, any concerns. I'm always happy to have guests at the Council House. I want you to know we are responsive to those needs as well, not just to the"—she hesitates—"misunderstandings about the rules."

I see. She's trying to tell me subtly that the current state of things in Canaan is not how she would have it. I lift my head. "I do have a concern," I say, "since you bring it up."

Her still, dark brows lift slightly, and she leans forward to hear.

"I'd like to know why my house was searched. What was the Council hoping to find?"

"Ah! Yes, I can see why you would ask . . ."

The people on Meridian are stepping aside, making way for Janis, and my eyes go straight through the parting in the crowd to First Bridge, where Gray is standing with Imogene, Eshan, Veronika, and a few of the others who were in the blacknut grove. He's beneath the streetlamp, hair tamed—he must have found another string—in a plain white shirt and dark green leggings, a cup in his hand. His eyes find mine as if I'd called, and he goes stock-still. I think it might have been mid-sentence. Janis pauses our walk, her brows drawn together.

"The Council," she says quietly, "seems to feel that random inspections are good for the city, to keep rules from being broken in the first place, to keep us from having to employ the sterner measures. I believe your family's name was drawn at random." She smiles at me. "Please don't take the search personally. If you do well in your work, I don't think I'm overstepping when I say there might be a position at Council for you someday. It's certainly something that's been considered."

She has to be joking.

Then she says, "Is that a piece of glass you're wearing, Nadia?" Janis reaches out a thin finger, touches my necklace.

I can feel the metal bracelet behind it, hanging down my dress. "Is it old, or is it new?" she asks.

"New."

"Pity. I am working on a project to compile a history of Canaan, a difficult subject for our city, as you know. I'm looking for anything old that might shed light on our origins. If you happen to find something, heirlooms, anything at all, will you let me know?" She touches the glass again. "This is extraordinary. Our glassblowers are quite skillful, aren't they? I'll have to compliment them on their workmanship. Now, please, enjoy your festival." And with that Janis makes her way through the path the crowd has left, leaving me in the emptiness of her wake.

I look to Gray again. I don't think he's moved, but his eyes have followed Janis. I watch them come back to me. His lips part. Veronika has her hand in the air, saying something irritatedly that neither of us pays attention to. I don't know what we're supposed to do now. I don't know what I'm supposed to do.

Someone bumps me from behind, people in their finery closing Janis's gap. My line of sight is broken and Gray is lost to the colorful clothes and the weirdly fancy hair that surrounds us. Then I realize that we're all surging forward, to the amphitheater and the speaking platform, where Janis is going to read before the moons come up. Then they'll start the dancing.

I'm pushed step by step, all the way down Meridian, trying to ignore being looked at. Being pressed by people like this is difficult; it makes me feel grabbed, panicked. I wonder if Mother is a bit the same way. I try to scoot my way to an edge, where I can escape if need be. Janis has gone all the way down the amphitheater stairs and is climbing up to the speaking platform, lit all around by torches, Jonathan behind her, the tower rising up above us all. The water clock rings out the hour. I see Karl of the Books, Jemma the Clothesmaker with Sasha, the little girl who was born early and who is blind. I see Hedda smile at me with her younger set of twins, and Delia, Gray's mother, on Nash's arm, frowning at me at the same time. Where is Liliya? I don't see Gray, or anyone who was with him.

I'm on the top edge of the amphitheater, against the sur-rounding wall, not anywhere near the edge of the crowd. I look back and they're still thronging. Janis opens the First Book of the Forgetting, and I forget about the people for a moment, strain my neck. It's hard to judge in the wavering lights, but it looks like an ordinary book. Dark, maybe black, a bit frayed or faded. It's not thick, but there are more pages there than are ever read aloud. *I'm going to find out what you say,* I think. *What you really say.*

The people hush, noise dying like a dropping wind. Janis looks down at the First Book, her voice ringing in the struc-tured space.

"At the first sunrising of the twelfth year, they will forget. They will lose their memories, and without their memories, they are lost . . ."

"Hey. You came."

The voice in my ear startles me, and I realize it's not the crowd pressed up against my back, it's Eshan. He's already been in the moonshine. I can smell it. I try to move away.

"Their books will be their memories, their written past selves. They will write in their books. They will keep their books . . ."

"You look really pretty, Nadia . . ."

Eshan is touching my hair. I try to turn my head, move his hand, move away, but the crowd is too close. "Eshan," I whisper. "Stop."

"They will write the truth, and the books will tell them who they have been. If a book is lost, then so are they lost . . ."

"You know what I think, Nadia the Dyer's daughter?" he says in my ear, slurring a little. "I think you're a lot more friendly than you act."

"I am made of my memories. Without memories, they are nothing."

"Stop, Eshan," I hiss. His hand is on my arm now, body tight against my back, voice close to my ear. I can't shake him off. I can't move. The crowd is too close. I'm going to scream if he doesn't stop touching me. I won't be able to help it.

"Excuse me," whispers a voice beside us. There's another hand, on my other arm. "Could I speak to you for a moment?"

I look up into the face of Anson the Planter. Eshan drops his hand, and I automatically move with the tug on my arm, follow Anson out of the crowd. I feel like I am walking through one of my nightmares.

"Books will be written in every day. In our books we are to . . ."

The crowd finishes the sentence: "*. . . write the truth.*"

"Truth is not good, and truth is not bad. When we write truth, we . . ."

The people say, "*. . . write who we are.*"

The familiar words echo off the buildings as the people of Canaan recite them. Anson maneuvers me out of the throng, into a side street, sits me down on the front steps of a weaver's house. Then he lowers himself next to me. I am stiff, frozen, nearly paralyzed by my father's nearness.

"Was that young man bothering you?" he asks.

I shake my head.

"It looked like he was to me. I'm Anson . . ."

I turn my face away. *Yes, Father. I know who you are.*

". . . and you're Nadia. Dyer's daughter, right?"

". . . *remember who we are,*" chant the people in the crowd.

Anson is not put off by my silence. "You see, the thing is, Nadia, I seem to upset you. Not just the search, or the counting, but me. *I* upset you. I just . . . I want to know if you can tell me why that is."

". . . *remember our truth,*" says the crowd.

I'm pushing down on the cold stone of the steps with both my hands. I think so I won't fall apart. Anson's voice is not calm anymore. He's the one upset.

"Nadia, I'm going to ask you a personal question. I hope you won't be . . ." I hear him breathe deep. "Do you know what happened to your father? Is it in your books?"

And then I'm not upset at all. I'm angry. At him.

"Who is Anna?" I say.

"What?"

"Anna. Who is she?"

"I . . . I don't know . . ."

I'm up and gone, skirting my way through the edge of the crowd, making for Meridian. I was wrong. I am upset. I'm shaking. Hard. I turn the corner, duck beneath the trees, and then a hand catches mine from behind and pulls me into an alley. I have one moment of panic before I realize it's Gray.

"Shhh," he says. He lets me lean against the wall, puts the hand that isn't holding mine on the back of my neck, and pushes my forehead onto his chest. "Just wait a minute," he says.

I breathe. I smell soap and the furnace, a hint of moonshine. He's warm in the chill. I'm not sure how much time goes by. I'm still shaking, though not nearly as much. The streets outside are quiet, the alley dark. I can hear the murmur of Janis still talking to Canaan.

"Better?" Gray asks.

I'm aware of the question inside his chest, aware of his breathing, which is faster than mine. His voice had sounded calm, but he is not.

"Tell me who Anson the Planter is," he says.

I don't even hesitate. "My father. But he doesn't remember."

"He did it on purpose?"

"Yes."

"Is he figuring it out?"

"I think so."

"He'd be crazy if he wasn't. You look just like him. Don't stand next to him if you don't want people to know."

I feel his heart beat.

"And this is why you don't tell that you can remember?" Gray says. "Because Anson would be condemned? For something he doesn't even know he did?"

I like that Gray always puts things together so quickly; it saves me difficult speech. It feels good to be here, surrounded, between him and the white stone at my back. Completely different from being trapped by the crowd. By Eshan. My shaking is almost gone.

"You have to make a decision," he whispers.

I don't want to make a decision.

"Who do you want me to hit first? Anson, or Eshan?"

"I thought you already hit Eshan."

"He was a bad friend and didn't offer me the opportunity." Gray lets my head up and searches my face. "You look good. Who did this to you?"

"And why do you think it wasn't me?"

"Because you wouldn't. Probably."

I look away. I think I'm smiling just a little. "Fine. It was Genivee."

"She's an artist."

"And she would agree with you." And then he's looking at me, really looking at me, and I know that Genivee was right. About everything she said.

"Let's go," Gray says, his voice low. "Right now. Over the wall."

"What?"

"Let's forget the festival. We have seven hours until resting. And I don't want to dance with you once and then pretend I'm not looking at you the rest of the time."

I wonder how much he's been drinking.

"Come with me," he says. "And we'll run up the mountain in the dark."

His hair may be tamed but he is wild today. Barely contained. I want to touch his face. And I do not want to go back to that crowd. He leans forward, voice near my ear.

"Go to Jin's," he says. "I'll tell people I'm going places I'm not and meet you there, and we'll climb the wall. Because we want to. Will you do that with me, Dyer's daughter?"

There is only now, I think. And this is exactly what I want to do. "Yes," I breathe.

I can feel his smile next to my cheek. "Don't let anyone see you."

⤳

I find myself standing on the rooftop of Jin's, breathing hard in the chilly air. I came here four festivals ago, with a long, stiff ladder made of fern, and while the music was going drove two iron rings into the stone with a hammer stolen from Arthur of the Metals. It was easier to drive in those rings than stone should have allowed. I'm glad I did it.

Then Gray is at the top of the stairs. He has a bottle in his hand. We don't speak. None of this feels real, and I don't want to think too hard about it. I hook the rope ladder, which takes longer to find in the dark, pull it to our side, watch Gray ride the ladder to the wall with the bottle in his shirt, which he miraculously manages not to break. He sits on the wall instead of lying flat, and I take the end of the flowing tunic, tuck it back through my low collar, tying the cloth tighter to my body. I come up after him, hair flying. We flip the ladder, and then we're over.

The dead grasses on the other side of the wall look silvery in the dark, as does the gray cliff face, but the fern fronds are lit with glowing strands, the flashflies emitting their brief stabs of light overhead. The world sparkles and smells of cold things. Gray takes the bottle out of his shirt, uncorks it, and stretches out his arm to me. I take a swig. "Strong" is not the word. Gray drinks after me, pops the cork back in, looks me up and down.

"Let's run," he says, and he takes off through the rustling grasses just like he did the first time.

I chase him, fern fronds whipping my face. He's weaving around the mountainside, following the natural opening in the forest, lit by the glowworms and their gleaming silks wound through the fern fronds above us. I don't think he's really that much faster than me. His legs are just longer, which is not fair. And he's deliberately leading me through soggy ground and mud holes. And he's making sure he stays in sight, turning around, running backward for a few steps to check my progress, grinning, his white shirt glowing almost as much as everything else in the forest. I leap over a fallen fern and feel the upward slope, amazed that he remembers the way to the canyon, to my little room at the top. In the dark. The cold air burns my lungs, and I am gasping when I get there.

"Knew you couldn't catch me," Gray says.

He's out of breath, too, splashing water on his face, which I can only tell from hearing and the dim clue of his white shirt. It's dark here, a shadowy dark that the glowworm light can't quite penetrate. The running of the stream and roar of the waterfall sound louder for it. I go to the opening and look out, and see that the canyon is lit, not like the strands we ran beneath, but like a city, alive with movement from the bugs or the wind, I don't know which. Pale moths flutter their wings, and there's mist on the pool below, mixing with the water spray. The moons will come soon.

"Come here, Dyer's daughter."

Gray is still beside the stream, by the rock where he sat and told me he'd been Lost. My white cloth must be glowing like his shirt because he has no trouble seeing me come. He offers me the bottle. I can't believe he ran all the way up here with it in his hand. I tip it up, hand it back, and he sets it beside the rock. He says beneath his breath, "Let's go swimming."

My breath catches, then comes faster. He wants me to jump the waterfall with him. In the dark. And I'm going to do it.

I kick off my sandals. Gray reaches down, still looking at me, and pushes his own sandals off his feet. Then he puts his hands on the skin of my waist, feeling until he finds the tether that holds my book, and begins working at the knot. I let him, running my hands over his chest until I find the buckle of his bookstrap. Even the silence is bigger in the dark. Just water and breath.

His book comes free first, and I hold it until mine is loose. We set them on the rock, and Gray pulls his shirt over his head, throws it on top of them. I start to take off the glass-and-metal necklace, but he stops my hand.

"Wear it," he says, and bends my head forward, moves my mass of hair to tie it up shorter, tighter. I put my forehead on his chest, like I did in the alley, feel his heart beating, this time not through cloth but through the warmth of his skin. He is so still. And there is only now, I think. I lift my head, lift a hand to his bare chest, slide it up, up to the softer skin of his neck, to his jaw, almost smooth because he's shaved, and back to where his hair grows. I am aching for him.

"Are you ready to jump?"

I nod. He takes my other hand in his.

"Tell me you're ready."

I raise my eyes to his. "I'm ready to jump."

"We're going to run and clear the falls."

"Yes."

"Run hard."

I turn and face the opening into the canyon. Gray still has my hand. I know we can't miss the pool. I know there are no rocks, but my heart is a thing I can feel trying to push its way out of my chest. Because I don't have my book. Gray doesn't have his book. And we are going to fly. Through the dark. I turn to look at him, and he is looking at me. I think the corner of his mouth is lifting.

"One," he says. "Two. Three."

We run, hard, and the ground falls away, and then we are the ones falling, soaring, and I catch a glimpse of the sparkling canyon, the misty pool below, the spray of the waterfall, three moons cresting the peak of a mountain. Then it all drops away, the air whistling by, consumed by the smack and roar of water in my ears.

I kick to the surface, and it's a long way to break up and into the mist. I suck in the moist air, laugh. I lost Gray's hand somewhere along the way and I tread water, circling for him in the fog. I hear a tremendous splash. A yell that for one second I think is pain and the next I know isn't. Gray yells again, echoing all over the canyon. I swim toward the noise and then I find him, floating on his back, still shouting.

"I'm thinking maybe you enjoyed that," I pant.

"You!" he says. He sends a wall of water at me. "You didn't tell me it was warm!"

I laugh, avoid another splash. The waterfall is cold, the air is cold, but the pool isn't. Gray sighs. "We'll never get out now."

"We're going to freeze," I say happily. "But it's warmer the deeper you go."

"Really?" He starts to swim in my direction, and I sense danger, like maybe I'm about to explore the warmer depths. I lift a hand.

"Oh, no. This is not the men's baths. We don't appreciate that sort of behavior on the women's side."

"That's not how I pictured it." He keeps swimming at me, curls plastered down, an evil glint in his eye.

"Do not! It's too hard to swim with all this on!"

He's skimming through the water. "I took off mine."

"Shut up!" I laugh. He attacks me anyway, and I splash him, but he doesn't even make me go under. After a minute, it's just an excuse to hold me. I let him do that, too. The water is buoyant; it wants to lift us, topple us. We settle in with Gray half floating, arms wide and head tipped back, eyelashes a smudge against his face, me above and hanging on with my legs. My body beneath the water is pleasantly warm, my body above the surface shivering. My hair is absolutely everywhere.

"Do I have paint smeared all over my face?"

He opens his eyes, smiles the tiniest bit, touches the water rolling down my cheek. "No," he says. "You are the single most beautiful thing I have ever looked at in my life."

I have no idea how to kiss someone. I lean down, and very gently touch my lips to his. I don't want to drown him. He is floating so still now, eyes closed, bobbing just a little in the waves from the waterfall. I bring one of my hands out of the water, put my palm on his chest like I did before, run my hand over the skin that is now water-slicked, up to his neck, thumb across his jaw to the back of his head. I hear his intake of breath. I lean down again, put my mouth on his.

This time he brings an arm up to hold me there, goes more vertical in the water while he pulls me in. I may not know how to kiss someone, but Gray does. His lips are soft and his mouth is warm, one hand keeping us afloat, the other twisted into my hair. I didn't know I could feel so sought after. Needed. He tugs on my hair to tilt up my chin, kisses my neck down to where the water meets my shoulder. I cradle his face and he kisses my mouth again, soft and then hard, and I hold his head, do not let him stop. I'm not sure that we can stop until he breaks from my lips and puts his forehead on mine. We breathe each other's air.

"Did that just happen to me?" he whispers.

"I think it did." It's me I can't believe it just happened to.

"Come here," he says, pulling me with him, slowly swimming me to one side. I feel the cold spray of the waterfall, and then the broken rocks and boulders that ring the pool appear suddenly from the mist. He finds a ledge where we can sit and still be mostly covered in the warmth of the water. It's darker here, more sheltered from the lit canyon. I go under and come back up, to slick back my hair, and he pulls me to him again.

Now he's playing, but it's expert play, like he did with the glass, touching my face, kissing my cheeks and my ears, and he lets me do the same. I can't believe he reacts to my touch, but he does. He revels in it.

"You know we can never actually leave," Gray breathes in my ear. "We'll die of exposure. It's a shame, but I think we'll have to stay in here forever."

"Forever?"

He's kissing my throat around the piece of blue glass. "We'll adapt."

I laugh, mostly because he's tickling me with his mouth on purpose, but then he's not tickling me anymore. I put my hands in his wet hair. This is bliss, and I know I'm like a child who has never had something sweet. One taste, and I crave more. Like sweetness might never happen again. I hold him tighter, tilting back my head, and then I see something, in the scraggly vines and bushes growing among the rocks. I pause.

"What is it?" Gray asks.

There's a round light on the side of one of the rocks, just out of my reach, a dot, small, like an insect glowing. Except it's the wrong color for an insect. Green. Gray gets more upright in the water, looking at the same place I am. I plant my hands on the rocks and push myself up and out, into an unpleasant blast of cold.

"Oh," he says. "I really can't believe you just did that."

I pad over to the rock, shivering and dripping, reach out a finger to the point of green light. Then the light is on my finger and I gasp, jerking it away, thinking a bug has jumped on me. But it's only light, except light that's not like flame or glow-worms, or anything else I've ever seen. The green dot shines on the rock again. I touch again, and the light is back on my finger. A beam of light.

I hear Gray splashing out of the water, cursing cheerfully as the air hits his body. I open my hand and let the green beam of light hit my palm. I'm shivering, but I've forgotten to feel cold. It's fear I'm feeling now. This light on my hand is not normal. Not natural. And it's coming from nowhere.

Except that everything comes from somewhere.

When I was a child, wanting to know the truth was called curiosity.

Now that I am grown, the truth I want to know is called a crime.

NADIA THE DYER'S DAUGHTER
BOOK 15, PAGE 81, 1 SEASON UNTIL THE FORGETTING

CHAPTER TWELVE

I t's a beam of light," I say, when I hear Gray behind me.

"What kind of light?"

Like cracking the door of a lit room when your hallway is dark, I think. I back away and let Gray touch it. The light makes me think of going to the dye houses, when the dyers mix different colors together, find shades that don't grow that way on their own. This green is deep and weirdly bright. Unnatural. It gives me a strange feeling. Repulsed, though I don't know why.

Gray straightens and shakes the water from his hair, looking around us. Searching for the source. We're in a shadowed strip of land between the cliff face and the pool, full of tumbled stone. I crouch, open my hand, and let the green light touch my palm. Then I start walking, toes first in the dark. Gray comes behind me. When I veer off course the light disappears from my hand. I stop until I find it, then move forward again.

"Watch out," he says.

We've come to a thicket of young fern trees, and the light seems to be beaming out from between them. Gray parts the stalks, letting me slide through, stepping in after me, and then looming up in front of us is the cliff face, and I don't have to crouch anymore. We're deep in shadow here, the light still on my hand. I bring my hand closer and closer to the rock. And then I stop. The light is coming out of the cliff. That is impossible.

Gray goes to the rock face, running his hands over the source of the light. "This isn't rock," he says.

"What isn't?"

"What I'm touching. Feel."

I put my hands where his are. Instead of cool stone I feel an area about the size of my hand that is warmer, smoother, not gritty. I trace my fingers around a tiny crack that is the change between rock and what isn't, where the light is coming out, a place near the bottom center. There is a bump, a bump that pushes in when my finger runs across it.

A short scream I didn't know was coming jumps from my mouth, and Gray jerks me back half into the ferns, like I've been attacked. The place that isn't rock is sliding open, on its own, alive and whirring like a hissing beetle. The light brightens, showing me Gray's face in livid green, and then the movement stops. Now there's an opening in the rock about the size of my hand, ten squares glowing inside, each with a number silhouetted black against the light. Zero through nine.

I can feel Gray's breath coming fast beside me. I don't understand what I just saw. I don't understand what I'm seeing right now. Nothing else happens, except that everything has happened. Gray gradually relaxes his grip on my arm. He approaches the shining numbers, squats down to look without touching.

"Someone made this," he says. "They had to. There's a flame inside, shining through something green . . . like green glass . . ." Then he stiffens. "There are words."

I come to stand behind him. Above the numbers, where there had been only black, there are now words in red, a red that is somehow deep and bright just like the green. Words made of light. That no one could have written. They say "Enter Code." I step forward.

"Don't touch it," Gray whispers.

I touch it anyway. The surface above the words is completely smooth, polished. The fire is on the inside, but it burns very steady, and it's not hot. But Gray is right. None of this is natural. Therefore it had to be made. By people. People from beyond the walls. "Do you think . . . The ones who came first, the ones who built the city . . ."

Gray shakes his head. "I don't know. This is nothing like the city. I mean, Canaan is huge; it would take all of us years and years to build it, even if we could find the stone. But we could do it. We might not know exactly how to shape it the way it's shaped, but have you ever seen what Jin used to carve out of fern stalks? It's not impossible. The whole city is something we could do, it's just so much more than anything we do now, it's hard to think of it. But this . . ."

I understand what he's saying. I can imagine someone carving blowing wheat from stone. What I'm seeing here is beyond imagination.

"Enter," Gray says. "Enter. So is there a door?"

He starts feeling all over the rock face again, still dripping, a tall shadow in a green-and-black dark. A door, I think. But to where? To inside the mountain? Gray stops and looks over his shoulder. "They're not attached."

"What isn't?"

"These rocks. They're not part of the cliff." He knocks one down, sending it rolling off into the thicket of fern stalks. "They're just piled up."

He sends another down, and now I'm helping him, dismantling a sloping pile of stones that had looked like just another part of the canyon walls in the dark. In the light they must have looked that way, too, especially with the fern trees in front of them. I've been in that pool at least six times and never noticed. Gray stops about two-thirds of the way down, stepping over the remaining rocks into a space beyond them. There's a hole in the cliff face. A fissure. Like a cave. I can just make out that he's reaching up, high over his head, squatting low and to either side, exploring by feel.

"Metal," he says.

"Is it a door?"

"I don't know. It's door-shaped, but it would be a big one. I can't find a latch. It's more like a wall."

A wall of metal in the cliff. But why put it there? Unless you were protecting something inside? And why protect something inside if you never wanted to get that thing out again? There must be a way in.

I step back over the rocks we've tumbled and toward the green lights. "They're gone," I say. Gray sticks his head out of the cave opening. "The lights and the numbers. It just . . . shut. By itself."

Probably while we were tumbling stones. And then I think of what Gray said about a fire inside, shining through glass. Someone has to light a fire. Tend it. Are there people in the mountain? Did someone shut that little door from the inside? I shiver again. Not from cold.

Gray comes to look at where the word lights had been. "What did you do the first time, when it opened?"

"I pushed something."

"Show me."

I take his hand, and together we find the smooth place. His hand stays with mine while I feel for the edges and find the bump. "Here."

"I feel it."

He must push it, because I jump at the whirring noise again, and there are the green lights and the numbers, no red words this time. This is so unthinkable. And yet it is. I run my fingers over the numbers themselves and jump again, this time at a noise. A note of music, a single blast, sudden, loud, and gone, and, like the lights and the little door opening by itself, completely unnatural. Wrong.

"Will you stop touching things?" Gray breathes, but I'm looking at the black space where the words had been. Now there is a green number 1. Gray sees it, too. I touch the 3. The sound comes again. A number 3 appears in green light.

"Let me try." Gray reaches around and pushes the 4, 5, and 6, all the way to 9. I push the 2 for good measure, and the 0. The numbers appear in a line. He pushes more, and when the numbers reach the end of their space, they disappear. Like a flashfly, red light suddenly spells "Invalid." Then flashes right back to "Enter Code."

Enter code, I think. Enter code. They use code at the Archives, and at the granary, for the rations. "What if it's not 'enter,' like 'go inside,'" I say. "But 'put in.' What if it means put in a code?"

Gray doesn't answer. He's gone very still behind me. Then he turns on his bare heel and walks out of the fern thicket, back to the edge of the pool, and stands there, hands on the back of his head, staring at the thunder and mist of the waterfall. He's thinking. And I think he's upset. The moons are rising in triangle formation over the mountain, and I can see the tension in his back in the silvery light. He is something unreal in that light, shirtless, bookless, wet hair curling against his shoulders. When the moonlight reaches the cliff wall, I wonder if I would have seen that green glow at all.

"Nadia," he says, "I need you to tell me the truth. Right now. It's important. Where did you get that piece of metal?"

My hand strays up to the necklace, the metal bracelet hanging behind it. He sounds afraid, but of the wrong things.

"Did your mother give it to you?"

"No."

"Then where did it come from?"

The little door whirs as it closes. It makes me feel like someone is here, listening. The green light is gone, except for the dot on the rock. "It came from a book," I say.

"What book?"

"My first one. The one I thought Anson had destroyed. I found it . . ." I pull out the metal from beneath my bunched and dripping tunic. The numbers, I think, scratched on the back. Code. But how could those numbers be this code? And why would they be in my book? Then again. Why not? So far, nothing has been the way I'd thought it would be.

Gray turns back, sits on the rock where the green dot of light shines. "Where is that book now?"

"Top of the waterfall." His gaze darts up. "I stole it from the Archives."

He puts his head in hands. I think he's actually laughing. "Of course you did, Dyer's daughter."

But I'm wondering how Gray thought of those numbers as code. Because they're on something else we don't know how to make? But he'd wanted me to hide the metal bracelet before the festival; he'd hooked it onto the necklace himself. He knows something. Something he hasn't told me.

"You're shivering," Gray says. It's true. "You should strip down and wring those clothes out so they can dry." And without even taking the obvious opportunity to suggest that he could wait while I do, he gets up and picks his way carefully in bare feet down the rocky edge of the pool. Now I know he's worried.

When I can't see him anymore, I step back into the dark shelter beside the young ferns, pull the end of the white tunic out of its collar and tug it over my head. Water splashes my feet as I wring it out. I shake it, hang it up on a fern, leave on the leggings—they're so tight to my body they're not holding much extra anyway—and lean over to twist my hair, squeezing the water downward until it runs onto the ground. There are still pins in there, I think, and maybe strips of blue cloth. What I'm really trying to do is not think about someone being inside the mountain behind me. And thinking of that is helping me to ignore the sprouting seed of doubt about what Gray hasn't told me. I never did ask him why he wanted to go over the wall.

I'm wringing out the lower end of my shirt for a second time when I hear a faint rustling in the ferns. From the direction Gray went. I yank the tunic back over my head. The rustling comes nearer, fast, and Gray emerges from the dark and instantly puts a hand over my mouth. He shakes his head once, telling me very clearly not to speak, grabs my arm, and pushes me back behind the fern thicket, over the tumbled stones, inside the opening in the cliff. There are more rocks left piled on one side than the other, and Gray pulls me behind them, presses me up against the cave wall, one finger against my mouth.

A rock falls somewhere near the pool, a big one, three sharp clanks of stone against stone before it settles. He leans down.

"Someone is here," he breathes in my ear.

I can feel his heart again, pounding inside his bare chest, my own racing to match it. Whatever Gray suspects, whatever he hasn't told me, he's afraid for me. I can feel that. I pull out my doubt like a weed. The waterfall rushes, and there's nothing but the quiet of being outside the walls. And then I hear footsteps crunching in the smaller rocks along the edge of the pool.

I put my hands on Gray's shoulders, catch his eye, and push, showing him I want us to crouch behind what's left of the rocks. We sink downward together. I kneel in the dirt, wince when I put my knee on a pebble, and get one eye between two stones in the pile, Gray somewhere just behind me.

There's a shadow at the edge of the moonlight, a person-shaped shadow, looking at the pool. I try to remember if I could see our pile of rocks from there, through the fern thicket, if it was obvious they'd been pulled down. I'm not sure I ever looked. But I'm hyperaware of that wall of metal behind me, like a gaze on my back, blocking up a hole into the mountainside. Maybe there's another way out. Maybe this is who was writing the words of light, raising and lowering the little door. I let my breath out slow, afraid it can be heard, but then there's a faint echo on the canyon walls. A bell.

The figure by the pool lifts its head, indistinct; I think they must be wearing a hood. Another bell, and then five more. The shadow person turns and walks quickly away, taking the same route Gray did among the rocks.

This is not someone from inside the mountain. This is someone from the city, someone who listens for the bells. My fear leaves me, only to be instantly replaced by another. Our books are up there, alone at the top of the cliff. Unprotected. I half stand and stretch a leg over the rock pile, pushing away Gray's restraining hand. Crouching low beneath the branches of the ferns, I creep up to the rocky strip beside the pool, find a line of sight around a boulder, and there is the shadow person, hazy but with a quick gait, the movement of long cloth rhythmic around the ankles.

Whoever this is, they know where they're going. Straight to the break in the canyon wall, up the mountainside and to the cliff. Or down the slope to Canaan. I remember how easy it was to see Gray's white shirt in the dark, so I step back into the branches to wait, and as soon as the shadow figure enters the glittering ferns below the canyon break I run. Just along the edge of the trees, away from the noisy stones that could cut my bare feet, around the pool, then straight into the forest.

I pause inside, listening, but I can't hear any movement. I inch forward in the light from the treetops, wary, climb the narrow gorge that takes me to the rim of the canyon. The city gleams in the open grassland before the walls. And in the light of the three moons I can also see my shadow figure, already down the slope and walking quickly through the grasses, but in the other direction, away from my ladder. Someone else, evidently, climbs Canaan's walls. And comes to my pool. The grasses rustle and then Gray is behind me. We both sit, in case the shadow decides to look back. Whoever it is, they're just a black patch in the moonlight now, almost to the city.

"Who do you think that is?" I ask before he can say anything about running off to chase people in the dark that I prefer not to hear. I watch the shadow disappear into the deeper shade beneath the walls.

"I never saw a face. But those were robes, I think. Black robes."

Council, then. Which Council member climbs the walls? And where? "Were you seen?"

"I don't think so. I was in the ferns when they came down from the gorge. Were you seen?" His whisper is tense.

"No."

He's relieved. Very relieved. So relieved that he's angry with me. "I'm going back up the cliff to get our books and our shoes. If I asked you to wait, is there any reason to think you would?"

My first reaction is to say no, there isn't, and I'll get my book myself. And then I look at Gray, wild-headed and shirtless, brows down and accusing, and I realize two things: First, that it doesn't frighten me to think of him touching my book, or carrying it down the mountain. Second, that Gray expects me to be frightened by this, and that the expectation hurts him. I don't know how much.

"I'll wait here," I tell him.

I hear him exhale twice before he says, "Okay. Then we'll go back down and try the numbers, yes?"

I nod.

"I'll be quick." And he's off through the grasses.

If the forest was lit like the city, then the city is lit like the forest, with hundreds of tiny, twinkling lights, white stone shining beneath the triangle of the moons, stars spattering the sky beyond them. I should think about what might happen when we try the numbers around my neck, about Anson and his questions, the Council member outside the walls, what kind of unimaginable force could make words out of lights, and how close we came to being caught. About stealing the First Book tomorrow. About the Forgetting. Instead I lie back in the grasses, out of the breeze, and watch the flashflies, thinking how the Nadia of the sunlight days would have never let another human touch her more than a pat on the hand. How Nadia of the sunlight had to force herself to speak. How Nadia of the sunlight would have never let the glassblower's son untie her book, would have never leaned down and kissed him in a warm and misty pool. Maybe Nadia of the dark days is more like she would've been if she'd never been forgotten. Or maybe not. That Nadia would have never been over the wall.

I hear Gray coming through the grasses. I turn my head and see that his white shirt is back on, though he hasn't bothered to tuck it or tie the collar, his book strap back across his chest. He must have left the bottle at the waterfall. I sit up at the last moment, make him stop short.

"I just about stepped on you. Here." He hands me my book, which I set beside me since I'm too damp to tie it on, and then my sandals. He's over being mad at me, I see. Or just happy to actually find me where he left me. He gives me a hand up after I tie my shoes and doesn't let it go, like he did in Rose's room. "Let's hurry."

❧

Now that I know what to do we get the little door open quickly. I felt nervous before, that someone might be behind me, inside the mountain. Now it feels like someone might be behind us at the pool. But I crouch down, holding the metal close to my eyes in the glow of the green light, calling out the numbers one by one while Gray touches the corresponding square. The false note of music comes each time he does. I get to the x scratched on the bracelet and pause. There are no options for letters on the green squares. But there's still a 2 scratched after the x.

"What do we do?" I ask.

"I don't know. There's no room for any more." The numbers of light have filled their space. Then the numbers disappear, exchanged instantly for a word in red: "Invalid." I hear Gray suck in a breath. It's uncanny, watching writing appear and disappear like that. Then "Invalid" is suddenly gone, replaced by "Enter Code."

"I guess it doesn't work," I say. I don't know whether I'm disappointed by this or secretly glad.

"Let's do it again," Gray suggests. "See if the same thing happens twice."

His words "again" and "twice" shake my thinking. "No, wait. Not an 'x.' Multiplication. 'x2.' Times two."

Gray thinks about this. "Push the numbers twice, or do we multiply it by two?"

"Can you multiply that in your head?"

"Not a chance."

"Me neither. Do it twice."

I call out the numbers and he pushes each one twice. Before we even get to the end the numbers disappear and the word "Invalid" takes their place, then "Enter Code."

"Okay," I say. "The whole thing, then, twice in a row."

We do that, and when we reach the end of the black space, instead of "Invalid" the space just keeps receiving numbers. I call out the last number, 1, and when Gray pushes it, all the numbers fade to black. It didn't work. I sigh, and then suddenly there's a new word on the screen: "Open."

We both turn to a noise, a clank that echoes over the roar of the falls. It echoes inside the mountain. And from inside the cave opening comes a streaking glare of pure white light.

I have been taught to write the truth. But is it still the truth when I cannot believe it?

NADIA THE DYER'S DAUGHTER
BOOK 7, PAGE 104, 8 YEARS AFTER THE FORGETTING

CHAPTER THIRTEEN

I stand, let the metal bracelet dangle from the string around my neck, blinking, our pile of tumbled stone etched into sharp relief by the sudden bright light. I can't believe that worked. It gives me the same feeling in my stomach as jumping over the waterfall. I take Gray's offered hand, my other still clutching my book in the cloth Genivee cut for it, and we step over the rock pile into the cave opening. The wall of metal has opened just a little, like a door swung on its hinges. I think it is a door now, though I can't see a latch, or anyone who could have opened it. I'm hardly even surprised by this. Gray looks to me, and I nod. He puts his hand flat on the metal and pushes.

The door creaks. Beyond is a kind of hall, rough rock walls that look like a natural shaft in the cliff, but the light, as always, is brilliantly unnatural. It comes from long tubes strung high up in rows along the passage. We step inside. The floor is dirt, smooth and polished with the passing of feet, air smelling of damp rock and stale soil. It's warmer in here, but other than an odd buzzing noise just on the edge of hearing, it's silent like the dead.

Gray lets me go, which I don't like, and turns back to the door we just came through, looking at it all around. I see what he's thinking. If we close the door, can we get back out again? If we leave it open, who might follow us inside? He finds something near the floor, like a small, upside-down cup made of red glass, set in a kind of base, colorful strings running out of it and along the rocks. He squats down, studying this. Then he pushes the door shut. I hear a click, like a lock, and the red glass glows with sudden light. Gray pushes on it, like we did with the numbers outside, and the door clicks and swings open again. He grins at me over his shoulder. These things are inexplicable. Impossible. Except that obviously they are not.

Gray stands up, shuts the door, lets the red light glow. I take his hand, and we start down the narrow hall inside the mountain. It's dark ahead, but never for very far, because as soon as we step near, another light springs into existence, and then the one behind us is gone.

"It's like they know we're here," Gray whispers. "Exactly where we are."

I don't like this thought. "Who does?"

"I think I mean the lights."

That doesn't make sense. We move forward, step by step, and I can't shake the feeling of hidden things. Of hidden eyes. Hidden people lighting the lamps, blowing them out again as we pass. Of someone or something waiting for us at the end of this hall. The last tube above us ignites, and then I can see another door. A regular door. Like ours, except the metal is not so shiny, no inner sparkles. This one has a latch.

"Ready?" Gray says. I can feel the tension in the muscles of his arm. I think my body is the same. I nod. He pushes down on the latch, there's a whoosh of air, and we step inside a room that is blacker than the moon shadows.

Until it isn't. Lights spring to a blaze, not only the glaring ones overhead but all around us. Blue lamps glow in flat, black squares, three large ones high up, a huge one as tall as I am on the opposite wall. Four smaller squares of blue light are on stands across the length of a long white table that is the wrong shape, curved like a scythe. I hear humming, whirring, buzzing, all soft or only just discernible, feel a faint breath of air that smells like . . . nothing. The walls aren't rock anymore, they're something shiny and solid, like the floor, overly bright, overly clean.

The blue squares high on the wall fade quickly to a black-and-white haze, little dots that move and crawl like insects. I'm reminded of Jin's walls, how he'd hung cloth in patterns, just for the look of it. I wonder if this is the same, though I've never seen cloth change colors before my eyes. Of the four squares of light on the curving table two have gone black, two have remained blue, and the huge one on the wall now says a word: "Welcome."

That word, so familiar, so human, and coming so obviously from nowhere, is more frightening than anything I've experienced. I don't feel welcome. I feel dizzy, disoriented, like a child, a little like I did on the night of the Forgetting. There isn't a single familiar object in this room; even the two chairs are large, cloth covered, oddly shaped. Gray lets his breath out slow. I'm holding on to his hand like someone might yank him away.

He checks for a latch, and the door shuts behind us. There are two more doors in this room. He takes the first step forward and I let him go.

"Let's not touch anything yet, okay?" he says.

I'm not going to. Or at least not anything that seems danger-ous. The floor is white like the walls, but not white like stone. It's impossibly white, like everything. I step across the shining floor, run a hand over the table, smoother than stone. No dust. It makes my fingernails look dirty by comparison.

"Two seconds," I hear Gray mutter, referring, I think, to my touching. I continue to run my hand along the length of the curving table while he looks underneath it. He's interested in how these things work. I want to know what this place was for. Then I glance back the way we came.

"Look," I whisper. Just down from the door we entered the entire wall is made of glass, from floor to ceiling. My eyes had been so full of everything else I hadn't even seen it. Behind the glass are things I don't have words for, things that remind me of the glowing number squares, only there's a wall of them, a mass of them, contained in some sort of silvery cabinet that's much taller than Gray and several times as wide. Colorful strings are twisted together in thick ropes, tubes going up and sideways to places I can't see. Tiny lights extinguish and ignite, extinguish and ignite. Like flashflies.

Gray is already at the glass, and I see that the center of the wall is a door. Made of glass. He tugs on the handle, but it doesn't open, and I'm a little glad. Gray got worried when I touched the table, when it's absolutely everything behind that glass wall that seems like the danger to me. He peeks through instead, blocking the reflections with his hands.

I wander to the other side of the room, where there's a door and another piece of glass in the wall, this time a win-dow. Inside I can see a mattress raised half a meter off the floor. I feel some of the tension in my middle relax. A mattress I can understand. I open the door, and now I hear the little pop before the light comes on when I enter. There are blankets on the bed, rumpled, a little partitioned area with what can only be a latrine. One or two unfamiliar tools are scattered on the floor, clothes draped across a chair, like someone just stepped out. Like they'll be right back. I don't think they'll be right back. On the table beside the bed is what I think was once an apple core, now dry and desiccated. Ancient.

I pick up the clothes. For a man or woman close to my height, I think, cloth sewn into one large combination of loose leggings and shirt with the whole front left open, the huge gap edged with tiny teeth of metal. It doesn't look very modest, or useful, in my opinion, but the cloth is extremely fine. And there, on the chest, are the letters "NWSE." Just like our knife. I set the clothes down exactly as I found them. Maybe someone lived here. I turn and see Gray in the doorway.

"Let's find out what's behind the other door," he says. "Just in case."

He means just in case someone or something might come through it. I follow him across the white room in silence. Gray tries the door latch. It's not locked. A soft pop for the light, and we see a very short hallway, another door at the end. Everything is so white.

"I'll hold this door," I say, "while you open that one." He nods. If we get locked in here, we'll never be found. He opens the other door, while I try the latch of the one I'm holding. It doesn't seem to be locked in any way. Gray nods again; I hold my breath and let the door shut. It clicks. I try the latch, and it opens again. I see Gray's shoulders ease down. He waits for me at the end of the little hallway and we step through the door.

The lights ignite, one, two, three, four, on and on down the length of a huge, open cavern, columns of natural blue and gray hanging down from a ceiling too high to see. The air is different here, damp, more dirt-and-rock-scented, like the first passage. And it's just as deserted. But where my eyes have landed is on a stack of white blocks. I run to them, put my hands on them.

"The stone!" I say. What the whole city is made of. Beside the stacked stone is a structure almost like a small building with an open room inside, made from more of the same smooth material as the curving table. Only this is black and yellow, shiny where it isn't covered in fine dust, huge molded letters saying "3-D Print Architect" across the top, almost too dusty to see. Gray is already beside it, doing his intent scrutiny without touching. We don't know what might decide to spring to life in here.

I wander past heaps of soil and pale sand, a cart made of metal with no way to pull it, also full of sand. The lights don't go all the way to the end of the cavern, leaving this area murky and dim, and when I look up I can just make out a broken tube hanging from the ceiling. I'm not looking at the wall of the cave, I realize, but an enormous pile of broken, tumbled stone. This whole side of the cavern has come down. Some of the boulders are huge, and blackened. They leave soot on my fingertips.

"Have you ever looked inside the water clock?" Gray calls. He's climbed up inside the black-and-yellow building, in the open-room part. We're not whispering anymore. It doesn't seem like there's anyone to disturb. I go back and peer upward, like he is.

He says, "The clock is just a machine, right? Cause and effect. You make one part do something, and that makes the next part do something, and the next, until you have a chain of things happening that makes the one thing you want to happen . . . happen. For the clock, it keeps up with the time. Rings the bell."

I think I know what he means.

"Well, I'm saying that all these things are machines. In the white room, and what I'm standing inside. Look." He jumps up, grabs hold of a metal bar that goes right across the open space. He hangs from it, wipes his hand across pieces and parts that are attached to it. When he drops down he shows me his hand, covered in the pale dust. It's the same color as our stone.

"I don't understand what causes what kind of effect," Gray said, "or what all those things in the white room are meant to do. But I would say this"—he opens his arms to the machine he's standing inside—"makes that"—he points at the piles of sand—"turn into that." Now he jerks his thumb at the pile of finished Canaan stone. "They didn't quarry it, Nadia. They created it."

"And the carving?"

"Maybe it came out that way. Who knows? Maybe that's why it's so perfect. Not sure how they got it in and out, though . . ."

"The other end of the cavern has collapsed. Exploded, maybe." I show him my blackened fingertips. "The door beside the pool seems to be the only way in or out, but maybe it wasn't that way before . . ."

My voice trails away. Gray has a little sheen of white dust over his hair; his expression is intense, excited by what he has learned. I look back toward the white room. I never imagined that so much knowledge could have been lost. How could we have lost this? How could the Forgetting have taken so much away? I'm already marching back across the cavern, angry. Despite the latrine and the mattress and the clothes, the white room just doesn't seem like a living space. It's a workspace, like Gretchen's, to do . . . something. Something I'm going to figure out.

I go through the door, down the little hall, let the second door whoosh and the lights and the squares all jump back into life. I feel the air that smells like nothing. Maybe that's why it stays so clean. I'm dry enough now to tie on my book, so I do that while the door whooshes and Gray comes in behind me. I'm done being careful. I walk over and sit in one of the chairs.

I nearly fall on the floor. The chair is moving, and at first I'm afraid it's moving by itself, like everything else, but then I realize the chair is on wheels on a very smooth floor. I'm halfway across the room, spinning in a circle before I know what hit me. I let myself slow to a stop. Gray is watching me, brows up. I put down my feet and spin myself on purpose. It's a little like swimming, or sliding, but not really like either.

Gray grins, gets in the other chair, and does the same thing, propelling himself fast across the floor, catching himself just before he crashes against the wall. He looks back at me. "Now this," he says, "is an incredible machine. Who could ever just sit on it?"

I laugh. The chair is stuffed with something soft, with the perfect place to lean back a head. I spin with one foot and cross my legs, close my eyes, feel the circles slow and wind down.

"And I thought we should go to the Dark Days Festival," Gray says.

No, sneaking over the wall, jumping a waterfall, finding a hidden door, and playing around inside a mountain full of machines we don't understand was clearly a much better plan, Glassblower's son.

"Are you sorry?" he asks.

"About what?"

"You kissed me."

I open my eyes. Gray is still in his chair, facing me, his brows back down, smile gone. "You kissed me, too," I say.

"You kissed me first."

"Well, you made me want to."

"Are you sorry?"

"Are you?" I counter.

He pulls my chair to him, puts a hand on my neck, his forehead on mine, and shakes his head just a little.

"Then neither am I."

He kisses me once, and there something's very intense about it. He's still, like when he was floating in the mist of the pool. "I don't want you to be sorry," he says, so soft it's barely words.

"Well, I don't want you to walk with Veronika anymore."

He leans back. "You want to talk about Veronika? Right now?"

"No. I never want to talk about her again."

I get a hint of his smirk. "But it's all part of my extremely clever plan to keep you a secret," he says. His mouth is back on my neck.

"Get a new plan," I whisper.

He laughs. And I wish I knew why he thought I might be sorry.

"What bell do you think it is?" I ask. He keeps his mouth where it is and points upward. I follow the angle of his finger to a dial on the wall, above the window to the resting room, a dial that is just like the one on our water clock. Of course it is. Why shouldn't it be? The dial says it's only half past the eighth bell. We have time. Unless Gray makes me forget what I'm doing. I kiss his cheek and his mouth, then sit back and shove him, sending his chair flying toward the other wall.

He leans back and sighs. "Was that necessary?"

I think it probably was. I've already turned and scooted to the huge square of light on the wall, the one with the word "Welcome." So if this is a machine, like Gray said, then it must do something, be for something. I cross my legs in the large, soft chair, run my hand over the black edge of the light square, like a window frame. Maybe it has a bump. Maybe it will open, like the little door over the numbers in the cliff face. Gray's chair rolls up beside mine.

"I really wish you wouldn't touch that."

"It says 'Welcome,'" I say.

He doesn't argue. I brush my fingers along the edge, and when they get near the blue light, suddenly little symbols appear, like wisps of colored fog. When I take my hand away, they're gone again. I look at Gray in triumph. He tries it as well, holds his hand poised over the light that has no warmth, and I try to understand the symbols. Circle, triangle, square, and more, all with a design inside.

I point at one, meaning to ask Gray if he thinks the design could be letters, when there's a sudden, trilling, false note of music. I sit back, craning my neck upward. The word "Welcome" has dissolved, like powdered sap in water, and the entire square has gone green, the circle symbol large in the center, with the letters "NWSE" entwined inside it. Words appear like blinking. I don't even know what all of them mean. "System," "Repair," "Utility," "Core," "Control" . . .

Gray is out of his chair to see what's behind the square. By his puzzled expression, I assume there's nothing but wall. I hover my hand and touch a triangle this time, and the same thing happens. The symbol rushes to the center and grows large, letters entwined, this time in yellow, words like "Language," "Security," "Camera" . . .

"Look at this one." The foggy shape resembles an open book. I touch it, the shape leaps upward, and this time the words that appear are "Archive—The Canaan Project." We both stare at the name of our city. Below it, one by one, appear "History," "People," "Statistics," "Curriculum," "Vlog," and "New World Space Exploration." The significance of that last one hits me.

"NWSE," I say beneath my breath.

"I see it," Gray replies.

"What kind of space? Like a workspace?"

Gray stands, and this time he hovers his hand over the whole lit square, to see if anything else might show itself. When it doesn't, he touches the word "Exploration."

A list of numbers appears, the number 1 brighter than the others. Then sound blasts into the silent room, and I cover my ears. Images roll across the screen, not drawings or designs but real things, a moon in a sky, some kind of moving white container spouting blasts of furnace fire, and people, so many people walking what I think are streets except they are nothing like the streets of Canaan. Metal buildings that stretch to the sky, carts that are enclosed, not pulled, zooming at unattainable speeds, hundreds at a time. Bizarre clothes, strange hair colors, one little girl holding a creature like an insect but huge, at least half her size, and covered with hair.

Then a man's face fills the square of light, five times bigger than any man's face should be, and he is smiling, his hair clipped so short it must have been done with a razor. It's not real, I have to tell myself. He's not here. But he looks real, and he's looking right at me.

He says, "The New World Space Exploration Corporation announces the Canaan Project, a historic joint venture to colonize the first known habitable planet in our galaxy . . ." The picture changes to another burst of fire, and another white container is now flying among stars. A flying machine?

"Seventy-five men and seventy-five women," he says, "the best of our world's best, will leave Earth and embark on a first-of-its-kind journey to expand the boundaries of human exploration." The square on the wall shows the flying machine hurtling through stars, approaching a green-and-yellow sphere, three smaller ones circling it. "39,413,958,467,871 kilometers," the man says, "4.17 light-years, 1.28 parsecs from Earth." The music is swelling, the green-and-yellow planet coming closer. "We will travel the galaxy. We will experience what has never been. We will build a new civilization. Because we dare."

The sound and the images stop. Gray is still standing. I'm not sure he's moved a muscle. He reaches out and touches the last image, and we watch the whole thing unfold again. It's easier to listen to the words this time, when I'm not as shocked by the sights. The man is saying that Canaan is the civilization they set out to build: a one-kilometer circle of stone 39,413,958,467,871 kilometers away from a place called Earth. The same numbers as the code I used to get inside this room.

Gray lifts his hands behind his head, still staring at the light square. Other than that, we don't move or speak. I'm not sure what there is to say. Everything? Or nothing. I thought the people who built Canaan might have come from across the mountains. They came across the stars. And then they forgot about it. The list of numbers reappears, and after a long time, Gray reaches out and touches "2."

We watch a similar grouping of images, like a story being told, this one about the vision for Canaan, with voices from people we cannot see. "This is our directive," a man says with confidence. "To build and to populate the first civilization created to exist in harmony with itself and its environment."

"To live without bloodshed, without money, without industry, without waste . . ." a woman's voice says.

"Self-sufficient and with respect for the land," another continues.

"A new world," says the next one, "where humans live in partnership by the work of their own hands. With peace, with justice . . ."

"With minimal technology," says the voice of a child.

"We will live off the grid, because there will be no grid."

"We will advance the knowledge of the human race. We will create the perfect society."

"Because we dare," they all say together.

I don't know what money is, or industry, or technology, or a grid. But I know I've seen bloodshed.

The next story is longer, showing the selection process for the people chosen to come to Canaan. Architects, engineers, mechanics, chemists, agricultural experts, doctors, physicists, psychologists . . . I don't know what half of these things are, either, and many of these people, I see, did not even speak the same words. Everyone had to learn to talk and write the same, in a way called English. I'd never even considered that one human could speak differently from another. And they had to pass tests, not just in their particular trade or skill, but for stress, resourcefulness, empathy, and health, and even for hidden malfunctions in their families.

Then the one hundred and fifty chosen members all trained as something called an "artisan." We watch a man who refers to himself as a "nutritionist" being given his first lesson on a potter's wheel. He's not very good at it, and he laughs, and the men and women gathered to watch his progress laugh with him. They're wearing the same sort of clothes I saw in the resting room behind us, though I can't see how they've managed to close up the fronts.

"Wait!" I say. "Gray, can you make it stay right there?" We've learned that if you hover your hand over the story being shown, it will allow you to manipulate the story itself. Gray touches the symbol that makes the images pause. It's like stopping time.

"Look," I say. "On the right, toward the back. Is that Jin?"

Gray stands back a moment, then steps forward and looks closer. "I think it is."

Jin looks so young. But his smile, and something about the way he's holding his hands, is exactly the same. Jin was born thirty-nine trillion kilometers from where we sit. And I don't think he knows it. I hate the Forgetting.

"Wait," I say again. I get up from my spinning chair and hover my hand to make the symbols come back. I touch the book, and when the words pop into existence, this time I choose "People." A list of names materializes. Everyone seems to have two, or even three, none of them having to do with a skill, all of them alphabetized by the last name first, which is odd. I touch one at random. Barkhurst, Amelia. Instantly a woman's face flashes onto the light square, and it tells me Amelia Barkhurst was born in a place called the United States, that she was a materials engineer on Earth and a weaver on Canaan, who she married, the children she had after they arrived. It doesn't say when or if she died. She doesn't look familiar.

"Look for Jin," Gray says. "Or no, we can't. That wouldn't have been his name before the Forgetting. We'd have to go through them all . . ."

I go back to the list and choose another at random. Gara, Ketan. Born in India, astrophysicist, with a note that his particular specialty would be the study of Canaan's twelve-year comet. The word "comet" is in a color, which I've learned means it can be touched. I do, and it shows me images of Canaan. I can see that from the fern trees, from the rocks, though these images are not clear like the others. These are a little distorted, like seeing through squinted eyes. There's the sky streaked for sunrising, but then it goes bright, too bright for the person's vision we're seeing through, sparkling like the metal in our doors and tables. Like glass. A broken-glass sky.

I step back. "Gray, that's what the sky looked like. Right before the Forgetting." I sit down. Deep inside my head, I am slipping, falling in the streets.

"What is it?" Gray asks. "Was there any noise?"

No. The sparkling sky had been bright and silent. Caused by something called a comet. Something that comes every twelve years.

"Is it like a storm?" he asks.

I don't answer this question, either. I just don't know. I stare at the image. I don't want to think that something like this could cause the Forgetting. Something we have no way of stopping.

Gray moves the image away, goes back to Gara, Ketan, and then back to the list. "What about Rose?" he says.

I stand. He's right. If Jin was one of the original people chosen for the project, then Rose should be, too. She's just as old, or she seems that way. Would it make her not Lost if we could tell her who she was? I start to scan the list, ready to touch them all, but one name near the top catches my eye. Surprises me. I touch it.

And there is Janis's face smiling out at us. She's very young, just a girl, but her looks are unmistakable. Striking, the eyes deep set, hair dark instead of white. The information says Janis Atan was not born on Earth, but on the *Centauri*, the flying machine they called a "ship," carrying the chosen members to

Canaan. Her parents were both chemists. Suddenly I want very much to know how old Janis is.

I turn to say this to Gray, but he's staring at the illuminated face, still, his expression almost blank, and it reminds me of two things: the way he'd stopped mid-sentence when he saw me with Janis at the festival, and the way he'd looked at me at the waterfall, the first time, when it came to him how I knew about his burns.

"Explain to me," Gray says, "how Janis still has her name?"

I look back at the smiling face on the wall. "She must have kept a book . . ."

Gray throws a hand out toward the light wall. "Why would a little girl keep a book before the first Forgetting, Nadia? All these stories, these things we've been looking at. The people who came here"—he emphasizes the next words—"they didn't know they were going to forget. They didn't know it was coming. They weren't prepared. And just who do you think that was at the pool earlier?"

I think about the shadow figure, hurrying away along the fern edge and down the grassy slope to the city. It could have been Janis in her black robes. But I can't be sure. Gray has his hands behind his head. He isn't moving, but it's a kind of stillness that makes me think he's going to explode.

"It was Janis," he says, "and you were right, dead right. Everything you said in Rose's room, about who must have written the First Book of the Forgetting, who could have figured it all out so quickly, who would have talked that way. You were right to try and steal the First Book, because Janis wrote it. She came to that pool today because she knows that door is there. And she knows that door is there for the same reason she still knows her name."

He looks at me then. "It's because Janis is like you. Because Janis never forgot."

Father always said to write the truth, but to write the truth we have to know it. And knowing the truth is what makes me alone.

NADIA THE DYER'S DAUGHTER
BOOK 14, PAGE 22, 3 SEASONS UNTIL THE FORGETTING

CHAPTER FOURTEEN

I don't understand," I say, which is the understatement of my life. Gray is a fast thinker, but this time I think he's making a leap. "If Janis never forgot, why wouldn't we know about it? Why wouldn't we know about all this? What could be the reason for it?"

Gray doesn't answer any of my questions. He's staring at the smiling face on the wall like he's being tied to the plaque on the water clock, and that little sprig of doubt I'd plucked before we opened the door springs back up from my insides like it's the first day of sunrising. Gray says, "If I asked you to do something for me right now, would you do it?"

I don't know how to answer that. He looks at me hard.

"If I asked, would you do everything I said without asking me why for half a bell? Trust me for half a bell more? That's all I'm asking. And then I'm going to answer all of your questions."

I almost tell him that I stayed on the slope and waited for him, didn't I? That he owes me seventy-four answers anyway; but my doubt has roots now, choking the humor. I don't want to feel this. I want things to be the way they were before. Gray comes and lifts the string of my necklace, rubs a thumb once across the blue glass. Then he unhooks the metal bracelet and puts it in my hand.

"Memorize it," he says.

I frown. "You want to leave it in here?"

"Why do you think your house was searched? And Anson's?"

I hadn't thought of this yet.

"Just do it, Nadia. Please. No questions. Not yet."

Maybe he's right. Somehow, all of this has to do with me, with my family, and I don't know why. And until I do, this room is the safest place I can imagine for the code besides my own head. Gray has turned away now, arms crossed, deliberately not looking at the numbers. I visualize them, make sure I can see them in my mind before I lay the bracelet on the table.

Then without another word Gray leaves the white room, letting me follow. The door shuts behind us. I imagine the lights blowing out, dying inside as we walk down the rock passage, the tubes overhead igniting just as we need them to. There's a sense of wrong here, of something impending, and right now I am more afraid than the first time we entered this passage.

At the door Gray says, "Say the numbers in your head." I have them, but I do as he asks. Then he pushes down on the round red glass with his foot, the door unlatches, and we leave the inside of the mountain, step over the rocks and out into the patch of young ferns.

The dark day flowers are blooming, a pungent, tickling spice that permeates the air like the roar of the waterfall and the mist of the pool. My mountain is glittering, the moons casting silver light. But I don't belong here. Humans don't belong here. We belong on a place called Earth. I wonder if Gray is thinking the same thing. Or if he's thinking of our jump. Of me. He told me in the white room that he didn't want me to be sorry. Like I might be sorry. I hear the door shut without our help.

We walk around the pool, up the gorge in the canyon to the grassy slope, around the foot of the mountain. Gray doesn't talk, and I don't ask questions, not because he asked me not to, but because right now, I don't want to know the answers. I see my ladder hanging down from the wall, like a posted sign. If that really was Janis at the pool, if she ever comes this way, she'll know someone has been outside. Maybe it's like Gray said. Maybe she's always known, maybe she's just deciding what day is my day to be caught. Maybe all of this is one enormous game.

Gray lifts me as I jump for the bottom rung. While I wait for him on top of the wall I can see the festival, all the torches glinting, hear a soft background of music and noise. The streets are empty, and when I land in Jin's garden it feels like we've run the images on the wall of the white room in reverse. Like I've gone backward in time.

I stand still, waiting. Gray pushes the ladder over the wall and hides the pole. Guilt, as I remember, is a bitter taste. Dread, however, is foul. He sits on the wall edge, leans over, elbows on knees, fingers tented over his face. He doesn't start speaking.for a long time.

"All that time we played our game," he says to the dead grasses, "and you never asked me the right question: Why was I in Jin's garden that day?"

I had thought the question. I'd thought I had the answer.

"On the twenty-fifth day of the sunlight, Reese came to the workshop when I was alone, and said I was wanted at the Council House. I didn't know what I'd done. I assumed it was Jonathan who wanted me, but when I got there it was Janis, sitting in a cloth-covered chair. She offered me food, asked me about glass. Said nice things to me. And then she said she was concerned about your family. That the Forgetting might have made your mother's mind malfunction, as if your mother might hurt someone else. She wanted information, but she wanted to get it discreetly. No worrying the neighbors, she said. And she wanted me to get it from you."

I can make guesses now, where he's going with this. The dread is becoming certainty, the certainty a deep ache in my middle.

"I told her no," Gray goes on. "That it couldn't be done. You wouldn't talk to me or anyone else, that it had nothing to do with me. And she just smiled and said she understood, and then she asked me about how I coped with the Forgetting, whether I ever went to the Archives or not, if I read my old books."

Gray looks up for the first time. "I've never looked at my old books in the Archives. I didn't think they were mine. I thought they belonged to the glassblower's real son, the one who died, or was Lost. And all I could think was what if there was something in there, something that didn't match? There was so much chaos after the Forgetting. I was young and dirty and burned. It was Arthur of the Metals who found me on that rooftop, but there were others, and even the Council members were confused, relearning faces. Rose cut off almost all my hair before I left, and I've always worn sleeves over my scars and avoided Arthur like poison. But what if I'd gotten careless? If he'd finally recognized me, after all this time? Me, my parents . . ."

He doesn't need to go on. I know what would have happened to them.

"Then Janis asked if I wanted to reconsider getting that information. And that's when I was certain. Janis knew I'd been Lost. Knew what my father had done. She had me. I spilled everything I knew about you and your mother. Anything I could think of."

I close my eyes.

"But she wasn't happy with my answers. It wasn't enough, and so she suggested I spend time with you. Ask you questions. She was interested in anything that might set off your mother's condition—words, numbers. An heirloom."

This makes my eyes snap open.

"So that we can help her, she said. So we can learn more about the Forgetting. But I think we both know now what she was really after. What she still wants. The code to the white room. She told me to come back in three days, tell her what I'd found out, that she wasn't writing our conversation down. That I wasn't to write it down, and I was relieved. That meant she was going to forget the whole thing soon. That she was allowing me to forget soon. If I could keep her happy, the situation would go away.

"So I followed you. Tried to find out what you do, to start a conversation with you, anything. But you were like a rock in a stream. I saw you going to Jin's, so I went to Jin and offered to help him with his writing, but at the end of three days I had nothing. Janis explained her disappointment until I was sweating. So I spent a resting on Eshan's roof, watching your house. And what do you think I saw you do? Leave. And what do you think I saw you do next?"

Climb the wall, I think.

"I couldn't believe it. I sat in that corner right over there and waited, and before you came back I'd made a decision. I wasn't going to tell Janis anything until you took me with you. I'd make you talk to me, tell me things about your family. Maybe I could get enough that she would let me stop. So I went over the wall with you, and you handed me my past like a gift. And I went straight to Janis, told her everything I could, lied about the rest. Which is what I've been doing pretty much every day since. Lie to you, lie to her. It's all a big lie."

I had a choice, I think. I made it in Rose's room, and I knew I would pay. I thought I'd begun the next day, when Mother took the knife to her arm, but now, I realize, is my time. Now I am paying, and I, who thought I knew pain, had not had an inkling of the agony the glassblower's son could extract from me.

"I'm not asking you to forgive me," he says. "I think I know what you're going to do. But I am going to tell you the rest of the truth first."

My chest heaves like I've been running. I lean against the archway, turn my head where I can't see him.

After a long moment he says, "Maybe I do have memories, at least a little, because the first time we went to the learning room after the Forgetting I didn't know who you were, but I wanted to. You wouldn't talk to me, or even look at me, and the more you didn't the more curious I was. And it stayed that way for years, and when I tried too hard you slapped my face. I probably deserved it. Everyone, all of them, they just assumed you hated us. That you thought you were better than us. But I know Lost when I see it, Nadia, book or no. I wanted to know why."

He makes a noise, an exhalation of air I think is a laugh, but there's no humor in it.

"So when Janis forced this situation down my throat there was a part of me that wanted to do exactly what she said. You fascinated me. I wanted to pursue you. And when I saw you go over that wall, I wanted to go with you. I wanted to make you want me. I knew she was playing a dirty game and I knew I had to betray you to it, and I wanted to make you come to me anyway. And I did, didn't I? What a plan. What a brilliant scheme."

I think of Gray floating in the pool, of leaning down to brush his lips with mine. I was much better off being the Nadia of the sunlight. When I was in control. When I protected myself from pain. When I was alone.

"So now you know the truth, and I'm going to go and let you decide what to do about it. I'm due at Janis's at the resting bell and I don't have much time to think up a new stack of lies. She doesn't know you've been over the wall, she doesn't know you remember, but you can count on her knowing just about everything else. I had to give her some truth. A lot of it, actually. And I don't think she's going to forget it, either, do you?"

He waits, but I don't say anything.

"If you want me to help you steal that book this waking I will. I'll be on this roof right after the leaving bell, before you have to be at the Archives. And if you don't . . . if you're not here, I'll know to leave you alone."

The music of the festival ends. The people clap, and the noise in the air is like a hint of thunder. My neck is wet, water running down from my cheeks. "Don't come tomorrow," I say. "I won't be here."

I hear Gray get up from the garden wall, move across the dry grass, pause at the top of the stairs. "And one more thing I should probably tell you," he says. "I think I love you."

❧

I walk home in a daze, among people who don't want to be going home at all, who don't know they are thirty-nine trillion kilometers away from it. I'm vaguely aware that I need to be in my bed by the resting bell so Mother can check, that I will need to talk to Genivee, who sent me out to stop thinking about tomorrow. That I don't ever want to think about tomorrow again. That I can't actually tell Genivee anything. I can't think anymore at all.

Maybe that really was thunder on Jin's roof. A soft boom rumbles in the distance, clouds slowly blotting out the stars above the mountains. The dark day rains are coming, maybe by the next waking. I wander into the alley between the houses, making for my front door, and when I look over my shoulder Eshan is going into his. His eyes meet mine. He takes a step, as if he's starting across the street. I fumble with the latch and get inside, dropping the bar as soon as I'm in.

The house is dark and quiet, stifling after my hours in the brisk air. There are no lamps lit in the sitting room, though from the dark hall I can hear Liliya talking to Mother. When I slip into my room Genivee is asleep sitting up, her book in her lap. I take her pen from her hand, set her book aside, and adjust her blankets. Now that I'm in the light I can see just how dingy and wrinkled the white tunic dress is, how bedraggled my hair. I'm grateful that Mother has exhausted Genivee today. My little sister will take one look at me and know that the Nadia of the sunlight is back. I don't want to see her disappointment. It will go away soon enough. When she forgets.

The resting bell rings and Mother sticks her head in the door. She counts bodies, smiles once, then leaves without noticing the state of me. I pull off the dirty tunic and leggings, hide them under the mattress until I can take them to be cleaned, put on a sleeping dress. Then I lift the string with the piece of blue glass over my head and set it on my shelf. My neck feels light, empty without it. I'd already grown used to the weight. The glassblower's son is good, so very good at making everyone love him. I blow out the lamp, lie on my bed counting the bells until Genivee wakes up for the Learning Center. I pretend to sleep until she's gone, until I hear Liliya take Mother to the dye house.

I don't go to the Archives. I really don't see the point. I don't go for four days. It rains and it rains. Gretchen sends a note and I don't answer it. I don't speak. I write, though, in my secret book beneath the floor, anything my mother and sisters might need to know if their books were to get lost. I see Genivee's disappointment. And her worry.

On the fifth day I put on an old tunic and see if Karl has my new requested book ready. He does not, and his shop is a mass of bodies, angry people, panicking to get new books, to write down everything before the Forgetting. I hear the potter accuse Karl of not making books for the people he doesn't like on purpose. So they'll become Lost.

I stop listening, wander down Meridian beneath the fat buds of the forgetting trees, dripping with rain, drop off my dirty clothes at the baths and sign in to run. I'm behind on my exercise, and prefer to do it in the dark days, anyway, in the wet, and when the wind is sharp.

I run the path around the walls twice, cold rain stinging my face, and the second time I pass the Archives I glance up, I can't help it, all the way to the roof garden of Jin's house. There's someone standing up there, in the rain, arms crossed, the clouds ragged across the moons. It's not Jin. Has he been up there every day?

I run harder, pretend my tears are rain, are sweat, and then I pretend the same thing in the baths, which are dim and flickering with the hanging oil lamps in the steam. I stay in until I'm almost too hot again, until Rose comes. She doesn't have my clothes this time; they'll take some time to dry now that the sun's gone. I put on the clean ones from my pack, and then she just sits behind me, squeezing the water out and braiding up my hair. I wonder why she comes in to take care of me. I close my eyes, think of Rose's wrinkled face and deft fingers, her soft voice. She was not born on this planet. She was chosen. Rose was inside a machine that carried her through the stars. I wish I could make her remember.

While her fingers fly through my hair, she says quietly, "I don't have the news you asked for about your mother, but I thought you might like to know that Chandi the Builder has come to the houses of the Lost, patching the holes and the fences. And we have new doors. Strong ones."

Her tone makes me uneasy. I can't tell if she thinks this is a good thing, or a bad. It is strange, to have work done, and done well, right before a Forgetting. Now that I listen, Rose speaks with just a touch of the accent I heard in the white room. Just a bit like Janis.

"Will you tell Gray?" she asks. "It won't be as easy to get in from now on." I nod as she finishes, start sliding into my sandals. She folds her hands in her lap. "It's only a short time until the Forgetting, Nadia the Dyer's daughter. Best not to waste it."

When I walk home I see a divide in the streets. Some laughing, drinking like it's still the festival, others with their faces pinched, hurrying with their supplies clutched to their chests. I take note of which is which. The ones who run to their holes are probably not the ones to be feared. Michael and Chi and Veronika have their heads together on Meridian, beneath the shelter of the trees. "Outside the walls . . ." I hear Veronika say. Thunder rolls.

When I close the front door there's a yellow glow in our storeroom, such a soft, comforting light compared to the glare of the white room in the mountain. Mother is inside, fiddling with the jam pots, tearing bread from a loaf. The knife must be in the potatoes. I ought to leave Mother alone. I tend to irritate her, but suddenly I'm starving. I think I've forgotten to eat. For a day. That must be why my hands are shaking.

"Liliya's here," Mother says, watching as I take the jam pot from her hands. "We're not working." I wonder if this means Mother didn't do well at the dye house today. When given a task she's used to, she's usually fine. I use a spoon to spread some jam on a piece of bread for her, then do the same for myself. She watches me, wary.

"You have the bracelet," she states.

I think of Gray unhooking it from my necklace. "I don't have it anymore, Mother."

"Don't write it down."

And then a tiny bit of breeze begins to blow through my mental fog. How does Mother recognize that bracelet? When could she have seen it? My book was gone when I let her out of her room after the Forgetting. *Nadia's book is wrong.* That's what she always says, but is she saying it because I did, or for another reason? "Where did the bracelet come from, Mother?"

"Potomu chto ya smeyoo," she replies immediately, the strange, harsh sounds I had taken to be nonsense the first time I heard them, when Arthur and Anson were searching her room. *"Potomu chto ya smeyoo,"* she says again, and then, very soft, "Because I dare."

She eats her bread, a little jam getting on the book around her neck, and I'm seeing the moving images on the wall of the white room, hearing the booming voice. *We will build a new civilization. Because we dare . . .*

And right here, in the storeroom, holding bread with jam, for the first time I truly understand my mother. She remembers. Not like me, the way I remember everything, or like Liliya, who has only a specific image, as far as I know. Mother's head must be full of vague bits and pieces, a confusion of people, places, half memories, the memory of memories, from what has to be at least four Forgettings. And they are driving her mad.

"Because I dare," I repeat. "What's the other way to say it, Mother?"

"Potomu chto ya smeyoo."

She smiles, and I'm thinking about those symbols on the bracelet, and how the chosen members of the Canaan Project had to be taught to speak the same words. My grandparents, or my great-grandparents, would have been born on Earth. Is that how they talked? It's bizarre to imagine. I look at Mother, curious. I've tried this before, but she was full of sleeping tonic then. I look at the bread in my hand, say very carefully, "Mother, who is Anna?"

I can almost see the struggle inside her head. Mother must have been so pretty once. Like Liliya. She whispers, "Anna was the first."

And I understand. Anna was the first. The first child, the oldest, who put me to bed when I didn't want to go. Who I was going to grow up to be just like. My oldest sister. Liliya would have lost the memory of her to the Forgetting, but I must have forgotten her naturally. I was maybe only two when she's last mentioned in my book. I gaze at Mother while she eats jam from the pot, think of her terror of an empty bed. Because something inside her almost remembers, knows there's a bed empty that shouldn't be. That she's missing a child. Letting out her own blood must seem less painful sometimes. And what does Mother see when she looks at me? Anson the Planter, and all the hurt that goes with him. I feel a sudden rush of grief for all of us—my mother, Anson, the sister I can't remember.

"We have to write the truth," Mother says suddenly. She's put down the jam pot, wiping my fingers with a cloth like I'm six. "Do you write down what's true, Nadia?"

I don't know. I try. But who can find the truth in Canaan? Janis doesn't tell it, the Learning Room doesn't teach it. My father has twisted it, Mother half forgotten it, and the Forgetting is the thief that steals it. Except the Forgetting didn't actually steal the truth from Janis, did it?

And if she's never forgotten, I suddenly realize, then Janis, our benevolent leader, the one who cares for us all and still carries her name, must know exactly what comes before a Forgetting. Knows, and lets it happen. How easy would it be for the Council to lock families in, to empty the streets, to write everyone down like they did for the counting, to mark each man, woman, and child? All it would take is for Janis to say it, for one Council member to understand it was needed.

But they don't understand what's needed, do they? They don't remember, and she doesn't tell them. We've been complacent, trusting, assuming that keeping a book is the solution, without ever asking why the solution isn't any better. Accepting the fact that this is the only way life has ever been just because we can't remember any differently. But it has been different, and Janis must know it. Just like she knew how to coerce and threaten Gray.

And now that the clouds in my brain have broken, understanding just keeps flowing, like rain pouring down the windowpanes. There has never been a reason, I realize, for anyone to be Lost. Janis knows who they are. They're Lost because Janis has let them be Lost. Or made them be. She's certainly allowed those unwritten babies to be taken from their mothers, boys like Gray from their fathers. And she has to know exactly who Rose is. Rose was with her on the ship, the *Centauri*, traveling a galaxy to build Canaan. Janis knows my mother, our names, where we live, and I'd be willing to write in my book that she knows who my father is, too.

But why? Why any of it? If she was searching for that code, if she was trying to get Gray to find the code, then I would guess that means Janis doesn't want anyone to know what's in the mountain. Or to know what she wants that is inside that mountain? Otherwise she could have knocked on my front door and asked for that bracelet. Probably I would've given it to her. But she's doing all this in secret, right before a Forgetting, telling Gray not to write it down. Using the knowledge she's collected, the things no one else remembers. To shape the truth as she pleases. To bend us to her will like a piece of melting glass.

But there's at least one person in Canaan who will no longer be bent. Who can shape the truth for herself. Me. *Write the truth,* Mother said. To write the truth you have to seek it, to know it, and the only person in this city who has ever handed me the truth, in all of its reality and ugliness, I have just rejected.

I look up at Mother, still scrubbing my fingers, scrubbing them raw, and I do something Nadia of the sunlight would never have done. I kiss her cheek. She doesn't hate it as much as I thought she would. Then I grab a bowl and an empty jar, hurry to my room, take the blue necklace from my shelf, and hang it around my neck. The weight of this is right. Then I am out the door and up to the garden, feeling in the dark around the dead, wet breadfruit stalks until I find the jar with the plant cutting. I hold it up, looking for light in the rain. The water is thick with waving tendrils of roots.

I walk deliberately down the stairs, soaking, set down the plant cutting, and smash the empty jar into a million pieces inside the bowl. Jemma the Clothesmaker stares at me through the pouring rain in the light of her open door. Plant in one hand, bowl of broken glass in the other, I turn down Hawking, make my way by the light of the streetlamps across Newton and down Sagan to Hubble Street. The day is dark without the moons. Clouds have consumed the stars, the wind driving water into my face brisk and chill.

This might have been rash, I think. This is rash. I'm not sure I care. I have lived my life so frightened of pain it's been paralyzing. I hate pain, but I hate fear more, and I've eaten fear every day of my life because of the Forgetting. Today I will spit it out. And what was Gray supposed to have done, anyway? He couldn't condemn his own parents. And he told me. When he didn't have to. When he didn't want to. When he thought the truth would make me walk away. It almost did make me walk away. It makes me think that everything he said might be true.

The door to Gray's house is coming closer. I can't see the workshop from this direction, but I can smell the furnace. They must be blowing glass. My breath picks up, a tingle of nerves dancing down my spine, different from the feel of water running down my back. I take the last step and knock on Gray's door.

Knowing the truth makes me alone. I wrote that once, but I think I was wrong. Fear of pain is what has made me alone. But today I realized that pain and love have a balance. I can feel so much of one only because I feel so much of the other.

NADIA THE DYER'S DAUGHTER
IN THE BLANK PAGES OF
NADIA THE PLANTER'S DAUGHTER
BOOK I

CHAPTER FIFTEEN

Delia the Planter answers the door. She's a head shorter than me, much rounder, with Gray's eyes and coloring, except that her hair is soft and very straight. She's a pleasant-looking woman whose expression is not all that pleasant when it lands on me. I'm the bad influence, I remember. And it's only just now occurred to me that I'm going to have to speak.

"Yes?" she says.

"I . . ." I pull myself together, hold up the bowl of broken glass. "I have some broken glass for you."

"Take it around to . . ." She glances once over her shoulder, toward the workshop. "Never mind," she says quickly. "I'll take it."

Good. That means Gray is here. "Actually, would you mind looking at this plant for me? I don't know what it is." I hold up the cutting, a piece of flora I'm fairly positive Delia the Planter has never seen. Her eyes widen a little, and at that moment thunder booms, shaking the air. Water is running down my face. "Could I come in?"

Delia hesitates, looks again at the jar in my hand, and opens the door a little wider.

"Thanks," I say, stepping inside before she can change her mind. I'm tracking water on her floor. "I wanted to see if it should be planted, but then no one seemed to know what it was, so . . ."

I'm so nervous I think I might be in danger of talking too much. Which would be a first. In my lifetime.

"These are nice," I say, stopping beside her dark day plants beneath the window. And they are. They've opened into pale, shining blooms now that the moons have risen, making her sitting room smell like my mountain in the dark. I try another smile. Delia does not cooperate. I go to her table, set down my bowl of broken glass, and put the plant cutting beneath the hanging lamp. She hands me a cloth before she bends down, pushes back her loose hair, peering at the purple leaves. I wonder if she wants me to dry myself, or the floor. I opt for myself.

"Where did you say you got this?" Delia says.

I hadn't. "I found it growing in our garden during the sunlight," I lie. "One of my sisters pulled it, but I saved a cutting. I think a seed blew in."

"No," she says. "Not this. This will seed with fruit, I think."

Well done, Delia the Planter. I struggle to think of things to ask her. "Is it ready for dirt?"

"Hmm . . ." She's smelling it now.

"Mum!" The door from the workshop slams. "Dad wants . . ."

I straighten, lower the drying cloth from the back of my neck. Gray is standing stock-still in the doorway to the sitting room, unshaven, sweaty, and sooty, and whatever thought had been in his head seems to be long gone now. We stare at each other.

"I brought your mother a plant to look at," I say. "I was afraid of doing the wrong thing. I'm not afraid of that now."

"Well, it definitely won't like the inside," Delia says, oblivious. "You'll have to take it up to the roof."

"Yes," I say. I see Gray's eyes slide down to the necklace on my chest and back up again. "Not going up to the roof would be a mistake. That was a mistake."

"It was a mistake?" Gray asks.

"Yes," I say. And then, "Because I love . . . plants."

He blinks slow, eyes on mine. "You're sure about that?"

"Yes, I'm sure."

"I love them, too."

Delia stands up and puts her hands on her hips, scoots her book around to her back, out of the way. "Well, I don't know about that, but it sure is an interesting one. Let me just go get my magnifier . . ."

Gray moves to let his mother through the doorway. She's talking nonstop about the serration patterns of leaf edges, and as soon as her sandal hits the storeroom he's across the sitting room floor with my head in his hands, kissing me, hard. He tastes of metal and smoke. I run my hands over his chest, around his neck. Delia's voice edges toward the sitting room and Gray steps back, dropping onto the long bench at the table as his mother comes through the door. Her voice trails away when she sees us not where she left us. I think for a moment she forgot who I was. I drop my hand from my mouth, trying not to breathe too hard.

"Gray," she says slowly, "did you want something?"

"Go ahead with what you were saying, Mum," Gray replies, but he's looking at me. "I love plants. I really do." His voice is rough, a little hoarse. I wonder if it's the smoke, or me.

Delia snorts. "Since when?"

"Since sunsetting," he says to me. "When I was seven."

"You're a terrible liar," Delia comments, amused now.

"Yes," he agrees.

He's not so bad at the truth, either. It occurs to me that I've forgiven the glassblower's son just like everyone else does. I guess it can't be helped. And anyway, I think he's just forgiven me. I want Delia to go away again.

"Gray," she says, looking at the roots through a magnifier, "run out back and get me one of those pots of soil."

"Where is it?"

"What do you mean, 'where'? You know exactly where."

"I don't even know what you're talking about, Mum." I'm not sure he's taken his eyes off me.

"Oh, never mind. I'll go."

And as soon as the door clicks I'm back in his arms. "What . . . is happening here, Dyer's daughter?" he whispers between kisses. I can feel him smiling.

"I'm telling you . . . I'm sorry."

"Accepted. Are we stealing a book?"

"Yes." My lips are tingling. I think they might be bruised. "I need the key."

I lean back to look at him. What I had taken to be soot is actually a fading purple bruise at the corner of his mouth. "What happened to—"

We break apart at the sound of the latch. Delia comes back inside with the pot, and Nash, Gray's father, wanders in right after. Nash the Glassblower is evidently better informed than Delia the Planter, and quicker to note the piece of glass around my neck. He smiles and casually hands me another cloth, and I think he means it for drying off until Gray, smirking, holds up his sooty hands behind his mother's back. I try to surreptitiously wipe the soot off my face and neck while she digs around in the pot of dirt, and then I tell her she can keep the plant if she wants, which makes her happy. She offers me tea, Nash goes back to work, and I sit with Gray at the table. We have our heads together as soon as she leaves the room. Gray has one of my hands, while I run the other over the scratchiness along his jaw.

"What's happened to your face?" I whisper.

"What, this?" He lifts a finger to the purple corner of his mouth. "Eshan hit me. As predicted. Took him long enough."

"He hit you?" Like Genivee, my emphasis is on the last word.

"Funny thing. He didn't seem to like being hit first. He was having a bad day. Anson the Planter had just given him all the details about what would happen if he didn't leave you alone, and then I demonstrated, and he hit me back. End of story."

I don't know how I feel about this. Anson must think he knows now. I wonder if his wife does. Delia comes in with the tea and Gray holds my hand, mother or no. She gives me the tea, but I think she's sorry she offered.

I stay anyway, and Gray gives me the key of glass, while I slip him a bottle of sleeping tonic that was very recently on my storeroom shelf. We go over the details of our plan to steal the First Book. I tell him about my mother, about Anna, what I've realized about Janis. He has to go to her before resting, and I help him decide to tell her more about my job at the Archives, that I've been spending time reading my old books, looking for any information or heirlooms about the history of Canaan, like she asked before the festival. Anything that might keep her satisfied. And when no one is looking he kisses me again, like he can't help it. Like he doesn't want to stop.

The Forgetting is going to try to take this away from me. I know that. I thought I could protect myself from it. But I cannot. I don't even want to. Tomorrow we steal the First Book, and then there will be twenty-four days to find a way for Gray to remember me.

❧

But there's no stealing books of any sort the next waking. When I come flying up the steps of the Archives, I push down on the latch and nearly smash straight into the fernwood. The doors are locked. The Archives is closed. And so I climb the wall with Gray instead. This is a risk during the waking, and in the rain. But it's dark, hard to see in the downpour, and when I went to tell Gray the Archives was locked and suggested going back to the white room instead, he agreed without hesitation. We're running out of time, and I'm afraid shutting down the Archives right before a Forgetting has everything to do with Janis. And me.

We go fast down the ladder, so wet the last meter or so is more of a slide. Gray pauses to make sure his book is covered, and I offer to put it in my pack, freshly oiled before I left. He unbuckles the strap and puts it in, and then he carries the pack, still tethered to my belt. I wonder what Genivee would have to say about that, letting Gray carry my book. Twice. She'd had plenty to say about him during those days I wasn't talking. All her efforts gone to waste, and it was his fault, she was very sure about that.

But when she'd seen me waiting for her after I left Gray's the waking before, standing beneath the dripping eaves of the Learning Center, leaning against the sign that says "Learn Our Truth," she left her friends and came bounding up to me. No flowers in her hair during the dark days, just two big bunches of yellow and blue braided cloth.

"You're better," she'd said immediately. "What. Happened."

Well, Genivee, I talked to Janis, and I found out that she's like me, that she doesn't forget, and I think Mother might be going mad from remembering. I think our father knows who he is, too, by the way, and I went over the wall with Gray, and I kissed him, and he told me that everything that happened between us was a lie right before he said he loved me. Only it wasn't a lie, not all of it, and I love him, too. Oh, and the mountain beside my pool is full of machines and we don't even come from this planet.

Genivee had just stared at me, eyes large, waiting for my answer in the rain. But no matter how much I might talk in my head, I knew I'd never be Nadia of the sunlight again. I bent down and hugged her, which she accepted for about three seconds before wriggling away. Then I opened my hand, showing her a piece of glass, clear, but long and twisted, a thin spiral of never-ending swirls, a loop at one end. For hanging.

"Gray says that when the sun comes back and you hang this in the window, it will make colors appear all over the room."

"What has he done to you?" she'd said, picking up the glass from my palm. "Never mind. I don't want to know."

"But I want you to write down that he made it for you, and that I gave it to you, if you would. So you won't forget you're an amazing little sister."

"And I thought I was just really good at eyeliner" had been her only comment, staring at the glass. "What happens if I hold it in front of a lamp?"

I wish we'd brought a lamp now. The clouds and the rain are thick, blocking the glow of the moons, and any light from the glittering strands in the treetops is misted and wet. But we can't call attention to ourselves, and we can't linger. We've seen Janis out here before. We find the gorge down into the canyon and make our way around the pool in the dark, breath smoking in the chill, stopping in front of the dark cliff face.

"You know it?" Gray asks.

Of course I do. I've been saying the code to myself twice a day. I push in the numbers.

It's a relief to step into the cave opening, to squeeze out the end of my tunic. I don't know why we have to be wet every time we get here. Gray shakes some water from his hair as the door closes, the lights just beyond us popping into existence.

Inside the white room the squares glow blue and the wall says "Welcome." I take off my shoes, hating to track mud into the pristine white space, and Gray does the same, handing me my pack while I untie my tether. He goes to the small resting room, looking for anything to dry off with. The dial on the wall says we have two and a half bells before we need to make our way back to the ladder. Gray has to see Janis; I have to make sure Mother sees me in my bed. Gray brings two blankets from the resting room, which will do. I wrap up and sit in one of the spinning chairs, bringing up my feet, chin on my knees, the chair swinging gently side to side.

"What," I say, "does Janis want so badly in this room that she would go to these lengths to find that code? Or maybe the right question is, what is in this room that she doesn't want anyone else to discover?"

We both look at the light wall. There's information in there. I suspect more information than any book could hold.

"I'll look for Janis," Gray says. He's already standing in front of it, wrapped in a blanket, deciding where to start. I scoot my chair to one of the squares on the table, touch the blue light, hold my hand over it, but nothing happens. I run my fingers over the edges, looking for anything to push, but there's nothing.

"Moose," Gray says.

"What?" I look up and there is an image on the wall of something freakish. I think there might be legs, but that's about all I recognize. "I thought you were looking for Janis?"

"I was. I chose 'Curriculum,' thinking there might be a history of Canaan, for the Learning Center, but instead it's a history of Earth." He looks back at the bizarre image. "I think it's . . . alive."

"No, it isn't!"

"I'm just reading what it says." He touches the image and the thing starts walking, leaning down to eat vegetation, or I assume that's what it's doing. I feel my mouth drop.

He starts touching words at random. "Cat," "frog," "elephant," "snake," and "eagle," which flies like a moth, only much better. Some of it is beautiful, and some is so strange I can't make myself look at it. Then he touches "shark." A legless, armless thing, like the snake, only this is breathing water instead of air. We watch it attack another swimming creature, tear it to pieces. And consume it. I cover my mouth.

"They eat each other," Gray says.

That is too horrible to be believed. Except I just saw it. Then he sees a word we both recognize: "cricket." He touches it.

"That's not a suncricket," I say, though I can almost see the resemblance. It does hop like a suncricket, but it's much too big, and doesn't have facial expressions.

"So after the Forgetting . . ." Gray says, staring at the cricket in the light square. "I would say no one from Earth had names for the things here. They wouldn't have known them long enough to remember. So they just used the names already in their heads? Like 'cricket'?"

That makes sense. "Same with the plants, too, I would imagine . . ."

We haven't looked at plants, but I've already seen growing things in the other images that aren't familiar at all. Wrong shapes. Wrong colors. Then we both recoil. Gray accidentally touched "chicken" while hovering his hand over the list, and there is a woman, looking thankfully recognizable and human, and like the shark, she's eating the body of something called a chicken. I can just make out what must have been a leg. Gray is fascinated; I am disgusted. I consider never eating—or swimming—again. No wonder a hundred and fifty people wanted to leave Earth.

I go to the next blue light square, trying to make it do something, anything, until Gray says, "There."

I look up and a woman is smiling out from the light. Erin Atan. Dark hair, deep-set eyes. A chemist, and a dyer. "Look at her children," says Gray. The oldest is Janis. Below her information is the word "vlog," in a different color.

Gray touches the word, and I jump as Erin Atan suddenly begins talking to us. Weirdly, she's in the white room, almost in the same place I'm sitting. I look around, I can't help it, but she's not here. She's just an image on the wall, a piece of time that has been caught and kept. There are dates below her face, as if they're written on the image.

Year One, and Erin is smiling and happy. She has two children, one born on the ship, *Centauri*, one on Canaan, and her husband is a weaver. Year Two, Year Three, Four, Five, and Six, just a few minutes for each, describing a life in Canaan. She talks about growing food with her own hands, the satisfaction of discovering how to make what's needed, what your neighbor needs, as if these are things she's never experienced. She has three, four, and five children now, and she watches them grow without the prejudices of Earth. I wonder what this means.

But by Year Nine, there is a subtle shift in Erin's tone. By Year Ten, the difference is marked. She has seven children, and doesn't know how many more might come. The harvest was miscalculated. The roof garden doesn't supply enough. Her sleep patterns have never adjusted to the long periods of light and dark. The latrines were not properly dug out, and over-flowed in the rain, fouling the water supply. Her education is being wasted. Her children's intelligence is wasted.

"On Earth, they could be living like kings," she says. "Here, they plant fields and scrub the dye vats. We've found what NWSE wanted us to find. It's time to send the signal, call Earth, and claim our reward. Let Earth see what they think of their perfect society. This was never supposed to be forever. Not if we didn't want it to be."

"Call?" Gray asks.

I shake my head. The word is confusing, like "enter" was. Call Earth. Send a signal. What does that mean? Shout to them? Bring Earth here? And what did she mean, *we've found what they wanted*? I don't know what a "king" is, but Erin Atan, in Year Ten of Canaan, must have been just on the verge of forgetting those children she was talking about. It makes me sad.

"We were the best of the best," she goes on. "If the Council won't send the signal, then we'll have to do something about it."

The image ends there. Gray looks for the word "signal," but he can't find it. He sits in the other chair, leans back his head. "If you needed to talk to another planet, where in Canaan could you do that?"

It's a good question. And the answer is probably here. The only place with machines we don't understand. Or at least, the only place we know of. It's incredible to think that we could be sitting in a place where we could talk to Earth. It makes me feel that Earth is real. Then I think of what Erin said, and the broken, blasted rock in the cavern.

"Do you think Janis's mother, and whoever else, tried to get in here to send that signal, to talk to Earth? But couldn't because—"

"They couldn't get in. Because they didn't have the code?" Gray finishes. "It could be. Janis must remember something about your family, something that makes her think one of you has it. Maybe your family was on the opposite side. With the Council."

I think of Janis asking me about heirlooms and history.

"But why now?" Gray goes on, thinking aloud. "I don't know how many years have gone by, but it's a lot." We listen to the faint hum of lights, and then he spins the chair to face me. "We know she comes to the pool. Could she have seen you out here, do you think? Remembering whatever she does about your family? How often have you been on the mountain?"

"Dozens of times. I've never seen anyone else, but . . . I wasn't looking, either."

"Maybe she thought you already knew about the door. And the code. Maybe she thinks you come in here all the time."

"But why not do anything about it? Why not send Reese to yank me from my bed? Have Jonathan flog me for rule-breaking?"

"I don't know. But she plays games, Nadia. She was asking me about your memories. I told her I'd asked you, that you didn't remember anything, and I think I convinced her, but . . . she was asking. You can still get out your window?"

I nod. But we both know that neither one of us is safe. And none of this gets us any closer to understanding how to stop a whole city from forgetting who they are. To stop Gray from forgetting me. We have to get the First Book.

But the Archives stays closed. Three more times we go to the white room, watching the vlogs without learning anything much different than when we watched Erin Atan's. On our fourth trip we sneak down Jin's steps in the rain, soaked again, hurrying down Copernicus. I think we haven't been seen until someone calls my name, and I turn to see Gretchen, standing beneath the eaves of the locked Archives.

"I assume you still work for me, Nadia?"

She's referring to my disappearance before the Archives was closed. I nod. Gray stands still just behind me.

"Then be here as soon as you can after the leaving bell. We're opening up next waking."

I exchange a look with Gray, and I see that he agrees. Tomorrow we steal the book.

Mother smiled at me today. So I asked a question. Why do some doors have keys and some don't? Why do there have to be locks? Mother said some things should be kept safe. I thought it was because some things were bad to let out.

NADIA THE DYER'S DAUGHTER
BOOK 3, PAGE 59, 4 YEARS AFTER THE FORGETTING

CHAPTER SIXTEEN

The day of our book stealing, Karl finally has my new one ready. I have to dash back home in the downpour to tie it to my tether, to put the stolen book I've been carrying into my hiding hole so that I can switch the new book with my real one on the Archives shelves.

I'm hurrying back down the hall when I see Liliya coming out of her room. I've hardly seen Liliya since before the festival, and only now do I think that maybe she's been avoiding me as much as I've been avoiding her. She looks dazed. Wrong. She glances at me once, then turns around to go back where she came from.

"What's happened to you?" I say sharply.

"Go away, Nadia" is her reply. I follow her into her room. Liliya's room has always been like a cross between Genivee's and mine. Decorated, but organized. With lots of things, but all things in their place. It's not like that today. It's a mess. How long has she been like this? I think I know why. Now that I know about Janis and Gray, I think Liliya might be in the same situation with Jonathan of the Council. It certainly would explain his interest.

"Cut it off, Liliya."

"Leave me alone," she yells, tired.

"Don't see him anymore. Cut it off."

She hesitates, then picks up her blanket, like she's going back to bed. Cutting it off is probably not that easy.

I lower my voice. "If you need me to, I can hide you." This makes her pause, brings her head up. I'm not sure I could get Mother over the wall, but I think I could get Liliya there. "Say the word, and I'll do it."

She looks over her shoulder at me, and I see the fear I saw there once before. Then I watch her expression change. Her chin lifts, searching for some of her former swagger. "I hear the Archives is opening back up today. How's that work going for you?"

This is a jab, but it lacks Liliya's usual punch. I ignore it. "Just tell me if you need to disappear, and I'll make it happen."

❧

All this makes me late and I run to the Archives, stopping outside beneath the tiny bit of shelter created by the thatch to catch my breath. To get ready for what I'm about to do. I run up the steps and push open the door.

The waiting room is already full, packed wall to wall with damp people. I have to wait in line at the desk for Imogene to write me on her list, behind Frances the Doctor and the potter's wife. The potter's wife looks me over, gaze lingering, and Imogene does the same as she finishes writing in Frances, her eyes finding my necklace and staying there. I've worn my blue

tunic with the lower collar today, so the necklace is promi-
nent, but I didn't realize that people noticed me this much. That
Gray had practically posted a sign around my neck, just like
when he sat with me at Eshan's whatever. I suppose I should
know these things. I suppose he did. While Imogene writes me
down she says quietly, "I want to talk to you."

I don't reply. I'm lifting my arms for Reese's search. Reese
has gotten lazy with me. He hardly looks in my pack, which
now has a brand-new, unused book in it. But his search is
taking a little long.

"Really, Nadia," Imogene says beneath the noise of the
room. "During your break?" I still don't answer. "Okay?" she
insists.

I nod in answer, she gives Reese a look, and he lets me go.
I take off through the door to the anteroom and into the
stacks, find my rolling table, and, as expected, Gretchen is
right behind me, cranky.

"Nadia," she says, "please arrive as close to the leaving
bell as possible. Is that understood?"

Or what? I think. This close to the Forgetting, she's lucky
to have anyone show up at all, and we both know it. But I do
feel guilty for those days I didn't come, so I nod my apology.

"I may need your help in the front today, if we have to
start turning people away."

She cannot turn anyone away. Not today. I need Gray
inside. But I only smile, accepting Gretchen's words. She leaves
with her book at a quick clip, and as soon as the door squeaks
shut I take off at a trot to the back wall of the Archives, to the
N shelf, closest to the locked door. I open my mouth and take
the glass key off my tongue, gasping once before I shudder.

Gray's key may be pretty, but it tastes terrible. I slide it just beneath the end of the N shelf and hurry back to my spot, though not to do Gretchen's inventory.

I realized before my absence that the book Gretchen wears strapped to her middle is what she's using to find requested books by name, which is disappointing, because I'd wanted to search it for Anna the Planter's daughter. The book is so small, though, compared to the massive one I'm using, I think it must be in some kind of shorthand or code, and wouldn't do me good anyway. So I search the huge book on my rolling table instead, pushing the cart slowly down aisles I haven't paid the first bit of attention to. The hours until my break stretch long and slow. I don't find Anna's name.

When Gretchen finally gives me my break I step out of the Archives into the chilly rain. I heard Imogene getting up for her break as well, while I was searched, and when I come back from the latrines, she's waiting beneath the shelter of the thatch, next to the sign that reads "Remember Our Truth," rain making a curtain in front of her. I dart through the water to stand beside her, and Imogene says, "I need you to talk to my brother."

I look at the water running down into the gullies that drain beneath the walls. I don't want to talk to Eshan. Possibly ever again.

Imogene lowers her voice even further. "He'd been drinking, Nadia. And I think maybe . . . I think you misunderstood, okay? But this is something different." She glances once around us. "There's a rumor at the granary. Eshan says they've gone through the counting, and next distribution day, rations are going to be cut by a third."

I blink once. I can't believe that's true. Surely the harvest couldn't have been that bad? If it is, it's a disaster, especially for Imogene's family. Their rations are too low as it is.

"Eshan told me you've been bringing us extra. We owe you, but . . . he doesn't think it's been coming out of your stores. Or your garden." She shakes her head. "He thinks you've been going over the wall. I know it's crazy, but . . ."

I see Gray coming in the light of the streetlamps, his book covered, hair curling in the rain.

". . . and now Eshan's going to the Council, to try and get them to let him go over. He thinks it's safe, because you've been going, don't you see? Tell him you haven't been doing anything like that, Nadia. Tell him he misunderstood."

I think you were just telling me how I'd misunderstood him, Imogene. I sigh. Imogene doesn't want Eshan to go because she's afraid of the other side. As we've been taught to be. I'm not sure what I can do about that. Gray pauses when he sees me talking to Imogene, takes shelter beneath an eave, partially obscured by a column. He won't go inside the Archives until he's sure I'm in.

"Please," she's saying. "Talk him out of it. If things are really that bad they might let him go. He doesn't know what's out there, and it's too close to the Forgetting. What if he doesn't come back in time? I know he'll listen to you."

I've got to let Gray get inside. Finally I settle for, "I'll talk to him, Imogene. If I can." I feel guilty saying it, because she won't like what I have to say if I do. Eshan is right. If the harvest was bad, we should be foraging beyond the walls. As soon as we can.

Imogene breathes her relief. She sighs, stares at the sheet-ing rain. "Don't you ever just wish the Forgetting would go ahead and come already?" My expression must be incredulous, because she adds, "You know, a fresh life. A new start . . ." Then her gaze focuses again on my necklace. "So," she says, smiling, "that's glass, is it?"

"Girls!" Gretchen's head is out the Archives doors. "What's wrong with you today?"

We both scurry up the steps, and when I look back Gray is making his way toward the Archives, shaking the water from his hair.

The second half of the day seems longer than the first. I search the book for Anna. I wonder where Gray is in the wait-ing room. I can feel the presence of the glass key beneath the N shelf. When Gretchen finally comes to tell me I'm done, she looks tired, which is to say, the tiniest bit mussed. I tell her I'm going to finish my row, and I pretend to. Very slowly. The first step of our plan should have already happened. If it worked. If what Imogene told me about Deming is still true. All I have to do is be the last to leave. I wait, and the absence of sound is a roar in my ears.

When I decide I can't wait longer, I ease out the door into the anteroom. The door to Gretchen's workspace is open. I peek inside. Empty. I'm hoping she's gone, that she's left Deming to see us out the door, but no. Gretchen is outside, going over Imogene's list.

"There you are," she says when I appear. Imogene shrugs at me. Deming is standing in his usual position halfway down the hall to the reading rooms. Reese is gone, the waiting room empty. "Deming," Gretchen calls, "can you come take care of Nadia's search?"

He shambles over, glances in my pack, and while he's patting me down, he says, "Room Three." Just a whisper. It's the most I've ever heard him say. I hold in a smile.

Gretchen seems inclined to keep Imogene talking about her lists. Someone did not get signed out. I think for a moment it's Gray, who is apparently in Room Three, and a cool trickle of fear slides down through my chest. Deming was supposed to have taken care of that. But the someone left off the list is from earlier in the day. A mistake. Imogene apologizes. Deming can't search me any longer without being indecent. I bend down and fiddle with the tie of my sandal.

Gretchen says good resting and, to my disappointment, heads back into the anteroom, toward her workspace. Imogene snatches up her things and goes, eager to get out the door. She hesitates, to see if I'm coming, but I'm still fixing my sandal. She runs out into the rain, and when I look up Deming is staring fixedly at the glowworms moving in the lamps. I take off to Room Three, before Gretchen can come back. The door is heavy, the walls to the reading rooms built thick for privacy. I get the door shut without a noise, drop the bar, and turn around.

Gray is sitting on the floor instead of at the reading table, back against the wall, his book open in his lap. He's got that little smile on his face, just verging on a smirk. He holds out a hand, setting his book to one side. "Come here," he says.

I come, letting him pull me down to sit where his book had been. "What did you tell Deming?" I ask him.

"That I wanted a place to be with you where my mother wouldn't find out."

Oh. That's embarrassing.

"We got a lot of sympathy, actually. I think Deming has a bit of a soft spot for love. And moonshine. And anyway, have you ever seen Deming's mother?"

I have. "How much sleeping tonic did you put in the bottle?"

"All of it. He's big. I left enough moonshine for taste, it's so strong, but it's mostly tonic and water."

When I think about our plan being completely dependent on Deming tipping up enough of a laced bottle of moonshine to knock himself out, I have that cold sensation in my chest again.

"Don't worry yet, Dyer's daughter. How'd you get the key in?"

"My mouth."

He kisses it. "Good girl."

"Here," I whisper, swinging my pack off my shoulder. "I brought us something to eat while we wait." I climb off his lap before I crush him, and pull out a wrapped half loaf of bread and a corked bottle of ginger water. He's ridiculously happy about this, and I'm suddenly worried about what Imogene said. That we won't be getting full rations. I may need to go without my share of the bread for a few days to make up for it.

While Gray is eating and talking I pull the book I got from Karl's out of my bag, slip off a sandal and use it to start scuffing the cover. To take away the new. Gray's book is lying open right beside us. He doesn't seem to mind. I try not to glance at it. I wonder what he's written to help himself after the Forgetting. If we can't stop it. I've got everything I can think of written in our extra book. Just in case.

"So what did you tell Janis last resting?" I ask him, starting in on my share of the bread.

"How I've spent all my time romancing you, slowly gaining your trust."

"So the truth? Clever."

"Then I said how flattered you were that she spoke to you, and that you really did hope to do well enough to be on the Council someday."

"Oh. Lies, then."

"I might've left out forty or fifty other facts she would've been interested in, yes." His brows come down. "I could lie to her better if I understood what she wanted." We wonder about this, until Gray looks up, glances once toward the door. "I think it's time."

I get our things back into my pack, slide the straps over my shoulders. Gray holds out a hand, pulls me to my feet, and I approach the door. The latch turns. I listen and, very cautiously, stick my head out. The open hall outside the reading rooms is empty. Quiet. I hold up a hand for Gray to stay put, slip out the door and into the waiting room. And there is Deming. Laid out on a bench in the room's only dark corner like he's going to his funeral pyre. Except his chest is rising and falling. Gray's bottle is beside him on the floor. Almost empty.

I pick up the bottle, cork it, and put it in my pack, to give Deming just a little less trouble than he's going to get. Hopefully he'll wake up with something similar to a hangover, the knowledge that he got into a strong bottle of moonshine, and the sense to keep quiet about taking a bribe. I motion Gray out, holding a finger to my lips. We can't be certain Gretchen is gone. We go quick to the door behind Imogene's table and then I open it, slowly.

I can't hear anything, so we creep into the anteroom. Gretchen's workspace glows with its usual light. I walk silently to the door and get an eye around the edge. The room is empty. My shoulders relax just a little, and I hurry inside, pulling out the book I've scuffed. Gray waits with me, tense and arms crossed while I get out the blue paint and mark the new book with the numbers of Nadia the Planter's daughter. I'm careful to wipe down the brush, leave all on the desk as it was before, wave my book in the air to let the paint dry.

Then Gray follows me out of Gretchen's workspace to the door to the stacks. I open it fast, and as little as possible. It barely squeaks. We slide inside, and I shut it the same way, minimizing its noise. I hear Gray let out a long breath. It's overwhelming the first time you see it. All the lives of Canaan, compressed into one room. I thought the lights in here were brilliant until I saw the lights of the white room.

I hurry to the R shelf, Gray behind me, untie the newly painted book, and take my book from the shelf. I switch them, and tying my own book back in its rightful place is a physical relief. Gray is running a hand over the spines.

"How do you stand not looking?" he whispers. "Or have you looked?"

I shake my head. "I was tempted once. But it's awful to think of someone looking at your book when you don't want them to."

"You can look at mine. If you want." He throws that out very casually, as if it wouldn't come as a surprise to me. "Come on," he says. "Show me where the key is."

I lead him to the N shelf, reach underneath, feel around until my fingers find glass. And that's when the door to the stacks squeaks. I grab the key; Gray jerks me with him around the edge of the shelf. Footsteps click across the stone floor, a fast, efficient gait that echoes just a little. Gretchen. Gray presses me flat against the end of the shelf, just opposite the locked door. We are hidden from the other side of the room. But if Gretchen comes down an aisle, if she comes all the way to the end of any of the shelf rows, there will be nowhere to hide.

I listen to the footsteps, clicking, clicking. It sounds like she's coming up the N aisle, the one we were just in. Gray has a hand against my mouth, as though I might speak, and I breathe against his fingers, letting the air out slow. The footsteps stop. I hear rustling. Movement. The dull thud of something heavy on the shelf. Did Gretchen just take a book? Or replace one? The footsteps move away again, the fast clip down the aisle. The door squeaks.

We don't speak. We just hurry. Straight to the locked door. I hand Gray the key, and he goes to his knees, putting his eyes on level with the keyhole. My body is tense, straining for the sound of the other door. What is Gretchen doing here? Is she sleeping here? She must have been in one of the other reading rooms, just a few steps away that whole time. Gray puts in the key, moves it about gently, feeling to see how it fits. If he turns it too hard, if he snaps the key, then all this is for nothing and we start again. And we don't have enough time before the Forgetting to start again. He tries a turn, very gently, stops, and adjusts it, his brows down in concentration. He does this twice more, tries a turn, and then, like a miracle, the lock clicks.

I watch a grin spread across Gray's face. I think he's as surprised as I am. The door swings open on silent hinges. Gray takes out the key; we step inside and let the lock click shut. Then I turn around.

We are in an old room, another huge circle, in a style I now know is from Earth's machines. One or two hanging glowworm lamps make a dim, shadowy kind of light across a large, open space, broken by columns creating a smaller inner circle, and rising up the full height of the back wall is an enormous plaque that reads "Without Memories, They Are Nothing." The floor is alternating blue and white squares, stone arches formed like interweaving vines fly up and out between the columns, holding up a roof that is half a sphere.

I tilt back my head, looking up inside that sphere, and I think there could be glass up there, in the ceiling, but the thatch has covered it over. Why would anyone build the Archives over this room? Is it forgotten, or deliberately hidden? I wonder if Rose or Jin ever saw this. The air is stale, stuffy, a little like the smell of underground, and at the back, there is a long, semicircular bookshelf, maybe half my height, curving with the shape of the outer wall, just below the plaque.

"Did they mean for it to be a meeting hall?" Gray says. "Is it where the first Council met?"

I don't know the answer. Gray's voice was barely a whisper, but the room has an echo. The walls seem thick, but I don't know what Gretchen can hear. What is Gretchen doing in the stacks, anyway? Then I remember it was Gretchen's book missing from the shelves, on my first day, and Gretchen that I heard Jonathan threaten when I was on the wall. I wonder if Janis is reading our books, and if Gretchen knows it. I start toward the bookshelves in the back of the room, and then I pause. A single book has been set on top of the shelves, a little askew, in the very center. As if it was just tossed down.

I move straight to it, like a dustmoth to a lamp. It's unassuming for a book, medium-size, the cover faded and a little torn. It could be the one Janis was reading from, but I can't be sure. As soon as Gray is beside me I open it.

The inside cover has two small words in the upper right corner: *Erin Atan.* We look at each other. That was Janis's mother. The name isn't written in ink, but in a soft, faded gray. I turn the page carefully, and there are numbers, equations, things I don't understand. Just jottings, for three or four pages. Then we read:

Something is wrong with us. With everyone. Those who are willing have stopped hiding and fighting and we are living together under one roof for now, to find food, to try and find some sense. The clock in the center of the city says we are in Canaan. There are dead people in the streets. We go out in groups to drag them to the fields, where the fires burn around the bells . . .

"So this is after the first Forgetting," I say. "And the clock was already there." And it sounds like it went badly.

There is a girl here who says she thinks she is my daughter. She might be . . .

And I'm willing to bet this daughter she mentions is Janis. I know how Janis felt at this moment, being the only one to remember.

There has been so much violence, and we don't know who's done it. One group is taking the stone from a ruined building, filling in the gates, for protection . . .

"Gates," Gray says. We weren't always inside the walls.

We go on reading, about how the people chose names for themselves, trying to determine which women had given birth, dividing up the children based on looks—I know I wouldn't have been given to my mother based on appearance—searching the city for information, supplies. Erin talks about the eerie strangeness of realizing just how much she knew about plants, particularly the ones that could be used for medicines and dyes.

I glance once over my shoulder, nervous about the door, and Gretchen walking in and out of the stacks. I flip quicker through the pages, getting an overview. Gray stops my page turning, his finger on a sentence: *We are made of our memories.* The whole entry describes the confusion of waking up, the marking of a family, a book tied to a wrist.

"The second Forgetting," he says.

And after that come all the words we learn in school, the same words read twice every year at the beginning of the dark days. How the Forgetting will come, how we will write truth, and *I am made of my memories.* A slightly different wording than in the entry before, but the handwriting here is different, too. And it stays different, for the rest of the book. At the end of the book are lists. Name after name. Then blank pages.

I run a hand over the last page, over paper that is starting to crackle. So this is the First Book of the Forgetting. I hadn't been positive until I read the words Janis spoke at the festival. If the first part was written by Janis's mother, is the other handwriting by Janis herself? Did she write those things we're supposed to recite? Gray thinks so, and it wouldn't surprise me.

I go back to the page with *I am made of my memories*, where she's describing the second Forgetting, and turn to the entry just before it.

> *Janis says it is coming. That we have to write down our lives, prepare. Sarah and Jorgan don't believe her, but I think I do. Janis is gifted. She sees patterns we don't . . .*

Gray shakes his head. "Because she remembers. That's why she sees. She wasn't telling them even then."

> *We have locked ourselves in, and it is sunrising. The light is so white, too bright to—*

The entry stops there. The comet, I think. That too-bright sky. This also means Janis had worked out the Forgetting was coming before the second time. Members of the Canaan Project had specialized in studying the comet; Janis would have remembered that it came every twelve years. What it does prove is that Janis, at least at this point, believed the comet and the Forgetting are connected. I think I agree. What does she do to shield herself from it? What did I do?

I start turning pages, careful but quick. The next section is all the rules and regulations of Canaan. How we're to be tested, how to write down an understanding, how to cross it out, how to write down a child's parentage. How we restart our city every twelve years. All the things I know. And then I come to the lists.

The first is large, numbered one through one hundred and fifty. Name after name, both the first name and the trade name, but almost every one of them has been crossed out, replaced with another name written to one side. Sometimes that second name is also crossed out, also replaced with another. It's difficult to read; the inks are all different, some of the names cramped to fit in the space.

There are five more lists after that, much shorter. More random. I stop on the third one, look up to where Gray has been motionless beside me, reading from over my shoulder. I say, "Your name is here."

He stares at the page. There are fifteen or sixteen names besides his. "Think," he whispers. "Do you recognize any names on this from before the last Forgetting? Anything familiar at all?"

It's not easy, with no context. Then, "Yes," I say slowly. I show him *Gregory, Teacher.* "He was our teacher in the Learning Center, the first year we went, the year before the Forgetting. I can remember having trouble saying his name . . ."

Gray looks at me. "You remember me at school, from before? What was I like?"

"A mess." I smile at him. "The man spent half his time with you, just trying to get you to sit still. He liked you, though." Everyone always has. "He made up extra games for you to play . . ." Now that I think back on it, Gray was just too quick for the rest of us. When we were half finished, he was ready to move on. I wonder what happened to Gregory the Teacher. I don't think I've ever seen him since.

Gray has gone serious again. "Now tell me, do you recognize any of those names from now, other than mine?"

I don't. Not one.

"Then I'll tell you what I think this is," Gray says. His voice is angry, surprising me with an echo. "A list of the Lost. The ones Janis decided would be Lost."

I stare at the names. Why Gray? At six years old? Why any of them? Gray reaches over my shoulder and turns the page to the last list. There are only a few names on this one, but the first one is *Sasha, Clothesmaker's daughter.* That is Jemma's little girl, who is blind. At the bottom are *Renata, Dyer,* and *Eshan, Inkmaker's son.*

I let the information sink into my mind like ink into the paper. Janis thinks she's going to make my mother Lost. And little Sasha, and Eshan, of all people. I don't understand. There's no reasoning, no logic for any of it. For anything. And then I think Jonathan of the Council must know about this, that he's been trying to warn Liliya about Mother for some time. But I will not let this happen.

I go back and look at the first list, the one of a hundred and fifty names, almost all of them crossed out. One of the crossed-out names is Erin Atan. I breathe loud in the shadowy silence, eyes scanning all the names, trying to categorize, to understand what they mean.

"Gray," I say slowly, "these names that are crossed out. I think all of these people are dead." It's the names that are not crossed out that I know. The ones that are alive. "If the other lists are for the Lost, I think this is a list . . ."

"Of the dead," Gray says, voice bitter. "Or do you mean the people she's going to make dead?"

That can't be true. Except that maybe it could be. And there, near the bottom of the list, not yet crossed out, is my name.

Janis came to our class today and watched us take our tests. The teacher was nervous, I could tell because she looked sweaty when it wasn't hot. Janis wrote down notes and picked out some of us to answer questions, and she liked it when we answered right.

I knew all the answers, and I was really glad not to be chosen.

NADIA THE DYER'S DAUGHTER
BOOK 3, PAGE 34, 2 YEARS AFTER THE FORGETTING

CHAPTER SEVENTEEN

y name. And there is Rose's name, too, also not crossed
out, but with a line drawn in front of it, connecting it to
the name before, Zuri Adeyemi. I flip the pages back.
Zuri Adeyemi appears on the first list of what I think are the
people that will be Lost. "I think this is Rose," I tell Gray,
pointing at the name. He puts his hand on my shoulder.

"Let's take the First Book to the white room," he whispers. "See if we can compare these lists with the original
names. We have to know what those lists mean. And it's too
dangerous to stay for long."

I nod my agreement, try to think. We have to leave while
Deming is asleep, but if Gretchen is still in the Archives, that's
a complication. A huge one. I wonder when she's going to
notice that her watching Council member is out cold. I wonder
how long it will take for someone to realize the First Book is
missing. I wonder how the two of us can fight both Janis and
the Forgetting at the same time.

"We should look at the rest of these books first," I say.
"Just so we know what they are."

Gray eyes the long bookshelf, then says, "I'll take the other end."

I slide the First Book into my pack. This feels impossible, and it makes me angry. Janis hides behind the Forgetting like a coward. Doing what she wants when it won't be remembered. But I can remember, too. There has to be a way to change this. To stop it. All of it.

I squat down in front of the shelves, glance over the spines. They're different sizes, different colors, different amounts of wear. No code or order. I take one off the shelf and look at it. The front says *Roland, Weaver*. I feel guilty, but I look through it. Notes on the size of the flax harvest and how much cloth we're likely to get out of it, descriptions of Council meetings. The book beside it on the shelf is also Roland, and beside that is *Johann, Teacher*, also Council.

So all of them seem to belong to Council, like I'd thought. And suddenly I'm having that itch of curiosity again. Anson is on the Council. He would have books in here, too, under the name Anson or Raynor, I'm not sure which. Maybe both. And now I'm having to physically resist rifling through this entire shelf to search for them. Maybe I'll pull one off accidentally. No one could blame me for looking then.

"Nadia." Gray is near the far end of the shelf, cross-legged on the colored stone. He beckons me over. "This is a grower, Mia. She's describing her job for herself, for the Forgetting, but look. It says here we used to vote. Once a year. Everyone who'd finished their apprenticeship could say who they thought should be on the Council." I reach over and touch the open page in Gray's lap. It's starting to yellow.

"Can you tell which Forgetting she's talking about?"

He shakes his head. Dates tend to get so mixed up in Canaan, the city basically works in twelve-year increments. Another thing the Council could fix, if they would only think to. It's just so easy to accept that this is the way life has always been, when you can't remember how anything has ever been before.

"Nadia," Gray says again. His voice has changed. He looks up at me, and I look down, to where his finger sits on a name in ink: *Anna*.

> *Today they found Anna, Raynor's daughter, in the oil plants in the west quadrant field. The doctor said she died of poison, and that she must have done it deliberately, that it would have been impossible to consume so much by accident. She was fifteen. Renata is devastated. I can't understand it.*

And that's all. I read it again and I am numb. I've never known anyone to deliberately hurt themselves. Except for my mother. And now my sister.

"Nadia," Gray says.

It might be the third time he's said it. I need to walk. I want to run. I get to my feet, move across the shadowy blue-and-white floor, lean for a moment against half of a stone column, sticking out from the wall as if a massive fern trunk had been embedded inside it. The coolness soaks through my leggings. I had another sister. She ate poison, and I can't even recall her face. Of all the memories swirling in my head, images I'd do anything to purge, this is the one that has to be gone. Why would she do it? Why is any of this happening?

I run my hand over the stone, like I always do. Crisp. Unworn. Unsurprising. We have to hurry. To figure out how to get out of the Archives. To go to the white room. To be back by the first bell of the resting so Mother can check my bed. So she won't see one of her children missing. Mother. For the first time I wonder if it might be kinder to let her keep on forgetting.

I put my hands on my knees, fighting the shaking, though not because of fear this time, or panic. What I'm feeling is fury. At this sister my old book said I loved, who destroyed my mother, and probably Anson, too, if he could remember. At Janis, who could help us and doesn't, who makes us Lost, maybe even kills us. At the Forgetting I don't know how to stop. At the thing that is sticking hard into my back. I straighten up and look behind me, and when I turn I find Gray standing a few feet away, watching. He's returned the books to the shelves, a thumb hooked in his strap.

"Gray," I say. "There's a door latch in this column."

He comes and stands next to me, looks at the door latch. And then, like in the alley at the festival, he puts a hand on the back of my neck, just below my pinned braids. I put my forehead on his chest, let him hold me in place for one, two, three, four breaths. Longer. He lets me go when I'm ready. Calmer. I breathe one more time, and when he gives me a nod, I push down on the latch.

The door opens easily, without noise, a curved piece of column swinging outward. Inside there are stairs going down, not white stone but rough-cut and gray, straight into darkness. I smell earth, and damp rock, like when we opened the door in the mountain.

"Cave," I whisper.

I take the first step downward, going slow, hanging on to the rough rocks that bulge out from the walls. Gray shuts the door behind us, and because he's Gray, I don't even ask if he's checked for a latch. For a minute I think I'm in complete darkness, but then as my eyes adjust, I catch the glow of dim light below. The steps are man-made and curving slightly, and the more steps I take and the more they curve, the more light I see. I hear the rush of water, and then the passage widens and we are walking down a slope of bare rock instead of stairs.

Something brushes across my face and we step out into a cavern, not of gray rock but of purple and blue, green and white, a wild array of colors illuminated by glowworm lights hanging every now and again from brackets driven into the rock. Then I realize it isn't the rock that's colorful. The cavern walls are covered in plants, waving in the moving air, and when I look back I see they're nearly covering the passage I just came out of. An underground river rushes loud beneath us, the rock and dirt below our feet sloping down to its level, and I think the water must be a bit warm because the air is humid, dripping.

Gray goes ahead of me, like he did the first time we went over the wall, but he's slower here, thankfully, because of the slippery rock. I follow him down, along the trail of lights, the rock matted with blowing tendrils. Gray's shoulder brushes one and the tendrils pulse, reaching out, a ripple effect that goes all the way up the wall, like a drop of water in a still bath, only vertical. We both stare at the wall, back a little away from it. There's not a breeze down here at all; the plants are moving on their own, waving their tendrils, pulling food, moisture, I don't know what out of the air. It's more than unsettling. It's creepy. Gray waits for me, brushing blue dust from the shoulder of his black shirt, that small smile on his face.

"We're following this?" He nods at the continuing lights, making a path into the ongoing dark. As if he had to ask.

"Let's be careful, then, and quiet. If there are lights, someone must use this way regularly."

He takes my hand in his and we go soft and quick beside the underground river. The plants on the rock walls grow thinner, until there's just one or two left, scattered like the last flowers of sunlight. Then the path splits, one set of lights following the river, another branching off to our left. Gray looks to me, and I look to the ceiling. I think we've been following almost a straight line through the city, but it's hard to tell.

"Left," I whisper.

We leave the water behind and the way becomes more rugged, with more tumbled rock to scramble around. But the lights go on, and eventually I can see a different kind of light. Diffused silver. The passage ends and all at once we are on a cliff, a little valley below us. The rain has slowed, the clouds thinned to show the luminescence of the moons. I look up and back, and there is the white stone of Canaan, rising high above, my mountain a black, glittering shape to our left.

We didn't have to go over the walls. We just went under them.

Gray shakes his head. Laughs.

"What?" I say.

"All that sneaking around. I made a key out of glass, drugged Deming; we nearly got caught. When all we had to do was follow the walls the way Janis showed us when she left the pool. It's not even locked. She thinks there's no threat out here."

I let this fact settle in my head. We don't have to get past Gretchen. We can get into that room in the Archives anytime we like. "Where do you think the river passage goes?"

"The Council House," Gray says immediately. "You can write that down, I think. It's the right direction." He looks around our cave opening, gets his bearings, tilts his head at the mountain. "Coming?"

I follow him up a narrow path, tracing the curve of the city wall above us until we reach the level of the grasslands and hike up the slope. Into the canyon and around to the hidden door, and when the lights blaze to life in the white room, I kick off my sandals and sit in the spinning chair, silent. Thinking. I want to know what happened to Anna. I want to know why Gray was Lost, why my name is on that list. I say, "Let's look up Zuri Adeyemi."

Gray hesitates. He knows I'm not all right. He probably isn't completely all right, either. But he goes to the light wall, hovers his hand, pulls up the list of people, and touches "Zuri Adeyemi." And there is Rose.

I go stand with Gray, in front of the enormous image of Rose's face. She was so young it seems impossible, like Jin. And Gray was right. She was a doctor, both before and after coming to Canaan. Gray touches "vlog" and then Rose is sitting right here in the white room. We start with Year 1 and watch her age year by year, five minutes at a time. Her voice was not soft then. She was a force. But it's Year Ten that's eye-opening, like it was for Erin Atan. Rose, called Zuri, is Head of Council, and her face is grim.

"It has come to the attention of the Council that when New World Space Exploration created and invested in the Canaan Project, they gave not one directive for this program, but two. The first directive was to build a human civilization capable of living in harmony with itself and its environment. We were to learn, build, and populate without damaging a virgin planet. This is what we agreed to. This has been our dream, and we have spent our blood, sweat, and tears to do it. But there was a second directive from New World Space Exploration, known only to a few, and directly opposed to the first. Some of us were sent to Canaan to explore its resources, to create ways to exploit them and open Canaan for trade. And they have found their resource. Metallic hydrogen is the deep bone of this planet, and to our knowledge has been found nowhere else in the universe.

"Those with this second directive have tried to send an arranged signal back to Earth, to call the ships and begin mining and exporting Canaan's metallic hydrogen. However, the destructive mining of the moons and other planets within Earth's own solar system is a disaster that must not be repeated on Canaan. This is our home now. The people have voted, and while I am Head of Council, Earth will not be signaled. We have asked those given this second directive by NWSE to adhere to their original agreements, to help us move forward by living on this planet and leaving it as it is."

We pause, and then Gray leaves Rose where she is, searching quickly for the word "mining." He finds it under "Earth Curriculum," and I see images of mountains stripped bare of their plants, flattened into wastelands of powdered rock, water silted and undrinkable. I can't imagine letting that happen to my mountain. And I can't understand why anyone would want it to, until Gray touches the word "profit," and then the word "money." Money, we see, is like a symbol, a representation of something you want. Sometimes it's just a number on a paper, but the more of it you have, the higher your numbers, then the more things you can have that you want. Metallic hydrogen, it seems, is one of the things that will bring people a lot of money, and a lot of what they want. It seems like everyone on Earth is trying to have more, even if they don't need it. I don't understand this, either.

"I do," Gray says, surprising me. "It gives you something to go after, to stretch yourself for. What can you do in Canaan but be good at your trade or be on the Council? There's nothing out there to go and get."

I watch him hovering his hand, finding the next image of Rose on the light wall, and wonder if this is one of the real reasons Gray wanted to go over the wall.

He touches the next image, and we both lean forward. This vlog is different. Rose—I can't think of her as Zuri—is again in the white room, but this is obviously unplanned. She's panting, her hair down, dust streaking her face.

"A record," she says, "if we do not live. Canaan is at war, between those who wish to mine this planet and those who wish to preserve it. We've sealed the bunker with the tech; they cannot get to the signal . . ."

The bunker, I think. That's what we're standing in now. With "tech." Is that what they call the machines?

"They've taken the granary, threatening to starve the city unless we open the bunker. We'll starve anyway if we can't get the crops in the field. They're taking Canaan street by—"

There's a deafening noise from the light square on the wall, a deep, sudden boom. Gray flinches beside me, and the image of Rose goes misty, then black, before coming back again. She's steadying herself, I think, with the chair I was just sitting in. Other people are in the room, running and shouting behind her, one man with a bloody head. Rose is shouting, too, the sound distorted, then she turns to look directly at us.

"They've blown up the side of the mountain, trying to get in the bunker. One side of the cavern has fallen in. The entrance is blocked."

The rockfall.

"We have three"—someone shouts at Rose—"no, four dead. There is only one way in or out now, and Sergei Dorokov has just changed the code . . ."

"Wait," I say. "How do you go back?"

Gray moves his finger along the bar that appears below Rose's image. Time runs backward, and she says the words again: ". . . and Sergei Dorokov has just changed the code . . ."

"Stop!" I say. Gray does, and I walk closer to the wall, peer at the image. Rose is frozen in the act of turning to look at a man crossing the room behind her. Gray spreads his fingers and it's like using a magnifier, or leaning forward in a chair. The image focuses to only one thing: the man's wrist, where I can just make out the links of a metal bracelet. I pick up the metal bracelet from the perfect, curving white table, hold it tight in my hand.

Gray makes the image return to its size, but it ends abruptly, then starts a new one. Rose is back. She looks very tired. She has blood smeared on her shirt. I think she's been tending injuries.

She whispers, "Something is happening to the city. We turned the cameras to the comet, but when we turned them back . . ." She spins whatever is capturing her image toward the three large light squares high up on the wall, the ones that right now look as if they have tiny flies crawling across them. In Rose's time, those squares show images of Canaan, moving images, like what we're watching now, a light square within a light square. I see Meridian Street beneath that horrible bright sky, the water clock and the amphitheater surrounded by free-burning fires. I think the granary is in flames. And there are people fighting. One person swings what I think is a board and hits another in the head, dropping him like a heavy sack.

"They're all either running or fighting," Rose whispers. "There are no sides. Children are just wandering . . . It's like everyone out there has lost their mind. I sent Ross out to forage and he hasn't come back. I don't know what to do . . ."

"It's the Forgetting," I say. Gray is peering at the screen, trying to see what Rose did, but she's spinning our point of vision back to herself.

"We can't last long in here. We're out of food." She winces visibly at something she sees in the city. "I think," she whispers, "that we can officially declare the Canaan Project a failure."

Gray stops the image. "That doesn't make any sense."

"What doesn't?"

"That the city is forgetting, and Rose isn't. And we both know she forgot. Everyone in this room must have. But not while they were in it." He looks around us. "What's different about this room?"

I turn, look at the white walls, the spotless table, the impossible images of light. Absolutely everything is different about this room. But then I know, and the answer came easy. I'd already thought of it before. "The air," I say. "It's blown in, filtered. There's no dirt in here, no dust. Whatever is keeping out the dirt is also keeping out the Forgetting."

"So when they went outside . . ."

"It happened. And this room was gone. At least in their minds."

"Except for the code, scratched into the bracelet on that man's wrist."

I hover my hand, go back to the list of people, and find Dorokov, Sergei. I can see bits of my mother in him, not exact, but there. I touch the image, distorting it like I've put my finger on a reflection in the water. This must be my grandfather, it's hard to say how far back, a chosen one from Earth. An astronomer and a teacher, from a place called Russia. A place he forgot. Or did he? Me, my mother, Liliya—the whole family seems to have a habit of not forgetting. Or not completely.

I think of that page in the First Book, written by Erin Atan, who seems to have been on a different side of this war from Rose. *Dead people in the streets,* she'd written. From the Forgetting, or the fighting that came before it? Or maybe both.

"Tell me what you saw," Gray says. He's looking at the three lit squares, high on the wall, where Rose watched the city forgetting.

I close my eyes. I know what he wants, and I don't want to tell him.

"Nadia," he says, very quiet. "I need to know what we're facing."

Whether the Forgetting is from the comet or if it's in the air, either way, we can't stop it. And Gray is right. He needs to know what happens, because he has to live through it. He can forget me all he wants, but he has to live. I leave my eyes closed, and for once I don't push the images away.

"It's because they know it's coming," I whisper. "They know that everything they are is about to disappear. That everyone who loves them won't remember they love them, and that they won't remember that love, either. It's like the end. Like death.

"So some lock themselves in with their families. Others . . . it's more like the festival, only . . . twisted. It's almost like they . . . celebrate. Do whatever they want. Whatever they've been denied. I heard screaming, and there were people . . . and they were laughing at the one who screamed. I saw two men breaking windows, taking bread and stores through the missing glass, and a girl being dragged out of her house. She was bloody, and she didn't have her book, and there were buildings on fire. I saw . . . a woman . . . laying a baby in the street . . ." I'm shaking, but only a little. Gray has pulled my face into his chest, his hand on the back of my neck, like before. Like a tether to the present. ". . . it was still in its blankets, and there was a row of three children, and later, when I remembered, I knew . . . they were dead, and I don't understand why—"

"Enough," Gray says. "That's enough."

I can hear his voice in his chest. And I can feel that he's angry. Angry because of my words and, I think, because we can't do anything about it.

"It didn't exactly turn out like they'd planned, did it?" he says. "Their new civilization . . ."

I think of the hope I saw on the faces in those images, Janis's smiling little-girl face. Gray's grip on me tightens.

"So we come in here. When it's time for the Forgetting. We bring food and we stay until it's over."

I lean back to look at him. "And when is it safe to come out? We can't stay in here forever."

He closes his eyes. Doesn't answer.

"And what about your parents? What about my—"

"Listen to me." He opens his eyes, and he is intent, so still he might explode. "You listen to me. I do not want to forget you. Do you understand?"

All this time I've been fearing the moment that Gray would forget me. What I hadn't realized was how much he was fearing it, too.

"Then don't forget me," I say.

His mouth is on mine before I know what's happened, like he's trying to imprint the memory of it there. My hands find his stomach, the skin of his back, and then I am undoing his bookstrap and he is untying my tether and kicking my pack away across the floor, pulling me to him until we stagger through a door and my back hits the mattress. I am pinned, pressed, covered, and he is wild and beautiful and I twist my hands into his hair so he can't get away. I want time to stop, to freeze like an image on the wall. His lips brush my shoulder, my collarbone.

"Gray," I breathe.

He kisses my mouth again, stopping my words.

"Gray," I say again.

He doesn't loosen his hold, but this time his forehead drops to the mattress beside my head. "I know," he whispers. "I know." He breathes in and out, our bodies tight together. He sighs again. "I don't even like babies."

It takes a beat before I laugh. Leave it to the glassblower's son to make me laugh at a moment like this. He laughs, too, against my neck while I stroke his hair. "You're terrible," I tell him, which is to say, wonderful. He rolls to the side and I roll with him, propping up my head on a hand. His hair is tangled, eyelashes a smear of dark brown like the stubble on his chin, and I wonder how he can exist. Our time is so short. He runs a hand down the curve of my side.

"Write me down," he says. He's not looking at my face, he's looking at his exploring hand. "Write me down," he says again. "So that when I forget, I can see it."

I roll away, get up from the mattress, and leave the little resting room. I sit next to my half-open pack on the floor, get out my book and my pen and ink. On the next blank page I write the sentence "I choose Gray, Glassblower's son."

While my pen is scratching I hear Gray coming, feel him sit against my back, watching me finish. He picks up his own book from the floor and opens it, flipping to find his page, sets it in my lap. It says "I choose Nadia, Dyer's daughter."

"When did you write that?"

"After you came to my house and told me you loved plants." He puts his arms around me, chin on my shoulder. I lift his right arm, lay my head on the scars from the last Forgetting.

"If you forget me," I say, "then I will remember for us. Okay?"

I hear him breathe long in the quiet. "Okay."

❦

I leave the bracelet on the table and put the First Book back in my pack. I want to study that list of one hundred and fifty. The book would be safer here, but it's occurred to me that's the same number as the original "best of the best" chosen for Canaan, maybe even seventy-five men, seventy-five women. And I can always put it in my hiding hole. I wish I had a hiding hole big enough for Mother. If I could get Mother into the

Archives, I could maybe get her out and under the wall, and I'm not sure Genivee doesn't need to come, too. With the history of our family, it's possible that Genivee might not forget, and if that's so, I don't want her anywhere near the city before the Forgetting. I'm talking to Liliya about it as soon as I get home.

Gray straps on his book, and we walk hand in hand down the rock passage, quiet. He has chosen me. I have chosen him. I never thought I would choose. I never thought I would be chosen. And when he forgets me, if he forgets me, I just have to make sure he chooses me again.

We stand for a few seconds in front of the door. Gray kisses my held hand before he presses down on the glowing red glass. The door whirs, clanks, and I hear the rain, a soft constant swish melding with the roar of the waterfall, the smell of dark day flowers spicy in the air. I follow Gray through the door into the cave opening, feel him freeze before I realize what's wrong.

There, just in front of the clump of young ferns, sitting quietly on a rock in the rain, is Janis.

"Children," she says. "What have you been up to?"

No one could take as many risks as I do and never be caught. I know this. But when my day comes, I will never say I'm sorry. Because I have been taught to say the truth in Canaan.

NADIA THE DYER'S DAUGHTER
BOOK 15, PAGE 54, 1 SEASON UNTIL THE FORGETTING

CHAPTER EIGHTEEN

Gray steps just a little in front of me. I'm still holding his hand, the open doorway behind me, the two of us filling the small space between it and Janis. She is not going through that door.

Janis shakes her head. "Nothing to say?" She sighs and gets up from her perch, straightening out her wet robes. The door behind us begins to shut on its own.

Janis makes a dash toward the door, surprisingly fast, and Gray blocks her. I push her when she tries to get around him, and Gray holds out his other arm. By that time the door is shut and the mountain is locked. I smile.

Janis drops her hands. Looks at Gray. "Open the door."

"No."

She looks to me. "And you say the same, I assume."

I nod.

"Very well. Come with me, then."

She turns, stepping spryly through the rocks and rain. Like we're going to follow her. I glance at Gray, and he hasn't moved. His eyes are narrowed, jaw set. Angry. Janis looks over her shoulder.

"Come. I have guests waiting for you. You need to tell me what to do with them." She looks back and forth between the two of us. "Delia and Genivee."

Gray holds my hand, immobile. I look back into Janis's pitch-dark eyes.

"Or do I need to decide what to do with them?" she asks. "I do have thoughts."

And that's it. We come. Janis puts up her hood, to keep out the rain. We are so much faster than her, so much stronger than her, but two names, and she holds us in her hands. My stomach is tensed to the point of pain. Genivee. What would she do to Genivee to make me give her that code? Maybe anything. We all have to get out of the city—Gray's family, too. Run right over the mountain into whatever is beyond. What we do is follow Janis through the rain. How was today my day to be caught? Right now? I'd thought my time would come at the ladder, or in the Archives.

At the cave entrance below the walls, Janis flips back her hood, showing her elegant twist of pure white hair. I stop, pull Gray to a stop beside me.

"I'm not going any farther unless you agree to let Genivee and Delia go when we get there."

Janis slows, turns to eye me. "Are you familiar with the concept of leverage, Nadia? Genivee is only required to make sure that you and I have a conversation. Nothing more. Once you arrive, of course she will no longer be needed. And the same for Delia," she adds, glancing at Gray. Gray's hand tightens on mine, and we exchange a look. As soon as we see my sister, as soon as we see his mother, we have to grab them, and we have to get over the wall. No waiting for conversations. Gray nods just slightly, and we are in agreement. What we'll do after the Forgetting I can't imagine. We step into the cave.

Janis knows her path, moves much more easily among the rocks than we did earlier. At the river passage she turns left, away from the Archives, as I thought she might, and we walk a long way in the blue-white glow of the lamps. There are no plants on the walls here, and though this is a natural passage, I think the way has been cleared somewhat, chiseled and smoothed for travel. The last glowworm light ends at another set of steps, these also carved from the rock, and at the top of them is a door, sparkling metal, and then we are in some kind of workspace.

The room is dark but for lamps, oil this time. I think we must still be belowground because there are no windows, and the floor above is supported by a row of posts, fern tree trunks that have hardened, running in rows down the long room, which is open but for the clutter. Dried plants, hanging plants, high tables with bowls and metal tubing, enormous vats, books, insects crawling in jars, a desk with ink and papers, shelves with bottle after bottle of colored liquids, and there's a faint smell I can't identify, a smell that burns my nose. This is not what I expected from the extravagant Council House. Gray is still holding my hand, muscles pulled taut like the rope of my ladder. Judging by his expression, he's never been here.

Janis smiles pleasantly at us, rings a bell just outside a door to a stairwell going up, and then she locks the door to the cave with a key hanging from a ring of keys on a string around her neck.

"Genivee?" I call.

"Patience," Janis chides.

"Where . . ." I start to demand, but Gray suddenly pulls me to one side, toward the door to the stairwell, shoving me toward it.

"Run," he yells, shielding my escape with his body. "Run!"

I don't know what's happening. But before I can even regain my balance, Reese is coming down the stairs, from what must be the main part of the house, Li behind him, and Jonathan of the Council. It takes both Reese and Li to subdue Gray, and only Jonathan to subdue me. Or Jonathan and the knife he holds to my throat, pushing me backward into one of the posts.

I hear the sound of fists hitting skin, Gray choking. The tangle of bodies is on the edge of my vision, but when I turn my head to see even a little the knife stings, and a trickle of blood runs behind my necklace and down to my chest. I keep my eyes on Jonathan. He stares at the blood on my neck, and it makes me think he'd prefer to see that trickle grow bigger. I stay very still.

The scuffle dies down. Gray is being searched now, and when Reese comes to deal with me, Jonathan doesn't move the knife, just changes his position to behind me. Reese yanks the pack off my back, tossing it to one side. The First Book is in there, now half under one of Janis's high worktables.

"Search her," Janis says. "We could be looking for something small."

He searches me, feeling all over, without any of the restraint he showed at the Archives. Then he pushes my feet back, one on either side, and goes round and round my ankles with rope, tying them to the post, pulling my wrists back and tying them together, too. When Jonathan finally takes the knife from my bleeding neck Gray is just a meter or two away, seated backward on a chair, head hanging over the back of it, his wrists tied to his calves. The glass key, I see, is still around his neck. I wonder if they think it's decoration, like my necklace.

Reese retrieves my pack and goes through it, tossing it back where it was, a little farther under the table. He doesn't mention an extra book. He just says, "Nothing."

Janis sighs. I don't know where Jonathan is. Somewhere behind me with that knife. I grit my teeth to keep my voice steady.

"Where is Genivee?"

Gray looks up and coughs. His cheek is purpling, swelling, much worse than when Eshan hit him, and there's a cut on the corner of his eye. But unbelievably, he's also smirking. He shakes his head. "They're not here. They never were." I see when he catches sight of the blood on my neck.

Janis waves her hand toward the stairwell, sending Li and Reese away without a word. Jonathan comes out from behind me, hesitating while they go. "I will entertain our guests," she says, dismissing him. His eyes meet mine for just a second, and there is no light behind them. None at all. I wonder how often she has guests down here, and how often her grandson stays to see them entertained.

"I spoke to you of leverage," Janis says. She is shedding her wet robes, beneath them a very plain, practical black tunic reaching almost to her feet. She doesn't have a book. "I find that most people are more cooperative when their decisions involve someone besides themselves. This is what we will be exploring today." She hangs her robes on a hook behind the desk. "But please, Nadia, don't be concerned with my concept of the truth. I can have Delia and Genivee here at a moment's notice, if I wish, so it hardly matters whether or not they were here already. It's this one"—she goes to Gray's head, pulls it up by the hair—"that has issues with truth. You have been lying to me, Glassblower."

My chest is slamming. It's hard to breathe against it. I can't believe we just followed her in here. That we believed her. But how could I run if there was even the slightest possibility that she had Genivee? I'd probably do the same thing again. Gray is stretching his fingers, testing his bonds, and somehow still managing to smirk while his hair is being pulled. "You should have taken me back to the Lost," he says.

"Indeed." She drops his head, *tsks* once, goes to a high table full of bowls and tubing and picks up a bottle of fluid. "There was no reason to think, back then, that you had a place among us." She glances at me, and adds, "Gray was a terrible test-taker."

"I was too bored to finish," he says, a little belligerent. I think I'm supposed to discern from this that Janis sent Gray to the Lost because of his test scores.

"And you were such a troublemaker," Janis says. "But there was a shortage of labor, and I admit that you made me curious after that. A mistake."

"Indeed," he replies, mocking. And there is the Gray I remember from the learning room. These two seem almost comfortable in their loathing for each other.

I wriggle my wrists behind me as Janis lifts something I've never seen before, a small tube with what looks like a sewing needle on its end. She draws up fluid through the needle and into the tube from a bottle, and suddenly my anger and fear congeal into panic, deep and basic. We have to get out. I can see no way out. She holds the tube up to the lamp, the sharp end glinting, flicks it once with a finger.

"You should both understand that I'm going to ask you questions, and you might as well answer, because I will make you answer. You're not going to remember that I asked, or remember that you answered, or that you were here at all. So you can see that there's no point in being brave or even spiteful. It doesn't have to take long. Or it can take long. I am very patient."

I think she must mean the Forgetting, that we're not going to remember after that, but that's still fifteen days away. Surely she's not that patient. Janis smiles at me.

"But I can see you don't believe me, Nadia. You have a very logical mind that requires convincing. I've noted this about you. Let me explain, so that when it's time, you will understand exactly why you should be candid with your answers."

She goes to the high, wide shelf on the other side of me and chooses a bottle. It has white powder inside, dusty and fine. My eyes are on the needle in her other hand.

"This," she says, holding up the bottle, "is Forgetting. Breathe the tiniest bit, and what happens in this room will be gone from your head. Along with everything else. This is not a terrible loss for you. It was going to happen very soon anyway. But understand that before you leave here, you will forget."

She thinks she can make us forget. And not just every twelve years. When she wants to. And she's right, I don't believe it. Not after getting tricked on the way in here. It also makes me realize that Janis does not realize I can remember. There's one of Gray's lies she hasn't seen through.

"Is it dust from a comet?" Gray says, trying to lift his head. He asked like he was in school, just to irritate her. But I can hear that he's in pain. His position has to be leaving his back and neck cramped. Janis laughs, as if his answer was wrong, but not quite as wrong as she expected.

"Very good, Glassblower. But no. Not from the comet. These are the live spores of the forgetting tree. Aptly named, don't you think? The spores are released into the air with the tree's blooming cycle every twelve years, perfectly timed, or perhaps triggered by, the passing light and radiation of our comet. The spores have three days to find a dark, moist place to replicate. And they do it fast, right before your eyes, which I must say is very intriguing. They're meant to travel in the wind, or on the backs and wings of insects, but when breathed by humans . . . they attempt their replicating process in the body, where in most cases they cause an inflammation of the brain that takes away memory. This"—she holds up the little bottle—"could make half the city forget."

I meet Gray's gaze. There it is. The answer to our questions. And I think I believe her, and I can't decide if that's stupid or not. But it does fit with what we saw in the white room. I think of those fat buds on all the limbs along Meridian Street.

Gray looks at Janis from the corner of his eye. "You said *in most cases.*"

Janis gives me her lovely smile. "He's paying attention today, isn't he?" she says, and I don't realize at first that she's coming at me with the needle. She jerks down the wide collar of my tunic and drives the sharp end into my upper arm, quick. I gasp.

"This will sting a bit," she says pleasantly. Gray struggles against his ropes while she holds in the needle, the liquid in the tube oozing, burning beneath my skin, her face beside mine. Up close Janis's skin is smooth but old, drying out like paper. I hold my breath. She jerks out the needle, wiping away a tiny bit of blood with the cloth of my tunic, not bothering with the blood that's drying all over my neck.

"What did you do?" I say. It's hard now to keep the shake out of my voice.

"Just experimenting, my dear. It's important to collect data."

I'm afraid of what's inside my body now. Afraid to the center of my soul. Gray is straining to hold up his head, to ask with his eyes if I'm all right. I suspect I'm not. Janis goes back to her high table, starts running her needle through some sort of solution.

"Every now and then," Janis says, going back to Gray's question as if nothing had happened, "the spores do not seem to cause inflammation in the brain. A body will hold them in the blood instead. In these cases, memories are retained with only a mild sickness while the body fights the spores in the blood. Too many in the blood, however, and the body is over-whelmed. Then the body sickens and it dies. There's still so much study to be done on this. It took me years to—"

"You leave those trees all over the city," I say. Janis turns around. Fury is overwhelming my panic for the moment. "You could have saved us, and you didn't. You don't. You just let us forget!"

"Let you forget? Let you? Nadia, my dear. Do you think the Forgetting is a punishment?" Her dark, dark eyes seem to pity me. "No, no, my dear. The Forgetting is a privilege. A gift. A rebirth. A chance for the wrongs of the past to disappear. The Forgetting stopped a war, brought us peace. A second chance to fulfill our directive and create the perfect society." She smiles at me again. "The Forgetting has saved us."

"How," Gray says, his voice thick and slow, "do you think that losing everything you are, every twelve years, makes a perfect society?"

Janis looks thoughtful. She sets down her now clean needle with a row of similar ones on a cloth, walks around her desk and sits behind it, sandals silent on the stone. There's a knife on the desk, with "NWSE" engraved on the blade. She wants to talk, I realize. She's eager to. This must be the only time she ever can. Because she thinks we're going to forget it. That she will make us forget it. I, however, plan to remember every word. Unless she's put something horrible in me.

Janis folds her hands and says, "Have you ever pruned a plant? We look at all the branches, all the leaves and the buds. And then we pluck one here, snip one there, say yes to this one and no to that. But what if the plant could remember its pruning? That would be most unpleasant for the plant. But is the plant not better off? Will it not flourish? Isn't it a much healthier plant for being pruned? And is the plant not fortunate to have never been conscious of its pruning at all?"

I stare at this beautiful old woman sitting behind the desk, describing how she picks and chooses people, tossing away the ones she doesn't want like discarded branches.

"Our directive," she says, "is to build and to populate. To create the ideal society, that Earth might learn from us. We were all born of the chosen, the best of the best. And now Earth is waiting for us to re-create that society. Needs us to re-create it. One hundred and fifty of us, the best of the best of the best, will return to Earth and transform it. We will be kings. As soon as we send the signal."

Janis picks up a book on her desk and opens it while Gray lifts his head to look at me. This is like what we heard in the white room, read in the First Book, only it's a distorted version, a child's perspective twisted into the logic of an adult. One hundred and fifty names on that list, crossed out, replaced. Gray slides his gaze to Janis.

"And so what happens when you send your signal?"

Janis looks up from her book, brows arched. "Why, Earth comes, of course. As was arranged. When we send the signal, we go home."

"And what about all your leftover branches?" he asks, heavy on the sarcasm.

She lifts a pen, dips it in ink. "When Earth comes there will be no extra branches, of course. They will find what they were supposed to find. The perfect society. One hundred and fifty. The best of the best of the best." She smiles as she begins to write.

A list of one hundred and fifty. Not a list of the dead, I realize, a list of those she has chosen. It's the rest of Canaan Janis is going to kill. As soon as she gets into that mountain.

Janis sits back for a moment in her chair, running one skinny finger over the open book in front of her. "It takes honing," she says, "and extreme care to keep one hundred and fifty always ready, to raise up replacements when one grows old or falls short. To find those with the right combination of intelligence, looks, mental health, physical health, the ability to bear children, and a thorough understanding of the common good. It takes firm management to keep the wrong ones out of the gene pool. Did you know the original chosen for Canaan had to pass very strenuous tests, not only the simple things I just mentioned, but for stress, resourcefulness, problem-solving . . ."

And empathy, the light wall had said. I don't think Janis is passing the test on that one. I wonder for the first time what the Forgetting has really done to her, being the only one to remember over and over while everyone else forgets. It devastated me once. How many Forgettings has she lived through? Maybe what she's forgotten is herself, squeezing and compressing her emotions until they were all but gone. Like I tried to do. Until Gray.

"I have to know the potential chosen well," she is saying, almost to herself, "put them in peril, under stress, in extremity, to see how they'll react. You must be very perceptive to know how to push them, to make sure they can pass the tests. That is why there is only one who can decide which buds to pinch."

Which is her, I suppose, because she can remember.

"There are three kinds of people born in Canaan," Janis says, "those who fit the directive, those who could fit the directive, and those who never will. And it is easiest, of course, to test them right before the Forgetting, a natural time of confusion and anxiety, to see how they will react. As the city has grown, I admit to having used it more and more. It is interesting to watch, to see what people do. To see how spectacularly they fail. The city weeds itself for me like an overgrown field."

I remember all the things I saw during the Forgetting, the cruelty, the fighting, the woman with the dead children. Could Janis have really sown all those seeds? Put those people under stress, pushed them to their limit? I think of the floggings, the way she manipulated Gray, the rumors that run rampant through the city. Hedda and her low rations. And now I believe Janis really is up in that clock tower, safe, watching the results. Watching as we weed one another out. And then we forget it all.

"But we are very nearly sorted," Janis says, satisfied, "our numbers almost done. It's time to move into the bigger field."

Gray says, "I think I might be looking forward to being Lost again. Sounds like I'll be in there with all the best sort."

Janis waves a hand. "Oh, I don't think we'll be having any Lost after this Forgetting. It's too difficult to keep them from producing children. And we have a food shortage, or haven't you heard? But, Nadia, how are you feeling?"

She comes around the desk to my post, lifts my chin, peers at my eyes, puts a finger to my pulse. I'm looking at her close up again. It's only our belief that's given her this power over us, and it's only the Forgetting that gives her the power to be believed. Janis steps back.

"Hmmm. I'm going to ask you a question, Nadia. Think hard, then tell me the first thing that comes to your head. What is your earliest memory?"

I blink. I don't know what to say. I don't know whether I'm supposed to be remembering or forgetting. My arms ache from being pulled back, from straining at the ropes, but I can't feel any reaction to that liquid she put inside me at all. And then I know what I want to say to this woman who remembers everything about everyone in Canaan, whether I should say it or not.

"Anna."

I get a reaction. Janis goes still, lifts a finger to her chin. "Really?" she says. She walks back around the desk, picks up her pen. "What about Anna?"

"Nothing much. Putting me to bed." Gray is trying to adjust his position to look at me better. "And then Anna was gone."

Janis is writing. "Yes. She was particularly sensitive."

I don't know what she's talking about. Sensitive as in personality or . . . sensitive to what Janis put in her? The doctor said Anna had too much poison in her for it to have been an accident. Did Janis kill my sister? Like this? Maybe Anna didn't feel anything, either.

"What happened to her?" I ask.

Janis dismisses me with her hand. "Anything else? What about Lisbeth?"

Liliya's old name. She's looking to see if I remember. "Who is that?"

"How about your father?"

"No."

"Well. That was helpful, Nadia, and rather interesting. Thank you."

She goes on writing at her desk, the pen scratching quiet across the page. I realize I can't smell the foulness of the room anymore. Janis sets down her pen, leans forward.

"And now, it's time to discuss the code. You will remember me saying that I want you to understand, so that you will know to answer my questions without delay. I need the code to the bunker door because at long last we have nearly completed our directive and it is time to send the signal. It took me years to find the door. I was never there as a child, and

Zuri blocked it up. Hid it. The Forgetting takes longer on the mountain, where the spores are not so concentrated, and when I finally found it, oh, the combinations I have tried. The books I read, the people I questioned. And nothing. I nearly lost faith. And then I saw you, Nadia, Sergei Dorokov's great-granddaughter, over the walls, coming down from the bunker door in the mountain. I thought you must have the code and so you do. And now you have shared it with this one . . ."

She comes around the desk, bringing a vial of blue liquid with her. She sets it beside the knife with "NWSE" and touches Gray's hanging head. I can see his shirt stretch as he pants. Shallow breaths. I think his ribs might be broken. She says, "You like him, I think." She sounds almost puzzled by it. "And your scores were so high. But your associations . . . I'm afraid those are all wrong now, Nadia. All wrong. Such a shame to have to cross you off."

She sighs, and I'm twisting my wrist bloody inside the ropes while she talks.

"I would have preferred not to alert you. It's so much easier when the plant doesn't know it's being pruned. But . . ." She jerks Gray's head up by the hair.

"Did you tell me Nadia the Dyer's daughter was going over the wall, Glassblower?"

He meets her eyes. Two dark gazes. Trust him to be smirking just a little. He shakes his head.

"Did you tell me you had the code I was looking for?"

He shakes his head.

"Did you tell me that you had been over the wall? That you had been inside the mountain?"

He shakes it again, still smirking.

Janis lifts the top of the blue vial, a dropper attached. She lets a single drop fall onto the back of Gray's right hand. I don't know what I thought was going to happen next. But it wasn't this. I hear him hiss, and then his hand clenches, and there's a small trail of smoke rising, the smell of burning hair and skin. He doesn't make a sound, but there are blisters already forming, a small amount of blood.

Janis sets the top back in the vial, still smiling. "One of you," she says, "is going to give me the code. Would you like to give it to me now?"

My gaze meets Gray's, and he gives me the tiniest shake of his head. The entire population of Canaan minus one hundred and fifty is going to die when she sends that signal.

"You do remember," Janis says, looking back and forth at us, "that I will make you tell me, one way or the other. That this could be short or long?"

I raise my eyes to her, my breath coming hard, keeping my face still while I twist my wrist. I can feel the blood running warm down my hand. Neither of us answers her.

"Then we begin with you, Glassblower," she says. "You're going to tell me the code. Or Nadia is. And then you will forget. You do recall me saying that?"

I lock my gaze with Gray's. That burn on his hand is terrible. I can see him sweating with the pain of it. I don't know what to do. I twist my right wrist. I've got my thumb halfway out.

"Are you ready to tell me the code?"

He looks at her with hate-filled eyes. "No." He doesn't even know the code. And he is so afraid of forgetting.

Janis turns to me. "Are you?"

Gray is telling me no vehemently behind her. I blink tears, undecided. We are going to lose, I think, and no one will remember it but me. And her. And then Janis decides I have taken too long. She takes the knife, slits the strap of Gray's book and lets it hit the floor, then slides the knife up the back of his shirt, slitting the cloth with a soft rip. He tenses as the air hits his bare back. He knows what's coming now, and so do I.

"Stop it!" I yell. "Stop!"

"There is a very easy way to make me stop," Janis replies calmly.

"Nadia," Gray says. "If I don't break, you don't. You promise me."

"Tell me anytime you're ready, Nadia," Janis says, picking up the vial.

"Promise me!"

I see his face when the first drop hits his back. A wince that becomes distorted.

"Stop!" I scream.

"Tell me the code," Janis says. Gray shakes his head, panting, and she lets the liquid drip again. Twice. Three times.

I could make up a code, but that's quickly found out. I could tell her the code. But who will remember for the people she plans to kill? To weed away? We are two of those people, and then I realize, with certainty, that forgetting or remembering, we are not walking out of here at all. Whether we give her that code or not. We never were.

The blue liquid drips. Gray yells and I go crazy in the ropes, pulling and sliding in the blood until my thumb comes free. I smell Gray's skin burning. His head moves back and forth, trying to escape what's inescapable.

"Are you ready to tell me the code?" Janis says. She leans closer to his head. "No? Then is it an ear next? An eye?"

I thrash, and my right hand is free, then my left. My feet are still tied. I can't even feel them, but next to me are the shelves full of bottles, and then I know what I'm going to do. I'm going to blot that code from existence. As far as Janis is concerned. I stretch for the bottles, grab the one I want.

"Gray!" I scream. He's shaking, smoke rising, blood running from his back. But he turns his head to me, raises his eyes. I show him the bottle of white powder in my hand.

"I'm sorry!"

"Don't . . . forget," he pants. "You have to remember . . . for us . . ."

Janis turns from her task, opens her mouth, but before she can speak I toss the bottle. It spins in a slow arc in the air. And then glass shatters, a white puff like a miniature cloud flying upward. A sweet smell, thick, like rotting honeyfruit, fills the room. The smell of forgetting. Janis runs, snatches her damp robe from the hook and holds it across her face.

"Nadia!" Gray's voice is ragged. "Do not . . . forget me. Do . . . not . . ."

His eyes fall closed. And when he opens them, he will not know me.

Pain spreads through me like the spores in the air, the sick sweet smell on my tongue, in my head. Gray's face is losing its expression and it hurts, hurts to be forgotten, to be blotted from his mind like a word is lost to spilling ink. To watch him lose himself. But at least she's stopped. Now Janis will stop.

I clutch my head, unconcerned with my bloody wrist, and then the pain inside me suddenly becomes something different.

More tangible. Very physical. I double over, gasp. I'd meant to mimic Gray's expression, to fake my forgetting along the lines of his, but this is like knives, knives in my head, knives in my back. I cry out, fall forward onto my hands, my feet still tied to the post. Then the pain doubles and I scream.

Dimly, I'm aware of Janis's feet walking slowly toward me.

"Oh, Nadia the Dyer's daughter," I hear her say, muffled through her damp robe. "It seems that you are a liar, too."

I hope I never again have to see someone die. I think it might be the same as watching them forget.

NADIA THE DYER'S DAUGHTER
BOOK 10, PAGE 74, 9 YEARS AFTER THE FORGETTING

CHAPTER NINETEEN

When I wake, I don't open my eyes. I feel heavy, like I'm part of the mattress. I have memories, unfocused, dim. Of lamplight, and of pain. A lot of pain. Of the glassblower's son's face. I stir, frown at what that movement feels like, and decide not to do it again. Something rustles nearby, a whisper of moving air. I open my eyes.

Brightly dyed cloth hangs at intervals over stone walls, and the matting has a pattern woven into it, red and blue, like the blanket on top of me. The bed is raised, and there's someone on the floor beside it, hair wild and untied. I relax. It's Gray, his shoulder level with my eyes. He has his shirt off, and for one second I think we've been swimming, that it's been raining, that we're in the white room, except nothing around us is white. I reach a hand from beneath the blanket and touch his arm.

He starts. Gets up and stands a few feet away, rubbing his hands on the black cloth of his pants. He has a bit of a beard, and it suits him. When did he grow a beard? The glass key is still around his neck.

I find I really can move my body, though I'm unbelievably sore and stiff. I swing my feet over the edge of the mattress, evaluate being upright. My head spins and I let it clear. The windows are high up, like a resting room's should be, but there's light coming in, pink and gold. Sunrising. I am missing something. Gray watches me.

"You've been sick," he says.

I decide that being sick is terrible. There's a pitcher of water beside the bed and I try to lift it, but I need both hands. Gray helps, handing me the mug when it's full. I can only drink a little. Sunrising. How can it be sunrising? My gaze darts up. The Forgetting.

"What day is it?" I demand.

"I don't know."

He seems embarrassed about that. A little angry. I reach for his hand, to say something more, but he walks away, to the other side of the small room. And then I see his back. Burns. Deep ones, like he's been spattered with boiling rain.

"Your back . . ." I start to say. Then the memories come. Janis taking us to the underground room, being tied to the post. Gray screaming.

He turns his back to the wall. "It doesn't hurt as much now," he says, defensive. He looks at me. Looks away again. Then he says, "What's your name?"

The shock of that question is like a blow, and somewhere in my head I am six years old, hearing my mother say, *Who are you?* I remember the white powder now, spraying up from the broken glass on the floor. I did it. I made him forget. I put an arm across my stomach.

"Where is your book?" I ask.

His brows come down, confused. I swivel on the edge of the bed, look around at the floor, at the corners. But there's no pack. No books at all. For either of us. I put my head in my hands. I'm shaking. Of course she took our books.

"Hey, you should . . ." Gray comes back across the room. "I think you should lie back down."

He doesn't know what to do. Doesn't want to touch me. *Time-out,* I want to say. *Free question* . . . But Gray won't know any of the answers now. I try to slow my breath. "My name is Nadia," I tell him.

He sits where he had been when I woke up, on the floor, getting down slowly, to spare the skin of his back. After a few minutes he says, "So . . . you know me?"

"Yes," I whisper. "Your name is Gray."

He nods, jaw clenched. "I thought it must be. That's what you called me. In your sleep, but you might've been . . . you were really sick." He sounds as shaky as I feel.

"You're the glassblower's son," I say. "You work with your father, Nash, and your mother is Delia. She's a planter. You're nineteen. You've finished school."

"Nash," he repeats. "And Delia. You're sure?"

That sounds like what he asked me that first day at the waterfall. "Yes, I'm sure."

"What's happened to me?"

"You've forgotten," I say. I'm holding my voice and my hands steadier, but there is one scalding tear running down my face, and it's making him uncomfortable, embarrassed. "You've lost your memories."

"When . . . I woke up, it was dark and I was tied down, and . . ."

In terrible pain, I think.

". . . and they cut me loose and brought me here, and you were on the bed. And that's almost all I know. A girl came once and cleaned my back. Food and water come every now and then."

Then we're still in Janis's house. "How many days have we been here?"

He shakes his head, such a familiar gesture. But his tone is unfamiliar when he says, "I don't know. Food has come four times."

My head is starting to clear, facts falling into their proper lines. Janis said that for a rare person the spores that cause the Forgetting can stay in the blood instead of the brain, and memories are retained. But too many spores, and it can be too much of a fight. I remember when I was a child, after the last Forgetting, how sore I was, how much I slept. I think I must have been sick. This time I think maybe I was nearly dead. Janis had said that bottle of live spores was enough to make half the city forget, and then, *Oh, Nadia the Dyer's daughter. It seems that you are a liar, too.*

So she knows how I react to the spores now. She knows I remember. That the code isn't forgotten. It's probably why we're alive. So she can drag it out of me as soon as I'm awake. I have to know what day it is. We have to get out.

I stand, like I'm going to run. But I'm not going to run. I've never felt so weak. I start a slow trek across the room, toward the door. I'm wearing someone's old sleeping dress.

"It's locked," Gray says.

I try it anyway. The door is heavy, sparkling metal. And then I have an urgent need for a latrine. I must look like I'm searching because Gray points at a blanket in the corner, hanging over a cord strung from window to window. There's a bucket behind it. This is mortifying, but necessary.

When I come out Gray is as far away as he can get, his wounded back turned. I sit on the bed again, exhausted, and he turns around, leaning against the wall, though not letting his skin touch. It's painful to see him so at odds with himself. To see him so uncertain.

"You've had to take care of me," I say. "All this time. I'm sorry." I'm guessing he strung that blanket. It matches the one on the bed. He shrugs a shoulder.

"Shouldn't have to apologize for that."

And that sounded a little more like Gray.

Then I say, "Could I look at your back? You said someone tended it, but . . ." Obviously he can't do anything about it by himself.

He hesitates, but he comes and sits on the edge of the mattress. The swelling on his face is gone, as is all the bruising he must have had after the beating he took from Li and Reese.

"Do your ribs hurt?" I ask. He shakes his head.

Looking at his burns hurts me intensely, then makes me so angry I can feel my face getting hot. That blue liquid has eaten round holes into his skin, one or two places streaked, where it ran. He's going to scar. Badly. There's a cloth beside the water pitcher, a torn piece of blanket.

"Is this clean?" I ask.

"Clean as it gets."

We're both filthy. I pour a little water from the glass and very gently clean his back, working around where each wound has run and dried on his skin, careful not to touch the burn.

He flinches, but doesn't say anything. I can see that he is tense, though. Uncomfortable with me. Now that I'm looking closer I realize that some of these wounds have healed more than others. In fact, there seem to be several stages of healing.

"Could I see your hand?" I ask slowly. "The one with the burn?"

He lifts his hand so I can see the back of it. The first place Janis burned is well on its way to healing, like half the burns on his back. But there are others not nearly as healed, a few more seem to be just now closed and dry. And then I know, and my breath comes hard, my weakened body not quite capable of dealing with my level of rage.

She has burned him again. At least twice. And he doesn't remember, because she's made him forget it. But why? If you're ruthless and cruel and you want something, wouldn't it make more sense to let him remember and dread the next session? She has to think he's forgotten the code, and it can't be leverage, because I wasn't awake. I set down the cloth and lie down before I fall, bunching the blanket beneath my head.

Gray moves immediately back to his spot on the floor. I hadn't meant for him to go. It pains me that he wants to. I try to think, step by step, about what happened in that room. Being tied, all Janis's eager talking, her questions. And what had she put inside me with that needle? Other than a sting and a burn when it went in, I never knew it was there. *Experimenting*, she'd said. *Collecting data*. Then she'd asked me my earliest memory, and I'd wondered if she poisoned Anna, and . . .

I rub an aching temple. Janis knows that Anna was gone before the last Forgetting. She knows everything like that about our family. Why was she only interested, not surprised, when I said Anna's name? That had been me giving in to my temper. It should have been a mistake. And then Janis had deliberately used the name Lisbeth.

I sit up again, realizations tumbling down like stones. I'd thought Janis was probing to see if I remembered, like her. But what if she was trying to determine if what she put inside of me had worked? To see what it made me remember? Janis doesn't just have Forgetting, I realize. She has the cure. Something to make us remember, and that's exactly what she's been using on Gray. Making him remember, burning him for the code, making him forget again, repeat the process, and won't he be confused and docile in the meantime? I close my eyes, my fury of a moment ago nothing compared to this new feeling in my chest. Cold, black hatred.

When I open my eyes I find Gray staring at me, watching me think. He looks away. I pull my knees up, set my chin on them. Maybe having that cure in my blood is what kept me alive. Either way, we are in trouble, just as soon as she knows I'm awake.

"Gray." His name startles him. "If someone comes in I'm going to pretend to be asleep. I don't want them to know I'm awake yet, okay?" I'm so tired it might not even be a lie.

Gray nods, brows down, eyes on the floor again. I want to stroke his head, touch that unfamiliar hair on his face. I am going to fill him so full of that cure. Just as soon as we get out of this room. "Who brings the food?" I ask. "Man? Woman?"

"Once a girl. Mostly a man. He's big. Older, hair slicked back . . ."

Reese. No help there. I look at the room, almost bare of furnishings. "Think," I say. "What could we use in here as a weapon? If we cut down that cord with the blanket, if you were behind the door when the man comes in, do you think you could get it around his neck?"

Gray's eyes move from the hanging blanket to me, open a little wider. And for the first time I see a hint of the glassblower's son in the corners of his mouth. "You know, suddenly it's a lot less boring in here."

"Could you do it?"

"I think so. I don't know."

He looks tired. How has he been sleeping? Certainly not on his back. Maybe facedown on the matting. "Do you want to come up here?"

He shakes his head.

"Don't be stupid. You'd probably rather be on your stomach, and not on the floor." I scoot as far as I can to where the bed meets the corner of the walls, to show him how much space he can have.

He doesn't argue anymore, just gets up, scowling. I can tell that it hurts. He gets his knees on the mattress, stretches out on his stomach. Even dirty, hurt, tired, and not remembering me, I think he is beautiful. Why can't I ever save him? I thought I'd helped save his book during the Forgetting. I thought I'd saved him from pain in the underground room. Instead I gave him what he feared most, and more pain. Guilt is more than a bitter taste. I think it's a sickness; it makes me ache all over. He lays his head on his arms, facing away from me, while I huddle in the corner, cold stone at my back.

Gray says, "Someone hurt me on purpose, didn't they?"

"Yes."

"Will they do it again?"

I don't want to say, because the answer is yes. She will use him to break me. Again. And again. And it will probably work. "We have to get out," I say.

He thinks about this. "I want to ask you another question."

"You can ask me any question."

He takes a breath. "What are you . . . to me?"

What should I say? *You're the best friend I've ever had, the best thing that ever happened to me. You lied for me and suffered for me and wrote my name in your book.* I settle on the simplest of the truths. "You loved me."

"I don't remember that."

I know. I close my eyes.

"Sorry," he adds.

"Not something you should have to apologize for," I whisper. He turns his head on his hands.

"Where did you get that?"

His gaze is on my necklace. I pull it over my mass of tangled, half-braided hair, and let him hold the blue glass. The string is bloodstained, though I think the cut on my neck is nearly healed. "Do you remember it?" I ask.

"No. But I looked at it, while you were asleep, and knew exactly how I would make it."

I nod. The Forgetting is so unfair. I wish he was remembering me instead.

"You said I made glass. Did I make this?"

"You did. And the key around your neck." I think of him that night, sweaty in front of the furnace, when I was still trying to resist him, and failing miserably. He puts the necklace back in my hand, lays his head down. I see one of his hands, stretching and clenching. I wonder if he's remembering being tied. "Nadia," he says, trying out the name. "Forgetting is awful."

The lock on our door clicks. I drop onto the mattress, shut my eyes as the door opens, creaking on its hinges. I hear foot-steps. They sound female, though I wonder how I can tell—maybe because of the sandal heels, or because they sound so light and small. The footsteps stop beside the bed. Gray doesn't speak.

"Nadia!" someone whispers.

My eyes fly open. It's Genivee.

"You're awake!" she says, clearly relieved.

I sit up. "What are you doing here?"

"Getting you out!"

"Who is this?" Gray asks.

"We have to go," says Genivee. "Can you walk? You've been really sick, but Liliya says you'll get better quick once you start."

"What does Liliya know about it?"

"Please," says Genivee with a roll of her eyes. I'm already half off the mattress, trying to stay decent while I get to the edge. "What happened to him?" she asks me. "Has he forgotten already?"

"Yes."

She looks at Gray again. I can see she wants to ask about his back, but doesn't. "Grab what you need," she says. "Do you have any shoes?"

Gray shrugs. I don't have any, either. "Where are your books?" she asks. She looks grim when I shake my head, and pulls me to my feet.

"Genivee, what day is it?"

She stills, and for the first time I get a good look at her. Her eyes are large, as always, but there's something different in them. Fear. This, and the pink light outside the window, is making my pulse speed. She says, "It's the Forgetting."

"How long?"

"Five hours. Maybe less. If you weren't awake"—Genivee tilts her head at Gray—"he was going to carry you out."

"Who are you?" Gray asks again.

"Her sister."

"I thought you were the girl with the soup."

"Just the once," says Genivee. "Now move. Reese is coming back."

I move, hand on Genivee's shoulder, weak, but stronger than the last time I tried. I look at Gray. "Stay with me." I'm not sure for which of our sakes I'm saying it. He looks uncertain, but he follows.

"We don't have to go far," Genivee whispers.

She sticks her head out the door, wary, and we creep into a hallway, where the matting is not only colorful but thick and soft underfoot, making our careful footsteps silent. The ceiling is tall white stone stretching upward, lit by a single hanging lamp. Genivee shuts the door we just walked through, locks it with a key from a string around her neck. I have no idea what's happening here, how or why Genivee could have a key to a room in the Council House. Then Genivee motions for us to follow her, past a stairwell, to a door at the end of the hall.

We slip inside, and instantly I'm reminded of the images I saw of Earth. Too much of everything. A raised bed piled high with blankets that are soft and thick and very bright, low windows showing the fields and the sunrising, a row of plants beneath them, pinched and clipped into harsh shapes. And things, little things, assortments of odds and ends that can have no function, piled in heaps or arranged in patterns over all the surfaces. The air is heavy, perfumed with flowers I can't see. I hate it.

"Janis's room," Genivee whispers, quietly shutting the door. "She's been sick, too, but not as sick as you. She only got up a week ago. She's gone now, to the Forgetting. And to see about the granary."

"What about the granary?"

"Eshan, Veronika, Michael, that whole group took over the granary after the second bell. Barricaded themselves inside. There's been fighting . . ."

Take the granary, wake up after the Forgetting in charge of the food supply, and the Council will have to listen to them. But I don't think Janis has gone to do anything about that at all. I think she's gone to her tower. To observe. To see the city "weed" itself. Gray has turned toward the wall beside us, where drawings surrounded by colored squares cover almost the entire surface. I see his back, and the hatred burns cold inside my chest.

"We're waiting for Reese to check the room and run off looking for you," Genivee goes on. She has an ear against the door. "And then Liliya will come get us when she's sure we can get out. And I'm really glad you're not dead, Nadia. Here." She tosses a bag I hadn't even noticed she was carrying. There's clean leggings and a tunic inside, and a shirt for Gray.

"Genivee, who's with Mother? Is she—"

But Genivee turns, waving a frantic hand at us. Heavy, muffled footsteps are coming down the hall, followed by the sound of a key in the lock of the other room. There's no way I can see to lock Janis's door without a key, and we don't have it. I turn, searching for anything we can use, and see something like an enormous, long knife hanging to one side of the drawings, just beyond Gray. I take it from its hooks. The other door opens, a pause, and then running steps come down the hall.

Genivee grabs the door latch, ready to push up with all her weight to keep it from being turned. Gray takes two silent steps and puts his hands over hers, adding his strength. I hold the long knife, not sure what I would do with it, except that Reese, Janis, none of them will be touching Gray again. I look down the length of the knife. Never mind. I know exactly what I'd do with it. I see the moment the latch moves, when Reese tries the door, but he doesn't try it very hard. He must assume it's locked. We hear him run down the hall, footsteps disappearing downward.

Gray lets go of the latch, and Genivee deflates with relief. The small rush of adrenaline has left me shaky. I lean back against the bed. The edge of the knife is not very sharp, but sharp enough, the name "Kevin Atan" engraved into the metal. This must be from Earth, too. Something from Janis's family. I've never seen anything like it in Canaan.

"Now we wait for Liliya," Genivee whispers.

"Who's Liliya?" Gray asks. I leave the knife on the bed and scoop up the bag of clothes I dropped, picking out the shirt and handing it to Gray.

"Could you just . . . stay turned around for a minute?" I ask him. I've spied a jug of water and a washing bowl, and I don't care if it is Janis's. I'm using it.

He sees the clothes in my hand and nods, takes his shirt and goes to stand in front of the wall of drawings. I watch him studying the shirt in his hand, rubbing the cloth between his fingers. I think he's trying to remember it, and something about the way he stands, about the slope of his shoulders, makes me realize he's afraid. Very afraid. And it's making him angry. I turn to the water basin, eyes stinging.

"What is happening, Genivee? Where's Mother?" I ask, a little more sharply than I'd meant to. I grab a clean cloth from a stack, get it wet, and start scrubbing my neck. Genivee holds her voice low, keeping one ear close to the metal door.

"Mother is with the Lost. She was bad when you didn't come back, Nadia, and we couldn't find the sleeping tonic. And everyone said that you and Gray had run off together over the wall and gotten yourselves killed . . ."

I close my eyes, tasting the guilt.

"Then Reese came with Li and Arthur of the Metals and took Mother and Sasha. It was awful. They tried to take Eshan, too, but they couldn't find him. And Liliya went to Jonathan of the Council . . ."

I jerk off the sleeping dress and pull the clean tunic over my head.

". . . and Jonathan told her where Mother was, and that you were in here with Gray, and you were sick, and he gave her the key to your room. He's sort of . . . in love with Liliya, I guess. It's creepy. And he told her when we should come to get you, and that we should get Mother, too, as soon as we can, and all of us go over the wall . . ."

I put a second foot into the leggings. "I don't believe you." Genivee raises a brow. Just one of them, and it's not the look of a little girl. "Liliya would go and get Mother," I tell her, "but she would never risk breaking into the Council House to come and get me."

"Things have changed," Genivee says calmly. "We read the books you had hidden under the floor. And don't look at me like that! You disappeared! And Anson the Planter came to our house, and said something wasn't right, and he's Council . . ."

I wonder if she realizes who else Anson is.

". . . and I'd seen you writing in the wrong book, a stolen book with numbers on it. So I thought about where you could hide something and looked until I found it. We know you never forgot. We know that something must have happened before the last Forgetting. That book, the old book from the Archives, we know that's yours. We know it's us, even though the names are a little different. Liliya understands now. And yes, she came to get you."

Liliya knows she is my sister. She knows. And she came. I lean against the bed, let out a long breath, and when I look up Genivee is beside me.

"What happened to Gray?" she whispers. She's looking at his back now, covered with a shirt I worry is too rough for his wounds. I've forgotten to tell him he can turn around. He's scrutinizing, the way he always does, this time a drawing with trees and plants that are all wrong, and a creature I think we might have seen on the wall in the white room, with hair all over its face. This must be Earth. All of them are Earth, I think, and I imagine Janis lying here in her too-soft bed, just looking. I wonder who drew them.

Suddenly, Gray turns to the table beside him, covered in little boxes and bowls of flower petals, and sweeps all of it to the floor, throwing down the table, too, for good measure. Genivee jumps, but she stays where she is. Gray just crosses his arms. He's breathing hard, and that probably hurts.

"We can't let them have him," I whisper to my sister. "No matter what."

"Okay," she says. And the tremor in her voice tells me that no matter how smart and capable, my sister really is just twelve, and understanding things I wish I could protect her from. Janis could use Genivee just as easily as Gray, I realize. If she found us here. We have to get out. Maybe we could wait out the Forgetting in the white room, like Gray had suggested, now that I know the spores can only live three days. Or will Janis be sitting on a rock with Reese and Li, or whoever else she recruits, the first time we open the door? She'll guess where I've gone, and she won't let that door close a second time.

Then I spot something in the mess Gray has made of Janis's table. I go and pick it up. It's a small bottle, a tiny amount of clear liquid left in the bottom. And there's a tube with a needle in the clutter, too. I feel relieved then. Certain. This had held the cure, and of course Janis was using it on herself, when she was sick. I show it to Gray.

"This had something inside that I think can help you remember again. I'm going to get it for you, okay?"

He looks at the little bottle, then so intently at my face. Trying to wring the memory from his mind. Then we all jump, but it's only Liliya, coming in the door. My sister and I exchange a look. There are many things we could say, and we both decide not to.

"Reese has gone," she whispers. "I think to the clock to find Janis. We can get out right now."

"Who else is in the house?" I ask.

"No one. Soon it will be the whole Council, though. They'll gather with Janis in the amphitheater, then come here for the Forgetting. Where are your books?"

"Gone," I say simply. "What time is it?"

"Four and a half hours." Until the Forgetting.

"Liliya, you and Genivee take Gray and get Mother out of the houses of the Lost and go . . ."

Where? Where are we going to go? And then I look at the bottle in my hand, and I realize something. Those spores make Janis sick. She must have somewhere that's like the white room, sealed, where the air can't get in, where she can hide from the Forgetting . . . And then I smile. I know why the Archives was built over that room, and I know why it smelled so stale.

"Go to the Archives. There's something here, in the underground room, that I need to get."

"You mean Janis's laboratory? Don't go down there, Nadia."

"I've spent quite a lot of time down there, actually." I turn to Gray, standing beside me like we're tethered. "When you get there, go inside and keep going back, as far as you can. Past the shelves there will be one more door. Use the key you have around your neck. Really gently, though. It might break. I'll meet you there."

Gray looks at me, at the empty bottle I still have in my hand. "No," he says. "I'm with you." He yanks the string over his head, holds out the glass key toward Liliya, moves his eyes deliberately to the bottle in my hand, and back to my face.

"I don't want them to find you again," I whisper. "I want you to get out."

"I'm with you," he says again. "Take it or leave it."

This almost makes me smile. "Okay," I say, thinking. I look at my sisters. "He's right. Bring Mother back here. There's a better way to get there, anyway."

Liliya almost looks like she wants to argue, except that I don't think there's any argument in her right now. She nods. It really is too bad she's going to forget this. Unless she doesn't.

Liliya and Genivee turn for the door while I grab the long knife from the bed. When my sisters are out and down the hall, Gray grabs my arm.

"Tell me. Am I about to forget again?"

I look at his face, at the rage and frustration simmering below the surface. "The day you forgot," I said, "we planned what we'd do. Right now I'm going to try and hide you from the Forgetting, and I'm going to get more of those bottles and put something into your skin that will make you remember. But . . . if it doesn't work, then I'll remember for us. Like I said I would."

Gray looks away from me. Jaw clenched. "That's not good enough."

"I know," I whisper.

"But you swear you'll try to help me remember."

He's breathing hard as I nod, only just under control. I want him to trust me again. Choose me again. But as we slip out of Janis's room and through the empty hallways of the Council House, I'm not at all sure that's what will happen.

I used to think that when the Forgetting came, my mother and sisters would need me. To remember. To keep us together. Then I knew that Gray would need me to remember, too. To keep us together.

Now I'm beginning to think it's all of Canaan that needs someone to remember. To keep our city from falling apart . . .

NADIA THE DYER'S DAUGHTER
IN THE BLANK PAGES OF
NADIA THE PLANTER'S DAUGHTER
BOOK 1

CHAPTER TWENTY

Liliya points my way to the stairwell that goes to the laboratory, uncomfortably familiar with the layout of the Council House. Gray follows me down. It's dim and dank in the laboratory, as Liliya called it, with that slightly foul odor burning in my nose. The broken glass has been swept away, but Janis's book is still on the desk, crammed with notes, the knife she used to slit Gray's shirt beside it. I see the cure on the shelf, eight bottles of Remembering, just above where the bottle of Forgetting had sat. The one that I threw. It looked like Janis gave herself an entire bottle from the empty one in her room, which is also the amount I'm guessing she put in me. So that's eight people I can make remember, maybe nine if there's another person as small as Genivee. I start counting in my head: Gray, Mother, Liliya, Genivee, Gray's parents. Rose, and maybe one more. I don't know how I could ever choose just one more.

"I need the needles," I say to Gray. "They'll look like a tube with something sharp on the end."

He goes to the other side of the high table and starts look-ing before I even finish the sentence. I want to stick a needle in his arm right now, but the spores need to get into the air and die first. Janis has proved that a person can be reinfected. There are no more bottles on the shelf, so I start opening the drawers on my side of the cabinet beneath the table, searching for more. A scrap of cloth catches my eye from underneath the cabinet. I touch it, then pull it out. It's my pack.

I can't believe it. I open the flap, and there is my book, the First Book, even the empty bottle from drugging Deming. In all the confusion of my tossing the Forgetting, whatever she'd had to do to drag us both upstairs, and then being sick, it seems that Janis has overlooked this. Or just hasn't found it. I doubt she'll have been as careless about Gray's book.

A voice from the stairway shocks me into stillness. "Well, look who's awake."

I whirl around. It's Reese, coming down the last two stairs. My heartbeat stutters into new life, racing. He has his eyes only on me, which means Gray must have been down, searching low and out of Reese's sight line. He needs to stay that way.

"I'm just going to take what I need and go," I say calmly. "None of this has anything to do with you."

"Oh, now she speaks. Now that she's afraid of me."

I make a move toward the door, getting his back to Gray, but he jerks me hard by my knot of tangled hair.

"It's four hours before the Forgetting," he says, walking me backward, steering me by the hair. "And you owe me."

"What do you mean?"

"I didn't tell her what you had in that bag, did I? She doesn't even know her book is missing."

"Let me go," I say. "Whatever she's promised to give you, she won't do it. You should just let me—"

He laughs. "Little girl, we're all about to forget. And right now, I don't care about promises, and I am not thinking about Janis."

He searches me with one hand, my hair held in the other, like we're at the Archives, like before he tied me to the post. Except it's nothing like that. And there's nothing but Reese and air within my reach. The long knife sits on the high table where I left it, the smaller one on Janis's desk. I try to push him away, to scratch his face, but I'm weak from sickness and he's built like a fern trunk. He slaps me, my head held almost immobile by the hair, and I feel strands rip from my scalp, see a burst of stars. Taste blood.

"Be still," he says. "You're not going to remember. No one has to—"

A thud stops his words, a dull noise, the sound of metal hitting something both soft and solid. The grip in my hair loosens, and Reese staggers, turns, and then Gray hits him again, this time in the side of the head. Gray has a small pot in his hand, metal and heavy-bottomed. Reese steps back, loses his balance, goes careening into the shelves, and when he falls, they fall with him, glass smashing, papers fluttering, smaller things rolling across the floor. For one moment, everything is still.

Then Gray throws down the pot with a clang that makes me wince. He's panting hard, otherwise immobile, and I know what that means. He is boiling, on fire with rage. "Are you all right?"

I don't think I am. But not because of a split lip, or the panic I haven't yet recovered from. I'm not all right because of the noise of all those breaking bottles.

"Help me get it off him," I say, and when we push the shelf back upright, balance it against the wall, Reese lies motionless in a scatter of detritus and broken glass, his chest still rising and falling. A sharp smell wafts up as I search frantically through the mess, something I've smelled before but can't place. In the end I hold up a one single, unbroken bottle of Remembering. And I know who it's for.

"This is yours," I tell him. "We have to wait until everything is out of the air, but after that, it's for you. Okay?"

Gray watches me getting up, hurrying my bare feet over the glass-strewn floor, tucking the bottle into my pack. He hasn't moved. I'm sure he's in pain.

"Will it give me my memories back?"

"I think it will."

"Good. Because if I'm going to try and kill the next man that touches you, it might be good to know a thing or two about you first."

I actually smile, just a little. "Come on," I say, sliding the straps of my pack over my shoulders. "We'll meet them upstairs and go the other way." In this room, with an injured Reese, is the last place Janis or Jonathan needs to find Gray.

He follows me up the stairs, and I am running now, not nearly as fast as I used to, but so much stronger than when I woke. We pass through the empty house, large rooms and corridors filled with more furniture than I've ever seen, and I wish I had Liliya to guide me. It takes several minutes to find the front door, and when I do, my sisters haven't come yet with Mother. The sky is streaked with pink, the air soft. I don't want to wait in full view of the road into the city, either.

I look back at the house, undecided, and that's when I stare out across the sunrising fields and see the thin trail of smoke rising from the houses of the Lost. The houses with the holes patched, and the strong new doors.

Oh, I don't think we'll have be having any Lost after this Forgetting. We have a food shortage, or haven't you heard?

"She's burning them," I say. "She's burning them!"

And I run into the fields, between the damp rows of the newly planted grain, all the way to the fences that surround the houses of the Lost. My knees are buckling when I get there, Gray coming just behind me. The new gates are open, not barred, and in one, quick glance I take in the biofuel stacked along the plaster walls, the thatch already flaming in one place, and Jonathan of the Council setting fire to the piles of fuel with a torch. Liliya chases after him, and Genivee kneels on the ground beside Jemma the Clothesmaker, who seems to be unconscious.

Smoke must be making its way inside from the burning section of thatch. I can hear the muffled screams through the walls. Mother is in there. Rose. And Sasha, Jemma's little girl. I wonder if Jonathan has hit Jemma. Gray takes the long knife from my pack and goes straight to the heavy new door while I hurry to Jonathan. The smooth facade he wears is gone.

"I have to!" he's yelling. "You don't understand. I have to . . ."

"No, you don't," Liliya says.

"Yes, I do!" He puts the torch to the next stack of fuel, and I see what my sister is trying to do. Jonathan has a key around his neck. Gray is beating at the latch with the handle of the knife, hollow, clanging thuds amid the noise of fire.

"Jonathan, you don't have to do what she says!" Liliya is moving closer to him. "Just stop doing what she says!"

"Don't!" He brandishes the torch at her, slowing her steps. "If I don't, it will be you! She'll make me do it to you!"

Liliya stops.

" 'Do it or the child will!' " Jonathan yells. " 'Look like you enjoy it, or it will be Liliya next time.' " His voice is almost singsong, reciting what he's heard. " 'You wouldn't want that to happen to Liliya, now would you?' And she'll make it happen. She always makes it happen! And she'll make me remember . . ."

"Jonathan," I say, startling him into looking at me. I don't think he knew I was here. The screams from the houses of the Lost are getting more frantic. "I have the cure. Liliya is going to remember this. She'll remember what you did here today."

Liliya has no idea what I'm talking about, but her gaze snaps back to Jonathan. Now he's the one who looks stricken.

"She swore to me," Jonathan says. "She swore this would be the last. That today I can forget. That I never have to remember again." He looks at Liliya and his voice breaks. "If I do it, your name is on the list."

And just like the day I understood Mother, for the first time I fully understand Jonathan of the Council. He's been manipulated and coerced, maybe more hideously than any of us.

"Jonathan," Liliya says, taking another step, "my mother is in there."

"I don't want you to remember," he says, hand on his brow. The torch has lowered to the ground. "She promised me you could be on the list . . ."

"I know." I watch as Liliya walks right up to Jonathan in the smoke, reaches around his neck, and lifts off the string with the key.

"She'll . . . she'll make me do it to you," he says.

"No," Liliya says. "She won't."

She holds out the key. I take it and run to the locked door. Gray is still banging on it with the knife hilt. He steps back; I put the key to the new lock and fling open the door. Lost women pour out in a puff of black smoke, some carrying children, some just running for themselves, all half blind and choking from the fumes. Genivee appears beside me, trying to see around the bodies, calling for our mother. I find Gray's hand and put the key in it, speaking low so he can hear me over the din.

"There's another door around the side, for the men," I say. He sprints away, and I see the shirt he's wearing is stained in the back. He's opened some of his wounds.

Flames are engulfing the roof thatch, one plaster wall fully on fire, heat scalding one side of my face. The women rush from the door like a breached dam, and then Rose comes stumbling out, coughing, Jemma's crying little girl in her arms, our mother hanging on to her shoulder. My relief is like gravity, buckling my knees, trying to pull me to the ground. Genivee runs to Mother, and Mother stretches out an arm, but her gaze passes over my face without recognition. She seems dazed. Then Rose is kissing my cheek.

"I thought you were gone for good," she says, her cheeks so smoke-stained her wrinkles are white lines.

"I thought the same thing about you. Is my mother all right?" I discover I have tears on my face, and I don't know where they came from. I wipe them away.

"She's as right as she can be. Gray?" Rose asks. She bounces Sasha, who is coughing more than she's crying, and almost more than Rose can hold.

"He's letting out the men. Sasha's mother is over there. Can you help her?" Rose sees Jemma getting herself upright on the ground, awake, but bewildered. Rose nods, taking the little girl with her as the men are streaming into the fenced yard. Mother sits on the ground with Genivee, unseeing in the melee of the milling Lost and the smoke and flames.

"Jonathan," I call quickly. He turns a bleary eye from Liliya. And I realize that except for the crying of the children and the crackle of the flames, bit by bit the courtyard is falling silent. Eyes turning to him and the torch still burning on the ground at his feet. "Jonathan, tell me when she's going to gather her list."

"As soon as they forget. She'll hold them in the Archives."

That's so soon. "She won't get the code first?"

Jonathan looks at me, and I have never seen a face so hopeless. "She knows she'll get the code from you. And she will."

His certainty gets its claws into me, difficult to dislodge. He waves a hand at Gray, coming up to stand behind me. "See? None of it means anything. All of them"—he runs his eyes over the now silent courtyard—"they'll only die later. Or sooner. She gets what she wants, in the end."

"And what about the rest? The ones not on the list. What does she mean to do with them?"

Jonathan smiles, nothing like his politic, public smile on the speaking platform. This is a crazed twisting of his mouth. "The granary," he says. "Haven't you heard there's a shortage?"

I step closer to Jonathan, conscious of the roaring fire, the silent, waiting Lost. "She pulled aside grain for the hundred and fifty?" His expression doesn't change, and it's confirmation enough. There, I think, is the source of our food shortage. But there isn't really going to be one, is there? What there's going to be is a shortage of people. Somehow. "What about the rest of it?"

He makes a noise almost like a laugh.

"Is it poisoned?" I ask him. "Jonathan, is the granary poisoned?"

But Jonathan is looking at Liliya again. "When she makes you remember, remember that I kept you safe. I got your name on the list, and . . . I didn't let things happen to you."

"Jonathan," I say again. "Tell me what Janis has done. Is the grain poisoned?"

"Will you promise me?" Jonathan says, ignoring everything but Liliya. He waits for her answer, face going slack with relief when she nods. He takes Liliya's hand, squeezes it once, smiles in a way that is not quite so crazed. Then he turns on his heel and walks straight into the burning houses of the Lost.

❧

I'm not certain how many minutes we stand there, watching the "Without Their Memories, They Are Lost" plaque burn to ash beneath a sky brightening for the sun. But when the noise has returned to the courtyard, subdued muttering and talk, I see clean streaks in the soot and dirt on my sister's face. "I was the leverage," she says. "Always the leverage."

"I know," I say. "Gray was mine." I'm aware of Gray just behind me, silent. I wish I could lean against him, just for a minute, but the barrier of my forgotten-ness stands between us, even more than the heaviness of my pack. The First Book is in there. And as many times as I looked over the list of one hundred and fifty, I never saw my sister's name on it.

I look at this courtyard full of undyed cloth, Rose examining Jemma's head while she rocks Sasha, the burning house that is the pyre of Jonathan of the Council. The silent, resentful glassblower's son. Eshan and my schoolmates fighting over poisoned grain. The anger inside me is both cold and hot. A calculated fury. We've all been taught in Canaan to write the truth. Now it's time to say the truth. When I was tied to that post I thought that Janis only has power because of our belief, and the Forgetting is what gives her the power to be believed. The truth, then, is the only real weapon I have. I have to topple their belief. And her.

"When you take Mother to the Archives," I tell Liliya, "shut all the doors. Seal it off. And once the Forgetting starts, you cannot open the doors, do you understand? For three full days. There's access to water but that's it. Get any supplies you can along the way." I look at the courtyard of people that Janis decided were unworthy, insufficient. "Take them all, Liliya. And anyone else you can convince to come. Get Rose from the baths to help you. The Lost will follow her."

I watch my sister gaze at the dirty faces and confusion around us, and I see her head come up, the curls flip over her shoulder. She's already organizing. Then her eyes narrow. "Where are you going?"

"To find Janis." I think I know where she is. In the clock tower. I run a hand over the back of my neck. It's where Gray's hand belongs, pulling my forehead onto his chest. I look back at him.

"I'm with you," he says, answering the unasked. As long as that bottle is in my pack, I think, he's not going anywhere else. I want to tell him to go with my sister. But this is his fight as much as mine, though he doesn't remember why.

"Take care of Mother," I say to Liliya. "And if I don't come before the sky is white, you have to shut the doors."

~&~

We see our first body as the field road changes to flagstones. A man, a sandalmaker, I think, struck on the head. It looks like he was running from the city. Maybe from the granary. I check, but he's not alive. I pick up our pace. I'm fairly sure that anger is the force moving my legs right now. Deep down, I can feel that I probably shouldn't be out of bed.

"Is it always like this?" Gray asks.

I look back at the column of smoke rising like a mountain in the air behind us, at the matching one over the city, dark against the sky's blushing gold. "No," I say. "Or at least, we didn't know it was."

"I wanted to kill him, you know." I think he means Jonathan until he says, "In the underground room. I didn't want to hurt him. I wanted to kill him."

He doesn't say anything more, but I know what he's asking. "You're not like that," I tell him. I want to say that somewhere, deep down, he is remembering me. I can't wait to put that needle in his skin.

The lane down to the granary is choked with carts, pieces of stone, rocks, a dropped scythe or two, and what I think is the shape of another body beside the granary walls. The gates are blackened, smoking. Someone has tried to burn them down. In the distance I can hear shouting, but right here, right now, it's eerily quiet, the air around me a held breath. I wonder if Eshan and Veronika and Michael and the rest of them are still in there, protecting vats full of poisoned grain. I wonder if Janis is watching them, safe in her perch while the sky lightens and the buds on the forgetting trees crack.

The amphitheater drops down like a hole before me, the clock tower rising, and the Council, or what's left of it, is huddled around the speaking platform. They have their families with them—husbands, wives, children. Grandchildren, some of them. Less than two hours to the comet, and the Forgetting. I turn to Gray.

"I don't know what's going to happen," I begin. I don't even know if I can do this. "But if it goes wrong, I want you to grab my pack and run to the Archives. Get inside, all the way to the back." I know he doesn't know where the Archives is.

He nods, looking at me hard, mouth twisting into that tiny smile. His gaze slides down to my necklace and back. "Don't be afraid," he says.

I'm not afraid. I've lost my fear. Or no, I think. That's not true. I'm just more afraid of not changing this than trying to change it. I take a deep breath, turn, and take the first step downward.

"Where is Janis?" I call. The channel rushes down its waterfall on one side, Gray on my other. The amphitheater was made for sound, and my voice had been forceful, echoing as we descend. I see black robes rustling, turning to watch my approach, muttering behind hands. "Where is she?" I demand.

Anson the Planter is coming up the steps to meet me, his wife staring blank-faced as he does. "Where have you been?" he says, voice held low, and for a moment he sounds like someone who is my father. I don't have time to talk about it.

"Where is she?"

He glances over his shoulder and up. I look out across the vast amphitheater, over the faces turning to me, up the latticed stone to Canaan's clock, a spike against a sunrising sky that will soon turn white. And I am going to speak, to shout, to tell them all.

"Janis! Come down!"

Every pair of eyes below is turned to me. Unlike the Nadia of the sunlight days, I don't care.

"Come down!" I demand. And then I see the black robes on the stairs through the stone lattice, coming down with slow, deliberate steps. Janis emerges from the tower onto the speaking platform, tall and elegant.

"Nadia the Dyer's daughter," Janis says. "How good to see you well. And the glassblower's son . . ." Her gaze on Gray is like a brief dose of poison. "We'd feared the worst."

I smile at her composure. Until very recently, as in just a few minutes ago, she must have thought me unconscious and locked up. I say, "You told me once that I should feel free to share my concerns with the Council. I have some concerns."

Janis smoothes her sleeve. "A strange time and place to request a meeting. The Forgetting is almost here."

"The concern I want to share with the Council is about your rule of Canaan."

"I do not 'rule' Canaan, Nadia. The Council and I work together for the good of the city."

"I disagree."

The Council stares back at me. Rachel the Supervisor, Arthur of the Metals, Tessa of the Granary, Deming, Li, and the rest of them, Anson just a few steps away. Everyone but Reese. And Jonathan. Janis smiles.

"What, exactly, do you accuse me of?"

"That you have never lost your memories to a Forgetting. That you remember, and have never informed the Council. That you understand exactly what causes the Forgetting, and that you know how to bring memories back, and that you choose to do neither. That you deliberately make people Lost by removing their books. That only a few minutes ago you almost succeeded in burning the Lost alive in their houses." I see her eyes widen just slightly at "almost." "That you manipulate, coerce, and kill when it suits you, and that you have lied to this city for longer than I've been alive."

I pause. A little out of breath. I don't think I've ever said that many words in a row at my own dinner table, much less in front of a crowd. Especially a wide-eyed, speechless crowd.

"That is much for one person to be accused of, Nadia the Dyer's daughter," Janis says gravely. She is perfect in her dignity. "But can you be certain those things are true? Truth is often as we see it, each to his own."

"Are you saying that if I didn't actually see the houses of the Lost burning down, that it didn't happen?"

"I am saying, Nadia, that there are nuances. When you say it is true that the houses of the Lost are burned down, is that a literal statement, or are they still partially standing, or did someone leave a fire burning and smoke up a room? Your perception of the words, you see, affects what you believe to be true."

"No, I think I'm saying that you stacked fuel against the walls and had it set on fire with the doors locked, and that the smoke is still in the sky." I point beyond the fields, where a mountain of black smoke billows into the air. "Are you denying you did it?"

"Nadia, I have been in the clock tower. You just saw me come down. How could I do such a thing?"

The Council stares up at me with varying degrees of frustration and dislike, and with confusion, as if I've been speaking in a different way, like Mother. I almost laugh. Janis is good, and she is enjoying this game.

"If you have something to accuse me of, Nadia, then I think you will have to prove it. Can you?"

A challenge. I motion for Gray to stay where he is, and I go to meet her, down the stairs one at a time, through the silent Council members, up the steps and onto the speaking platform. A scream echoes from somewhere in the city, and no one looks around. Our eyes are on Janis as she glides to her chair, lowers her body into it. For the first time I can see she's been sick; there's a hint of frailty in the movement. But her smile is strong, dark eyes glittering in the new light. She includes the watching Council with a sweep of her hand.

"Prove your accusations, Nadia the Dyer's daughter."

Truth has to be written, because it is. The hard part is when and how to tell it.

NADIA THE DYER'S DAUGHTER
BOOK 6, PAGE 87, 7 YEARS AFTER THE FORGETTING

CHAPTER TWENTY-ONE

I think of all the things Janis is guilty of. Her precious one hundred and fifty. Gray. The countless others she made Lost or had killed because they didn't pass her tests. The ones who weren't healthy enough, or smart enough, who would not or could not reproduce, all because of her childish, warped view of Earth's directive. Of Canaan's purpose.

And I stare back into the serious faces of the Council and know I can't tell them any of that, no matter how true. How can I ask them to believe they're standing on the wrong planet? To understand what I've seen in the mountain? It's too much to take in, too much to believe on my word alone. Anything I talk about here, anything I say to shake their belief, will have to be about Canaan itself.

"We are waiting, Nadia. What do you have to accuse me of?"

This is something out of my nightmares. On the speaking platform, all eyes on me, everything to gain or lose based on my words. I look at Gray, seated now, elbows on knees, tense. Watching. Angry. Afraid. I hear his screams in my head. Janis still smiles. I stand a little straighter, face the Council. Anson gives me a brief nod.

"I say that Janis has never lost her memories during a Forgetting, and has never shared this information with the Council. That she is using a name she's had since before the first Forgetting, because she can remember it." .

I lower my pack to the ground, open it. "This is the First Book of the Forgetting"—I only just see Janis's flinch of surprise—"which originally belonged to Erin Atan. In it she talks of her daughter, Janis Atan. And this"—now I pull out the long knife with the engraving—"belongs to Janis, and has the name Kevin Atan engraved in the metal. And it's not a thing we know how to make now."

I see Tessa of the Granary and Arthur of the Metals put their heads together, others frowning, talking among themselves. Janis adjusts her robes in the chair.

"I do not deny that I am using the name I was born with," she says. The murmuring stops. "But my mother was always very particular about our books, that our books would never be lost. I don't understand what Nadia means by the 'first' forgetting, or why she thinks there were no Forgettings before this book. Haven't we always forgotten?" She looks at me kindly. "I've always taken 'first' to mean 'most important,' Nadia, because in this book we learn to live with our forgetting. The knife you have there was made by a metalworker in my father's time. His name and skill are forgotten."

These are all lies, and we both know it. But the rest of them don't. And then I see the last thing I expected, something that makes some of my hope extinguish like an unneeded light in the white room. Jonathan of the Council steps up onto the platform to stand beside his grandmother, as if what happened at the houses of the Lost just . . . didn't. He must have walked right through that burning building and found his way out the other side, to escape that accusing crowd. I remember his certainty when he said Janis would get that code out of me. That she would have her list and kill the rest. That she would make it happen, in the end. He slides into his place behind his grandmother's chair.

"What else do you accuse me of?" she asks.

I close my eyes for just a moment, face the Council again. "I say that Janis knows the cause of the Forgetting, has always known the cause, and has deliberately not protected Canaan from it. Gray the Glassblower's son has forgotten already. He was made to forget. By Janis."

I see Gray sit up, look again at the woman in the chair.

"Wait," says Arthur of the Metals, "are you saying Janis understands the Forgetting, or that she can cause it?"

"Both," I reply.

Arthur looks at Gray, and then back at me. Gray stands, unsure of what's required of him.

"I think I should inform the Council," says Janis, "that Nadia and the glassblower's son have recently begun an understanding, or something like it." The tiny note of derision was expertly done. "I'm afraid Gray would do or say nearly anything for Nadia."

"The glassblower's son," I snap, losing my temper, "is covered in wounds you gave him while making him forget." I see Anson glance at Gray. He would have seen the stains on the back of Gray's shirt. He frowns. Janis looks at the Council, and then back at me. With pity.

"If Gray is injured I'm sorry to hear it. But everyone knows you've been hiding with him over the wall. If Gray was attacked, that can hardly be blamed on me, and only reinforces my position that our city should stay as it is, behind the walls that keep us safe."

I cannot believe the smoothness, the way she wriggles out of every turn. The truth is here. I'm saying it. And they cannot see it. I dig through the pack and hold up the last clear bottle of Remembering. Gray's bottle. "I also accuse Janis of knowing how to cure the Forgetting, and withholding this cure from the people. Your memories are hidden, not lost . . ."

"The Council knows I study this subject, Nadia, and have had no success."

"This will bring all of the memories back. It goes beneath the skin . . ."

I hesitate, lower the bottle. It sounds fantastic, even to me. Janis doesn't even respond this time. She lets the Council murmur. There's a boom from somewhere in the city, up Meridian, though I can't quite see where, only distant smoke. The sky is lightening.

"How many on this Council has Janis coerced?" I say. "How many have heard Janis suggest that she knows something about you, or someone you love, and that it would be best to vote the way she wants?"

If they have, they don't want to admit it. Not in front of the rest of them.

"If it's not true," I shout, "then why would I be telling you this now, when you're about to forget it again? I have nothing to gain! No reason to be standing here. Unless what I'm saying is true."

There's a beat of silence as the idea is considered. Then Janis says, "Children Nadia's age often don't think their actions through. They are impulsive. I'm sure some of you have experienced this with your own—"

"I'll try it." The Council looks around, and it takes me a moment to focus on the one who spoke. Anson the Planter is coming down the amphitheater stairs like I did, through the Council, up the steps of the platform, his eyes on the bottle of Remembering still in my hand. "If that's the cure, then put it inside me and let's see if I have any memories. You say it goes beneath the skin?"

Lydia the Weaver says, "No, Anson," but it's soft, like she knows he's going to do it anyway. She has my half sisters by the hands.

"If Janis wants her to prove it, then let her prove it," Anson says to the Council. "Then we'll know." He looks at me and says, "I want to know."

He wants to help me. He wants, I tell myself, to remember me. I could know why he left us. I could know what happened to Anna. To my mother. I blink long. But this dose is meant for Gray. Gray's arms are crossed, watching me.

"Oh, Anson," says Janis. She sounds old, sad. The Council's attention instantly sweeps back to her. "I appreciate your position, and what you're trying to do. But your feelings of loyalty here are regrettably misplaced." She turns to the Council. "Anson has become aware that"—she pauses, as if trying to think what to say—"that he is Nadia's father. I'm sure you can all see the truth of it."

Because I look just like him. I glance around at the staring Council, their families, then at Lydia the Weaver. I've never felt sorry for her before, but I suppose this isn't exactly what she'd hoped for, either. I also see that she's not shocked. She knew.

"It doesn't matter," Anson says, looking at me, "assuming what she's saying is true. I'll try the cure."

"Oh, but it does matter," Janis says, voice softening, "because there is the issue of how you have your current identity. I don't believe Nadia or any of her sisters have books that say Anson the Planter is their father, do they?"

"Which makes me the liar, and not them," Anson replies. "If I've falsified books, then someone write it down quick, before the Forgetting, and I'll take your punishment after. In the meantime, let's see if I can remember doing it."

My eyes are stinging. He's trying to help me. I look at Gray. This was meant for him. This bottle is his. He deserves it, and without it, I don't think he'll choose me. Not again. But his credibility has been compromised by Janis just as thoroughly as my father's. I sit down right where I am, pull the tube with the needle out of my pack. My hands are shaky.

"Jonathan," Janis is saying, "the clock is moving and I believe we need to detain Anson. We cannot tolerate rule-breaking or lies in Canaan . . ."

She doesn't want me to put this in Anson, I think. That's a good sign. I hurry, draw up the fluid into the tube. I don't know exactly how to do this, and I'm a little clumsy at it. I don't know how much to give. I'm not even a hundred percent certain that it works. Jonathan is coming across the platform. If this doesn't convince them, then the Forgetting will happen and nothing will have changed. Only everything will have changed, because Janis will massacre three-quarters of the city with poisoned grain.

I stand, the tube full of clear fluid, sharp end out. Jonathan grabs Anson by the arm. I look up at my father. "Help me," I whisper.

His brows come down, and I turn and plunge the needle into an upper arm, right through the black cloth. Only the arm belongs to Jonathan. Anson turns and grabs Jonathan quick, holding him in place while he struggles. Janis hisses, stands up, but it's too late. I've pushed in the fluid, and the cure is inside him.

Something booms again in the city, close this time, amplified to an earsplitting noise inside the half hole where we stand. Fire, huge and sudden, shoots upward from the high ground outside the amphitheater, I think near the entrance to the granary. I hear shouts, yelling, a scream of pain. Jonathan doesn't even react. His eyes have gone wide with fear. I saw Gray afraid of forgetting, but what Jonathan faces by remembering must be beyond belief.

"Jonathan," I whisper, "I'm sorry. But it's not for long. The Forgetting is almost here. Help me," I say, just like I asked my father. "If they don't believe her, she has no power over them. Or you . . ."

"Liliya has to . . . stay on the list . . ."

"There won't be a list if you just help me end her. All they have to do is believe you. Say the truth. Don't let it happen to anyone else."

Anson lets him go and Jonathan falls to his knees. He's already sweating.

The gathering in front of the speaking platform has shrunk into a tighter knot, some eyes on Jonathan, some on the flames at the granary. We can hear the fighting. Janis doesn't even look up at it.

"Council members," she says, pulling their attention back, "let them fight. They will forget soon enough . . ." I see Tessa of the Granary frowning at that. "We must get to the Council House so we can wake together and rebuild our city. Arthur, Li, would you help me detain Nadia and her father? And, Deming, if you would help me with the glassblower's son . . ."

"Nadia," Anson's voice behind me whispers, "when I say go, you grab the glassblower and you run. Get over the wall."

I lift my eyes to Gray, standing still, arms crossed. Betrayed. I promised him his memories. Lydia looks stricken, her girls confused. Jonathan pushes himself to his feet.

"I'm not her grandson," he says. He's smiling, almost laughing. The Council falls silent.

Janis says quickly, "Council, what I have been trying to develop, what Nadia has so naively named as a cure for the Forgetting, is the result of my experiments to take away pain. But sadly, all this substance seems to do is bring on hallucinations. Like Nadia's . . ." I look at her in disbelief, but the Council has only paused again, interested.

"She made it all up," Jonathan says, "because she never had children. Everyone has to have children. The right children . . ."

"Jonathan." Janis says it like a reprimand, still managing to sound hurt. "Like I said, hallucinations . . ."

We flinch as a group at another explosion from the granary. They must be using barrels of oil.

"Jonathan," I say, as gently as I can. He's sweaty, manic. "Tell them what you remember."

"Deming, Tessa," Janis orders, "please detain Nadia and—"

"You," Jonathan says suddenly. He's looking at Tessa of the Granary. "How's your back?"

Tessa's face goes blank.

"She likes backs," Jonathan says, "because it's hard to see the scars. After the Forgetting, you might not even know they're there unless someone tells you. But at the time, you scream and scream." Jonathan puts his hands over his ears. I can guess what he's hearing. Then he looks at Tessa's husband. "Describe her scars."

I don't know Tessa's husband's name, but he is not a brave man. He shakes his head.

"Jonathan, sit down. You're not yourself," Janis commands.

"Did you know she reads your books?" Jonathan says. "All the time. She gets yours from the room in the Archives whenever she wants, the rest she makes Gretchen bring to her. That's how she understands how to push you. How to test you. See what you're made of. See if you're worthy of the list." He looks at Emily, wife of Arthur of the Metals. "Describe the scars on the back of Arthur's thighs."

Emily glances at Janis, evidently made of stronger stuff than Tessa's husband. "Long slashes," she says. "Thin . . ."

"Six on one side, five on the other," says Jonathan. Emily nods, and Jonathan looks sick. I wonder if Janis made him do it, whatever it was.

"Council," says Janis quietly, "I owe you an apology. Jonathan is seeing things that did not happen. Or . . ." She looks accusingly around the half circle. "Or is there a plot here to discredit me?"

"I don't see any plot and I don't see any hallucinations," says Arthur practically. "I've had those scars since before the last Forgetting, and I've never told a soul except my wife . . ."

"Emily," asks Janis, "is this what you were discussing with Jonathan in private the other day?"

"I didn't have any discussion with Jonathan!" says Emily. Arthur turns to his wife, a look full of accusation, and I think Janis knew there was mistrust there. Emily lifts up her book.

"Here, you can read—"

"As if you'd write that down."

Jonathan sinks down to his knees again, meets my eyes. And he is laughing. The bell above us tolls. First hour of the waking. Before the next bell it will be the Forgetting, and none of them will know this ever happened. I see Jonathan's eyes find the First Book of the Forgetting at his feet. There's a third explosion at the granary, and someone goes head over heels over the wall at the top of the amphitheater and down the terraced seats, bouncing until they roll to a stop halfway down. It's a woman, and she doesn't move.

"Arthur, Li," Janis begins, "get Nadia and the glassblower to the Council House. We have delayed too long. Deming, you take Anson."

Deming is already easing his family away from the platform, and Arthur hesitates, but Li starts to come for me, Rachel the Supervisor taking Arthur's place.

"Run," Anson says to me. Then, "Lydia, run! Do you hear me?"

Lydia backs away with her girls but I don't run. I stay where I am. I can't believe Janis just won. I told the truth, everything I knew that they could possibly believe. I broke my promise to Gray. I made Jonathan remember. And she turned all of it to her advantage. My eyes meet Gray's, and he is motionless, so still that I know he's full of rage. I can hear glass breaking, see the orange of the flames, smoke hazing the pink-and-gold sky. How do you stop someone like Janis, when the ropes she uses to tie us are all in our heads?

"She's not here," Jonathan is muttering. I look down. He's turning the pages of the First Book, left sitting on top of my pack, frantic. "She's not here . . ."

Anson is practically pushing my frozen body off the platform, Li coming to take him by the arms. "Get them inside the Archives," I whisper to my father. "Seal yourselves in and you can escape the Forgetting . . ."

"Liar!" Jonathan shrieks, voice echoing, booming, bouncing around our heads. He stands, dropping the First Book to the ground. "You promised!"

He means Liliya, I realize. Liliya isn't on the list. Then I see that Jonathan has a knife in his hand, the one that says "Kevin Atan."

"Jonathan!" Janis's voice is a warning, but she takes a step back.

"You said the Lost were the last ones!" he screams.

"Jonathan," she says again, soothing.

"Wait," says Arthur of the Metals, "did she have you burn the Lost?"

"She said getting rid of them saved her!" Jonathan replies. Then to Janis, "You said I was saving her!"

"Let the Forgetting come, Jonathan . . ."

"I want to know why we're standing here talking and not protecting the food supply," says Tessa.

"Because it's poisoned, that's why!" yells Jonathan. "Isn't it, Janis?"

"How many of us are ready to admit she forced us to vote her way?" asks Anson.

Jonathan screams, "You didn't write her down!"

"Council," Janis shouts, and everyone pauses. "The Forgetting is on us. Come! Leave Anson if you must, but I will have the Dyer's daughter and the glassblower. They are needed." She smiles as Li resumes his stalk toward me, Rachel heading up the stairs toward Gray. Then she turns to Jonathan, looking for all the world like a grandmother. "Just a little while, and all this will go away," she says. "You won't remember any of it. Or her . . ."

Jonathan lunges. Janis leaps back, Li grabs for Jonathan, and Jonathan swipes with the knife, catching Li's forearm, sending him to his knees as blood wells through his sleeve. Jonathan doesn't even look at him. He just walks toward Janis. No one moves. No one tries to stop him, his footsteps making the platform creak, smiling like he's tying someone to the bloodstained plaque. Janis watches him come, studies his face as if it were a specimen in a jar, and then she is off the platform, not seeming old or frail at all, sprinting up the steps of the amphitheater.

Jonathan watches her go for a brief second, his smile getting bigger. Then he chases after her, Gray darting across the seats and up the stairs to go after him. And I am running, too.

Past my father's shouts just like the last Forgetting, up the stairs, cresting the top edge of the amphitheater into a fiery chaos.

Smoke blacks the growing light from the sky, and the air is loud with shrieking, shouting, nothing looking as it should. Down the street to my right I see the gates to the granary are truly on fire this time, flames shooting, roaring into the sky, half shapes of dark figures looming over the top of the granary wall. They must be on ladders. To my left a group of ten or twelve people, women and men, hide behind overturned carts, the area between littered with broken pieces of harvest equipment and a pool of burning oil and shattered glass. Another group is using what I think might be a table to ram the flaming gates, trying to knock them in while the figures on the walls drop stones on them. Three or four bodies lie still in the mess. And this, I think, is the Forgetting, and I don't even have time to fear it.

I can't find Janis, but silhouetted against the light of the gate fire I watch Gray catch Jonathan of the Council by the back of the robes and throw him to the ground, the knife skittering across the flagstones. I run to him. A bottle sails over my head, bursts in a small explosion of yellow fire. I dodge it, stumbling over and through the cluttered street.

"Tell me how to remember!" Gray is yelling. He's got a knee on Jonathan's chest, hands around his neck, hitting Jonathan's head against the ground. "Tell me how to remember!"

"Gray!" I shout. "Stop!"

"Tell me!"

Jonathan is laughing. I wonder if remembering has made his mind snap. "You should let yourself forget," he pants, flat on his back, arms splayed wide. "We're all going to forget . . ."

He's not even defending himself. His eyes roll to me. "She knows. She knows how to remember . . ."

Someone is burned at the gates. I can hear it. A stone or another bottle goes whizzing past my head. I take a few steps more into the battle zone, wave my hands in the air. "Stop!" I scream. "Stop fighting!"

The group behind the overturned cart pauses, as do the rammers in front of the gate.

"The grain is poisoned!" I shout. I wave my hands and the air goes still but for the roar of the flaming gates. "You're fighting over nothing, do you hear me? Janis poisoned the grain!"

"You tell me!" Gray screams. Jonathan's eyes bulge as his neck is squeezed.

"Gray, stop! Let him go . . ." I look to the fighters, still for the moment. "We can escape the Forgetting," I shout. "You don't have to forget!"

"Nadia!" Eshan is coming over the top of the granary wall, dropping down to the clutter below. "Nadia, we thought you were—"

Then he sees Gray throttling Jonathan of the Council and stops short. And in the middle of smoke and fire and violence I look at the expression on Eshan's face and know instantly that Imogene was right. I did misunderstand at the festival, completely misinterpreted Eshan's reaction the night he found me at the glassblower's. And I know why he was on Janis's list of the Lost, too. It wasn't me Eshan was looking at across that fire in the blacknut grove. It was Gray.

Eshan stutters, "I . . . We thought you were . . ." But he doesn't finish the sentence.

"Tell me how to remember!" Gray screams.

I put a hand on Gray's shoulder, reach down, and break the lock of his hands around Jonathan's neck. Jonathan gasps, coughs, and Gray rolls off him onto the glass-strewn street while Jonathan sits up, rubbing his neck and his bleeding head, laughing. I see Imogene and Veronika coming over the granary wall, Karl of the Books and Roberta from next door craning their necks from behind the harvest carts. Eshan hasn't moved. I stand between the two sides.

"Listen to me!" I yell. "The grain is poisoned. We need to set it on fire so it can't be used after the Forgetting." The faces around me are blank. "You can believe me right now or not, but this is truth. The grain has to be burned, and then we need to get to the Archives. If we can get inside and seal ourselves in, we can escape the Forgetting. But we have to go. Right now. Before the sky turns white."

Imogene comes to stand next to her brother, a bad gash on her cheek. Eshan looks directly at me, not at Gray. "You were going over the wall, weren't you?"

I nod. "Everything we should be afraid of is inside the walls, Eshan, not out. But we don't have to forget. It's not inevitable."

I can see him thinking, see him make a decision. "I'll set the grain on fire. You take the others where you need to go."

Imogene says, "And we won't forget at all, inside the Archives?"

"No." I glance at the sky. "But you have to hurry. And, Eshan . . ." He turns to look at me, already on his way back into the granary. "I'm sorry."

He looks confused, but only for a moment. He glances once at Gray, almost says something, and then doesn't. He just nods once before he runs back to the granary. Gray is still sitting where I left him, panting hard. Jonathan and the knife are gone.

"He's right," Gray says. "I should forget." I realize he's talking about Jonathan. "If this is all there is . . ." He holds out an arm, showing me the fire, the broken things, Karl of the Books weeping over the body of his wife. "If this is all there is to remember, then I don't want it!"

He can't do that. Not again. "Don't forget," I say. "Please. Not again. You marked me." I hold up the necklace. "You wrote my name in your book. You told me to remember for us."

He stares at my face, intent, trying to remember. He can't.

"I know it's not good enough," I say, "but it's better than nothing. I can be your memories. But you have to come with me."

"Why should I trust you?" he asks. I have no answer for him. Because that bottle of Remembering went into Jonathan of the Council instead of him.

He gets to his feet, moves away from me. I drop my out-stretched hand, rub it over my tear-streaked face instead. I look up at the blushing sky, then back at the little group forming around me.

"We have to run," I say.

❧

We take off down the streets. Gray, Chi, Veronika, and the rest of Eshan's band, Karl of the Books, Roberta, and Pratim, Jemma's husband. I don't know what happened to the rest of the fighters around the granary. Or the Council members. Or Janis. I lead them up Meridian and across First Bridge.

"Don't touch the trees!" I shout back at them, ducking beneath a limb. The buds look ready to burst. We pass the man I'd seen walking with Frances the Doctor, yelling and banging on his own door. He has his book, but he's locked out of his house. We take him with us, and on the turn down Einstein I step over a body below a broken window. There's a party going on inside, music and drunken singing. Veronika bangs on the door, trying to get them to come with us, but they won't answer.

We hurry on, past the Learning Center, which has been ransacked, the word "lies" painted in red, scrawling letters over the word "truth" on its sign, and then I find the potter's wife, huddled behind a row of porch columns. I'm not sure what's happened to her, but she doesn't have her book, and her hair has been cut, nearly to the scalp. Roberta helps her run.

We turn onto Copernicus and suddenly we are in the back of a crowd, a throng of people, in cloth both dyed and undyed, a few scattered black robes present, choking the street from one side to the other. I start to push through the bodies, and then I see why everyone is standing so quiet, so watchful. The Archives doors are shut, and right in front of them, arms spread wide, is Janis, a knife in her outstretched hand. And the knife she holds is pressed against Genivee's chest.

For those who forget, I think the loss must feel a little like death.

CHAPTER TWENTY-TWO

I push through the bodies, burst from the crowd into a moment that is a held breath. A piece of glass, teetering too close to the edge.

"Nadia." Janis greets me with a smile, her elegant hair the slightest bit mussed. "I suppose this is all your doing?" The hand not holding the knife gestures to include the gathered crowd, the pockmarked doors of the Archives. It looks like they were trying to break in. Genivee stands perfectly still, eyes closed, her back against the sign that says "Remember Our Truth," Liliya just a meter away, tears running from her eyes. Mother sits behind her, on the ground, face hidden in her hands.

"Get away from my Archives," says Janis. Her voice rings down the street. "All of you! I will be the one to say who goes in and who does not." She glances at the sky. "But first, you must all forget . . ."

I've had enough. Of talk, of twisting words. Of her. I'm on her before she sees me coming, pushing her body away from my sister, grappling with the arm that holds the knife. "Run!" I yell at Genivee, and then suddenly I have help. Liliya is with me, forcing Janis down by the hair until I can step on the arm with the knife. Janis lets the knife drop.

"Council!" Janis calls. But Li and Reese are not here, and none of the other Council members move, still unsure, maybe, about what they heard in the amphitheater. I see Lydia and the girls, but not Anson. Genivee has disappeared to our mother. I reach down and yank off the key Janis is wearing around her neck while Liliya holds her down, run for the Archives door, and put it to the lock. The key doesn't fit. I try again. And then I bang on the door.

"Gretchen!" I scream, bruising my fists. "Gretchen, open the door!"

I hear Janis start to laugh, a slow, gleeful chuckle, and when I turn my head she's thrown Liliya off, the knife back in her hand. The crowd in the streets does nothing. Just watches. Waits. Like the people of Canaan have done since the first Forgetting. They could storm this building, overwhelm her if they wanted. But they are firmly tied. Inside their heads. I glance up to the golden sky, to the beams of light that look ready to shoot out from beyond the mountains.

"You, Nadia the Dyer's daughter," she says, "are out of time. Any minute now, no one here is going to remember this."

And when that happens she is coming after me, I think. Because I remember. Because she knows I have that code. As soon as the Forgetting happens and I have lost my allies, she will try to take me. And I will suffer before I die, knowing that all but one hundred and fifty of our city are dying. I see Gray sidling up to the edge of the crowd, and Janis smiles, suddenly becoming our own grandmother, the beloved leader of Canaan who cares for us.

"And why," Janis is calling, sweeping her arms to everyone, "would you ever want to escape the Forgetting? The Forgetting is your gift. Your birthright. Your chance to leave your cares behind and start again."

I see a subtle shift in some of the crowd.

"You," Janis says gently, "Glassblower's son."

Gray stiffens just a little when he realizes she means him, and I hear a cry from the middle of the crowd that I think must be Delia, only just now realizing her son is alive.

"Wouldn't you like to forget the things you have seen today? The city after the Forgetting is nothing like the city before. All those unpleasant memories could be erased from your mind. And you . . ."

I see the potter's wife flinch beneath Janis's gaze, bookless, hand on her shorn head.

"Perhaps you would like to become someone else? A brand-new person, with no wrongs that need righting. Or you"—now she's addressing the husband of Frances the Doctor—"you might like to forget the betrayal of your wife. Blot it from existence. And, Roberta"—if possible, her voice becomes even more kind—"you have a child with the Lost, don't you? Aren't you ready to lay aside your pain? And where are you, Karl of the Books? Would you like to forget that your wife lies dead at the granary?"

I feel sick, so much more than when I was unconscious on a bed. One way or another, Janis has made all these things happen. Or pushed people until they could.

"There is no need," Janis says, hands up, imploring, voice ringing down the street, "to live with the past. The Forgetting allows us to create our perfect society without regrets. Now go to your homes, await the Forgetting in peace, and start your lives again."

I open my mouth to speak, to shout that she will kill everyone she hasn't chosen. But another voice speaks instead.

"And what about me?"

Jonathan of the Council is on the edge of the crowd, pushing back his black hood, face bruised and bloodied, robes covered in dirt. I don't know where he came from, but he's not acting manic now, or crazed. He's calm, and it's like all Janis's composure has been transferred to him. I see her face twist with rage. And hatred.

"What about you?" she spits. "I gave you all the skills to be the next Head of Council, trained you from a child. But your mind is weak . . ."

"And you are a liar," Jonathan says. "You didn't write her down."

Liliya steps toward him, a hand out, but Janis brandishes the knife, motioning her back. "Of course her name isn't there! What made you think Liliya was worthy of our society? What family does she come from, after all? And what makes you think that you should be chosen?" She practically spits the next words. "Weak. One girl, and your mind is weak. Worthless—"

I never saw it coming, any more than Janis saw me when I attacked her. All I know is that Janis is suddenly against the plaque, across the "T" in "Truth," arms out, like Hedda and the others, only Janis is facing forward, eyes wide and open in surprise, pinned not with ropes, but by the knife that says "Kevin Atan," thrust all the way through her middle. She gasps.

"That," Jonathan shouts, "is for my little brother." He puts a hand on her neck, pulls out the knife, making her eyes go wide, and plunges it again while someone screams. "For Liliya," he yells, and does it again. And again. "And for every single person"—each word gets a stab—"you made forget. And this . . . is for Canaan, and this"—he thrusts in the knife one more time and leaves it there—"is for me." He lets Janis's body slump into the little gully around the Archives, very dead.

I blink, shocked into nothingness. The plaque is smeared red, and Jonathan is panting as he turns to look at us. He's spattered, a few places on his face running with blood. He reaches down, picks up the knife Janis has dropped, and uses it to cut the tether to his fancy-stitched bag, the one that holds his book. He tosses away the knife and then his book, its corner landing in the pooling blood. Then he approaches my sister.

"I'm going to go forget now," he says to Liliya, smiling, "but when you remember, remember that I kept you safe."

Liliya nods. And then my hands clutch the sides of my dirty tunic as I realize he's coming to me. I've never seen Jonathan so relaxed and contented. It's an odd expression beneath all that blood.

"And you. You won't ever make me remember?" he asks.

I think of that last vial, gone into his body instead of Gray's. I can't think of anyone who deserves to forget more. "No, Jonathan. I can't make you remember. I can't make anyone remember, even if I wanted to."

He cocks his head to the side, still smiling. "Why not?"

But whatever he was going to say is lost as he's tackled by Karl of the Books, Rachel the Supervisor getting his hands back, tying them with what is probably someone's hair string. He doesn't fight them. He doesn't care about anything but forgetting now. The far mountain peak glows, edged with a nearly risen sun. Any minute and the sky will turn white and the Forgetting will come. The crowd starts to scatter. I turn and bang on the dented, splintered door.

"Gretchen!" I call. "It's Nadia! Let us in. They're not coming for the books! We can escape the Forgetting! Gretchen!"

I hear a muffled, frightened voice on the other side of the door. "What's happening?"

"We need to get into the Council room, Gretchen. Now! It's not about the books. You don't have to forget!"

"I don't have a key . . ."

Liliya has her ear to the door. She holds up the glass key beside me. "I have it!" I yell. The first beam of sun falls soft and warm on my back. "Open the door, Gretchen!"

I hear the bar across the door lift.

"Gray!" I turn and find him just behind me. "You have to unlock the door. You know how to use the glass key without breaking it. You can't break it, do you understand?"

He looks unsure, but he nods. Liliya puts the key in his hand, and I hear the lock inside the Archives turn.

"Move, Gretchen!" I yell as the door creaks open. I come through with Liliya and Gray, the first of a flood of people gushing through the doors of the Archives. Gretchen jumps to one side as I lead the way through to the anteroom, to the stacks, and to the door in the back wall.

"Liliya!" I say, and she understands, moving back to organize the crowd, keep them from stampeding until we get the door open. They fill the enormous room. I hear both Gretchen and Liliya telling people not to touch the books.

Gray is on his knees at the door, carefully inserting the key. He tries it, and the lock doesn't turn. I see him wince, and I'm afraid the key has broken, but maybe that was only the pain in his back, because on the next try the lock clicks and the door swings open. He looks up at me, smiles, and for one moment, he is my Gray. The Gray of the dark days and Jin's garden.

I go still for a heartbeat, then turn and run back the way I came, pushing against the stream of bodies. How could I have forgotten Jin? I run out the front door. Sunlight beams from the mountain peaks. Almost all of the crowd is inside the Archives now. I'm halfway to Jin's door before I realize Gray is with me.

"What are you doing?" I shout at him. He doesn't answer. But I know. I am his memories. I don't dare let myself think it's something more. I bang on Jin's door, then try the latch. Locked.

"Jin? Jin!"

He probably can't hear me. I find a stone and use it to break Jin's front window. When I push aside the curtain and climb inside, I find him, calm in his sitting room, with his book and a lamp and some tea, waiting to forget. He looks understandably surprised to see me.

"Come!" I yell, giving him no time to argue. I lift the bar on the door and Gray helps me run with him, though Jin really can't do more than hobble quickly. The sun rises, a beautiful sliver of gold, and when we reach the Archives, the people are gone. It's quiet, nothing but the stained sign and the mutilated body that was Janis. Jin stares at it and I push the latch of the Archives door. Locked. And then the sky bursts, a blinding, dazzling white sky moving over us, eating the golden light of the sunrising.

I bang on the door and it opens immediately, while my hand is still in the air. Gretchen drags us inside. I catch a glimpse of the forgetting tree across the street opening its petals, imagine a hint of the first, faint, sweet scent before Gretchen slams shut the door. She starts to lock it but I take the key from her.

"Run!" I shout at her. "It's not sealed here!"

She helps Gray with Jin and they hurry to the anteroom. I shut each layer of doors behind them as they pass, until we're through the stacks and opening the door into the inner room. Noise is the first thing I notice. And then an incredible press of bodies, some milling around, most sitting in groups. There must be three hundred, I think. I slam the door shut. Gray has the glass key, and he works it carefully in the lock, sealing us in.

"You cut that rather fine," says Gretchen, as if I'd almost been late for the inventory.

I do take inventory then, though of people, not books. Jin has found a place to sit with his back to the wall. He looks confused. Not far away is Mother on the floor, eyes closed, Genivee with her. On the other side of the room I see Lydia and my half sisters and Anson the Planter. I'm not sure where he came from, because he wasn't in the crowd outside when Janis died. I don't want to think about how Janis died. Seated near him are Deming and Veronika, who I thought we'd lost on Einstein Street, and then I see the potter's wife and a whole section of undyed cloth. I don't see Li, Jemma the Clothesmaker, or any of her family, or Eshan and Imogene. I don't think they got here from the granary. Rose hands a baby to Roberta, and Roberta sinks to her knees beside Arthur of the Metals and his wife.

Jonathan is against the bookshelves on the back wall, screaming, "You have to let me forget! You have to let me forget!" guarded by Karl of the Books and Rachel the Supervisor, the enormous words "Without Memories, They Are Nothing" rising tall over his head. Keeping him in here is cruel, I think. Just as cruel as keeping the others out. I clench my fists, stand a little straighter.

Someone shouts Gray's name then, and Delia and Nash are running to us, threading their way through the people. Delia crashes into Gray, knocking his back into the wall beside the door, making him hiss with pain. Nash hangs back, again the more observant.

"Where have you been?" Delia starts. "We were so . . ." Then she says, "What's wrong?"

Gray is looking at me, asking the question. "This is your mother," I tell him.

"Delia?" he asks.

I see the moment when it hits her, the realization that Gray has forgotten her. Her face twists, the hurt evident in every line. I know this feeling. Well. Nash puts a hand on her back.

"I'm sorry . . ." Gray says.

"Where's your book?" Delia turns her eyes on me before he can answer. "What did you do?"

I wish I could say I didn't do anything. But this . . . I did this. And none of them will forgive me for it. And how can I blame them? "I'll give you a minute," I say to Gray. He narrows his eyes at me.

"Where are you going?"

"Just over there, to see about my mother and sisters," I lie. I move away. I don't want him to see me cry. And I don't want him to know what I'm about to do. Liliya is instantly by my side. "Is Mother all right?" I ask her. "Genivee?"

"As right as they can be. Where's your book?"

"Lost." I left it on the speaking platform in my pack.

"Did you know this place was stocked? Blankets, and food. Not enough but . . ."

Enough for a hundred and fifty, I think. How long had she meant to keep them in here? Until everyone else was dead? Many people are dead. Gray is where I left him, his mother trying to look at his back, but he doesn't want to let her. He's stiff, arms crossed. If it's horrible to be the only one who remembers, I can also see that it's horrible to be the only one who forgets. Oh, yes. Guilt is a sickness. Jonathan's yells are echoing in the dome above our heads. I have to go.

"I need you to distract Rachel the Supervisor," I whisper.

Liliya looks at me. She has a smudge on her cheek, as if someone touched her with a bloodstained hand. Then she glances toward Rachel and throws back her head.

❧

Liliya pulls Rachel the Supervisor away to talk about organizing the people in the hidden room, and as soon as she goes I sneak up behind Jonathan, half-hidden by the bookshelf he sits against.

"I've come to help you forget," I whisper behind him. "Keep yelling."

I can feel that Jonathan hears me, because his body goes straighter. He continues his constant burble of begging to forget.

"Is it safe to open the door to the cave?" I hiss. He nods his head up and down, still talking, and I slit the string around his wrists with a sharp piece of broken glass, retrieved, unfortunately, from my foot. When his hands are free I give him the glass, let him slit the tie around his feet. Then I help him up. Not slowly, just unobtrusively, we make our way to the column. I don't think anyone has realized there's a door here yet. I crack it open and we slip inside, shutting it against the first hue and cry. The realization that Jonathan is gone.

He's off down the dim stairs of the cave, familiar to him, I can see, a well-traveled path. I run after him, the rock slippery beneath my bare, cut feet, down into the cavern. The water rushes outward, the bright, waving plants covering the walls. I wonder about those plants now, pulling things we can't see out of the air. Now I think that might include spores.

"Jonathan!" I say, trying to catch up to him. "Jonathan!"

He pauses, surrounded by the bright, bizarre plants, looking back half-afraid, like maybe my letting him go is a trick. I listen; but except for the flow of water, the silence feels deep, stretching in every direction. I don't know if they saw us going into that column or not.

"You are going to let me forget?" Jonathan asks. "You won't ever make me remember?"

Now it's my turn to pause. Why does he keep asking me that? *I can't make anyone remember, even if I wanted to*, I'd told him. And he had said, *Why not?*

Jonathan starts off down the cavern, me trotting to keep up. The soft bluish light of the glowworms is only just enough light to see by.

"Wait, Jonathan. Please. I have to ask you a question. I broke all the bottles of Remembering on the shelf. Is there another way to make someone remember?"

He looks back over his shoulder in the strange blue light, smiles at me, a little crooked and funny. I wonder if this is his real smile. And then he says, "Anna."

I'm so surprised I nearly lose my footing. But of course if he has his memories, he might remember Anna. "What about her, Jonathan? Do you know how she died?" I'm stumbling to keep up with him.

"She killed Anna," Jonathan says, matter-of-fact. "With too much Forgetting. Your family . . . some of you remember." Jonathan laughs, without humor. "She used to say how good it was that Anna died. Because it helped her to understand. To make the cure. Vats and vats of it . . ."

"Vats?" I pick up my pace, heart beginning to speed to the rhythm of my feet. "Jonathan, can you show me?"

He stops, looks back at me, a little frightened.

"I don't want to use it on you. I promise."

He nods, smiles at me. And I do think it's his real one. But when we reach the passage that goes under the walls, I catch the faintest whiff of sweet. I grab the end of my tunic, put it over my face, but Jonathan begins to wander. I take his hand, talk to him, try to get him to tell me what he meant by "vats," if that's where the cure is, but when we reach the door to the laboratory I have a slight headache, and Jonathan almost doesn't remember his name. I open the door, the smell of the Forgetting is everywhere, and Jonathan of the Council is gone.

I keep the tunic over my face, keep his hand in mine. The lamps have gone out, and there are no windows, but the door from the stairway is open, spilling down a little light. I tell Jonathan his name, tell him he's in his house. He's so docile. Not worried, or even upset. I send him up the stairs and tell him to stay there until someone comes for him. He thanks me. I can't go up with him. My head is splitting open. I'm sick.

I get a flame going. And that's when I see Reese, right where we left him, in a spray of broken glass. Cold. Dead. Gray must have hit him hard, or just right. I turn away from him and search. Quickly. Before I get too sick to walk back.

I find a cloth wrapped around several needle tubes lying on the floor, what Gray must have dropped when Reese came in the room, and all sorts of bottles and vials. I'm very careful with these, remembering what that blue liquid could do to skin. My body hurts, joints aching and sore. I wish Jonathan had said something besides the word "vat." I don't know what I'm looking for, except that it's clear. And then I think maybe I do.

On top of the counter, in plain view, is a pot with a lid, connected to twisting tubes and open bottles of glass, little pans of fuel for flame, things I don't have the first notion how to use. But when I lift the lid there's a smell—a sharp, fresh smell that clears my head, the odor I noticed when the shelf fell on Reese and the bottles broke around him. What I smelled every time I rubbed the leaves of that plant I brought down from the mountain, the one I gave to Delia.

I draw some of the liquid into one of the needle tubes straight from the pot. I have to drop my tunic to do it, my pulse throbbing, stabbing at my temples. I hold my breath. It's harder than I think to plunge a needle into my own skin. Something inside me insists that I shouldn't. I do it anyway, pushing the needle hard into my leg, and probably not fast enough. It bleeds, but I can feel the sting of the clear liquid getting inside me. I breathe through my tunic and wait, not looking, but also not quite able to turn my back to the body on the floor. If that was Janis's poison I just shot inside me then Reese and I will probably lie here a long time. But I think it isn't. I think my headache is easing.

I fill the rest of the needles and hurry out of the underground room, back through the cave, every step I take stronger. When I reach the waving plants I stop, set down my cloth with the needles, take down my hair, unbraid what's still braided, run my fingers through the tangles, and then slip into the rushing river. It's warm, as I suspected, but with a strong current. I have to be careful. Hang on to the water-slicked rocks. But I also can't risk bringing any spores back into the inner room of the Archives. I even rinse the cloth and the needles.

When I creep back in through the column I'm dripping, and everyone I know is angry with me. Anson is talking to Liliya and Genivee, all three of them stopping their conversation to stare when I come back through the door. "In a minute," I say, pushing past them. Rose has Gray to one side, his shirt up, tending his back while Delia watches. They're all three looking at me like they wish I'd just stayed wherever I went to, though I think Rose's anger might have something to do with the wounds she's washing.

"Did you just turn that murderer loose?" Delia says at the same time Gray tells me, "You said you weren't going to leave." I ignore both of them. I'm leaving a puddle of cave water on the floor. I hold out a hand to Gray.

"Come with me," I say. "Now."

We are made of our memories. I've read those words every day of my life. Today I decided that they're true. We are who we have been. But it's my choice today that is the memory of tomorrow. It's my choice that determines what I will become. Not the memories of the past.

NADIA THE DYER'S DAUGHTER
IN THE BLANK PAGES OF
NADIA THE PLANTER'S DAUGHTER
BOOK 1

CHAPTER TWENTY-THREE

I take him back to the bookshelves, to the other side, where I untied Jonathan, and when I look back I see Rose put a hand on Delia's arm, stopping her from coming after us.

"Sit," I tell him.

He does, and I sit down cross-legged in front of him, laying my wet bundle to one side. And least we're slightly away from the crowd here. But now I don't know exactly what to say. I have to give him a choice, and it's coming hard.

"You are so irritating," Gray says. "You're always saying one thing and doing the other, and I can't understand you at all. And then you run off, and I'm so worried, I can't understand *me*. Then you come back and I'm mad at you all over again."

I've hardly allowed myself to meet his gaze since he forgot me. It's been too painful. But I do now. I reach up and touch his face with the unfamiliar beard. And then I lean forward and kiss him, not for long, but for long enough. He pulls back, confused, embarrassed, and a little angry. But not unaffected. I can see it in his face, in the way he breathes. I felt it, when, before he had a chance to think about it, he'd kissed me back.

"Why did you do that?" he asks, voice low.

Because, Glassblower's son, I want to know if you refuse this cure, if there is any chance you might choose me again. And I think, just maybe, that you might. That somewhere, deep down, you remember me. Just a little.

I don't answer him with actual words, though. I just open the wet bundle beside us, show him the tubes with the needles. He goes very still.

"Where did you find it?"

"Do you want to remember?" I ask him. "Some of it's terrible." My insides clench at the thought of him saying no, then at the thought of him remembering some of the things I've done. I watch the smudge of his eyelashes as he thinks.

"Some of it may be bad, but I'm guessing a lot of it isn't," he replies, still very quiet. I wonder if he's thinking about that kiss I just gave him. But he doesn't say anything else, just pushes up his sleeve. I run my hand over the back of his arm, feeling the skin, trying to find the place I think will hurt the least.

I push the needle in, quicker this time. I watch his face, a slight wince as the liquid goes inside, and try to hold the tube steady. Then I set the empty tube with the others and we wait. We are knee to knee, alone in the small space in a very full and noisy room. Gray leans forward, head in his hands. He's panting, starting to sweat. I could lay my cheek on his wild hair if I wanted to. I close my eyes, hear him breathe so hard that it's almost a groan. I wonder what he's seeing in his mind. If everything comes at once, or if time is running backward for him, like when we played with the images on the wall in the mountain.

His hand comes up, finds the back of my neck. Then he lifts his head, puts his forehead on mine. After another long minute, he says, "Did you go swimming without me, Dyer's daughter, or is it raining outside?"

I laugh once, but I am crying, water running down my face and all over his scarred arm. I reach up a hand, touch the beard I'm getting used to.

"She told me where the cure was," Gray says. "Showed me how to use it, how she made it, explained exactly how to remember. Because she was going to make me forget. Because I knew she was going to make me forget, and I knew that as soon as you woke up it was going to be your turn, and I wouldn't be able to do a thing about it, because I wouldn't even know it was coming . . ."

I haven't had time to feel it, but I'm glad she's dead. "I'm sorry I made you forget," I say into the curve of his neck. "You really do remember me?"

"I remember the first time I saw you at school," he says in my ear. "I remember you in the workshop, before the Forgetting, when you hit Jonathan of the Council for trying to take my book and throw it in the furnace. I remember when you slapped my face. I remember watching you play with the honeybees in the south quadrant field when you were ten. I remember the waterfall, and the white room, and when you wrote me down in your book. I remember everything about you."

"I tried to save you, and I couldn't save you." *I can never save you.*

He strokes my head. "This, Dyer's daughter, feels very much like being saved."

"Gray?" This is from Delia, standing behind us now with Nash and Rose.

I lean back, wiping my face while Gray talks to his mother. And when he gets up to hug her I find someone else has come looking for me behind the bookshelves. Anson the Planter is just a meter or so away, my pack in his hand, the one I left below the clock tower. But his eyes are on the needles. Waiting his turn.

❧

Anson is nervous as he rolls up his sleeve, and so am I. All this time I'd wanted my father to remember me, to explain why he did what he did, and now I'm not so sure I want to know. But he does. He's determined. I plunge in the needle, not daring to look at Anson's face as the Remembering goes in.

It's strange to be this close to my father. He has lines on his face I hadn't noticed before, that I don't remember. Gray is still near me, facing the opposite direction while he talks to both Nash and Delia. But he is aware of what I'm doing. He offers his hand as soon as I put down the needle. I take it, holding it in my lap. I see the same moment in Anson that I observed in Gray, a few seconds when memories overwhelm, when the images have to be sorted. After that, they seem to run in order, a quick, backward tour through time.

"My name was Raynor," he whispers, sounding surprised. Then he says, "Anna. Anna was the first . . ." I was expecting to hear the name, though not the exact phrase my mother had used. "I took Anna to the Council because we realized she could remember. Just images, here and there. But they were clear. It was amazing." Anson looks up and I drop my gaze. "What do you remember, Nadia?"

I hold Gray's hand with both of mine. "Everything. I remember everything."

He runs a hand over his face. "I didn't know that was possible. Until today. So you've known? All this time?"

I nod.

"Then you listen while I explain," Anson says.

I blink. He doesn't sound apologetic. He sounds angry. Bitter. "I took your sister to the Council because I thought it meant something about the Forgetting. That we could learn not to forget. When Janis wanted to talk to Anna I didn't think a thing of it. I thought it was good . . ."

Now I hear the bitterness meld into grief.

". . . but then Anna was gone, and they said she'd poisoned herself. I knew it wasn't right. And your mother . . ." Now he tents his hands over his face. "Renata had been struggling, just short bouts at first, nothing I thought was serious, but when Anna was gone from her bed . . . I went to Gretchen and begged her to let me read Anna's books." He looks up suddenly. "Gretchen is my sister."

Aunt Gretchen. I hadn't expected that. And she broke the rules for her brother. I hadn't expected that, either.

"Anna wrote that Janis had put a needle into her arm, asked about her great-grandfather and heirlooms, but that her mother had told her it was a secret, to never tell, and then I knew exactly what she meant. Renata's bracelet, from her father. Anna had it on her when we found her, wound beneath the string in her hair."

The code. My sister was wearing it when she died.

"Anna also wrote that Janis had asked her about Nadia. Not you," he says, "but who you were named for, Renata's sister, lost to a Forgetting when they were children. I read Nadia's books, too. And she had memories as well. Talks with Janis. And then she was just . . . gone. Something was wrong. People with memories were not surviving, and memories were cropping up all through the women of Renata's family. In my girls, and, I suspected, in Renata, too. It was why she was confused. And what could I do? The Forgetting was coming, and Janis would have all of this written down. You, your sisters . . . what would she do to you?"

I bring up my knees, trapping Gray's hand against my neck. I'm beginning to understand, finally, after all these years. None of this had anything to do with Lydia the Weaver.

"I hid you," my father says. "Made new books and wrote myself out. Changed your mother's skill, changed your sisters' names, though I didn't change your mother's. It's a common name, and I was afraid she would remember. And I didn't change yours, either. You were named for a girl who had almost been completely forgotten. Like Anna would be. It should have been enough. You would be Nadia the Dyer's daughter, nothing to do with Raynor the Planter, so that when Janis looked for the family she'd written in her book, the family with memories, they wouldn't be there."

Except that Janis remembered everything. Like me.

"It was the worst thing I've ever done," Anson says, "taking away your books, knowing I was going to forget you. I had to lock up your mother and sister, but you still trusted me. I hate"— he says this word with vehemence—"that you remember it."

He cried when he took my book. I remember.

"And you ran, and the streets were a mess and I couldn't find you and I had to get all your books to Gretchen so she could hide them before we both forgot. My real book, it had everything inside, just like it happened . . ."

But she didn't get mine hidden. The one with the bracelet inside. Gretchen must have found it after the Forgetting, registered it, and shelved it, like an archivist does. And there it sat.

"But none of you were hidden at all, were you? And look at how she kept an eye on me. Putting me on the Council. And I'm sure she was reading my books . . ." He runs a hand through his hair. "I'm so sorry. I thought I was saving you, and I wasn't. I didn't."

Like father, like daughter.

∽

I step out the door of the Archives into air that is soft, warm with the rising sun, into a quiet street strewn with debris, a group of twenty or so people behind me. We've waited nearly four days to open these doors, just in case the spores needed longer to die. But the people in the Archives are restless, worried about friends and family who were left outside, and we've exhausted the supplies Janis had laid out for her chosen one hundred and fifty. There are three hundred and seventeen of us who escaped the Forgetting, and with the newly formed team of Liliya and Rose, the hidden room has been functioning like a well-run city. It's been surprising to see how well the two of them have gotten along.

Rose also taught me how to give a better injection. No one inside has forgotten the past twelve years, but for some, the remembering from before those years has been hard. Harder than forgetting was, maybe. The Council members inside the Archives made the decision to give anyone over fifteen years the choice to remember. Or not. Most made the choice to remember, but Lydia the Weaver chose not to, as did my mother, along with a smattering of others who had all their books archived. Who saw no need to risk who they'd become.

I've made trip after trip to the underground room, cleaning and filling needles with a wet piece of blanket over my face, Janis's robe over Reese. Some have been happy after their injection, ecstatic to find out who they were, who they are, to find family that had been forgotten. Some have been less so, others needing time for thought. I don't know what memories Rachel the Supervisor had, but she slipped out the door to the cave during the resting and we haven't seen her since. I think maybe she threw herself into the river.

I breathe the fresh air of Copernicus Street, air that is not the sterile emptiness of the cave, or the sweet, foul scent of the underground room, or the stagnancy from the close contact of too many bodies. I will always miss the dark days and the light of the moons, but right now the sun feels almost cleansing on my face. We fan out, heading our different ways, going out in teams to identify the dead, do an inventory of the stores, and find those who have forgotten. To ask them if they want to remember. Figure out what to do with them if they don't.

I am with Gray and Delia, an arrangement that has Liliya's fingerprints all over it. Disappearing for three weeks with the son Delia now knows she gave birth to has not endeared me to her, no matter how many times Gray has explained. I think it's actually the healing wounds on his back she can't get past. She needs someone to blame. I've slept beside Gray every resting we've been in the Archives, Delia always planting herself about a meter away. After the third resting Gray had shouted, "Mum! Enough! It's written down and done," to the amusement of half the room. She's been sulking ever since. But Liliya is certain, as only Liliya can be, that this is just a temporary obstacle to my happiness, and that she will be the one to remove it.

We step into the first house on Copernicus. It's empty of the dead, of anyone who's forgotten, anyone who remembers, and any stores. In the next house we find the same, and in the next we find Rhaman the Fuelmaker, not in his own house, but close. He has his book, chooses to remember, and is off to the Archives to find his Lost girl before he even stops sweating. Delia makes the notes. In the next empty house, Gray catches my eye behind his mother's back, eyes straying up to the roof garden. We slip out the door one at a time, while Delia records the meager contents of the cupboards, and I'm in his arms as soon as my feet hit the grass, careful not to touch his back. We haven't been alone once since he remembered me.

He takes his time with me in the way he's very, very good at, and this is different from any other time I've been kissed by the glassblower's son, because even though we're hiding from his mother on a roof, this isn't a stolen moment. The Forgetting is not going to come and take it away.

"Let's go over the wall," Gray says in my ear. "This resting. Jump the waterfall with me."

He needs to let his back heal. But after that, I don't know why we shouldn't. There's nothing to stop us. But then I stiffen, pull away from his arms. He follows me to the garden bed, where the tall, dry stalks of the oil plants are starting to flush orange with the sun, where a bare foot is sticking out from beneath the leaves. It's a child's foot, very still, and when

I part the stalks a little boy blinks, sits up, tries to scramble away. It's Eshan and Imogene's younger brother, one of the twins, I don't know which.

"Wait," I tell him, "wait. Don't go. Are you hungry? Thirsty? Would you like to come with me and get something to eat?" His eyes are large, so confused, and a little glazed. He considers, then reaches out his arms. I scoop him up and his hands go around my neck. He has a very dirty book tied to his waist.

"Gray, find water," I say, and he's off as I carry the boy down to the storeroom, find some dark days bread, a little stale. I make him drink the water Gray brings slowly, let him eat bits of bread while I clean him.

"Who is it?" Delia asks. I don't know when she came in behind me.

"James, Inkmaker's son," I tell her, after a quick look at his book. I'm sure he's too small to read it. "Your name is James, okay? We're going to take you to your house."

He has one hand filled with bread, the other on my neck, gripping tight while I wipe his face. He keeps on clinging, head on my shoulder as I carry him with Delia and Gray across the city, back to Hawking Street.

I'm relieved to see my house, door still closed and windows intact. Most of the streets are littered with paper and stores and broken glass. Hawking, however, seems to have been somewhat organized, swept, and I can smell food cooking inside the Inkmaker's house.

When Hedda answers the door, I explain who we are, explain about James. Hedda looks surprised.

"Well, if that's James, who is this, then?"

I step inside, Delia and Gray behind me, and there is Jemma and Pratim's son, playing on the floor with the other twin.

"This is Joshua, from next door," I tell her. Hedda nods in sudden understanding.

"They were looking for a boy, but I told them this one was ours. He was in our house." She's a little defensive. She doesn't try to take James; she doesn't remember him and he doesn't remember her. But she does look through his book.

James doesn't want to let me go, so we sit on the floor for a little while with the other children, until we can get things sorted, Gray on the bench beside us. Delia talks to Hedda, explaining to her about Remembering, and then Eshan comes down the stairs. He stops at the bottom.

"Who's this?" he asks, nodding at James. He comes to squat down beside us, puts a hand on James's head. He smiles at him, and James smiles slightly back.

"Eshan, I know you don't remember us, but we remember you. I'm Nadia, and this is Gray."

His mouth forms a kind of "ah" shape, though he makes no sound. He's read his book, I see. I watch him look at Gray, at me. There's knowledge, but no recognition.

"Glad you're okay," Gray says. "We were worried when you didn't make it to the Archives. Is Imogene here?"

"Upstairs. My sister and I . . . we decided not to go to the Archives, actually. That's what the book says. We came here instead."

Gray and I exchange a glance. They chose to forget. I look up as Imogene comes down the stairs, then stare as the last person I expected to see in Hedda's house steps down behind her. Jonathan of the Council.

"Oh," says Jonathan. "Are there more of us?"

He comes across the room with a spring in his step, bends down, ruffling James's hair. James smiles at him and, to my astonishment, lifts his arms. Jonathan takes him and sits on the floor beside us, pleased, picks up a toy block from the floor for James to play with. The other twin, Jeffrey, tries to take it away. I see Eshan filling in Imogene on who we are.

"So you know them?" Jonathan asks casually. "Do you happen to know me?"

"You're Jonathan," Gray says, and Jonathan bursts into a grin. "Hey, did you hear that?" he calls to Hedda. "I was right! I'm Jonathan!" Then he looks closer at me. "You're the girl in the house, in the underground room. You told me my name."

It's true, I did. But I have no idea how he ended up here, and I don't have a chance to ask. Hedda looks grave, comes to stand in the middle of the room with her hands on her hips, and I see what Delia has done. Of course she has. I've seen the scars on Hedda's ruined back, too. But something in me sickens, wishing with every part of me that Delia had said nothing. Right now, I think Jonathan of the Council is who he would've been if there had never been a Janis. Who he could become. Why should even this second chance be taken from him?

"Jonathan," Hedda says, "this lady here says that we can all remember if we want to, and that when we do, there are going to be things that make us . . . not like you quite so much."

Jonathan bounces James in his lap, his brows coming together.

"Actually," I say to the room, "I promised that Jonathan would never have to remember again. He made me swear to that, and I stand by it." I turn to him. "You threw your book away because you wanted it that way. And you were right to do it. I'll never be the one to make you remember." I might actually fight anyone who tries.

Jonathan frowns, thinking about this. "But there will be others who remember?"

"Yes," I tell him. "That's going to be true."

I see Hedda reaching around to find the ridges on her back, and my heart breaks for Jonathan.

"Well, Imogene and I are not going to remember," Eshan says. "We decided it before, and I think we'll stick to that." I smile at Imogene. *A new start.* That's what she'd said to me a lifetime ago at the Archives.

"Fine," says Hedda. "None of us will, then. We'll read our books if we have them, and we'll just start over from here. Let the past be gone."

And I watch Jonathan of the Council smile, playing with James on the floor.

❦

I thought of that phrase the rest of the day, even as Gray and I returned a confused and crying Joshua to Pratim and Jemma, helped people remember both the good and the bad, or not, as they chose, discovered and burned the dead. Let the past be gone, I thought. It felt true when we took Mother home to Hawking Street, even when she went to the potatoes to look for the knife. It seemed true as we dug out every forgetting tree, planted the gardens, re-formed the Council, had Canaan's first vote since before the Forgettings, and knocked down the wall where Jin showed us, where the gates had been, careful to reuse every piece of the stone. But the past is never really gone, I've realized. It only lies in wait for you, remembered or forgotten.

It comes for me most often in my nightmares, when I wake up screaming and sweating during the resting. I am always tied, unable to stop whatever happens next, which usually involves Gray, or my father, or the sister I don't remember. Genivee comforts me when she's there, but more than half the time she's with Lydia and Anson now, enjoying being the older sister, as she should, enjoying not having to care for our mother. As she should. Lydia is helping her write a new kind of book, without any truth in it at all. Or, at least, only the kind you can find for yourself. Mother has adjusted slowly to Genivee's empty bed, but not to me. I think she'll always associate my face with my father's, my name with her sister's, and the half-remembered pain that goes with it all.

I see the past in the people who still wear their books, just in case, in the bruises that appear every now and again on Jonathan's face, in my time at the Archives, helping Aunt Gretchen separate the books of the living and the dead. We use the books of the living with permission, the books of the dead without reservation, trying to connect families together, identify the people who were Lost. Create a history. Sometimes Gretchen goes to Anson's with us, which helps ease the awkwardness. Liliya and I have memories that Genivee doesn't, and no matter how much we try, or how good the intentions, twelve missed years can't be overlooked.

For Rose, though, it's easy to think time hasn't gone by at all. Right after I injected Gray and Anson in the hidden room of the Archives, I'd found her staring at my needles. "I don't need to remember," she'd whispered. "I decided that a long time ago."

"But I think we need you to remember, Rose," I'd told her. "To know who you are. You were a doctor before you forgot. And probably with a lot more skill than you're remembering right now."

And with that Rose had sat down beside me, picked up one of the Remembering-filled tubes, pulled up the cloth of her undyed smock, and popped the needle into the side of her thigh, sharp and quick.

"I would have done it like that," she'd said. And it was then I met the woman from the images in the white room. A woman not unlike Liliya, which made perfect sense when Anson the Planter walked past our spot behind the book-shelves and greeted Rose as "Grandmama."

Gray and I walk with her now out the new opening in the wall, up the natural way through the ferns that I realize must be the old road. Up the slope, down the gorge, and around the pool to the hidden door. Rose has been working nonstop since remembering, training our doctors to heal internal malfunc-tions, to make and use the medicines that had been re-created in Canaan before the Forgetting—anything from not having headaches to not having children. Helping Jin teach everyone about Earth. She's also been going through Janis's notes, using Gray's memories and the equipment in the laboratory to wring the cure from the purple plant samples I've collected for her. Her days are so full I thought she'd be tired, that we'd need to help her through the rough terrain up the mountain, but she doesn't need us. She is my father's father's mother, a doctor born on Earth, and her name is Zuri. I still think of her as Rose.

"How old are you?" I ask as she makes the little door rise, showing the squares with the glowing numbers. The lights are not near as bright now that the sun is up. Her wrinkles deepen all over.

"My dear," she says, which sounds very "Earth" to me, "I am one hundred and forty-eight."

"Is that normal?" I ask.

"It's completely ridiculous," she replies.

"How old was Janis?"

"She was born on the *Centauri*, so she must have been, oh, a hundred and twenty-four. And yes, before you ask, that's also not normal and completely ridiculous."

I give her the code, and then Gray helps her step over the rocks and into the mountain. I watch a mix of emotions play over my great-grandmother's face as she walks into the cavern with its collapsed wall, picks up the clothes with "NWSE" sewn on the front, sits down at the curving white table, showing us how to make letters of light appear on the table, to write any word we want to, to tell the machines what to do.

She shows us how there is a special generator, taking energy from the waterfall outside, explains that as long as it's maintained, the lights and "tech" should never stop. She explains what a camera is, how it captures time, and how Earth's sun rises and sets once each resting and waking, every single day. This seems blindingly fast, and when I tell her I don't see how Earth can get a harvest in a day, she laughs. She shows us pictures of metallic hydrogen, what the original chosen of Canaan made our tables and doors from.

"Your front door," she says, "could fuel a planet for a year."

But she doesn't laugh when she gets into another part of the machine, looking at the words appearing in the light square, what she calls a "screen." There's a symbol there, and a green dot, pulsing.

"Well, now. Who did that?" she says, leaning back into the chair. "I suppose we'll never know."

Gray bends forward, scrutinizing. "What is it?"

"That," she says, "is the signal. And it's on."

"It's already sent?" Gray comes to stand beside me.

"Yes, it's sent. And it's been sending for"—she adjusts the screen—"about one hundred and eight years."

"I don't understand," I say.

"Well, neither do I."

"Is there an answer to the signal?" Gray asks. "Can they answer back?"

Rose looks. "No answer. Either it's not working, or . . ."

Earth isn't answering, I think. I wonder if Earth is even still there.

Rose shakes her head. "Part of me wants to say what an incredible failure all this was. On the other hand, here we are. Rebuilding. And a whole planet none of us have even seen."

I meet Gray's gaze, and I think it's right then, without saying anything, that we are decided.

"How long would it take them to get here?" Gray asks. "If they came?"

"Now? I'm not sure. It depends on how the technology has changed. But back then? About four and a half years."

Thirty-nine trillion miles, I think.

"We'll have to put this to a vote, you know," Rose says.

She sounds unhappy about it. I don't blame her. The last time Canaan had a vote like that it had ended in bloodshed.

But when the city was given the choice, it was peaceful, and almost unanimous. Rose went back to the mountain and turned off the signal.

∽❧

It takes us the rest of the sunlight and the dark days to get ready. Nash needed Gray's help getting windows replaced and sealed before the dark and the rain. And to train someone new, which turned out to be Jonathan. Nash is as forgiving as Hedda, it turns out. Delia takes longer, but she'll get there. Maybe.

I pin up the last of my braids, fasten Sergei's bracelet around my ankle, and pick up my pack, a new one, large and heavy. Genivee's side of the room is nearly empty, not only of herself, but of her things, most of which are at Anson's. I look at it one more time before I steal out the door, shutting it quietly and moving down the hall so as not to wake Liliya and Mother.

Which was foolish, because Mother and Genivee are at the sitting room table, waiting for me, and Liliya is just coming in the front door. "Where have you been?" I ask, when what I really mean is, *What are you all doing here?*

Genivee rolls her eyes at me. "She's been with Jonathan, of course, and did you really think you were just going to walk out and we wouldn't say good-bye? You are so naive, Nadia." The "so" gets most of her emphasis. Then she sounds like a little girl again when she says, "Why do you have to go?"

"You know I'd have a house for you soon," says Liliya. Liliya is in charge of housing now, so I don't doubt it. Mother just frowns at her hands. Rose has been giving her some special teas, for calmness, but they only go so far. I'm careful with my words when I answer Liliya.

"I think when we come back we'll be going to Jin's, actually. He's fine for now, but . . . he will need someone with him soon. Will you check on him?"

Liliya nods, and Genivee says again, "Why do you have to go?"

I try to think of how to answer my little sister. *Because the city is too small. Because there should be something else to strive for. Because I dare?* I settle for, "Because I hate not knowing."

"Oh, that is so very Nadia," says Genivee, annoyed.

I kiss them all, and before I shut the door Mother looks out at Hawking Street, and the normal bustle of a day. "You're not like the first one," she says.

"No, Mother. I will come back."

❧

Gray is waiting for me at the opening in the wall, his pack looking heavier than mine. He smiles, holds out his hand, and we walk out of the city, this time not up my mountain, but around and beyond it. The sun is only a few days risen, low at our backs in the violet sky, ferns and grasses opening to new-foliage yellow. The suncrickets sing, the exposed rock glittering blue and silver with what Earth would have considered so valuable. It's prettier where it is.

We leave the city far behind, walking through a fern forest so ancient the trunks are like smooth, rounded walls, the new growth stunted beneath the vault of fronds. We've been climbing a gentle slope upward for a long time. Gray reaches the top first, turns back to look for me, motions me forward.

I join him and gaze down. A flat plain spreads out below us, a river twisting through it, and in the center of it is something . . . unnatural. We climb down, hike across the grassland, setting dustmoths rushing to the air in lacy white clouds. It's not until we get close that Gray recognizes what we're seeing.

"It's a ship," he says, incredulous, and I realize he's right. Just like what we saw in the white room. Only the planet seems to have claimed this ship, slowly making it a part of itself. Vines have grown over the metal, making it hard to see from far away, little plants growing in the dimples where soil has collected, and one whole side has sunk downward, submerged in the soft soil, leaving the ship at an angle that resembles a mountain slope. It's vast, so much bigger than I thought. We pull, tug, and push on anything that looks like a window or door, but we can't find a way inside, though Gray does wipe away the grime and we see the word *Centauri* painted on the side.

"Let's leave it to lie," I say. "This is where it belongs now."

We cross the plain, up the next set of rolling hills, through deep moss and quiet trunks, and when I stand on the top, back in the hot air and wind, I just breathe, unbelieving. I never imagined the unknown could be so beautiful. I want to write it down. Gray turns and grins at me.

"Let's run," he says.

And we do.

ACKNOWLEDGMENTS

This book was written because I am blessed with an army of encouragers: Genetta Adair, Susan Eaddy, Amy Eytchison, Rae Ann Parker, Ruta Sepetys, Howard Shirley, Angelika Stegmann, Courtney Stevens, Kristin Tubb, Jessica Young, and more. Every one of you said, "Yes, you can," and you're all so smart, I had to believe you. Thank you for knowing I could.

All my love and thanks to:

My critique group. We have spent a decade together. What an adventure we began.

Margaret Peterson Haddix, who waltzed into town and gave me the perfect advice at the perfect time. Thank you, my friend.

SCBWI Midsouth, my tribe.

Lisa Sandell, the most patient and insightful of editors and the most supportive of friends. You love me and my words, and I'm not sure I deserve it. Thank you for stretching me.

Kelly Sonnack, you are literally the most excellent agent a writer could have. I am so, so lucky.

The beautiful people of Scholastic: Ellie Berger, David Levithan, Rebekah Wallin, Elizabeth Parisi, Bess Braswell, Lauren Festa, Caitlin Friedman, Saraciea Fennell, Tracy van Straaten, Lizette Serrano, Emily Heddleson, Antonio Gonzalez, Michelle Campbell, Christine Reedy, Leslie Garych, Lori Benton, Olivia Valcarce, and all the other faces in sales, Book Fairs, Book Clubs, and foreign rights who are such incredible cheerleaders for my work.

Christopher, Stephen, and Elizabeth. I love you.

And Philip. You didn't write the words, but you made this happen. Every day. Page by page. You are, simply, the best.

ABOUT THE AUTHOR

Sharon Cameron's debut novel, *The Dark Unwinding*, was awarded the Society of Children's Book Writers and Illustrators' Sue Alexander Award for Most Promising New Work and the SCBWI Crystal Kite Award, and was named a YALSA Best Fiction for Young Adults selection. Sharon is also the author of its sequel, *A Spark Unseen*, and *Rook*, which was named an IndieBound Indie Next "Top Ten" selection, a YALSA Best Fiction for Young Adults selection, and a *Parents' Choice* Gold medalist. She lives with her family in Nashville, Tennessee, and you can visit her online at sharoncameronbooks.com.